Off the Air

Running on Air Book One

By L.H. Cosway

Copyright © 2019 L.H. Cosway.

All rights reserved.

ISBN: 9781794233430

This is a work of fiction. Any resemblance to persons living or dead is purely coincidental. No part of this book may be used or reproduced in any manner whatsoever without written permission from the author, except for the use of brief quotations in a book review.

www.lhcoswayauthor.com

AUTHOR'S NOTE

Dear Reader,

The start of this book contains the prequel novella, *Air Kiss*. The main events of *Off the Air* take place 3 and a half years after *Air Kiss*, and a number of months after those described in *Hearts on Air*. The prologue takes place several months after *Air Kiss*.

I apologise if this is confusing. The writing part of my brain often refuses to adhere to the rules of linear time.

To those of you who have waited almost two years for Callum and Leanne's story, thank you for being so patient and wonderful. And for those who are new to the world of Running on Air, welcome! I'm thrilled to have you and I hope you'll fall in love with these characters just as much as I fell in love with writing about them.

Best wishes,

L.H. Cosway.

Air Kiss

A Running on Air Novella

By L.H. Cosway

"They were stars on this stage. Each playing to an audience of two."

- F. Scott Fitzgerald, *The Beautiful and Damned*

One

Leanne

"I've never seen you this nervous," Paul commented as he ran his attentive gaze over me. "Are you sure you're feeling okay?"

The bloke was my best friend, but man, sometimes I hated how perceptive he was. I thought I was doing a good job of covering my nerves. Obviously, I wasn't.

"I'm fine," I told him and kept walking. We were on our way to an informal interview for an up-and-coming reality TV series, showcasing a group of freerunners from London. And yes, being that parkour was my life, I wanted to be a part of that group so badly it practically seeped from my pores. Maybe that's why I was so on edge. I couldn't remember a time when I wanted something more than this.

Paul was friends with some of the guys involved, and when they contacted him in their search for people to come on board, he was kind enough to put my name forward, too. That was Paul for you. Always thinking of others. He was the nicest person I knew, if not a little quirky. Anyway, it was too bad we didn't have romantic chemistry, because he would've made the perfect boyfriend.

Paul chuckled, the sound deep and attractive. His blue eyes made a distinct contrast with his bright auburn hair. "You look like you're about to shit a brick."

I tugged on the hem of my T-shirt. "Can you blame me? I'm about to meet Trevor Cross, Callum Davidson, and James Khan. They're like, the holy triumvirate, the frickin' parkour Gods of London. I know they're your buddies, but to me, they're these illusive mythological creatures only few have had the fortune to know."

"Okay, you're building this up way too much in your head. They're just normal blokes. When you meet them, you'll see."

I wasn't so sure about that. In my world, those three were spoken about but rarely seen. If you were lucky, they might show up when you were at the park one day. I'd watched them from afar several times but never had the nerve to introduce myself. They were like those obscure indie bands with cult followings, who only played secret gigs that spread through word of mouth. Or graffiti artists known solely by their name and work.

They had this aura of untouchability.

I shrugged as I glanced up at Paul. "Yeah, maybe."

He grinned and teased as he poked me in the arm. "If anyone else knew there was such a soft centre underneath that tough exterior, you'd lose all your street cred."

I poked him back with a lighthearted threat. "It's a good thing you're too much of a loyal friend to ever tell."

He winked. "I'm pretty fantastic, aren't I?"

I chuckled at his playfulness and focused back on where we were headed. We were meeting said "holy triumvirate" at a café on the South Bank. Paul wanted to take a taxi from the Tube station to avoid being late, but I insisted on walking. I needed the extra time and fresh air to get my shit together. Unfortunately, by the time we arrived, my shit still hadn't found itself. Fortunately, I put up a good front. Paul was the only one who knew me well enough to see through it.

I spotted them before they saw us, sitting at a table chatting casually. They were just like Paul described them, three regular blokes. Trev Cross was fair-skinned, dark-haired and light-eyed, while James Khan was dark-skinned and dark-eyed, his hair shaved short. Then there was

Callum Davidson. He had honey-brown hair, piercing green eyes, and ink covering every inch of his arms and neck. I was sure it extended to the rest of him as well, but since he was clothed, I couldn't see.

More's the pity.

I was a sucker for tattoos.

His arms were attractively muscular and he had the cheekbones and jawline of a catwalk model. I watched as he pulled a pair of black Ray-Bans from his pocket and slid them on, shielding his eyes from the sun. He might as well have been in slow motion, with "Sexy Boy" by AIR for background music, what with all the fluttery fangirl feelings I was having

"Hey!" Paul greeted as we approached, drawing the attention of the three.

All eyes came to us and those aforementioned nerves caught in my throat. I felt like I was meeting the Queen. My hands grew clammy and my stomach flittered with butterflies.

The pale, blue-eyed one stood first and pulled Paul into an enthusiastic man hug. "Paul! Good to see you," he said before turning to me. "And you must be Leanne. I've heard great things. I'm Trev."

With the attention of all of them on me, I felt a wave of self-consciousness. I wore a pair of black jeans, a white T-shirt, and my favourite Asics trainers. It was what I wore most days, because I was a low maintenance sort of gal. I didn't really wear makeup and kept my hair cut short. In fact, I was pretty sure the last time I wore a dress was my tenth birthday party. Because of this, people often mistook me for a lesbian, which was a ridiculous stereotype because I had lesbian friends who were more glam than half the straight girls I knew.

I shook hands with him as the next guy approached and offered his hand, too. "I'm James. Paul's been telling us all about you. I'm excited that we might get to work together," he greeted me warmly and my nerves started to subside. They were nice guys; open, friendly, welcoming. All my worries had been for nothing.

Just as soon as I had the thought, it was quashed by the fact that Callum Davidson sat there surveying me from behind the dark lenses of his sunnies. His mouth formed a hostile slant.

"Hello, we've not met before. I'm Leanne," I said, hoping to break the ice.

His gaze dipped to my hand, then up to my face as he replied in an unimpressed voice. "Yeah, I know."

Well, I guess all three of them being happy to meet me was just wishful thinking. Perhaps I should be thankful that Trev and James seemed nice. I could deal with Callum's less than friendly attitude. Since my day job was working at a Starbucks in Canary Wharf, I was no novice at handling egos. Those financial types were dead fussy about their coffee.

I withdrew my hand and shoved it in the back pocket of my jeans, unwilling to let his hostility phase me. "My reputation precedes me then," I joked but it didn't make a dent in Callum's antipathy.

"Please, take a seat," James said, clearing his throat as though to squelch the awkward vibes. He gestured to the two empty places at the table. A waiter sidled over and took our drink orders, then left as swiftly as he'd arrived.

"So, I guess we should get down to business," Trev said. "The three of us have been signed for a new reality show with Channel 4, but they want another two freerunners to come on board. Paul was a top choice for all of us, and since he suggested you above anyone else, we feel like we can trust his judgement. This meeting is just a little get to know you so we can decide if we all gel together as a group."

Callum quietly scoffed and I bristled. What was his problem? Trev either didn't hear it or decided to ignore him, because he continued talking. "The big question is, are you both interested? It's important that you thoroughly think this through. You'll be filmed twenty-four seven, and they'll have free reign to include details from your personal lives, so if you've got any skeletons in your closets, they're likely to come out. This isn't just about parkour, they want to show everything we do in our day."

"I'm okay with that. No skeletons here," Paul said.

"Yeah," I added breezily. "Me neither. Well, not unless you count that one weekend I spent with Charlie Sheen," I went on and everyone laughed except for Callum. Perhaps dark humour wasn't his thing. I wondered if maybe he was just having a bad day and endeavoured to break the tension by way of a compliment. I slid forward in my seat and gestured to his arms. "Wow, your tattoos are amazing. Are they all done by the same artist?"

He arched a derisive brow, like I was being nosy instead of polite. "You writing a book?"

I sucked in a breath as my stomach twisted with unease. Okay, I was reverting back to my original impression. He was just a dick.

"Christ, Cal, don't be an arsehole." James shot me an apologetic look.

Callum cast his attention to James. "What? It's none of her business." He paused and glanced back at me, assessing. "Wait, you *are* a girl, right? It's kind of hard to tell."

Jeez, cut me to the quick with a rusty blade, why don't you. It wasn't that the insult was particularly offensive, because I'd heard the same shit a hundred times before. It just hurt coming from him. As a freerunner in this city, I'd looked up to Callum Davidson, not to mention crushed on him like mental.

Paul glared at him angrily in my defence. "Who pissed in your cornflakes?"

"Watch it, Sheridan. I might like you, but that doesn't mean you're in yet," Callum threw back.

"If this is how you talk to people, then I'm not sure I want to be in," Paul replied.

"Listen, can everyone just calm their tits," Trev intervened as he levelled his gaze on Callum. "And Cal, try to tone down your inner dick, just for the next half an hour, yeah?"

"Can you blame me for being pissed? The show was supposed to be just the three of us. Now we're bending over backwards and letting them change the format. I'm sorry, but that's bullshit."

Ah, now I got it. Callum didn't like the idea of more people coming on board, more mouths to feed, so to speak. Not to mention more people to cut in on his potential airtime. Huh. I couldn't tell if he was egotistical or insecure. Possibly both.

"Are you worried we'll take the shine off your apple? Or is this a money thing?" I asked bluntly, never one to beat around the bush.

Callum barked a hostile laugh. "Honey, do you seriously think I care about you outshining me? I mean, look at me," he said and gestured to himself.

Okay, that was possibly the most unattractive thing I'd ever heard from an undeniably attractive man. "Wow, arrogant," I muttered under my breath.

I knew Callum heard when he pulled off his sunglasses to level me with a challenging look. Damn, his eyes were far too beautiful for someone so conceited. "I'm not arrogant, I'm confident. I know for a fact that I can outshine anyone who tries to come at me."

I'd always been a defiant person. Some would even say stubborn. Put me under depraved methods of torture and I'll be the very last person to break, which probably explained the next words out of my mouth. "I could outshine you without even trying, *honey*," I said, throwing his own sarcastic endearment back at him.

Now he looked at me, considering, his gaze astute. I got the sense what I just said interested him.

He made a sweeping hand gesture as he replied, "Go for it, then. Outshine me."

I scoffed. "I'm pretty sure you have to shine first, and so far, all you've done is sulk."

Trev barked a laugh. "Ha! She's not wrong. You've been a right moody bugger all morning."

Callum narrowed his gaze. "You're not my target audience, Trev. I'm shining for that blonde over there." He indicated an attractive woman sitting a few tables away. "She can't take her eyes off me."

He was right. She was staring at him with marked interest.

It was incredibly irritating, and my urge to take him down a peg or two increased tenfold. Standing from my seat, I walked toward the banks of the Thames and with several strides jumped atop the wall that ran along it.

I did a quick handstand then completed three flawless backflips, the final one landing me back on the path. Several passersby clapped at my performance and I grinned in triumph. On my return to the table, I made a show of dusting my hands as I levelled my new nemesis with a cocky look, "Top that, sunshine."

Parkour was the living, beating heart inside my chest. I wouldn't allow Callum Davidson to taint it for a single second, even if he was one of the sexiest men I'd ever met. Come hell or high water, I was going to be a part of this show.

Two
Callum

Bloody hell, she was sexy.

And I wasn't talking about the leggy blonde eye-fucking me several tables away. I was referring to the petite tomboy with the peachy arse and gorgeous blue eyes. I'd resigned myself to being pissed about the TV people wanting to bring on more freerunners, and since Leanne was one of those interlopers, I wasn't going to give her an easy time.

I knew Trev and James thought I was just being selfish, and in a way, they were right. I *was* selfish, and that was because I knew where the opposite got you: nowhere. If I was going to create a better life for me and Mum, then I had to be ruthless. I didn't want her living in that shitbox apartment block any longer than necessary. We'd both spent way too many years there already.

So yeah, I needed every penny I could get out of this TV deal, and bringing on another two people was going to cut into it.

Just think about the Polyphonic Spree. There were way too many motherfuckers in that band for them to have gotten a decent cut. And remember So Solid Crew? I bet none of those bastards were living the high life right now.

"Top that, sunshine," Leanne said as she sauntered back over, lowered herself into a seat and crossed one leg over the other. Too fucking cute. She was sexy and adorable and somehow tough in one completely tempting package. I'd never give her the satisfaction of knowing it though.

I was a stubborn prick like that.

Judging from the firm set of her jaw, I was willing to bet she was stubborn, too.

Maybe that was what I liked about her.

Or maybe it was just that peachy arse.

I folded my arms and flashed her a wicked grin, satisfied when the tiniest flush marked her cheeks. My grin always worked, even on women who didn't fancy me. It was my greatest weapon.

"I will," I replied casually. "When I'm ready."

"Ha! That's a cop-out," she taunted, but I didn't rise to it. I *would* show her up when the time was right, and she'd admit I was the better freerunner willingly.

"Maybe we should get back to the matter at hand," said James.

"Yeah. I'm already sold on the fact that you two are going to suck viewers in with your rivalry," Trev chuckled.

Leanne raised both eyebrows but didn't say anything. I wondered what she thought of all this. And I thought about what Trev said. Maybe he was right. Maybe this odd rivalry between us would make for good TV. I wasn't sure why, because I didn't even know her, but there was some natural instinct in me that wanted to rub her up the wrong way.

Then again, it probably just went back to the money.

"So, you both work at Starbucks in Canary Wharf?" James said. "You'll likely have to give those jobs up if you get signed."

Both Paul and Leanne shot each other looks as if to say, *oh no, please don't make us leave our beloved coffee slinging behind*. I resisted the urge to smirk, because I knew all too well how shitty it was working in the service industry. I was still an assistant manager at Urban Outfitters. Don't laugh. As soon as this TV thing was set in stone, those pricks could kiss my arse goodbye.

"Yeah, that's not going to be a problem," Leanne said with a healthy dose of sarcasm, and I hated how much it made me warm up to her. Appearance-wise, she was the exact opposite of the usual girls I went out with, so the fact I was attracted to her was surprising. And inconvenient.

I was grumpy about them bringing more people in, but I kind of wanted to see where this whole thing went. Not to mention I'd always liked Paul, even if he was a little *too* nice for his own good. Usually, when people were that nice, it meant they were up to something.

I realised I'd been staring at Leanne for too long when she arched an eyebrow and shot me a questioning look. I frowned, slid my sunglasses back in place and stared at a random spot in the distance.

She had nice skin.

I wouldn't mind touching it.

"There'll also be some travel involved," James continued. "We'll be in Manchester and Newcastle for the filming of several episodes."

He kept talking and the conversation progressed. I didn't really take part, still mulling over the idea that maybe it wouldn't be *so* bad to have Paul and Leanne around. At least when I got bored, I could amuse myself by checking out Leanne's arse.

"So, how about we all meet for a run on Saturday?" Trev suggested as we got up to leave. "That way we can get a proper feel for how we work together."

"Sounds good to me," Paul said.

"Me, too," Leanne added and I was oddly looking forward to seeing her run. If those backflips she did earlier were anything to go by, she was no novice. I noticed her cast me one last contemplative glance before we parted ways.

"Well, that was interesting," Trev commented wryly as we headed to where he'd parked his car. "I'm impressed by your ability to pull a strop in front of strangers. Toddlers everywhere should look up to you in awe."

"Piss off," I grunted.

"Seriously though," James said. "What was with you? You were a total arsehole to Leanne and she was only trying to be friendly."

"It's not your job to give me a lecture, James, so leave it out."

"He just wants to know why you showed us up like that," Trev said. "Leanne's a badass. My buddy Dan said he saw her running in Hyde Park one day and she blew everyone out of the water. We're lucky to have her. Plus, we need a bird on the show so it's not a total cockfest."

Great, now they were tag teaming me. "Fine, I'll be nicer next time," I allowed. He was kind of right about the cockfest thing.

"See that you are," James said just as we reached Trev's car.

Several days went by and when Saturday came, I had a spring in my step. I hated to admit it, but I was looking forward to seeing Leanne. With her tough exterior, pretty face, and stubborn personality, she intrigued me. I kind of liked the fact that she took my shit and gave it right back to me.

"You off out today?" Mum asked when I emerged from the bathroom, dressed and showered. She sat by the table in the kitchen, nursing a cup of tea and a smoke, which was her usual Saturday morning habit. Weekdays she left early for her shifts at the nursing home. I was determined to see the day when she didn't have to clean out bedpans just to make ends meet.

"Yep. Heading to Crystal Palace for a run with the lads. You need me to bring anything back on my way home?"

She checked her cigarette box. "Could you grab me a pack of ciggies?"

"Sure. See you later," I said and gave her a quick kiss on the temple before I headed out. I wasn't the biggest fan of her smoking, but she'd tried quitting several times and always went back on them. I tried encouraging her to give it another shot, but she told me sometimes you just had to leave people with their vices.

I ran down the stairs two at a time, grunting irritably when I saw someone left their works lying on the lobby floor. I mean, come on, kids lived here. Remembering I had a spare plastic bag in my rucksack, I pulled it out, picked up the drug paraphernalia without touching any of it and threw it in the rubbish bin outside.

See, I wasn't lying when I said this place was a shitbox.

We'd all agreed to meet at the Italian Terrace in Crystal Palace Park, one of my favourite places to practice. It had a bunch of stairs and inclines to jump between, not to mention there weren't usually many people around, so you could run without being gawked at.

I got there a little early, but I wasn't the only one. Leanne sat on a step staring down at her phone, oblivious to my presence. She was wearing black trousers and a dark polo shirt, which I realised was her Starbucks uniform. She must've come straight from a shift. I had a moment of indecision, as I decided whether to approach her or wait for the others to arrive.

Knowing it'd be weird to just stand there and not say hello, I walked towards her and called out, "Nice uniform."

Her finger paused on the screen of her phone and she glanced up, doll-shaped lips flattening in a straight line when she saw it was me. Obviously, she wasn't my biggest fan and I didn't blame her. I hadn't made the best first impression. It also irritated me that I was attracted to her, because the feeling clearly wasn't mutual.

"Thanks. Some of us have to work for a living, pretty boy," she shot back and I resented the assumption.

"I work," I replied and her mouth formed a smirk.

"Let me guess, you're an underwear model. It must be real tiring getting snapped in designer jocks all day long."

"Assistant manager at Urban Outfitters, actually," I fired back, annoyed by how defensive I sounded. Leanne barked a laugh.

"No offense, but I'm not sure that's better. You sell overpriced Ramones T-shirts to twenty-somethings with more money than sense."

"Coming from the girl who slings overpriced coffee to douchebags in suits."

She laughed again and I grudgingly appreciated the sound. "Okay, you got me there. We're both complicit in everything that's wrong with the world. Have a seat," she said and patted the step beside her.

I sat and pulled my phone out to check the time. Ten minutes before Trev and James got here. Guess it wouldn't be so bad to have a conversation. I did need to atone for the shitty first impression I made.

"Listen, I'm sorry for being a dick the other day. You didn't deserve that."

She gave a casual shrug. "No worries. It'll take a lot more than a bad attitude to put me off. This TV show is the gig most of us have been waiting for. You could call me a lesbo bitch every day of the week and I still wouldn't walk away. I don't scare easily."

Hold up, she was gay? Not to sound conceited but it'd certainly explain why she wasn't giving me any interested vibes. I arched a brow. "You like girls?"

She shook her head. "Nah, it's just an assumption a lot of people make because of how I dress." She paused and chuckled. "Wow, you look disappointed. Were you hoping to see me snog my hot girlfriend or something?"

That wasn't disappointment she saw. It was relief. Still, I didn't correct her as I shot her a flirtatious grin. "Something like that."

"Well, too bad."

I was about to reply when Paul approached us, his smile wary. "Are my eyes deceiving me? Are you two actually having a civilised conversation?"

"I'm trying to make up for the other day," I answered and glanced at Leanne. "How am I doing?"

Our eyes connected and her cheeks got a hint of colour. Wait a second, was she blushing?

She looked away as she replied, "So far so good."

"Well, that's a relief," Paul said. "I was worried I might have to break up some fisticuffs if you both went at it again."

His wording made my mind wander. I wouldn't mind going at it with Leanne. Not at all.

"Hey man, I don't hit girls."

"Yeah, besides, I'd beat his arse from here to Sunday," Leanne added cheekily. Cute.

"Now, why doesn't that sound like a bad thing?" I replied with a lopsided grin.

Again, with the cheeks. She *was* blushing. Maybe my attraction wasn't so unreciprocated after all...

"Oh, please don't tell me you're one of those blokes who likes women to wear PVC and punish them with whips and chains," said Paul, feigning horror.

I glanced at him, then focused on Leanne as I answered, "Nah, but I don't mind a bit of roughhousing every now and again." I grinned happily when I saw how my words made her breathing shallow. She seemed relieved when Trev and James showed up.

"Hey, you lot, ready to get moving?" Trev called as they approached.

"Ready as we'll ever be," Paul answered.

"Good to hear. We thought you and Leanne could do some freestyle stuff for us to start and then we'll join in," James said. "We want to see how you move together, then how we all move as a unit."

"Sounds good to me," said Leanne as she stood and began to stretch. She drew one arm up over her head, and I swear to God she had the cutest little triceps muscles. She was small, but every part of her was in perfect shape.

She stepped over to Paul and they exchanged a few words, then Leanne led the way as she ran up a set of steps before leaping onto a pillar. Paul followed behind her as she jumped from one pillar to the next, her execution perfectly controlled. I pulled out my phone to catch some video, thinking it'd make for a good YouTube upload later.

Then they reached the other side of the terrace, where there were two large Sphinx statues adorning either side of the steps. Paul climbed atop one and Leanne the other. I caught it all on camera as they shared a nod, then in perfect synchrony completed a backflip down onto the grass.

"That was fantastic!" Trev enthused as he hurried over to meet them.

I stood in place, frowning down at my camera as I tapped the button to end the recording. He was right. It was fantastic. They both were, but Leanne especially. She had something unique, a natural flair that you couldn't achieve through practice.

I was both jealous and a little turned on.

And that was why her being a part of the show was going to be a serious problem for me.

Three
Leanne

Paul and I trained with Trev, James, and Callum almost every day for the next month. Aside from the odd flirtatious or intentionally antagonistic comment, Callum mostly kept his distance. And that was a good thing, especially since I didn't know how to feel about his flirting.

It was difficult to tell whether he was being serious or taking the piss.

Since his comment about whether or not I was a girl still niggled at me, I was inclined to believe the latter.

Paul and I completed several auditions with the TV show creators and were subsequently approved to join the cast. We signed countless contracts and endured numerous meetings. It was a nerve-racking time, but it would all be worth it in the end. In just two weeks we were going to officially start filming and I couldn't wait. I was so ready to show the world what I could do—what *we* could do. Because I couldn't deny there was a special sort of chemistry when all five of us ran together. Not to sound corny, but it really did feel meant to be, even if I didn't know what to make of Callum sometimes.

I mean, most days I was driven to distraction by his body and pretty face, but then he'd open his mouth and irritate/embarrass the living hell out of me.

Tonight was James' twenty-seventh birthday and we were heading over to his flat for a small get together. He lived with his girlfriend, Diana, so I was interested to meet her for the first time. Paul picked me up at my flat at seven-thirty and we caught the Tube over to James' neighbourhood. Since it was a special occasion, I'd dressed up in my best pair of skinny jeans, heeled boots, and a tight black halter top. I also spruced up my hair with some product. It was as fancy as I ever got, but I was in a mood to look my best.

"What did you get him?" I asked Paul as we stepped onto the lift that went up to James' flat. He was carrying a gift bag and I was curious to know what was in there. I, personally, had gone with the old reliable bottle of reasonably priced wine and a birthday card.

"A clock," Paul answered and I shot him a look.

"You bought him a clock?"

He shrugged a shoulder. "He seems like a clock sort of person."

"What exactly is a clock sort of person?"

"I dunno. Someone like James."

"That makes no sense."

He cast a glance at my wine bottle. "At least I put in a little creative effort."

"Hey! I've known him a month. We haven't exactly entered into the engraved cuff links stage of our friendship yet, and I wager it'll be a few years before we reach the clock stage," I went on teasingly.

"Oh, go on, slag me off if you want. You'll be eating your words when you see how much he loves it."

I chuckled and lifted a hand to knock on the door. It was answered by a pretty, dark-haired woman in a stylish blue dress. I guessed this was Diana, the girlfriend.

"Hello, you must be Paul and Leanne. Come on in," she greeted, ushering us inside. "I'm Diana, James' other half. I'm sure he's told you all about me."

Paul and I exchanged a quick look, as was our habit when someone said something curious. It wasn't what she said exactly, but more *how* she said it. She sounded full of herself, like James couldn't possibly help bragging to everyone about how amazing she was.

"Oh yeah, he never shuts up about you," Paul answered, a blatant lie that seemed to please her.

"He's such a doll," she preened as we stepped inside the living area where Trev, Callum, and James sat chatting and drinking beers.

"Jayjay just wanted a nice quiet little party here at the flat, so I resisted the urge to invite all our friends on Facebook," Diana chuckled and *I* resisted the urge to mouth a questioning "Jayjay?" at Paul. Some people loved their nicknames.

"Can I take your coats?" she asked and I shrugged out of my jacket.

"Hey, thanks for coming," James said when he saw us. "I see you've met my better half."

"Yes, she's gorgeous," I answered, because it wasn't a lie, though better half was debatable. "Happy birthday," I went on, handing him the wine and card.

Paul greeted him next and gave him his clock, but James only set it aside to open later. I thought Paul looked a little disappointed that he wasn't going to tear it open right away. I loved how odd he was sometimes.

Diana returned with a tray of drinks for everyone and I took a glass of wine when I sensed someone's attention. Callum sat on the couch nursing a beer, eyes on me. He wore a dark shirt that fit perfectly over his muscular form. He looked sexy and gorgeous, as always, which was a big source of irritation for me.

Why couldn't he just be hideous?

If all went to plan, I was going to be on TV with these guys for at least the next year. Feeling horny about any one of them was a recipe for trouble.

Diana perched on James' lap, Paul took a seat next to Trev, which left me with just one option, the space beside Callum. I decided I was a big girl and could handle sitting next to him for a little while. I didn't greet him when I sat, but I could feel his eyes wandering over every inch of me. Clearly, he wasn't used to seeing me dressed up.

Diana started telling a story about how she surprised James with a trip to Ibiza on his birthday last year, going into detail about the beaches and the party boats, and how wonderful she was as a person for organising the whole thing. I was veering towards the conclusion that Diana had far too much of the wrong sort of confidence, and wondered what James saw in her. He was so kind and modest, so understated. I imagined him being with a demure librarian, or a sexy, intelligent scientist lady. I didn't know what Diana did for a living, but I was willing to bet it wasn't any of those.

I got a surprise when Callum bent in and murmured, "You think she installed mirrors on their bedroom ceiling so she can look at her own reflection when they fuck?"

I almost spat out the mouthful of wine I just sipped but managed to hold it down. My body shook with restrained laughter as I replied, "I have no idea, but I'm willing to take a bet on it."

Callum rubbed his jaw. "How will we find out though? One of us will need to sneak in their bedroom to see."

"I nominate you."

"Ah, but I could just lie to win the bet," he whispered, leaning close. His breath hit my skin, soliciting goosebumps. "No, we need to figure out a way for both of us to go in there."

"We could just wait until they're too drunk to notice."

He grinned, a boyish glint in his eyes. "I like your strategy. So, you don't think it's true?"

"I just can't see James agreeing to that, even if Diana really wanted it."

"You underestimate her ability to nag him into submission. Believe me, I've witnessed it firsthand."

"Hmmm, I still can't see it. He's too classy."

Callum chuckled. "Okay then. You're betting no, I'm betting yes, but what does the winner get?"

"A chocolate cake made from scratch by the loser," I suggested with a grin.

"Too boring. The stakes need to be higher."

"Chocolate is always high stakes," I argued.

Callum nudged me with his shoulder. "How about the winner gets to do the loser's laundry for a month?"

"Seriously, that's high stakes for you? You're really not living up to your bad boy appearance."

He raised a single eyebrow. "I hate doing laundry. And what do you mean about my appearance?"

I waved a hand in his general vicinity. "I thought maybe you'd want the loser to get their nipples pierced, or have something embarrassing tattooed on their backside."

His mouth curved into a calculating smile. "Well, now that you mention it, I'm not opposed to the idea."

"That's because you've spent like, a million hours under a needle. I'm not so keen on marking this virgin skin," I said in protest.

He looked surprised. "You've never gotten a tattoo?"

I shook my head.

His gaze turned speculative. "Scared of needles?"

"I just never got around to it."

"So, you have something in mind then?"

I shrugged. "I've always liked the idea of getting the solar system on the inside of my arm, but, like I said, I haven't gotten around to it."

Callum leaned closer, interest marking his features. "Why the solar system?"

I heaved a sigh, not too keen on exposing my inner nerd girl, but I answered him anyway. "My favourite subject at school was science, but I particularly loved astronomy. Then I discovered Carl Sagan's *Cosmos* and I became obsessed. I even had my parents buy me a telescope for my fifteenth birthday. Stargazing is a *huge* hobby of mine."

"So that's what you do when you're not jumping between rooftops?" Callum questioned, a fond note in his voice I hadn't heard before. It made me feel weird and fluttery.

"Pretty much. I think it's a travesty more people don't take an interest in the universe. They're all too busy looking at their smartphones."

"You look at your smartphone," he teased.

"Not as often as some people," I countered.

His eyes crinkled at the edges affectionately and again my insides went haywire. What was with him tonight? He was being so…friendly.

"Yeah, I guess you're right about that. But back to our bet. If I win, you have to get your tattoo of the solar system—"

"And if *I* win, you have to get "Leanne is the queen of everything" tattooed somewhere you actually have space left."

He barked a laugh at that, which solicited the attention of the others.

"What are you two snickering about?" Paul asked.

"Astronomy," I answered with a straight face.

"Ha! That's a lie. They were talking about anal sex. It's obvious," Trev teased.

"You clearly don't know Leanne. She's obsessed with the planets," Paul said. "I swear she gets aroused when she finds Jupiter on her telescope."

"Interesting," I heard Callum mutter under his breath just before Trev exclaimed, "Really? You have a telescope? Can I see it?"

I laughed at his enthusiasm, but I was beginning to learn that was just his personality. Trevor Cross was the most excitable person I knew.

"Sure, come over some night and I'll show you," I said.

Trev waggled his brows. "Some night, eh?"

"Well, you can't exactly see the stars during the day."

He made a show of looking sad, but I knew he was only playing. "Damn, I thought there was a side of sexy with the invitation."

I shook my head. "Sorry to disappoint."

"Well, you're both single, right?" Diana interjected. "There's no harm exploring the idea."

"Trev isn't single, Didi," James said. *Oh no, now he was at it, too.* Jayjay and Didi. Man, I hated cutesy nicknames. "He just started dating a girl he's been friends with for years."

"Oh, juicy!" Diana squealed, turning her attention to Trev. "Tell us everything."

He frowned, which wasn't something he did often, but it was only for a second. Then he plastered on a cheeky grin and replied. "A gentleman never kisses and tells."

Diana pouted. "Boo! You're no fun."

"Bet's on, by the way," Callum leaned in to whisper. I gaped at him in disbelief. No way was he going to get

'Leanne is the queen of everything' tattooed on him. He was bullshitting. He had to be.

"I don't believe you," I whispered back.

He stared at me intently. "Wait and see."

With that he stood and went into the kitchen, probably to get another beer. I stewed for several moments then hopped up and went after him. I found him by the fridge perusing his options. He was bent over slightly, affording me a nice view of his backside. I grew flushed and started rubbing my neck to chase it away.

"You need something, Leanne?" Callum asked, not turning around. How had he known it was me?

Suddenly, I couldn't think of a single thing to say, so I just stood there, silent.

Callum exhaled and turned around, opening a bottle of Budweiser and shoving it into my hand. "Here, have one of these."

"Uh, thanks," I said and busied myself taking a long gulp. At the back of my mind I knew I shouldn't mix my drinks, but I was too flustered to refuse.

He popped another one open for himself and nodded behind me through the doorway, his expression sultry. "Bedroom's that way."

My eyes bugged and I spat out half the beer I just drank. Callum chuckled as I went to grab some paper towels to clean up the mess. "You've got a dirty mind. I meant so we could find out the result of our bet."

"I know that," I grumbled, turning back to him as I wiped the wet from the front of my top. Luckily it was black, so it didn't show a stain.

"Why'd you look ready to bolt then?" he asked, seeming pleased with himself.

I glanced at the floor, embarrassed, before shaking myself out of it. Instead of answering his question, I walked by him out of the kitchen and straight into James and Diana's bedroom. Boisterous chatter sounded from the living room, so I knew the others were occupied enough not to catch me.

Stepping into the room, I discovered a pretty normal set up. King-size bed, linen sheets, dressing table, and mirror by the window, built-in wardrobe by the opposite wall. Then I looked up and swore profusely. How the *hell* had he known?

Laughter sounded from the doorway, where Callum stood leaning against the doorjamb, arms folded, smug expression in place. "Guess I'm the winner."

I narrowed my gaze at him. "You knew!"

He smirked and tipped the beer bottle to his mouth. "Maybe."

"That's cheating."

"No, it isn't. We never made any rules about whether I'd actually been in here before."

I huffed an irritable breath and looked up again. "I can't believe they have a mirror on their ceiling. That's just so kinky. James is a dark horse."

"It's always the quiet ones," Callum said.

I arched an eyebrow. "If that's the case, then you must be as vanilla as they come."

He feigned an offended look. "Are you saying I've got a big mouth?"

"I'm saying you talk a lot."

Now he grinned. "It's not a hard and fast rule, you know. I've got a few kinks."

"Oh?" I said, hating how curious his statement made me.

He crooked a finger at me. "Come closer and maybe I'll show you, little one."

Hmm, was he drunk or serious? I couldn't tell. If he was tipsy, he didn't look it, though that was the advantage of being a big bloke. You could hold your alcohol well. The inviting look in his eyes had a pull, but I resisted, walking towards him only to slip by and into the hallway.

"You're drunk, so I'll give you a pass for that one. Also, if you remember this in the morning, don't feel embarrassed. I get beer goggles all the time, too."

Callum's expression hardened. "Beer goggles?"

"You know, when alcohol makes you think you're attracted to someone you wouldn't look twice at sober. Like I said, I've been there."

At this he reached out and softly grabbed my elbow, stopping me in place. "I'm not drunk, Leanne."

I looked at his hand, stunned by the sizzle of attraction that ran through me. This was the first time he'd touched me and the results were...interesting. My belly flipped over on itself and my chest tightened. I had a sudden urge to link our fingers together, maybe stroke my open palm along his jaw just to see what it felt like. I wanted to feel the scrape of his five o'clock shadow.

"What?" I croaked, throat dry.

His eyes flickered back and forth between mine when he said, "I'm not wearing beer goggles, so please believe me when I say this, I think you're sexy as fuck. If we didn't have to work on this show together, I'd be propositioning the hell out of you right now."

I stared at him, taken aback. "But you always act like I'm a nuisance."

"That's because you are. You're a very, very pretty, distracting nuisance."

Um, what?

Aaaand back came the butterflies. Callum Davidson fancied me. What alternate dimension was this? Sure, he made a lot of suggestive comments, but I thought that was just how he acted around women. Typical flirt. But maybe that wasn't it. Maybe his flirting was simply that. Maybe he actually…had a crush on me?

This was certainly turning out to be an eye-opening evening.

I was still digesting the information when his phone rang. He pulled it from his pocket and stepped away to answer, a smile in his voice when he said, "Mum, hey, everything all right?"

In an instant his demeanour changed, his shoulders tensing, body going still.

"Slow down. Where are you now?"

A pause.

"Okay, stay in the flat. I'll be there in twenty minutes."

He glanced back at me as he shoved his phone in his pocket. "Something's come up. Can you tell James and the others I had to leave? I'll fill them all in later."

"Sure, but, um, do you need any help? Is your mum okay?" I asked with concern.

He chewed on his lip, conflicted, then grabbed my hand and pulled me out of the flat with him.

What was happening?

When he spoke, his words were frantic, rushed. "Actually, since you mention it, I might need your help. My mum's in a bad state and I think she'll like you. You might be better at talking her down than I am."

"What happened to her?" I asked as we arrived outside and Callum strode towards his Ducati. Oh yeah, did I fail to mention he drove a motorbike? It was kind of hard not to notice him rocking up to all our training sessions on it, an unapologetic mix of James Dean and Jax Teller.

Though I had to wonder where he got the money to afford it.

Before I could question him further, he shoved a helmet on my head. I was momentarily distracted by how it smelled like him when he studied me and asked, "Fit okay?"

I swallowed, my stomach tightening as I nodded. He stared at me a moment, like the sight of me wearing his helmet interested him somehow, then climbed astride the bike. He revved the engine and gestured to the space directly behind him. "Get on."

Swiftly, I did as requested. It wasn't like I hadn't imagined this scenario one or twenty times over the last month. I felt annoyed at my own predictability. Fancying a bloke because he drove a Ducati was just so typical.

"You'll need to hold on," he continued and I awkwardly wrapped my arms around his waist. There was a brief moment when he turned his head, gave me a strange look then focused his attention back on the bike. He revved the engine again and we were off. As soon as he picked up some speed, I held on tighter, not surprised by how much I enjoyed being close to him. My body was a traitor like that.

His smell infiltrated my senses and since his jacket was open, I could feel his warm, hard abdomen just beneath the fabric of his shirt. I had a brief thought of licking my way across those defined muscles and got a little lost in the visual for a moment. By the time we reached our destination, I'd run through way too many fantasy scenarios in my head to be considered healthy.

I climbed off the bike and Callum came and helped me remove the helmet. "You okay?" he asked. This new, caring version of him was hard to get my head around.

"Yep, all good."

Now he frowned. "My mum got into a fight with one of our neighbours. She's pretty upset about it, but I'm shit at comforting people. I always say the wrong thing. Do you think you could sit and talk to her for a while, maybe try to calm her down while I go deal with this fucker?"

I nodded. "Of course. What was the fight about?"

He grabbed my hand and led me inside, moving too fast for me to properly contemplate the hand holding and how nice it felt. His palm was soft, but with a roughness around the fingertips. "He keeps leaving his garbage in the corridor instead of carrying it downstairs to the bins, the lazy arse. It pisses everyone off because it attracts rats. Mum's been at him for months to stop doing it, but he won't listen. When she confronted him tonight, he called her a nosy slag and threatened to give her a slap if she didn't leave him alone," Callum grunted angrily. "Let's see if he's so brave when he's got me to deal with."

"He sounds like a bully."

"Building's full of them. As soon as I have enough money I'm getting us out of this dump for good."

I studied him, remembering our first meeting, and how he'd been pissed about splitting the money for the show five ways instead of three. Now I got why he was pissed and my gut twisted because I empathised. I didn't like empathising with people I thought I'd made my mind up about. I'd relegated Callum to the category of self-centred douchebag, but now I saw he did, in fact, have a heart. It softened me towards him and I wasn't sure if I liked it.

When we reached his flat, he slotted his key in the door and led me inside. The place was tiny as we stepped into the living room/kitchen area. His mum sat at the table and looked to be in her mid-fifties, with shoulder-length brown hair and green eyes. They were the exact same shade as Callum's, except right now they were rimmed in red. There were a bunch of crumpled tissues in front of her as she shakily lifted a lit cigarette to her mouth and took a drag.

"Cal, honey, you didn't need to come back."

"The fuck I didn't. I'm going to kill that rat bastard for talking to you like that."

"Please don't. You'll only make things worse. I still have to pass by his flat every day on my way to work. He could make life difficult."

"He's already making life difficult by being a lazy prick. We need to show him some teeth," Callum shot back and disappeared inside one of the bedrooms. His mum's attention fell on me and I gave a little wave.

"Hey, um, I'm Leanne. I'm a friend of your son's."

She mustered a smile. "Right yes, he's mentioned you. You're going to be on the TV show together."

I was surprised that he talked to his mum about me, though it was probably only in passing. "Come, have a seat," she went on and I approached the table to pull out a chair.

"Cal thinks you're fantastic. Says you run rings around him and the lads," his mum said, again surprising the hell out of me. I had no idea he thought so highly of me and couldn't imagine him complimenting me like that. At least not to my face.

Then I remembered our moment back at James' flat and felt conflicted all over again.

You're a very, very pretty, distracting nuisance.

"I'm Judy, by the way. Sorry, I'm such a mess. I wish we could've met under better circumstances."

I waved her away. "Don't worry about it. I've had a few problems with shitty neighbours in my time, too."

Before she could reply, Callum emerged from his room with a hockey stick.

"Where do you think you're going with that?" Judy questioned anxiously.

Callum's gaze was steely. "To teach Mr. Greenhall a lesson," he answered in a hard voice, then turned and strode from the flat.

Judy let out a noise of distress and I swore under my breath. I patted her on the arm and tried to be reassuring. "Don't worry. I won't let him do anything stupid." Then I ran out of the flat as fast as my feet would carry me.

He was halfway down the corridor by the time I caught up to him. "Hey! Wait up, Callum. Maybe we should leave the hockey stick out of it and talk things through the old-fashioned way."

He cast me a dark look. "I'm not going to attack him, so you can quit worrying. He just needs to see I mean business."

"Oh, right, well eh…" Before I could say anything else, we stopped outside the door to flat 7C and Callum gave it several loud thumps. Seconds later the door swung open, and a greasy looking bloke emerged, talking before he saw who it was.

"I swear to fuck, Judy, if that's you again—" He stopped in his tracks when he clapped eyes on Callum, vicious smile in place as he held the stick over one shoulder.

"You're gonna give my mum a slap, are you?" he questioned, jaw tight.

Mr. Greenhall started waving his hands in the air. "She was being hysterical. I only said that to get her to leave me alone."

Callum took a step closer so that his six-foot frame practically dwarfed that of his neighbour. "You ever talk to her like that again and I'll give you more than a slap, you hear me, you slimy fuck?" he threatened.

"Yes, yes, of course. I'm sorry," the man apologised, backing away inside his flat.

"And if I ever see you leaving your rubbish out here again you'll have more to worry about than a few complaints from the neighbours."

"I won't. I won't do it a-again," the man stammered, shutting his door in our faces, obviously scared witless. When he was gone, Callum exhaled a gruff breath. He let the stick fall to his side and started walking back the way we came. I hurried to keep up with him.

I didn't know whether speaking was a good idea, because he still seemed on edge, so I stayed quiet. When we reached his door, he paused to glance at me. "Sorry you had to see that. I just get so fucking angry when shitheads in this building try to intimidate my mum. I'm gone a lot, so some of them think she lives alone. It pisses me off how they think they can walk all over her."

"That's completely understandable. If I were you, I'd be angry, too."

His lips turned down at the edges, and for the first time, I saw how tired he was. Tired of struggling. Tired of living in this place. "Can you text Paul and explain why we left? I'm going to talk to Mum for a bit."

I nodded. "Sure, no problem."

I stood in the hallway and dialled Paul's number while Callum went into the kitchen. His voice was softer, more careful, as he spoke to his mum and I concentrated back on the ringing phone in my ear.

Yep, tonight really had been an eye-opener.

Four
Callum

I watched Leanne sitting next to Mum, talking and sharing a cup of tea like she'd known her all her life, and something about it just felt right. I liked her being here, liked having her close to me in whatever way she allowed. On our way over, with her chest pressed to my back and her arms around my waist, I'd never felt so turned on in my life.

I wanted her. Badly.

The last month had been nothing but a lesson in willpower.

I tried to figure out what it was about her that I found so attractive. I mean, she was hot, had a great little body and a pretty face, but there was something else, too. I just couldn't put my finger on it. Maybe it was the simple fact that I couldn't have her that made me want her even more.

"I should get to bed," Mum said with a yawn. "But it was lovely to meet you, Leanne. Don't be a stranger."

"I won't," Leanne replied and Mum shuffled by me, patting my shoulder as she headed for her room. As soon as we were alone, the atmosphere changed. Leanne wasn't looking at me the same as usual. There was a softness around her eyes, an affection that was the obvious result of getting a glimpse of my home life with Mum. We were all each other had, since my dad did a bunk when I was still a toddler. I promised myself if I ever had a kid of my own, I'd never be like him.

"I like your mum," Leanne said, still sitting by the table while I remained by the door. I worried if I came any nearer I might pick her up and carry into my bedroom. I was *this* close.

"She likes you, too," I replied, my voice unexpectedly hoarse.

This wasn't good. We started filming in two weeks. If I shagged her tonight, it'd change the entire dynamic of the group and right now we were on fire. When the five of us ran together, it was fluid, perfect, almost too good to be true. I wanted to keep that magic, and I didn't want to create any unnecessary "vibes" by having sex with my soon-to-be co-star.

Up until now, I was almost certain Leanne didn't fancy me back. But the way she was looking at me tonight, I was sure if I so much as crooked a finger, she'd come. Deciding the best course of action was probably to get everything out in the open, I took the seat on the other side of the table and clasped my hands together.

I looked her in the eye. "You mind if we talk?"

She shook her head. "Not at all. What's on your mind?"

"I'm attracted to you," I said and she sucked in a nervous breath before lowering her eyes to the table. I wished she wouldn't do that. I loved her eyes.

"You said that back at James' place," she muttered shyly.

I reached across the table and took her hand in mine. "Leanne, look at me." Her gaze flicked up. "I wasn't lying. If I had my way, we'd both be naked in my bedroom right now." A flush coloured her cheeks as the visual obviously got into her head. Christ, this was harder than I expected.

"Right," she said, embarrassed.

"But I don't want to fuck up the show. What the five of us have is too good. I know you feel it, too."

"Yeah, it's pretty spectacular when we run," she agreed.

"And with that dynamic, the show is going to be amazing. So, I guess what I'm trying to say is, I want you and I think you kind of want me, too, but we shouldn't act on it."

"No, I agree," Leanne nodded profusely, biting her lip. "This…thing between us, it'll pass."

I let out a shaky breath, and nodded back, hoping to convince myself she was right. "Yeah, of course. So, we're good, right? Let's try not to have any more weirdness between us. I just want to focus on the show."

I watched as she swallowed. "Me, too." A pause as she glanced at me. *Those fucking eyes.* "So…friends?"

I mustered a smile, even though there was an uncomfortable twist in my gut. "Yeah, friends."

***

Just as I expected, the five of us were *on fire* when we started filming. Everyone was convinced the show was going to be a massive hit when it went to air, and I couldn't disagree. I could already visualise the swanky new flat I was going to buy as soon as the money started rolling in. Mum would be living it large in no time. No more arseholes like Mr. Greenhall to bully or push her around.

Our director, Barry, had set us up with our own private gym in Shoreditch, kitted out with ramps, walls of varying heights, pillars and even a half-pipe. It was a dream to work out in and we were all there most days practicing. Usually, the film crew would hang about to catch footage, but they were off today since it was Sunday.

I could hear someone going at it on the punching bag when I arrived and thought it was probably Trev. The bloke worked out every single day to the point of obsession. However, when I came around the corner it wasn't Trev I saw, but Leanne.

Fucking fantastic.

Ever since our agreement to keep things friendly, life had been interesting. Real interesting. I swear, now that I knew she fancied me back, my attraction to her was even more out of control. The last two months filming had been insanely frustrating. Watching her run, work out, jump, hell, even her sweat was sexy. Somewhere along the way, my attraction became an obsession. She was all I ever thought about.

I had dreams about her.

When she was close, I fantasised about reaching out and touching her.

"Oh, hey," she said when she noticed me standing there. She was breathless, chest heaving from her efforts on the punching bag. She wore a sports bra that cupped her tits to perfection, and a pair of workout shorts that showed every inch of her toned, shapely legs. I stared for a touch too long, transfixed.

"Hey, uh, are you the only one here?" I asked, swallowing tightly.

Please say no. Please say no.

Trev, fitness freak that he was, *had* to be around somewhere.

She grabbed a towel to dab the sweat from her neck. I was officially jealous of a towel.

"Yeah, the others decided to go to the cinema. There's a new Jason Statham film out."

"Ah, right," I replied and turned in the direction of the locker room. "Well, I'm just going to get changed. Give a shout if you need me."

She nodded. "Sure, will do."

Instead of going to the locker room, I made a detour and headed straight for the showers. Once I was under the icy cold spray, I closed my eyes and thought of every unsexy thing I could imagine. Then I thought of all the reasons why having sex with Leanne was a bad idea.

Stepping out of the shower, I dried off, threw on my workout clothes and headed for the half-pipe. I ran the length of it, back and forth, up and down, without even warming up. Leanne was on the treadmill and I promised myself I wouldn't look at her. Looking at her only made things worse.

In my pants.

Man, this was bad. I'd been reduced to cheesy innuendos. Though if I couldn't express my desire physically, then at least I could be dirty in my own head.

I glanced to the side and saw she'd stopped running to readjust some part of her sports bra. *Good. God.* I caught sight of some side boob and tripped over my own two feet. My fall made a loud bang and Leanne came running over.

"Cal, are you all right?"

I loved how she'd started calling me Cal.

I sat on my backside, inspecting the ankle I'd just busted, when she climbed onto the half-pipe, her expression concerned.

"You fell," she breathed, sucking in a harsh breath when she saw the damage. My ankle was red and throbbed like a bastard.

"Yeah," I said, voice strained. "But I don't think I did any permanent damage."

Her pale, delicate hands lifted my trouser leg, folding it up so she could get a proper look. "It's swollen. There are some ice packs in the fridge. Stay here while I go grab one."

Before I could tell her it was fine, she was gone. About a minute later she returned, her features drawn in concentration as she pressed the ice to my ankle. She was so naturally gorgeous, it was almost hard to look at her this close. And if she bit that lip of hers one more time, I was seriously going to kiss her.

Fuck the consequences.

"How does that feel?" she asked, glancing up at me.

"Better. You're beautiful," I blurted and her cheeks coloured instantly. Great, now she was making me babble.

She looked away shyly, focusing back on the ice pack. "The pain must be making you delirious," she said quietly.

Nah, that's just you.

"Actually, I'm completely lucid," I countered and reached out to caress her cheek. She went utterly still, her breathing choppy, and I knew by the look she gave me that she was turned on.

Without thinking, I asked a very, very stupid question, "Do you want to fuck me, Leanne?"

Five
Leanne

"Do you want to fuck me, Leanne?" Cal asked and I swear to God I stopped breathing.

I was kneeling in front of him, but all of a sudden, he grabbed me by the hips and pulled me astride his lap. "This is a bad idea," I croaked as he ran both his hands up my spine to curl around my shoulders. His palms were warm as he started to dig his fingers into my tight muscles. I resisted the urge to moan.

"Such a bad idea," he agreed, leaning in to nip at my lower lip. "But let's do it anyway."

"W-what about the agreement?"

"Eff the agreement," he swore, his voice a husky rasp. Quick as a flash he flipped us so I was on my back, legs spread wide as he nestled himself between my thighs. I could feel his pants stiffen, the length of his cock hardening against me, and swallowed down a gulp.

This was actually happening.

Ever since filming started, Cal had been testing my willpower with his subtle flirting and little touches. Sometimes he'd help me down off a wall, even though I was perfectly capable of getting down on my own. His hands on my waist would practically burn through the fabric of my clothes. Other times he'd get too hot and sweaty during a workout and pull off his top, revealing toned muscles and miles of inked skin.

I'd become obsessed with memorising all of his tattoos, from the Virgin Mary on his right arm that looked almost like stained glass, to the anchor that said "Mum" on his inner wrist, to the black demon skull that spanned the entire width of his shoulder blades. Every time I looked I noticed something new.

I stared into his eyes, imprisoned in their sea-green depths, and wondered how I even managed to last this long. He was too beautiful for words, and though he often enjoyed riling me, he was a good person. Flawed yes, but still good. Cal was loyal to the ones who deserved it, but an all-around prick to those who didn't. I had to give him his props though. At least he was brave enough to call people on their bullshit.

"I think about you all the time," he went on and my breath caught again. "I dream about you. You're under my skin so much you might as well be one of these bloody tattoos," he laughed, a sexy, intimate sound.

"It's a good thing you lost that bet, or I actually would be."

His smile was affectionate. "You never did get your solar system."

"Haven't found the right m-moment," I said and whimpered when he pushed his hips in so that his erection was flush against me.

His hand cupped the back of my neck, fingers digging into the base of my skull and sending electric shocks all down my spine. My mouth opened on a gasp and his attention went to my lips. He stared at them with all the focus of a neurosurgeon when he bent forward to brush his mouth over mine, featherlight.

"I'm going to kiss you now."

"O-okay."

I barely got the word out when he crushed his mouth to mine with a hunger that was startling. His tongue dove in, no preamble, and explored every inch of my mouth, sliding along my tongue all hot and wet. I moaned into the kiss and squirmed beneath him. His deep, rumbling groan set a fire low in my belly and he reached down to slip his hand inside my workout shorts.

He cupped me right between the legs and I lost the ability to function. I simply lay there, allowing him to kiss and touch me, his fingers skilled and sure. When they dipped past the barrier of my underwear to touch me bare, my eyes rolled back in my skull.

This was weeks of foreplay coming to fruition.

Reluctant attraction finally finding an outlet.

I needed him so bad I ached.

"More," I begged, gasping as I broke our kiss. His eyes were open, watching my every reaction while he fingered my clit.

When I came, it was with a loud cry of pleasure that I barely managed to stifle. Something came over me as I fumbled for him, tugging up his shirt and practically yanking down his pants.

We were all instinct, completely mindless for each other.

I guess that's why you shouldn't deny yourself sexual pleasure when you want someone as badly as I wanted Cal. Because then you did silly, stupid things in the heat of the moment.

I gripped his firm, muscular arse as he positioned himself then pushed inside me. His thrusts were hard and fast, and I was too lost in my need for him to even realise he wasn't wearing protection. I saw him experience the exact same moment of realisation when he paused mid-thrust and stared into my eyes; panic, horror, and apology all in a single look.

I reached up to cup the side of his face and pulled his mouth down to mine. "It's okay, I'm on the pill," I reassured him, half of me knowing I was being reckless and the other half too lost in pleasure to care. Besides, since meeting Cal I'd never seen him with another girl, and we'd gone on nights out during filming. Sure, women flirted with him, but he never went home with anyone.

Believe me, I noticed.

And wondered.

Was he just not the one-night stand type? Or was he too pre-occupied with our weird connection to pay attention to other women?

"Are you sure?" he asked, breathless. He looked so handsome and sexy right then, strong arms braced as he held himself above me. I'd never been much of a submissive type, but I certainly didn't mind Cal being the one in charge.

I pressed a soft kiss to his lips and whispered, "I'm sure."

Those two little words were like a red rag to a bull. He pushed into me, building an impressive rhythm as I gasped for breath. I'd never had sex like this before, so passionate and reckless.

Someone could walk into the gym at any moment.

Luckily, they didn't.

Cal came with a rough groan and buried his face in my neck. It was such an affectionate gesture that my heart gave a quick, lung bashing thump that said, *Oh Leanne, we're in sooo much trouble here.*

I stroked his hair away from his face as he wrapped his arms around my middle and held onto me tight. His eyes were closed, his breathing deep and content as he just lay there and held me.

My brain was still scrambled by the sex when I felt him press a kiss to my neck and murmur, "We should go get you that tattoo."

I arched a questioning brow. "What? Right now?"

He smiled devilishly. "No time like the present."

Before I knew it, we'd cleaned up and dressed. Cal dragged me from the gym and outside to his motorbike. He helped me on with the helmet, just like he had that night we went to his flat to check on his mum, forgoing his own safety to ensure mine. It was one of those little gestures that endeared me to him.

"Just out of curiosity, how the hell can you afford this thing?" I asked, knowing the bike must've cost a pretty penny.

"Payment plan," he replied, like it was obvious.

I chuckled. "I thought you might have some story about how you got it on the cheap and fixed it up. I like the idea of you in a greasy T-shirt working on an engine."

He turned his head to me and reached out to give my thigh a light slap. "I bet you do, you dirty bird."

I chuckled again and wrapped my arms around his middle as he started the engine and sped off. About fifteen minutes later, we arrived at a tattoo parlour that looked like it was about ready to close for the evening. Cal led me inside, where there was a heavily tattooed bloke sweeping the floor. He was tall and muscled, and just looking at him made me nervous. I'd never been particularly scared of needles but being faced with the immediate prospect of some intimidatingly inked up bloke repeatedly sticking one in my arm had me breaking out in a cold sweat.

"Hey, Cal, how's it going? You're not in for a new piece already, are you?"

"Hey, Kev. No, actually. This is my friend, Leanne. She wants to get her first tattoo and I couldn't take her to anyone but the best."

Kev grinned at me with a gleam in his eye, like he enjoyed the prospect of untouched skin. "Well, you've certainly brought her to the best. What you got in mind, hon?"

I gestured to my inner forearm. "I want to get the solar system here, but I have no idea about colours or style."

"Let's have you look at some artwork and see what you like then," Kev said, motioning me over to a stack of folders.

Almost an hour later, Kev had sketched an original piece for me and I was sitting down to get my very first tattoo. The needle was sharp and uncomfortably stingy at first, like it was dragging and pulling at my skin, but after a few minutes, it became bearable. Kev sat on one side of me, diligently working on my arm, while Cal sat on the other, taking it all in. I swear he was getting an odd sort of enjoyment out of this, though judging from the amount of ink he had, he had to be just a little bit obsessed with tattoos.

"Stop staring at me. You're making me nervous," I said, voice tight. Just because I'd gotten used to the needle, didn't mean it didn't still hurt.

Cal shot me a dreamy smile and suddenly I was back at the gym, under him, completely at his sexy mercy. "Can't help it. You're gorgeous."

"Shut up," I grumped, trying not to smile as Kev chuckled at our interaction.

By the time he was done, I was a simmering pot of arousal, mostly from the way Cal watched the entire process, his attention going from the needle and to my body then back to the needle. I stood and walked towards a full-length mirror, admiring Kev's handiwork. The tattoo was beautiful, even better than I could've imagined. He took my vision and surpassed all expectations.

"It's amazing. Thank you so much," I said, smiling at Kev. He didn't seem half as intimidating now as when I'd first walked into the shop.

I was busy reading through the care instructions and admiring my tattoo, when I glanced up and saw Kev working on Cal's wrist. I'd been so engrossed in studying my new work of art that I hadn't even heard Cal asking Kev to tattoo him as well. It must've only been a small piece, because he was almost done by the time I came over.

"What did you get?" I asked, tilting my head to see. It was difficult to tell since Cal's arms already had so much ink.

Kev sat back, all finished, allowing Cal to hold out his wrist to show me. My mouth fell open when I saw the tiny crown with a swirly "L" inside the design. My mind backtracked to the night of James' birthday and our bet, when I said if he lost he had to get "Leanne is the queen of everything" tattooed on him.

This wasn't exactly that, but it was still shocking. The L obviously stood for my name. What on earth was he thinking?

"Is that...?" I whispered, trailing off as he levelled me with a serious expression.

"Today was important. I wanted a reminder," Cal said, like it was no big deal.

"Callum Davidson, there are plenty of ways to remind yourself of special days. You don't need to go and get someone's name tattooed on you. That's just...it's...God, it's insane."

"It's not your name, it's your initial. Besides, if you ever stab me in the back I can easily get a cover-up."

"That's not the point."

He arched a brow, lips twitching. He was clearly enjoying my fluster. "What's the point then, gorgeous?"

"Don't call me that, you know it makes me weak."

"That's funny, because you make me feel invincible."

I folded my arms and huffed a breath, while at the same time my heart did tiny somersaults. "Now you're just being silly."

Cal stood from the bench and approached me. Kev was on the other side of the studio, cleaning his instruments. "Leanne, believe me when I say this, because I won't repeat myself. I think you're incredible. These last two months I've seen just how talented and funny and smart and brave you are. I'm literally in fucking awe of you. So, if I want to memorialise that awe with a tiny tattoo of a crown, then that's what I'm going to do." He paused, smirking as he teased, "Now get over yourself."

I shook my head, exasperated, irritated, and charmed all at once. "No, *you* get over yourself," I shot back grumpily.

Cal chuckled, the sound low and sexy as he wrapped his arms around me and pulled me close. "Don't ever let anyone put you in charge of comebacks, because you fail at them. Big time," he said, all playful.

I was about to disagree when he shut me up with a kiss, and I let out a soft, dreamy sigh. Somewhere in the back of my mind, I had a premonition our road would be a rocky one, but I pushed that thought aside for now and focused instead on his kiss. His kiss was better than jumping fifteen feet to land in a perfect roll. It was better than a triple

backflip performed in front of a captivated, adoring audience.
　　His kiss was better than running on air.

Off the Air
Running on Air Book One
By L.H. Cosway

> *Trust your heart*
> *if the seas catch fire*
> *(and live by love*
> *though the stars walk backward)*
> - E.E. Cummings, "Dive for Dreams"

Prologue
Callum
Three years ago

Leanne blew me away. Her movements were lithe, fluid, fucking *graceful*.

We were in the London docklands, filming on top of hundreds of sea cargo containers. Giant coloured blocks went on as far as the eye could see. You could jump from one to the next like you were running through a game of Tetris.

We were all in our element.

I chased after Leanne, with Trev, James, and Paul just behind me. Some of the film crew were situated on cranes so that they could capture us from up high. It was a pure adrenaline rush. Leanne twisted around to wink at me before she precision-jumped ten feet through the air, then made a perfect landing on the next block of containers.

I swear she was the most perfect, wild, free thing I'd ever seen.

Trev caught up to me, his smile wide. Like me, these were the moments he lived for, the rush. None of us felt more alive than when we were doing parkour.

"She's in the zone today, isn't she?" Trev said, breathless.

I flashed him a grin and kept going. When Leanne ran, there was a pull deep inside that urged me to follow. Up ahead, she'd almost reached the end of the block and was readying herself for another precision jump. She leapt fluidly through the air, but then, something went wrong.

"Leanne!" I roared, fire blazing through me.

Time moved in slow motion. Every part of me rejected what I saw. Leanne had miscalculated the distance of the jump. Her body slammed into the container with a soul-crushing, metallic clang, her hands gripping the edge as she struggled to hold on.

I'd never been so terrified as my body sprang into action, propelling me forward with the need to get to her.

Within seconds I'd made the jump, and I pulled her up to safety, my arms cradling her body. "Jesus Christ." I stared into her wide, blue, terrified eyes.

She was pale as a ghost, like she couldn't believe what just happened. Shock rippled through both of us in a tangible wave.

"Are you okay? Are you hurt?" I asked, frantic, as the others reached us.

"Callum," someone said, but all my attention was on Leanne.

She opened her mouth, but no words came out. The sight of her slamming into the container kept playing on repeat in my head.

"Callum," someone said again. I realised it was Paul, but I couldn't pull my focus away from her. I needed to know she was okay. I needed to hear her say the words.

Leanne's eyes trailed down to her lap and I followed their descent. Something dark and wet stained her jeans. There was a moment of disconnect before I comprehended.

She was *bleeding*.

Panicked, I picked her up and moved by pure instinct. I had no idea how I got us down to the ground. All I knew was we were suddenly surrounded by crew members. Leanne was unnaturally quiet, and it killed me to know she was in pain. I couldn't think straight, my head too wild. Why was she bleeding? Had she been cut when she slammed into the container? Had she broken something?

The ambulance arrived, and a paramedic asked very gently if I could let go of Leanne. In the end, Trev and James pulled me away from her. They put her on a stretcher, and I followed them into the ambulance. Everything they said was medical talk, and it made no sense.

"What's wrong with her?" I asked, tugging on strands of my hair in agitation.

"We don't know yet," the paramedic replied, her expression sympathetic and kind.

Just fucking help her, I wanted to yell. Until this moment, I hadn't known just how much I felt for Leanne. I knew I lusted for her and that she was constantly on my mind. But the idea of losing her never occurred to me, and it was the scariest feeling. I refused to accept it could happen. She meant more to me than just sex. We'd been sleeping together in secret for a few months, but she was in my head and my heart now.

At the hospital, they wouldn't let me go any further than the waiting area. It was only when I sat on the uncomfortable plastic chair that I realised I was covered in her blood. The sight of it made me feel raw and chaotic inside, like I could thrash the world.

When everyone else arrived at the hospital, they wanted to know if Leanne was okay, but I had no answers for them. A sharp, heavy weight pulled on me. It took me a second to discern it was fear.

Everything I was made of rebelled against the idea of her not being okay.

About an hour passed. Trev took me into the bathroom to clean up, handing me a fresh T-shirt.

"Where did you get this?"

"Gift shop."

"Right. Thanks."

"Cal?"

"Yeah?" My voice was flat as I pulled some paper towels from the dispenser.

"There's something between you two, isn't there?"

I exhaled heavily, my entire body slumped, and I nodded. Trev swore.

"Right now, I just need to know if she's okay. You can shout at me for being stupid all you want later."

"That's not what I—"

I left the bathroom before he had a chance to finish talking. A doctor approached Paul and James, her face grave.

"Are you Miss Simmons' family?" she asked.

"We're her friends," Paul replied. "Her parents are on their way."

"I'm her boyfriend," I announced, and everyone's expressions seemed to ask the same question, *You are?*

"Oh," the doctor replied. "Are you Callum?"

I nodded, wondering how she knew my name. "Leanne asked me to talk to you. Come with me," she said and I followed her to a small office. She closed the door and levelled me with a kind expression.

"Callum, am I correct in assuming you were unaware that Leanne was pregnant?"

Just like that, my world stopped turning. My pulse pounded in my ears like I was under water. It took me a second to properly digest what she had said.

When I didn't reply right away, her tone softened. "Leanne has suffered a miscarriage, but she's in a stable condition right now. She's also broken two of her ribs…"

The thoughts in my head were so loud they tuned out the rest of what she said. When she finished talking, I turned and left the room. In a daze, I walked to the end of the corridor, then slid down onto the floor. I was going to be sick. Hands on my stomach, I willed myself to keep my lunch down.

"What the….what the hell?" I said out loud, confused and hurt. My voice didn't sound like mine.

I clenched my fist and punched the floor as I cursed at the top of my lungs, "Fuuuuck!"

A door opened, and a nurse stuck her head out to shoot me a concerned look. I stood and found an exit, pushing my way outside. My throat was heavy, my chest on fire, like something was trying to claw its way out. A man stood by the exit, wearing hospital scrubs and smoking a cigarette.

I rubbed a hand down my face. "Can I get one of those?"

"Sure," he replied, handing me a smoke and a lighter. I lit up, gave him back the lighter, and took a long drag. I never smoked. My mum did and I was always on her to quit. But how I was feeling right now, in the absence of alcohol or hard drugs, some nicotine would have to do.

How the hell could Leanne be pregnant? How could we not know?

Wait…did she know?

The thought of her hiding something like this from me made me feel unhinged. I refused to accept it. She wouldn't do that. She couldn't…

I was the bad guy here, not Leanne. I hated myself for doing this to her and I hated how the entire situation felt so out of my control. She'd been pregnant with *our* child, and now she was lying in a hospital bed and our baby was gone. Our baby I didn't even know existed. My eyes filled with tears as I choked down a furious drag of the cigarette. It tasted like ashes on my tongue. I stabbed it out and stomped back inside the hospital.

I needed to see her, to hold her, tell her how fucking sorry I was.

I used to think life was hard, but I'd never known pain like this.

Earlier today we'd been running like we hadn't a care in the world. Then just like that, it all came crashing down.

I found Leanne's room, but through the narrow pane of glass, I saw that her parents and sister were already inside. I couldn't go in there, couldn't face them when I knew this was all my fault. What do you say to the family of the girl you got pregnant? We were both way too young to become parents. Being a dad wasn't something I'd even considered yet. So why did it feel like someone had just torn out one of the most vital parts of me? Like a clawed hand had ripped my heart right out of my chest? Like I'd just lost a person I'd loved my entire life? A tiny little possibility of a person that I'd now never get the chance to know.

I skulked at the end of the corridor until I saw them leave. Her parents walked ahead, but her sister spotted me. I swallowed down my guilt to face her. Leanne's older sister, Lorna, was her complete opposite, long blonde hair, girly clothes, lots of makeup. Unlike Leanne, she was open and friendly, always smiling. Leanne was wary, difficult, suspicious of strangers, sarcastic, *perfect*.

I knew she'd told her sister about us when I saw her face. "Callum," Lorna said, her eyes full of sympathy that made the fire in me burn hotter.

"How is she?" I asked, scratching the back of my neck in agitation. My voice still didn't sound like mine.

Her sister inhaled a deep breath. "She's…still a little out of it. You should go in and see her."

"I'm going to, I just…wanted to wait until you and your folks were gone. I'm the last person you want to see."

Her blue eyes, the only part of her that was like Leanne, turned sad. "This was an accident, Callum. It's nobody's fault."

Tell that to the guilt eating me up inside.

When I didn't say anything, she came forward and threw her arms around me. I barely knew her, but something about her warmth eased some of the fire. She stepped back, her expression earnest as she gave my shoulder a soft squeeze. "I can tell that you care about my sister. Go see her. Talk to her. She needs you right now. You need each other."

With that, she went, and I stood glued to the spot. Forcing my feet to move, I went to Leanne's room and hesitated outside the door.

Just fucking go inside. I dropped my forehead onto the hard panel surface, drew a deep breath, then pushed it open. Leanne lay in the narrow bed, wearing a hospital gown, her short hair pushed back from her face. I expected to find her awake since her parents had just been here, but she'd nodded off.

She looked so small.

I hated that she was suffering, wished with every fibre of my being that I could swap places with her.

Then my mind went to a much more painful place. If we hadn't been filming today, if she hadn't taken that jump, our baby would still be alive.

No, don't think it.

It was futile to wallow in what-ifs, and yet, I was drowning in them, my heart and soul wishing to be transported to an alternate reality. Anything would be better than this.

Leanne's eyes flickered open. "Cal?"

In a flash, I was by her side. I sat on the chair next to her bed and took her hand in mine. "I'm here."

Just like that, she started to cry. I couldn't take it. Rising from the chair, I climbed into the bed beside her and, careful not to move her too abruptly or damage any of the bandaging around her ribs, pulled her into my arms. She turned her face into my chest and wept. I cried too. For a long time, we stayed like that, drowning in our shared misery.

When I spoke, my voice was choked, broken. "How can it hurt this much to lose something you didn't even know you had?"

Her reply was hollow. "It just does."

I had to force myself to ask the next question. "How long were you—"

"Three months," she replied stiffly.

Jesus. My voice went so quiet it was almost a whisper. "Do they know if it was a boy or a girl?"

Leanne stiffened again. I knew my questions were making her hurt more, but I had to know.

"They can't tell this early."

We were both quiet for a long moment. I ran my hands up and down her arms and she sank into me. "I think she was a girl."

"Cal," Leanne begged. "Please don't. I can't..."

"Hush," I murmured. "I know."

"If I'd known I never would've taken that jump," she said, trembling, tears streaming down her face. "I never would've—"

"If this is anyone's fault, it's mine," I interrupted, full of self-hatred. "I should've been wearing condoms."

"But I was on the pill," she swallowed thickly. "I think I missed a day. And we've been so busy with the filming schedule I didn't even notice I haven't had my period. This is all my f—"

"No," I refuted. "I'm older. I shouldn't have been so careless, so selfish."

She squeezed my hand. "Cal." The quiver in her voice when she said my name shut me up. She didn't need to hear my self-recriminations right now. There was nothing either of us could do to change this and talking only made it hurt more. So, I shut my mouth and held her. I must've drifted off because some time later I felt a tap on my shoulder. I blinked my eyes open. It was a nurse.

"Visiting hours are over, pet. You have to go," she said quietly.

It hurt to tear myself away from Leanne, but I knew she needed rest, and this bed was barely big enough for one person, never mind two. I climbed out, then fixed the covers over her. I stroked her hair away from her face and pressed a kiss to her forehead.

It killed me to leave. I walked to the door and the nurse's expression was sympathetic. A lot of people insisted they didn't want sympathy, but I did. Her look said *I'm sorry for what happened to you, but it will get better.* I needed looks like those because everything inside of me screamed that the opposite was true. Our lives were changed now, and no matter how much we might want it, this was never going to get better.

I barely slept for days. I was at the hospital every morning to see Leanne, willing her recovery to be as quick and pain free as possible.

Then, on the fourth day, with dark circles under my eyes, I headed to the hospital first thing. When I reached

Leanne's room, it was empty. The nurse who'd gotten used to my presence approached, her voice gentle.

"Her parents took her home about an hour ago, love."

"Oh. Right. Thanks," I said, panic rising in me. I didn't know why, but I just needed to see her. I'd gotten into a routine and it felt like bad luck to break it. I drove to Leanne's flat, but she wasn't there. Her parents must've brought her back to their house, so I called Paul to get their address.

The urge to hold her and not let go took over. I wanted to make her better, no matter what it took. I wanted to bring her back to her smart-mouthed, feisty tomboy self. If I could just do that, then maybe everything else would be okay again.

I hesitated when I saw my reflection in the window by their front door. I looked like shit. Felt even worse. I couldn't let her mum and dad see me like this, sleep deprived and manic. They'd just think I was even more of a scumbag.

I turned around, changing my mind just as the front door opened.

"Callum?" Leanne's mum asked gently.

My shoulders slumped as I turned back. "Sorry. I shouldn't have come here. I just…"

A heavy silence hung over us, then she asked, "Would you like to come in for a cup of tea?"

The simple offer made my throat heavy. I nodded and she led me inside the house. Leanne's dad wasn't around so he must've been at work. I pulled out a chair at the kitchen table while Leanne's mum put the kettle on.

There was a creak on the stairs and I looked through the doorway. Leanne was frozen on a step midway down.

"What are you doing here?" she asked shakily.

"Leanne," her mum said. "You need to go back to bed, you can't be walking around."

"I'm fine," she replied, but I could see the stiffness in her posture, the pain behind her eyes.

I stood and walked out into the hall. She stared down at me from her place on the stairs. I reached out to take her hand, but she pulled away. I frowned.

"I came to see how you're doing."

"I'm doing fantastic, better than ever," she replied sarcastically and I winced. Her frosty tone was like a knife to my throat.

Her mum moved by me, heading for the living room. "I'll let you two talk," she said then closed the door to give us privacy. Leanne came down the last few steps to join me. She was significantly shorter than me. In fact, I was much bigger, much stronger, and yet, in this moment she had the ability to crush me. I'd never felt so vulnerable. Then, without thinking, I asked a question that had been punching holes in my brain for days.

"Did you know?" My voice was choked.

Leanne frowned. "Did I know what?"

"Did you know that you were pregnant?"

Her tone was sharp. "Of course I didn't know! You think I'd keep something like that from you? I already told you I've been so busy with work that I didn't realise—"

"I'm sorry," I said, cutting her off and raking a hand through my hair. "That was a horrible thing to ask. It's just…my head is all over the place." Again, I reached out to touch her, but she recoiled like I was diseased.

She closed her eyes. "Please, don't."

"Why won't you let me touch you?"

"Because it just reminds me of how we got into this mess in the first place. I don't think I can be with you anymore, Cal," she blurted, and just like that, the knife at my throat pressed in, drawing blood.

I shook my head. "You don't mean that."

She opened her eyes. They were steady, unwavering. "I do mean it. I always knew we'd end badly. I should've trusted my instincts."

Agony twisted around my organs. "You're breaking me in two here."

Her words were barely audible as she stared at the floor, her voice watery. "I'm sorry. I really am."

"You're not in the right frame of mind to be making this kind of decision." I refused to accept this. I couldn't.

She swallowed as if for courage, for a second seeming fragile before the steel shutters came down. "That's not true. In fact, my head has never been clearer. I can't be with you anymore. Every time I'm with you, I'll be thinking of what we lost, and it hurts so much to think of it."

She was making a rash decision, and no matter how clear she thought her head was, she was wrong. She was in pain and lashing out. I needed to be calm, patient, but that was hard when my impulses fought tooth and nail against my logic.

"Don't fight me on this, Cal," she begged.

"I'm not fighting you."

"Then please, just go."

I saw the desperation in her and logic won out. She was drowning, but for whatever reason, she didn't want my help swimming to the surface. I felt completely and utterly useless. Disposable. And I knew there was no talking to her. Not right now.

Without another word I turned and left, leaving my heart behind on the hallway floor.

One
Leanne
Present

Don't judge, but sometimes I liked to re-watch the final rap battle scene from *8 Mile*. It helped when I was in a particular mood, or having a particular kind of day. Or when I had to deal with a particular *someone*.

That someone being Callum Davidson, my co-star/ex-lover.

I also liked to re-watch the poem scene from *10 Things I Hate About You*, but that was for a whole different type of day. And don't even get me started on Heath Ledger's "Can't Take My Eyes Off You" scene. That right there was a *mood*.

Some people had soundtracks for their lives. I had a memorized library of movie clips.

But yeah, today was an *8 Mile* sort of day.

It was Cal's birthday, and I was going to need all my mental armour to attend. This year he'd chosen a forest party to celebrate the occasion. I used my phone as a flashlight while our new assistant, Michaela, and I trudged along a dirt path trying to locate the party.

"Maybe we should go back and call James for better directions," Michaela suggested. "I can't get a single bar on my phone out here."

"No, we'll keep going for a little bit. It's got to be around here somewhere," I said, my trusty stubbornness kicking in. It often worked to my detriment. For instance, causing me to get lost in the middle of the woods and be eaten by wild animals. Or forcing me to continue working on the reality TV show that also starred my ex.

Constantly being around someone who hurt you, and hurt *with* you, was a painful experience. One I was still living in.

I was now accustomed to it though. Emotional turmoil was as familiar as the collection of scars and callouses on my body from years of freerunning.

"I think I can see lights up ahead," Michaela said.

My stomach tightened. I was here purely out of loyalty to the group. James, Paul, Trevor, Isaac, Cal and I were the six stars of the popular reality TV series, *Running on Air*. All of us were experienced in parkour, freerunning, and urban exploration, and each season we tried to create bigger and better stunts.

In a couple of weeks, we'd start filming Season 4, so we were currently enjoying some downtime. I hadn't seen Cal in five weeks, (*long* story), so I anticipated tonight would be an experience. Whenever we didn't see each other, we built up a reserve of antagonism and desire. Then when we were finally in each other's company, we let it rip.

It was exhilarating yet exhausting. Too addictive to give up. I'd tell myself tomorrow was the day I wouldn't take Cal's bait anymore, and every time tomorrow came, I said tomorrow again.

It was completely dysfunctional. I was aware of that. But weren't junkies also aware that they were addicted to drugs? It didn't mean they were going to quit. Besides, this was how our relationship had been for a long time, and it was hard to change old habits.

When Paul and I had first joined the cast of *Running on Air*, Cal and I developed something of a competitive rivalry. Midway through filming the first season, that rivalry turned to lust, something that had always bubbled under the surface between us. The lust led to heartache and loss. I pushed him away, he pulled me back. We fought, broke up, then found our way back to each other again. Wash, rinse, repeat. Fighting was natural to us. It meant we didn't have to acknowledge other issues and pain.

Over the course of almost four years, I'd taken a chance with him three times, and three times it ended in heartache. The first breakup was the hardest. The second added another crack, and the third, well, the third taught me never to be a fool again. It had been a year since I was last with Cal. I was strong now, and the control felt good, safe. Cal made me wild, he made me take risks, and I wasn't going back to that ever again.

"How long do you think we'll be out here?" Michaela asked, swiping away a midge.

"We can leave early if you want. I just need to show my face for an hour or so," I replied, and she seemed relieved.

Michaela started working with us a couple of weeks ago. She was perfect PA material, organised to a T. Our other assistant, Neil, was still training her, but she already felt like an integral part of the group. She also felt like a friend, and in my world, female friends were few and far between.

Michaela was very prim and proper, so it was no surprise she didn't seem too comfortable attending a party in the middle of the woods. With her neat ponytail, pencil skirt, cardigan, and ballet flats, she hadn't exactly dressed for the occasion.

I, however, had come in jeans and a hoodie. Casual attire was my usual, but I also didn't want to dress up and give Cal the idea I was trying to impress him.

Fairy lights came into view, leading to an open space surrounded by trees. I had to admit the party was impressive, especially since the location was so remote. There was a makeshift bar and a DJ booth. People were dancing and drinking, lots of barefoot girls dressed up like hippies and blokes with no shirts on.

"Is this legal?" Michaela asked, taking it all in.

"I have no idea. Come on. I think I spotted James and Paul over by the bar."

Her eyes lit up. I'd noticed she had a little bit of a crush on James, but I was pretty sure he was oblivious. It was a good thing too, since he was getting married to his long-term girlfriend, Diana, later this year. Michaela clearly didn't plan to act on her crush, but I felt bad for her all the same. I knew what it was like to want someone you couldn't have. Or, well, someone it wouldn't be *healthy* for you to have.

Cal and I were like Sid and Nancy, albeit, the less crazy, less famous version. When we were together, we burned bright but always self-destructed in the end. Nowadays we just tried to endure each other's company for the sake of our jobs.

Paul had his back turned to me, so I tapped him on the shoulder.

He turned around, grinning, and pulled me into a hug. "I thought you weren't going to show. Callum's been in a right mood."

"Don't blame me. It's not like it makes a difference to him if I'm here."

"We both know that's not true," Paul said, eyeing me meaningfully.

Paul and I were best friends. We'd met years ago, when we were just a pair of teenagers who loved parkour and had bonded over our dreams to do something bigger with our lives. With his red hair, bright blue eyes, and handsome features, people were always surprised to discover I'd never fancied him. But Paul was a dreamer, and well, a little quirky. Those were appealing attributes in a friend, but not so much in a boyfriend. Then again, I didn't exactly have great taste in men. Cal being exhibit number one.

And speak of the devil... I spotted him sitting with Trevor and his girlfriend, Reya. On the other side of him was Isaac and James' fiancée, Diana. As soon as Cal and I locked eyes, he rose and strode toward me. My pulse sped up the closer he got.

"You're late." He spoke low, and I shivered. His voice had always been one of my weaknesses.

My eyes wandered over him, from his sleeve tattoos to his ripped jeans and black T-shirt. He was every inch the sexy bad boy, every inch a cliché, and yet, I'd been a sucker for him from the start.

"Michaela and I got lost," I complained. "I'm surprised anyone managed to find this place. It's the middle of nowhere."

He gave a slight grin. "Yeah, sorry about that."

He lifted his foot to show a pair of brand-new Puma Faas 500s. They were Cal's favourite trainers for running in, though personally, I preferred my Asics Onitsuka Tigers. They had a better grip in my opinion.

"Thanks for these. Paul said they were from both of you."

Did he now? Paul was a little meddler, and I was going to have a word with him. I hadn't bought Cal anything for his birthday. Mostly because I couldn't think of what to get him. Everything felt either too personal or not personal enough. So, in the end, I went with nothing.

"Um, yeah, happy birthday."

"And what about my birthday hug?" he went on, a teasing glint in his eye.

I looked around for an escape, but everyone else was occupied. Reluctantly, I stepped forward and brought my arms around his neck for a quick, *friendly* hug. Then without warning, he pulled my body flush to his. A whoosh of air escaped me, and his smell invaded my senses. He always smelled like soap and well, something that was uniquely him. His skin had its own scent, a clean muskiness, and for a second I couldn't help sinking into him.

I miss his smell, the unbidden thought jolted me to my senses. I reminded myself that I hadn't seen him in five whole weeks. More specifically, *why* I hadn't seen him.

I straightened and stepped out of his arms. "Probably not a good idea."

He scratched his jaw and looked away. There was a flicker of shame behind his magnetic eyes when he brought them back to me. "You know I'm sorry for what happened, right? I was in the wrong and you didn't deserve to be at the centre of all that drama. I've wanted to come over to your place every day since to apologise properly, but Barry warned me off trying to see you."

Barry, our director, could be a bit of a hard bastard, and he wasn't shy in putting his foot down. In this case, I was glad of that. After the scene he caused, Cal was the last person I'd wanted to see. Only now that the storm had settled could I bring myself to be around him. I'd been upset for days before I finally got my anger under control.

When I didn't speak, Cal continued, "I've not been drinking. Trev suggested I cut back. Get my head on straight."

Cal always listened to Trev. He was like the big brother he never had and one of the few people who could make him see sense at times. "Oh? How's that been?"

His expression was self-deprecating. "Rough. I've limited myself to two drinks a night from now on. That way I can't get too…out of control."

"Seems like a good idea." He'd definitely been out of control the last time I saw him.

"Yeah."

A silence fell. I didn't know what to say, and Cal didn't seem in any rush to leave, still standing there staring at me, those green eyes of his bright with possibility. I could see the cogs turning in his head clear as day, like he was conspiring against me. Seduce me or tear me down. It was usually one or the other, though the twinkle in his eye said tonight it might be the former.

I was relieved when Michaela showed up, phone in hand.

"Oh, you're together. Good. I just received an email from Legal that both of your contracts are being renewed. You need to attend a meeting at nine tomorrow morning."

As soon as she said it, relief swept over me. Everybody else's contracts had been renewed over a month ago. Mine and Cal's were scheduled to be renewed, but then the big drama happened and the network postponed our meetings. I'd been driving myself crazy, wondering if all the negative press meant they'd decided to kick us off the show once and for all. My agent, Tanya, reassured me Season 4 was a go, and that they were just ironing out a few details. It turned out she was right and all my worrying had been for nothing.

"Good news, eh?" Cal said and I suspected he was just as relieved as I was.

I nodded before something occurred to me. "Wait, why are we both being put in the same meeting? We normally discuss our contracts separately."

Michaela gave me a perplexed look. She didn't appear to know the answer.

Cal shoved his hands in his pockets, his expression remorseful. "I'm sorry about the delay. It was all my fault."

I eyed him steadily. "Yeah, it was."

He blew out a breath and gave a low chuckle. "Tell it to me straight why don't you."

Some of the anger I'd worked so hard to let go of the last few weeks resurfaced. "Do you expect me to take it easy on you? You could've gotten us both fired."

His remorseful expression deepened. He looked like he was about to say something else when Paul joined us.

"Cal! I have a challenge," he said as he threw his arm around my shoulders.

A hint of annoyance thinned Cal's lips into a hard, straight line. He'd always been irritated at my closeness with Paul, even though there was never anything romantic between us.

Our friendship had been the catalyst to my second breakup with Cal. He discovered Paul spent the night at my place, *in my bed*, and lost his shit. And okay, it sounded bad, but Paul and I were the definition of platonic. I was pretty sure if you looked the word up in the dictionary there'd be a picture of us. Unfortunately, Cal never could quite get his head around the fact that we were friends and nothing more. Paul might as well have been a girl, but Cal didn't see it that way.

"Oh yeah? What's the challenge?" Cal questioned. I noticed his attention going to where Paul's arm rested on my shoulder.

Paul, either oblivious to Cal's hostility or deciding to ignore it, gestured to a gigantic oak tree about ten yards away. "The first one to climb to the top wins."

"But what does the winner get?" I asked with interest. Wagers always got my blood up. I loved challenges, both as a spectator and a participant.

Paul shrugged. "Bragging rights."

"How about the loser has to do the winner's dirty laundry while we film Season 4?" Cal suggested, smirking as he held my gaze.

I was reminded of a bet we'd made a long time ago. In fact, making bets was sort of our thing. Maybe that was our problem from the beginning. There always had to be a winner and a loser.

"We'll be staying in a guesthouse with a laundry service," Michaela put in.

"I have a good one," Paul said. "The loser has to strip down to their undies and run around the forest doing a primal scream."

"Is that a punishment? I love a good primal scream, and I look fantastic in my undies. Don't I, Leanne?" Cal winked at me.

I arched an eyebrow. "Modest much?"

His grin was wolfish. Somebody was definitely in the birthday mood.

"Well, are you in?" Paul nudged.

"Yes, I'm in," Cal replied, and they headed for the tree.

A group gathered to watch them, while Reya, Trev's girlfriend, came to stand next to me.

She nodded in the direction of Cal and Paul's antics. "What's going on there?"

"They're betting on who can climb to the top first."

"Of course they are." She paused as she took me in. "How have you been?"

I shrugged. "Touch and go. Mostly I'm all right."

She gave me an empathetic look. Reya knew all about the ongoing drama between Cal and me. She'd come on the road with us while we filmed Season 3 and experienced it for herself firsthand. At least no one could ever say life with us wasn't eventful.

"Has Callum apologised for the TV Choice Awards?" she asked.

I blew out a long breath. "Yes, actually. He seems pretty ashamed."

"Good. A little bit of shame will do that boy good."

"Here's hoping."

We watched Cal and Paul for a minute before Reya spoke again, "Trev said you and Michaela have been getting along."

I nodded. "It's definitely nice to have her around. Sometimes I feel like I'm going crazy around all the guys. Jo decided she wanted to try being a stay-at-home mum for a while, so we needed to find a new assistant. I liked Michaela as soon as she walked into the interview."

Reya lifted an eyebrow. "Oh?"

I chuckled. "She mistook Paul for James. She was completely embarrassed, but it was a plus in my view. It meant she didn't watch the show. A lot of people who apply for jobs with us are fans trying to get close to one of the guys."

Reya nodded. "Makes sense. Trev always tries to downplay the fan mail he gets from girls."

"Hey! You have nothing to worry about. Trev is completely besotted with you. He doesn't even look at other women."

She grinned. "I know."

All of a sudden there was a lot of cheering. Cal and Paul were neck and neck. I wasn't surprised they'd managed to get so high up. Anyone else might've worried someone would get injured, but we did much more dangerous stunts on a daily basis. Climbing was our bread and butter. Truth be told, I was kind of disappointed I hadn't taken part. I was smaller and more agile than both of them and could climb way faster. My competitive streak groaned at the missed opportunity to beat Cal. There had always been something intensely satisfying about besting him, more so than anyone else, which was an impulse I did *not* want to analyse too deeply.

In the end, Cal climbed the highest, which I guess meant Paul had to strip and run around the forest while primal screaming. I was just glad it wasn't Cal. Him being naked often tested my willpower.

The two of them began climbing back down, and I went with Reya to get a drink. We joined Trev, James, Diana, Isaac, and Michaela, who were all sitting on a picnic blanket enjoying the party. Reya lowered herself to sit next to Trev, and I took the space beside Michaela.

"You surviving okay?" I asked quietly.

She shot me a grin. "Yeah, just about."

There was a wolf whistle, and I turned to see a bunch of people egging Paul on as he stripped down to his boxers. Cal was in tears laughing, and I couldn't help my small grin. It was nice to see him having a good time. In spite of everything that had happened between us, and in spite of how difficult he could be, I still cared for him, still wanted him to be happy.

I just knew that it would never be with me.

"Oh, my God, what is Paul doing?" Diana asked. "Why is he taking all his clothes off?"

"They had a bet," I told her. "He lost."

"Well, it's a good thing the weather's warm today,' Diana replied, "Otherwise he'd catch his death."

"Actually, when we run our core body temperature increases," Michaela countered shyly. "Technically, it's better for him to run naked in the cold than in heat. It puts him in less risk of heatstroke and dehydration."

Diana frowned at her, annoyed. "Who are you again?"

"That's Michaela, babe," James said. "Remember, I told you? She's our new assistant."

"Oh, really? How cute," Diana chirped. Not surprisingly it came out disingenuous.

Diana was someone whose cattiness always bothered me, but I tolerated her for James' sake.

Cal and Paul came to join us, with Paul dropping breathlessly down on the other side of Michaela and Cal taking the spot next to me.

Paul winked at Michaela. "What do you think? Do you like blokes when they're all sweaty?"

She fought a smile. "Not particularly."

"Not even when they've got the body of a Greek God?"

She shook her head and let out a nervous giggle. I was sure if it were James flirting with her right now she might spontaneously combust. "Not even then."

"So you're saying there's a chance," Paul continued to tease, his grin amiable.

"You'll have to keep an eye on him when you come with us to Joburg," Trev said to Michaela. "Paul's got a habit for sneaking into girls' bedrooms at night."

"Hey!" Paul protested. "I'll have you know sleepwalking is a serious disorder."

"Oh, is that what they're calling it?" Trev chuckled.

"Speaking of Joburg, I can't wait to show you all around," Isaac put in. "My cousin Thato almost lost it when I told him we were coming. He's excited to meet you all."

Isaac was the newest and youngest member of our cast. He grew up in a township on the edges of Johannesburg, and he'd fascinated Trev with tales of his upbringing. So much so that Trev managed to convince our director, Barry, to shoot the fourth season there.

We'd never filmed so far afield, and I for one was eager to explore the city. I adored going places that looked and felt distinctly different from London. It gave me a thrilling rush to be in a part of the world I knew nothing about, to learn about the customs and culture, the history. Joburg also looked like an incredible place to freerun. Since Isaac was born and raised there before he and his family emigrated, I was hoping he could show us the real side of the city, rather than the usual tourist spots.

And the fact that I'd be living in the same house as Cal? Well, that was the only thing I wasn't looking forward to, but I could handle it. I'd managed to keep a professional distance from him for almost a year. I wasn't going to let a few weeks of filming break me.

"Have you been seeing anyone?" Cal spoke low, and I jumped a little. I hadn't noticed how close he was.

Then, I frowned, because he knew good and well that wasn't a question he should be asking after all the drama that went down. "Are you referring to Ben Young?"

Cal's facial muscles moved in a way that told me even mentioning Ben's name pissed him off.

"He's an arsehole, you know that, right?"

"And what are you, some kind of saint?"

"At least I'm upfront about it. Ben's the sort of bloke who acts like an altar boy then shags your best mate behind your back."

"I'm pretty sure Paul wouldn't be interested," I scoffed.

Cal shot me an aggravated look. "You know what I mean."

I let out a heavy sigh and relented. "I'm not seeing Ben Young. I was never even interested in him to begin with. You just blew everything out of proportion, like always."

I could tell what I said irritated Cal from the tight set of his jaw. He eyed me closely. "What if I told you I've been seeing someone?"

I tried to ignore the sting in my chest at the idea of Cal having a girlfriend. "You are? And where is she tonight?"

"She had to work. She'll be here later."

There was that sting again. I rubbed my sternum, knowing I had no business feeling jealous. He and I were over, and we both needed to find other people eventually, so why not now?

Cal continued to watch me until I grew uncomfortable. "Why are you staring?"

"You're jealous," he stated.

"No, I'm not."

"You forget I can read your facial expressions like a book."

"Well, if you think I'm jealous your reading technique is off, because I could care less if you're dating someone," I bluffed.

"Oh really? So how would it make you feel if I told you I lied just now?"

That little shit. I shoved him in the shoulder. "That was manipulative."

Cal grinned. "You're relieved, though, right?"

I was, but I'd never admit it. My jealousy and subsequent relief weren't logical. They were *illogical*. And that was why I refused to let how I felt for Cal control me. I could never feel free if my emotions were constantly dependent on the actions of someone who'd proven themselves to be unpredictable.

I made sure to look him directly in the eye. "Cal, believe me when I say this, I want you to be happy. I want you to find someone."

His expression sobered and he didn't speak for a long moment. When he did, he looked away and picked up a fallen leaf, smoothing his fingers over its lined surface. "Yeah well, I don't think I'm ready for a relationship. I've got a lot of issues with my temper that I need to sort through. What happened with Ben Young helped me realise that, so at least something good came out of that shitshow."

I studied him. It was unlike Cal to admit he needed to work on himself. I'd more expect him to claim he was perfect and that the rest of the world had the problem.

"Are you telling me you're turning over a new leaf?" It seemed poetic that he was holding one in his hand.

"Maybe not an entire leaf, but I am trying to change my ways, starting with drinking less."

Hmm, Cal did always do his worst damage when he was drunk.

"That's good. I guess... I guess I'm proud of you."

His expression softened. My statement seemed to mean something to him. "I really am sorry for what happened, Leanne. I never want to feel that out of control ever again, or put your career in jeopardy just because I'm a jealous twat."

Maybe that was why I always felt like I lost control when we were together. His wildness was contagious.

"You know I…" I coughed, my throat suddenly tight. Why was I feeling so emotional all of a sudden? "You know I meant it when I said I want you to be happy."

His eyes brightened, his voice almost wistful. "I want you to be happy too."

For a second, the emotion in his voice plunged me into a memory.

How can it hurt this much to lose something you didn't even know you had?

Cal's question from three years ago still echoed in my head regularly. It was the reminder I needed to stay away from him. If not physically, since we had to work together, then at least emotionally. I needed to constantly remind myself of all the reasons why letting Cal back into my heart was a bad idea. He took me on these crazy, exhilarating rides, but it always ended in pain. I couldn't do it again. I *wouldn't*.

What happened several weeks ago was a prime example of the chaos Cal brought into my life. I kept it at the forefront of my mind so that I wouldn't slip.

My heart had taken too many beatings over the years, and I wasn't sure it could survive another.

Two
Callum
5 weeks ago

I was in a foul mood.

Maybe it was the flashing cameras and the shouting reporters. Maybe it was the fact that Mum was still recovering from a nasty viral infection. Or maybe it was because Leanne hadn't spoken to me since I entered the limo taking us to the TV Choice Awards.

This year *Running on Air* had received four nominations, but I couldn't seem to focus on how amazing that was. Instead, I fixated on Leanne. It had been a rough year since our last breakup, and even though she was civil, I knew deep down she still hadn't forgiven me. The worst part? She'd broken up with me for something I *didn't even do*.

That was the problem with being famous. People liked to twist things, make you look like a prick when you were just trying to do your job.

I was first to step out of the limo, followed by Trev, Paul, James, Isaac, and last but not least, Leanne. She wore a pair of tight black pants and a fitted black waistcoat with, get this, nothing underneath. Her wardrobe generally consisted of monochrome—that was nothing new—but she'd stepped it up a level tonight. I had a hard time looking away.

We arrived on the red carpet and posed for pictures. I stepped up beside her, my hand grazing her elbow as I asked, "Who are you trying to impress?"

Because it certainly wasn't me.

She cast me a quick, assessing glance before she replied, "No one," then smiled for the cameras. I blinked at the blinding white light. Leanne didn't put her hand on her hip or tilt her head like the models and actors ahead of us. Instead her hands were in her pockets. Her posture said, *this is what you're getting, take it or leave it.*

It was one of the things I admired about her. She didn't give in to pressure to follow the pack. Before I met her, I thought I knew what I wanted in a woman. Then Leanne came along and flipped all that on its head. Now I was ruined for anyone else and she didn't even know it, let alone give me the chance to make her understand.

"Speaking of being out to impress," she said, eyeing my designer suit. "Is Mia Popov going to be here tonight or something?"

It was a low blow, but I tamped down my bitterness. "How many times do I have to tell you? Nothing happened with Mia."

Leanne rolled her eyes. "Cal, I saw her interview. When they asked her about you, she flushed, giggled then coyly responded that you were close. Just how many gorgeous Russian tennis players have you been "close" with?"

"She's an up and comer who lied for publicity. I met her once and we had a brief conversation, then I never saw her again."

"She was sitting on your lap. There are pictures, if you haven't forgotten," Leanne replied tersely. We'd had this conversation a million times, but I refused to quit having it until she finally believed me. I'd been doing a paid appearance at a night club. Unluckily for me, the tennis player Mia Popov had been in attendance. She sat on my lap uninvited and tried to flirt with me. Leanne and I had just gotten back together after our second breakup, so I wasn't even remotely interested.

"Just because a picture paints a thousand words, that doesn't make them true," I said through gritted teeth.

Leanne turned to look at me, eyes moving back and forth between mine. For a second, I thought she saw something she could understand, but then her expression went blank.

"I'm not talking to you about this anymore."

"Leanne—" I started, but she'd already turned around to walk away.

I ran a hand over my jaw. Yeah, tonight was not going to be my night. A bunch of reporters called my name, but I stalked by them without responding. We were supposed to stop and give interviews, but the others could take the slack. I needed a drink.

I was on my fourth whiskey before I even made it to our table. We were seated next to a bunch of actors from a popular TV drama. I took the empty seat beside Trev and grabbed the bottle of Prosecco, filling my glass to the brim.

I hated this bubbly shit, but I was miserable enough to drink it anyway.

A couple of seats away Leanne sat next to a blond, smug looking actor in a black suit. I already didn't like the look of him or the way *he* looked at Leanne. The fact that their outfits matched only pissed me off more.

The ceremony began, but I barely paid any attention to what was going on onstage. I wanted to know what that smug arsehole was whispering in Leanne's ear. She laughed at something he said and he briefly touched her arm. I wanted to break his hand.

A bunch of people started clapping, the cameras zooming in on our table. We'd won Best Reality Show. In a drunken daze, I followed the others up onto the stage, skulking in the background while Trev made a short speech to thank everyone who voted for us.

When it came time to announce the award for Best Actor, guess who won? That's right, the smug fuck who'd been chatting Leanne up all night. His name was Ben Young and never in my life had I encountered a more punchable face.

The ceremony was coming to a close and I was drunk enough to do something stupid. I stood from my seat and approached Leanne.

"Can we talk?"

She glanced at me, saw how shitfaced I was and pursed her lips. "Callum, not now."

"I just need to talk to you for a second," I slurred.

Ben Young shot me a dirty look, but Leanne didn't catch it. "She said she doesn't want to talk to you. I think you should go back to your seat."

I eyeballed him. "This isn't your business."

"You're drunk and harassing this woman," he said, like he was some kind of white knight. Fuck that noise. "So I'm making it my business."

He got up to stand toe-to-toe with me. The idiot clearly didn't know a lion when he saw one because I was two seconds away from mauling him. If his expression was anything to go by, he thought he could take me.

Were all actors this stupid?

"Stay out of this," I said, giving him one last chance to back down as I levelled my gaze on Leanne. My eyes pleaded, *don't make me argue with this arsehole. Just talk to me.*

She let out a heavy sigh. "Ced, you've got two minutes."

She started to stand up, but Ben gestured for her to sit back down. "You don't need to go with him."

"Still poking your nose in other people's business," I tutted.

Now he glared at me. "You're a bully. I don't like bullies."

"You don't know what you're talking about. Now, get out of my fucking way."

His expression oozed smugness. The piece of shit had the nerve to take his time as he gave me a slow perusal up and down. "Tell me, are you trying to compensate for something with all those tattoos?" He glanced disdainfully at my mum's name that was inked across my knuckles. "Who's Judy? Don't tell me you were dumb enough to get a girl's name tattooed on you?"

"Ben, maybe you should leave him—"

Leanne didn't have time to finish her sentence because I drove my fist into Ben Young's face. *Congratulations on winning Best Actor, you smug fuck.* It felt good for a couple of seconds before I was tackled by three security guards and escorted roughly from the room.

That was the last thing I remembered before I woke in my bed the next morning, head throbbing. My phone buzzed on my nightstand, but I ignored it. I struggled to recall how I'd gotten here, but my memory drew a blank. Trev or James must've brought me home. My phone vibrated again and this time I picked it up. My stomach dropped when I saw all the notifications and stories I'd been tagged in.

Running on Air Star Callum Davidson punches Actor Ben Young at TV Choice Awards.

There were at least a dozen headlines, each one worse than the last.

Ben Young to Have Callum Davidson Charged for Assault.

I'll admit that one made me panic. Why the hell had I let my temper get the best of me? I tried to remember the events of last night more clearly, but all I could see was Leanne's shocked and upset face after I'd hit him. Guilt and regret roiled inside me. I wanted to puke.

I was such a fucking idiot.

For over three years I'd been trying to win Leanne's trust, convince her that we could be something great if she let it. It dawned on me all at once that I'd been going about it all the wrong way. She was never going to trust me after last night.

But I refused to let this be the end of us. I just needed to make amends.

No, I needed to change, grow up, be a mature adult.

It was simple yet profound. I couldn't just keep telling Leanne we should be together. I needed to show her *why* we should be together. And the only way to do that was through my own actions and behaviour. Behaviour that didn't involve punching smug actors in the face when they tried to come at me.

Speaking of which, I swallowed my pride and pulled up my lawyer's number. I needed to convince Ben Young not to press charges. Yep, this was going to hurt like a mother, but I'd do it if it meant showing Leanne I could be the bigger person.

Bringing the phone to my ear, I pressed 'call'.

Three
Leanne
Present

I arrived for my 9 a.m. meeting five minutes early and Cal was already there. He stood outside the building holding two takeaway coffee cups. I'd expected him to blow the meeting off and have Neil reschedule at a more reasonable hour, but no, there he was, bright-eyed and bushy-tailed. He must've really stuck to his two-drink rule last night.

I wished I could say the same. I'd gone home early, crawled into my pj's and drank a whole bottle of wine before falling asleep. Red wine sent me into a blissfully dreamless sleep, but it wasn't so great for hangovers. I currently wore my hood up to avoid the glaring light of the sun.

"You look like you could use this." Cal held out one of the coffees.

I gave a nondescript grunt and took the offered beverage. He chuckled at my grouchiness, and I sipped the coffee, pleasantly surprised that he got my usual order right. Black with a drop of milk, no sugar. Cal was one of those people who remembered the small details.

I felt uneasy after our heart-to-heart last night and couldn't decide how to be with him. When I gave him attitude, he kept his distance. But as soon as I showed a bit of softness, he snuck right under my deceptively flimsy skin.

On the surface it looked thick, but on closer inspection, it was thin as paper.

"You're a ray of fucking sunshine today, Leanne," he commented wryly as we entered the building and stepped onto the lift.

I gave him a sour smile. "Aren't I, though?"

More chuckling from him. His chipper mood started to grate on me.

Our agent, Tanya Sanders, was waiting for us at reception. I liked Tanya. She was no-nonsense and always up-front. She told the truth, not just what you wanted to hear. Tanya currently represented all members of the *Running on Air* cast, mostly because she was an excellent negotiator. All six of us earned a very good living because of her.

"Fantastic, you're both here." She stood to greet us, giving us each a hug and peck on the cheek, as was her habit.

"Are you going to tell us what's going on?" Cal asked.

Tanya worried her lip. "I was literally only given the information last night, but I think it might be best if I let the lawyers explain it to you. Then we can discuss things in more depth."

Hmm, that sounded ominous. Cal and I shared a look before Tanya led us into a room where two men in suits were waiting. "This is Ted Pilkins and Ryan Kent. They're going to go through your new contracts for the upcoming season," Tanya said.

"Wait a second," Cal cut in. "Don't you mean upcoming seasons plural? The others have all been signed for three more."

That was a very good question.

"We'll get to that," Ted replied. "But first, I'd like to thank you both for coming at such short notice. As you know, we normally set up separate meetings for each of you, but an unusual request has popped up."

Cal sat back and clasped his hands together, eyeing Ted with growing suspicion.

"An unusual request?" I asked curiously.

Ryan cleared his throat. "In light of the recent events involving Mr. Davidson and Ben Young, the network would like to make an addendum to both of your contracts."

"What kind of addendum?" Cal questioned, leaning forward.

Ryan glanced at Ted. They shared a somewhat tense look before Ted spoke. "Throughout the last few seasons, there has been a lot of press surrounding your relationship. In the past, this has been great for bringing in viewers, but since recent events have gotten Mr. Davidson into hot water, we would like you both to take a step back from any romantic involvement."

"I'm sorry, but that's a highly unethical request to make of my clients," Tanya cut in.

I frowned so hard I could feel an indent form between my eyebrows. "Cal and I are not romantically involved. Not anymore."

"You don't need to explain yourself, Leanne," Tanya said. "Who you see or don't see should be no concern of the network." She shot Ted a sharp look.

He cleared his throat. "That may be true, but unfortunately, since there's been so much bad publicity surrounding the aforementioned event, we would like a guarantee that it won't happen again. We've included a new clause in your contracts that stipulates there will be no further romantic relationship between Miss Simmons and Mr. Davidson."

"That is very fucking weird," Cal said.

"Yeah, I second that," I added.

"We need to ensure there won't be any further legal matters," Ryan said. "Surely, you can understand the concern."

Cal eyeballed him. "It's not like there was some big lawsuit. The whole thing was settled out of court, and the money came straight from my own pocket. The network didn't have to pay a penny."

"That might be so," Ryan said. "But with this kind of scandal, we can lose the support of our sponsors, which in turn means we lose money. We will also be renewing your contracts on a yearly basis from now on, instead of every three years."

Tanya appeared to be thinking. "If my clients agree to this amendment, would you be prepared to sign them for three seasons like the rest of the cast, instead of only one?"

"We can't budge on that," Ted responded. "The one-year contract is a preliminary period. If your clients manage not to violate the terms, then they'll be signed for two further seasons."

I shifted uncomfortably in my seat. It felt very invasive to have my personal relationship with Cal looked at in such an impersonal manner. Cal was frowning down at his clasped hands. He clearly didn't like any of this either.

"Can you give me a private moment with my clients?" Tanya requested.

"Yes, of course," Ryan said as he and Ted stood up. "We'll be just outside."

They left the room and Tanya exhaled heavily. "Okay, tell me what you're thinking."

"I'm not doing it," Cal stood firm.

Tanya nodded then looked to me. "What about you, Leanne?"

I took a second to think about it. My initial reaction was similar to Cal's, but the more I thought about it, the more I realised this might actually be a good thing. The past three seasons I ended up sleeping with Cal at one point or another. I obviously had no self-control when it came to him. Maybe I needed something like this. Something much more serious than possible heartbreak. Maybe I needed to know that if I gave in to him, I could lose my job, my livelihood.

I opened my mouth to respond. "I...I actually think it's a good idea."

Tanya looked surprised, while Cal scowled at me so hard I thought his face might crack. "What the hell?"

On instinct, I reached out and touched his hand, speaking steadily. "I agree with you that this is weird, but just think about it. We both know our relationship is over. What's the harm in signing a contract that says the same? Besides, if it means keeping our jobs, I think we should do it."

He stared at me a beat longer than I was comfortable with, like his eyes were trying to tell me something he couldn't say out loud. Finally, he grunted, "This is such bullshit."

"It is bullshit," Tanya agreed. "And if you want me to fight this for you, I will."

Cal considered her, then me. I saw his internal struggle. He wasn't someone who backed down easily, and he'd had to swallow a lot of pride when he paid off Ben Young. I worried this contract might be the straw that broke the camel's back.

Then, an idea appeared to spark behind his eyes. He folded his arms, his attention starting at my feet and hitting every inch of my body before finally resting on my face. Surprisingly, he smiled. "Okay, I'm in."

Huh? That seemed a little *too* easy.

"You are?" Tanya questioned. She sounded just as surprised as I was.

He shrugged, and I didn't trust his calm façade. Something untoward was afoot. I could feel it. "Like Leanne said, what harm can it do?"

Tanya studied him a moment longer, then said, "All right then. I'll go grab Ryan and Ted and then we'll have both your lawyers come to look over the contracts."

She briefly left the room and I narrowed my gaze at Cal, whispering, "What are you up to?"

He plastered on an innocent expression. "I don't know what you mean."

Tanya, Ryan, and Ted re-entered before I could say more and took their seats.

"Tanya tells us you've come to a decision," said Ryan, seeming pleased.

Cal tilted his head, emitting pure attitude. "We're going to sign. But you can tell your network bigwigs I said fuck you for being such ruthless bastards. Feel free to quote me."

I tried not to smile at him freely using the F-word in front of these straitlaced suits. Tanya appeared to be holding in a laugh, while Ted and Ryan looked red-faced and uncomfortable over how to respond. Finally, Ted gave a stiff, "Very well then."

When our lawyers arrived we spent the next few hours going over the contracts. Once we both signed on the dotted line, Cal and I headed back down to the lobby together. I still suspected Cal was hiding something, but I couldn't think of what it might be. A silence hung over us when I pushed the button inside the otherwise empty lift.

Cal cocked his head to me, a cheeky slant to his mouth. "What is it about rules that makes me want to break them?"

The sultry look in his eyes put me on alert. I bloody well knew he was up to something. "That's a problem you'll have to figure out for yourself. I have no issue following rules."

"Want to bet?"

I froze, because those words were my kryptonite, especially coming out of Cal's mouth. Trying to appear nonchalant, I rolled my eyes and willed the lift to move faster. "Don't start."

"What? You have to admit this is a very interesting situation we've found ourselves in."

"Not particularly," I lied.

Cal continued speaking as though he hadn't even heard me, his tone ponderous. "We both just signed a contract stating we won't get involved in a romantic relationship, but what exactly does "romantic" entail?"

"It's an umbrella term. It entails everything you might associate with two people who are involved. Don't go getting ideas."

"Fucking isn't very romantic though, is it?" he asked, and a shiver coursed through me. "Sure, it's primal, animalistic even, but it's certainly not romantic."

I shot him a look. "I thought you were turning over a new leaf. Why are you searching for loopholes?"

He ignored my comment about his new leaf. It might as well be a shrivelled brown husk right now for all the effort he was making to try and change. I knew it was all too good to be true.

"We've always enjoyed our little on/off friends-with-benefits thing," he said then tutted. "It's sure going to be tough abstaining. A real challenge." His eyes flicked to mine, almost goading me. "You could say that for us it's the *ultimate* challenge."

The doors slid open when we reached the ground floor, and I stepped out before turning around to face him. "It won't be tough abstaining. Like I said, I have no problem following rules."

Cal's eyes shone with mirth. "If you're so good at it, then you should put your strength to the test. And what better way to test it than with a bet?"

I groaned loudly and turned to walk away, while at the same time my risk-taking heart thrummed at the opportunity to win something. The very thrill of it rushed through my veins. Cal gently caught my arm, stopping me in my tracks.

I closed my eyes and spoke low. "Stop trying to tempt me with a bet. It's a sly move. You know betting is my weakness."

When he didn't speak, I opened my eyes and found him staring at me in the strangest way. For a brief moment, there was no bravado, just affection.

I levelled him with a serious look. "We could lose our jobs, Cal. This isn't something to play around with."

"Some things are more important than jobs," he spoke low, his voice thick.

I frowned at him. "What are you talking about?"

Wherever his head had gone, he shook himself out of it. The tenderness I saw in him a second ago was gone, replaced with the mischief I knew so well.

"We won't lose our jobs. Trust me."

"How can you know that?"

His eyes wandered to my lips then back up. "Because even if we do violate our contracts, no one is going to know unless we tell them. And why would we ever do something like that?"

The huskiness in his voice sent a tingle down my spine. He had a point. Nobody had to know about the bet but us...

Oh God, Leanne. Shut up. You're being stupid.

When I didn't speak, Cal continued, "This will be the highest stakes we've ever had. You think we can hack this, but I disagree. I think it's only a matter of time before we break. If by the end of filming this season, we end up doing anything that falls under the umbrella of "romance" I win. If we don't, you win."

Like an untamed beast inside my chest, my competitive side thrashed and fought to break free. It was the same beast that got a thrill when I jumped between rooftops, the one that purred in satisfaction when I defied death and broke records during our stunts. It whispered seductively in my ear, telling me that this really would be the ultimate challenge. If I won, I'd get to keep my job, but I'd also prove to myself that I was finally in control of my own instincts. That Cal couldn't tempt me anymore with his irresistible wildness and chaos.

Then, just like it had already been decided, I asked a pertinent question. "What's the prize?"

Cal's grin grew so wide and satisfied that I again questioned if something else was afoot. He loved his job, and it just didn't add up that he'd risk losing it to play out some little wager with me. A part of me was going along with it merely to find out what his game was. Another, admittedly bigger part, wanted to win.

He appeared to be thinking, then finally he said, "The winner gets a month-long trip to Japan, paid for by the loser."

Japan was on both of our bucket lists, but neither of us had the opportunity to go yet. Everything else aside, it was definitely a prize worth fighting for.

I shook my head. "There's something seriously wrong with us, you know that, right?"

He smirked, like he had me right where he wanted me. He was so, *so* wrong. "That's why we aren't going to be able to stick to this rule, Leanne, and I'm going to win the bet."

"Fat chance. I won't be touching you with a ten-foot pole."

His expression turned heated and I hated how it set a spark alight in me.

"Game on, little one," Cal said before he turned and left me standing alone on the street. There was something about his confidence, the sure set of his shoulders as he walked away that made me start to freak out. Just a little.

What the hell had I gotten myself into?

Four
Leanne

The VIP lounge at the airport was my happy place.

When you were on TV, you got those first-class privileges. I always arrived early since, you know, free food and drink was a big passion of mine. It was a far cry from the working-class background I came from.

I looked completely out of place in my ripped jeans, T-shirt, hoodie, and trainers, but I didn't let that stop me. I sipped a Bellini and nibbled a croissant, while two businessmen a few tables away shot me side glances like I'd snuck in or something. I cocked an eyebrow and lifted my glass at them. They frowned and looked away, pretending they hadn't seen.

I looked over by the entrance just as Trev and Paul arrived. It was our tradition to meet here whenever we flew out of Heathrow. It was an eleven-hour flight to Johannesburg, so I planned on getting good and sauced by the time we took off.

There were few things better in life than drunk napping in first class.

"Hey, Leanne," Paul pulled me into a hug, jostling my cocktail. Some of it sploshed over the side and onto the table.

I returned his hug with gusto, since I really, really loved hugs. They were nutrition for the soul, especially when you were on your third cocktail of the morning.

"Are you excited for this trip?" I asked.

He smiled, his ginger hair uncombed, like he'd just rolled out of bed. "Of course. I even came prepared with my brand-new signature flight kit."

Trev shot him a look. "Oh?"

Paul started listing off items. "Sleep mask, flight pillow, eucalyptus spray, whale sounds on my iPhone."

I chuckled. "That actually sounds pretty good, but my plan is simpler: get drunk then enjoy the peaceful slumber of inebriation."

"Ah, a classic," Paul laughed.

"Hey," Trev began, his tone becoming serious. "Paul filled me in about yours and Cal's contracts."

My stomach tightened, not because of the contracts, but because Trev mentioning them reminded me of the bet. I was pretty sure my co-stars wouldn't approve. "Yeah, it's crazy, but they didn't leave us much choice," I replied.

"It's definitely a bizarre scenario," Paul added. "If you get back with your ex, you lose your job? What kind of sick twist comes up with this stuff?"

"They're just trying to cover themselves. Honestly, given what Cal did at the awards ceremony, I can kind of understand," I said.

"Well, we'll all keep a close eye on the two of you," Trev added with a wink. "Cal's penis will be steering well clear of your vagina if I have anything to do with it."

Paul faked a grimace. "Please reserve your penis and vagina talk for after 5 p.m. Some of us like to keep an air of decorum this early in the day."

Trev barked a laugh.

"He's right though," I said. "You all need to watch me like hawks. Don't let Cal get his hooks in."

Speak of the devil, Cal walked into the lounge right at that moment, a small backpack slung over his shoulder. My pulse spiked like it always did, pitter-pattering away inside my fragile chest. In spite of everything, my insides still got all fluttery and anxious whenever he was around. Mostly because we had a habit of rubbing each other up the wrong way. Other times rubbing each other up the right way, which obviously was half the problem.

He pulled a paperback from his bag and plopped it down on the table in front of Paul. *The Book of Joy* by the Dalai Lama and Desmond Tutu. "Pretty sure you left this at my place," Cal said, shades covering his eyes. I sometimes wondered if he wore sunglasses indoors just so you couldn't see what his eyes were saying to you.

"How do you know it's mine?" Paul asked.

"Well, it's obviously not his," I interjected cheekily. "Since it's not *The Art of War* or Machiavelli's *The Prince*."

Trev chuckled. "I think she just called you a douche, Cal."

Cal turned his attention to me, though I couldn't tell his expression past the dark lenses of his Ray-Bans. Then, his lips curved into a sexy smile. "Leanne's just mad because I can close my eyes whenever I like and see her naked. Oh hey, I'm doing it right now."

I fought a grin. So he wanted to play? Okay, then. "I'm not mad. I've got a great body and men like to think about it. I mean, you have a great body too, except for, well, your whole baby carrot situation."

Paul laughed and clapped him around the shoulder. "Aw, don't worry, Cal. It's not about size, it's about technique, am I right?"

Just as a sidenote, Cal did *not* have a small penis. But just like our bet, I wanted to win this battle of wits. After all, I was the one who started it. Our banter was one of the things I missed most about being with him. Maybe I had a masochistic streak, but it was fun to see who could come up with the best put-down.

Cal still stared at me, finally pushing his sunglasses up to level me with a heated expression. "Can baby carrots make you see God? Because I'm pretty sure that's what you called me last time."

Paul and Trev chuckled while I blushed hard and Cal saw it. My mind drew a blank. I did not have a comeback for that one. And now he had me thinking of the last time we had sex.

This trip was getting off to a *fantastic* start.

A minute later Isaac and James arrived, and the rest of the crew trickled in.

I did my best not to engage Cal, instead talking with James, who was all wrapped up in wedding preparations, which sounded pretty full-on. Diana was, well, high maintenance. She wasn't exactly my kind of person, but she and James were in love, so that was all that really mattered, right?

When it was time to board our flight, I was irritated to find my seat was across from Cal's. Since we were in first class, there was enough privacy so that I could ignore him if I wanted.

Unfortunately, ignoring him had always been a problem for me.

I turned around and bumped into our producer, Linda.

"Whoa there, girly," she said, holding up a hand. "Where are you rushing off to?"

I blew out a breath. I liked Linda. She was always around when I needed someone to unload my drama on. And she always went out of her way to fix whatever problem I was having.

"My seat is across from Cal's," I sighed. "I was going to ask one of the flight attendants if it's possible for me to switch."

Linda's eyes turned sympathetic. "I think I heard them say this flight is fully booked."

I chewed my lip, frustrated. "Will you switch with me? You're sitting next to Ken, right?"

Linda shook her head, shifting awkwardly as passengers passed us by. "Sorry, honey, but Ken and I have a tonne of work to do on this flight."

I blew out a breath, resigning myself to the fact that I was going to have to sit across from Cal. I'd just put the privacy partition up if he tried talking to me. Simple.

"Hey," Linda called as I went to retake my seat. "If he gives you trouble, you tell him where to stick it. You're tough. Leanne Simmons cowers to no man."

I wished her pep talk bolstered me. Instead it fell kind of flat. She just didn't understand the complicated tangle of history and feelings between us. There was also the little matter of the bet, and I knew he was going to take advantage of our close proximity during this flight to play with me.

It didn't take long. I was strapping on my seat belt when I sensed Cal's attention. I feigned preoccupation with the flight magazines. "Have I got something on my face?"

I shouldn't have given him an opening, but sometimes I was my own worst enemy.

"No. Just wondering how you've been," he replied softly.

Often, Cal was in a mood to fight, other times he was uncharacteristically caring. Right now, he'd decided to play nice, and since I was feeling defensive, he'd caught me off guard. Then again, this could all be a part of his plan to win the bet. I played along purely out of curiosity to see what his angle was.

"I've been fine," I answered, still not looking at him. It had been two weeks since our meeting about the contracts. Two weeks in which I'd gone out of my way to avoid him. I'd almost convinced myself our bet hadn't taken place at all. But when I looked at him, the hint of mischief in his gaze told me it was very much still on. He'd taken off his sunglasses, and his startlingly green eyes always smacked you like *pow!* They were eyes you could get lost in.

"Haven't seen you at the gym much," he went on.

We had our own private, specially kitted out gym in London, paid for by our sponsors. I actually *had* been there, but I'd been going at 5 a.m. with the specific intention of avoiding everyone. Mostly Cal. When we filmed, we had to live in each other's pockets, so I valued my alone time.

"I've been going early in the morning. You know I never miss a workout," I said then finally looked at him. For a second his eyes flashed with a rare glimpse of the shared pain we tried not to talk about. Chasing away our demons through exercise was something we both had in common.

I blinked and looked away. A flight attendant came by offering drinks, and I got a double vodka. Cal watched as I downed it in two gulps, but he didn't comment. That was one good trait he had—he didn't judge.

I pulled my flight pillow around my neck and closed my eyes, hoping sleep would come. It was at that moment that Trev, whose seat was directly in front of mine, decided to engage Cal in a long and detailed conversation about one of the stunts we had planned for this season.

It went on for nearly twenty minutes when I let out a long, beleaguered sigh and opened my eyes, glancing between the two of them. "Do one of you want to switch seats with me? I'm trying to sleep here."

Cal frowned. "Why would you want to sleep? Johannesburg is only one hour ahead of London."

"Because what else am I going to do for the next eleven hours?"

"I can think of a few things." His expression heated, his voice low.

I pointed my finger at him. "Don't start with that face and that voice. I'm not in the mood." Also, if he thought he was going to win our bet that easily he had another thing coming.

"Hey! You keep your mile-high club aspirations to yourself," Trev warned Cal. "You have a contract to uphold, remember? No shagging Leanne. At least not for the next year."

I shot Trev a serious look. "We are definitely *not* shagging."

"Maybe we should be," Cal said quietly, leaning on his armrest. "You seem tense."

I grumbled and turned away, endeavouring to ignore him. He enjoyed riling me way too much.

"I'm going to have to keep my eye on you, aren't I?" Trev said to Cal.

"Any excuse to check out my arse," Cal shot back.

Trev was unfazed. "Well, it is a fantastic arse."

Oh man, this was going to be a *long* flight. In fact, I had a feeling this season was going to test me like no other.

***

To my surprise, Cal didn't talk to me again for the rest of the flight. He must've been trying to make some kind of point.

And I didn't sleep either. Nope. I was wide awake the entire time. I thought being legally obliged not to be with Cal would make things easier, but I only found myself more aware of him. Every time he took a swig from his water bottle, I was mesmerised by how his throat moved as he swallowed. When he pulled off his jumper and his T-shirt rode up underneath, my eyes instinctively wandered to his exposed midriff.

One time he even caught me looking, and the satisfaction on his face was intensely aggravating. Yep, my willpower was definitely going to get tested over the next few weeks.

On the drive from the airport to our guesthouse just outside the city, I sat beside Michaela, my attention glued to the window. I was fascinated by the bustling city at night. The air felt different here, thicker somehow.

The guesthouse wasn't hugely fancy, but it was private, and it had been rented out to accommodate the entire cast and crew. It had twelve bedrooms, a private garden, and a pool, plus a view over the city. I was delighted to discover I'd been assigned a bedroom all of my own, while the boys had to bunk up in pairs. Our assistant Neil gave me a little wink, and I smiled. The solo bedroom had obviously been his doing.

Neil had a bit of a soft spot for me. We never spoke about it, but I tried not to take advantage of the fact, though I could never tell if his affection was platonic or romantic.

I wanted him to know I appreciated the room, so I gave him a brief hug. When I turned around, Cal was glaring at him, chewing on a toothpick. He wasn't looking at me, just eyeballing Neil. I marched up to him, grabbed his hand and pulled him into an empty lounge room just off the reception area.

He took his time pulling the toothpick from his mouth and stared down at me impassively, arching an eyebrow. "Yup?"

I made sure to look him dead in the eye. "Leave Neil alone. He doesn't need you giving him a hard time."

"Why would I do anything to Neil?" Cal replied like butter wouldn't melt. He was well aware of Neil's soft spot for me. "Is there something I should know about?"

"Of course there isn't. Neil is our assistant, that's all."

Cal stared at me for a long moment. "He does these little favours because he fancies you. You realise that, right?"

"He does things for me because he *works* for me," I tried to keep my voice down, even though I really wanted to start yelling. Cal had that effect on me. I turned to walk away.

"So, you don't think he booked you your own room because he's hoping to be invited in some night?" he called.

I swung back around. "Just because all you think about is sex, doesn't mean everyone else is the same." I left the room before he had the chance to reply.

In my bedroom, I flopped down onto the mattress and let out a tired groan as I snuggled into the pillow. After the stress of dealing with Cal, I definitely needed a good night's sleep. Though I'll admit a deviant part of me *loved* fighting with him. It was messed up, but I just couldn't seem to stop rising to the challenge every time he prodded.

Normally, I woke up every few hours when I slept anywhere that wasn't my own bed, but I was so exhausted I slept right through. When I woke up, I had a bit of a hangover from all the drinking I'd done before and during the flight. Maybe some exercise would help.

Right outside my window was the pool, and it was delightfully empty. I pulled my plain black bikini and flip-flops from my suitcase and headed downstairs.

The décor in the house was very distinctive, something I was too tired to notice last night. There were a lot of mismatched patterns and exotic potted plants, but it had air conditioning, which I was thankful for.

I'd completed several laps and was sitting on the edge of the pool, enjoying the early morning sun when a voice said, "You're all wet."

I rolled my eyes and turned my head to glare up at Cal. "Good one."

He chuckled, pleased with himself, and dropped his towel down on a sun lounger. He only wore a pair of swim shorts, his entire tattooed upper half on display. Without preamble, he jumped into the pool and started swimming laps.

Such a fucking peacock.

I should get up and walk away, not give him the satisfaction of sitting here and watching. But when it came to Cal, I did all the things I shouldn't. I was drawn to him in a way I'd never been to anyone else. Even before I joined the cast of *Running on Air*, I'd admired him. I remembered going to meet him, James, and Trev for the first time and being completely starstruck. My old crush seemed so innocent compared to our current dynamic.

How I saw him back then was so different from how I saw him now. It wasn't that the fantasy didn't live up to the reality, but simply that getting to know him as a person made me see there was more to him than a pretty face. Cal was loyal, unwaveringly so. He also told the truth, even when it wasn't fun to hear. He had a cutting sense of humour. But mostly, he had a good heart. The problem was his affection could border on obsessive. To the point where he often self-destructed when things didn't go his way.

And that was reason number one why our relationship never worked out.

I closed my eyes and turned my face up to the sun, trying to push Cal from my thoughts. I was giving him way too much space in my head. I felt something move past my foot and knew he swam right by me, trying to get my attention. So much for getting him out of my head.

I opened my eyes and let myself admire his athletic movements through the water. His tattooed, muscular form was closer to a work of art than a mere body. He reached the other end of the pool, then started to swim back to me. I glanced away, annoyed to be caught looking.

He hitched himself up onto the edge of the pool right next to me. When his wet arm brushed mine, I suppressed any kind of reaction. Not only would he not be winning our bet, but I refused to give him a single hint that he could.

I noticed he still wore the pendant I bought for him when we were first together. This was before we lost the baby, and before we broke up two more times. The piece of jewellery only functioned to remind me how happy and obsessed with each other we'd once been. We had so few worries back then and we didn't even realise it. We had no clue of the troubles that lay ahead.

"I'm sorry for being a dick about Neil last night. It was uncalled for," he said.

I scoffed. "Is this a tactical apology or a real one?"

"It's real. I'm trying to stop being so argumentative, but it seems old habits die hard."

I cast him a speculative glance, unsure if he was being truthful. When I didn't reply, Cal exhaled and let the subject drop. "Barry wants to get some footage of us out and about in the city today. Could be fun."

I sighed. "I thought we didn't start filming until tomorrow. I planned on spending the day relaxing."

Out the side of my eye, I saw the edge of his lips twitch. "Yeah? What did you have in mind?"

I yawned. "Mimosas, a workout, some sunbathing, maybe a nap."

We both had our hands braced on the edge of the pool. He brushed his pinkie finger against mine. "Want some company for that nap?"

I quickly drew my hand away. "Like I'd risk losing my job just because you want to share a nap."

"But naps with company are nice. I thought you'd appreciate me offering to do something kind for you." He stretched out now, droplets of water glistening on his inky torso. It was incredibly distracting. An unusual looking bird swooped by and I admired its pretty colours. It had a black head and a bright yellow body, its wings a mixture of black and white stripes.

"I'm fine napping alone, thanks," I replied, focusing on the exotic bird in the sky because it was safer than looking at the beautiful creature who sat right next to me.

He made a tutting sound. "Your loss. I offer extra benefits with my naps."

I couldn't help it when I said, "Yeah?"

He smirked. "Now she's interested."

"I'm curious, not interested."

He turned his head to me, eyes on my chest when he ran a finger along my shoulder. "I specialise in intimate massage."

My nipples beaded at his touch. I was sure he noticed. Memories surfaced, particularly of what Cal could do with his hands…and his tongue. I barked a carefree laugh to cover up how he affected me, my tone sarcastic. "Wow. Never heard that one before."

His eyes were hooded. "It's very relaxing. You'll be a new woman afterwards."

"Answer's still no. Now leave me alone."

There was a beat of silence then his voice turned tender. "You know I can never leave you alone, Leanne."

The rest was left unsaid...*no matter how much it hurts.*

***

After breakfast, the entire cast and crew drove into the city. Barry wanted to capture some footage of us walking around, gazing up at landmarks and such. We walked the streets and ran for a little bit, the cameras following us until we ended up at a park called The Wilds. It had an amazing view over the city and I tried to remind myself how lucky I was to be here. I mean, there were exotic birds and plants I'd never see at home, and here I was spending most of my time fixating on Cal, on the contract, on the prospect of losing my job. I wasn't living in the moment and I needed to rectify that.

When we stopped for lunch, I found Michaela sitting on a nearby bench eating a sandwich.

"Mind if I join?"

She shook her head, and I took a seat next to her. Another thing I liked about Michaela was that, like me, she didn't mind sitting in silence. I looked out at the view, the lush green terrain with apartment blocks beyond. Far in the distance, I saw the recognisable Telkom Tower.

"Can you believe this is the first time I've ever been outside the UK?" she said and took a bite of her sandwich.

"We have that in common," I admitted. "I'd never been abroad until I joined the show either. The furthest my parents ever took us on holiday as kids was Southend."

Michaela grinned. "I love Southend."

"Well, yeah, me too, but driving to a seaside town in Essex isn't the same as jetting off to Ibiza, now, is it?"

Michaela chuckled as her gaze wandered across the park. Cal stood talking with James and Trevor, and I could tell by their serious expressions that they were making plans for our first stunt. The camera crew filmed their discussion, but I was too far away to hear.

We were training to free run in Ponte City, a giant apartment complex close to the Hillbrow neighbourhood. We'd visited briefly this morning, but I was eager to go back and explore more.

Isaac told me that Hillbrow could be dangerous, especially at night, and that when he lived here, his mother always forbade him from going there. The tower had once been akin to a tenement or an urban slum, but it had undergone regeneration in recent years.

The structure itself interested all of us because it looked like nothing we'd ever seen before. The cylindrical skyscraper with its hollowed-out centre reminded me of something from a dystopian future. It also reminded me oddly of a telescope looking up into the sky, the vast white light of the sun pouring in during the day, then darkness and stars at night.

Astronomy was a big hobby of mine. My parents even got me a telescope for my fifteenth birthday because I was so obsessed. I still loved to study the stars and find constellations from my bedroom window.

A tiny, high-pitched squeak from Michaela broke me from my thoughts. I glanced at her. "What? Did you see a spider?"

"Um, no, sorry. It's nothing. Don't mind me," she replied and looked away.

I realised what had solicited her reaction when I saw James had taken his shirt off. With the exception of Cal, I sometimes forgot just how hot my co-stars were. As part of our jobs, we were all constantly working out. For me, that meant abs and toned arm and leg muscles. For the guys that meant that they were *ripped*. In particular James, the biggest of the group, was impressive when he decided to whip out the guns.

"James has a fiancée," I reminded her, my tone almost commiserating.

Michaela stiffened. "I know that."

I eyed her meaningfully as I continued, "Diana's not somebody you want to cross."

She once told me I'd be so much prettier if I let my hair grow. She also said my baggy clothes made me look like a boy. I'd responded by pulling off my hoodie, revealing my tight tank top underneath and showing her exactly how much of a woman I was. Yep, Diana might've been a mean bitch, but I was a tough bitch, and I didn't back down. She learned quickly not to aim her cattiness at me, but Michaela was kind and lovely. I didn't want Diana setting her sights on her.

"Leanne, I don't like James," Michaela said, her tone fervent, eyes downcast. She looked embarrassed that we were even talking about this, so I decided to drop it. Besides, given my current situation with Cal, I was in no position to be giving anybody advice, romantic or otherwise.

Back at the house, Barry called us all into one of the lounge rooms for a meeting. There was a stack of boxes on the table, containing what appeared to be top-of-the-line handheld video cameras.

"What are those for?" Trev asked, motioning to the boxes.

"We're introducing a new facet to the show this season," Barry said. "Diary cams."

"Oh, fuck off." Cal folded his arms irritably.

Barry shot him a look of warning. "Say that again and see what happens."

Cal stared him dead in the eye and enunciated slowly. "Fuck. Off."

Barry ran a weary hand over his face. "Jesus Christ, it's like dealing with a ten-year-old. Look, say what you want to the camera. Just give it a try. You might even end up enjoying it."

"I'm not talking into a camera about my feelings. End of." Cal stood firm.

"It's more about going over what you've achieved each day, and your goals for the coming days," Barry said.

"Yeah," Paul added. "I think it could do you good to keep a diary, Cal. It will help with all those repressed emotions."

"I'm not repressed."

"Oh yeah? When's the last time you had sex?" Paul questioned.

For a brief second, Cal's gaze flashed to me, and I tensed. He returned his attention to Paul. "You can fuck off too."

Paul grinned. "Telling everyone to fuck off is the first sign of repression."

Cal stood up. He looked like he was about to pop off, but then, for some reason he caught himself. His cheeks flushed when he glanced at me, and then, miraculously, he sat back down.

Had Cal just consciously stopped himself from making a scene? This had to be a first.

Feeling a little bad for him, I stood to address the room. "Look, I'm not happy about these diary cams either, but the least we can do is give them a try."

"I'm up for it," James said.

"Yeah, me too," Trev agreed.

"And me," Isaac added.

Paul shot Cal a look. "Seems like you're the only one not willing to play along."

"Fine, I'll do it," Cal allowed, and I was admittedly impressed that he hadn't resorted to throwing all his toys out of the pram. Or at least, he'd caught himself before he did.

Several cooks had been hired to cater for us while we were staying at the guesthouse. I was feeling like some alone time was on the cards, so instead of joining everyone else in the dining room, I grabbed a plate and a bottle of wine and headed out to the poolside. I sat down on a deck chair and dug into the dish, which consisted of delicious spicy sausage, mash, and vegetables. It was exactly what I needed after a long day of training.

I pulled up one of my playlists on Youtube and poured a glass of wine. The playlist consisted of three of my favourite movie clips.

1. *My Best Friend's Wedding* – "Say a Little Prayer for You"
2. *Strictly Ballroom* – "Final Dance"
3. *Good Will Hunting* – "My Boy's Wicked Smart"

I loved triumphant, feel-good moments. They lifted my spirits. If I was feeling down, a well-chosen movie clip could always cheer me back up again.

I'd finished eating and was onto my third glass of wine when someone took the sun lounger next to me. I knew it was Cal even without looking to confirm it was him. Instead I gazed up at the night sky. In this spot outside the city, there was blessed little light pollution. Above my head, a galactical masterpiece shone bright like diamonds. The sky was nothing but a sheet of sumptuous black velvet, the stars clearer than anything I'd ever be able to see back in London.

I liked the idea that there were things out there far bigger, older, and greater than myself. It helped put daily trivialities into perspective, which you needed when you were on TV and people were constantly commenting on your appearance and your private life.

Looking at the night sky was my version of meditation.

When I received my first paycheck for *Running on Air,* I went out and bought myself an Orion Skyquest Intelliscope. It was my favourite thing I owned. Like, I actually missed it when I travelled, as though it were a friend or a beloved pet.

"You doing some stargazing?" Cal finally spoke. His gentle tone put me on alert. He was trying to lull me into a false sense of security.

"Uh huh."

"What can you see?"

"Stars."

His low, deep chuckle simmered into my bones, just like it always did. I needed to steel myself. I was several glasses of wine deep and feeling less inhibited than if I were sober. In other words, dodgy fucking territory.

Cal looked up, silent a moment before he said, "I think I can see Centaurus."

My eyebrows shot all the way up into my forehead. "Since when do you know about constellations?" Also, he was right. Centaurus was clearly visible tonight, the shape half man, half horse. It wasn't something you could pick out unless you knew what you were looking for.

Cal shrugged, his tone casual. "I might've read a book or two. You used to talk about this stuff all the time. I wanted to find out what all the fuss was about."

I continued to stare at him. Had he actually gone to the trouble of reading astronomy books just because I used to talk about it? My chest felt flush all of a sudden, and I didn't know what to say. I brought my attention back to the sky and sensed Cal studying my profile.

"This diary cam business is some bullshit though," he said after a minute or two.

"Yep." I was determined to keep my responses short so he couldn't lure me into a long conversation.

Reaching out, Cal picked up the bottle of wine and took a gulp. Unable to resist, I turned, watching the way his throat moved. Like I said, it was one of many things I found intolerably sexy about him.

I didn't say anything about him stealing my wine, mostly because the bottle was almost empty, but also because I could tell he wanted a reaction. I heard the sliding doors at the back of the house open before Trev called out, "Hey, what are you two doing out here all by yourselves?" He stood about ten yards away, hands on hips. It seemed he was following through on his promise to keep me and Cal apart.

"None of your business," Cal shouted back.

"It's my business if you get yourselves fired," Trev responded.

I got up, a little unsteady on my feet, and headed toward the house.

"You don't need to let him boss you around," Cal said, eyeing me.

I glanced back at him. "I was planning on going to bed anyway."

"No, you weren't. You're avoiding me. You don't trust yourself around me."

I rolled my eyes. "If that's what you'd like to think, go ahead." I continued on to the house. Though I feigned confidence, his statement held true. I didn't trust myself around him.

And that was why I planned to spend as little time with Cal this month as possible.

Five
Leanne

I woke up the next morning with a vague memory I'd done something stupid. I just had this itchy feeling that I couldn't seem to shake. Noticing the video camera plopped at the end of my bed, I scrambled to grab it, then checked the recordings.

Yep, I'd made a six-minute video, though what I'd said I couldn't for the life of me remember. Alcohol often made me black out, which okay, was half the appeal.

At least I could delete the video before anyone else got their hands on it. But first, my curious side couldn't resist hitting play.

The video showed me sitting on the bed, bleary-eyed and tipsy: *"This is my first diary cam entry. Feels weird to be talking to a camera like this, but fuck it, I promised myself I'd give it a try. Anyway, we've barely been here a day and already Cal's been getting on my nerves. He thinks he's so sexy and irresistible, which yeah, he kind of is, but whatever. That doesn't mean I'm interested. Been there, done that. No thank you to a repeat."*

Jesus. I cringed and hit delete, unable to watch any more. I needed to make a rule for myself: I would hide this camera somewhere I wouldn't find it before I started drinking at night. If Barry ever got his hands on footage of me bleeding my heart out on a diary cam, you bet your arse he'd use it in an episode. Our director could be pretty ruthless when it came to stuff like that.

We spent the day practicing for Ponte City. In the evening, I shut myself in my room and visualised the stunt. I tried to envision myself climbing between window ledges.

This challenge was going to be easier for the guys because all of them had the advantage of longer legs.

I was significantly shorter, but I was good at jumping and had excellent grip. My stubborn side was determined not to be the one who couldn't finish. That had only happened to me once before, but that was a situation out of my control.

A pang of grief hit me at the memory, but I pushed it away and focused back on my visualisation. Paul told me that when something bad happened, it wasn't the thing itself that caused us to suffer, but the way in which we reacted to it. I tried to keep that lesson in mind when bad memories surfaced. I managed my reactions rather than allowing myself to wallow in the pain and let it overwhelm me.

The next day was more practice and more dodging Cal until I fell into another exhausted sleep. I avoided drinking this time, since I couldn't afford to be hungover during our stunt in the morning.

Michaela knocked on my door at the crack of dawn to get me up for filming at Ponte. I drank a giant oat smoothie, then joined the guys for a warm-up in a shaded part of the grounds outside.

Barry and the film crew, along with the show's producers, Linda and Ken, were already setting up when we arrived at the mammoth tower block. It was one of those structures that was simply amazing to stare up at. The crew followed us as we ran and explored the ground floor, where there was a massive hill of broken rock.

We completed a preliminary run through several of the lower floors, then headed higher up. Most of the residents went about their business, but a group of adults and kids followed along to watch. They seemed intrigued and excited by the camera crew, though I also knew a number of residents, including the security company that managed the building, had been paid handsome fees to allow us to film around their apartments.

Our challenge was a race. We'd work in pairs to climb in a circle, from one window ledge to the next, with the pair who completed the full circle quickest being the winners. The tricky part was that the window ledges were incredibly narrow, not giving us much space for error. Also, we'd all be at least fifty floors up, so a single misstep meant, well…it was probably best not to think about it.

"Right, a bit of a change of plan," Linda said. "I want Paul and Isaac to pair up, so then Callum can pair with Leanne."

I frowned at her, hand on hip. Didn't she know about our contracts? "But Paul and I have practiced together. Changing things now is only going to mess up our whole system."

"The ratings go up when you and Callum have scenes together, so this is how we're going to do it," Linda replied evenly.

I considered her a friend, sure, but she could be particularly ruthless when it came to manipulating situations for ratings. It wasn't her concern if putting me in close proximity with Cal meant testing my ability to resist him. Her main goal was to make the most exciting and interesting show possible, and apparently, our personal struggles didn't factor into it.

"Besides," she went on, "you two are incredibly in sync. You've worked together countless times, and those episodes are always the most popular."

I huffed a frustrated breath. "Fine, let's just get things moving." Standing around arguing about it only meant losing valuable production time. Paul sent me a sympathetic look that said he didn't like the last-minute change of plan either, but we didn't have a choice. I resigned myself to pairing up with Cal.

We took a lift to the fifty-second floor, and I was suddenly very aware of how high up we were. A thrilling rush coursed through my veins. My inner adrenaline junkie was more than ready for her next fix.

Cal came to stand next to me. "Don't worry. I won't let you fall."

I suppressed a shiver at his husky promise, then narrowed my gaze and scoffed. "I think you've got that twisted."

He tilted his head and winked. "You're right. Maybe you'll be the one to save me."

I fought a grin, refusing to be charmed. "Whatever. How do you want to do this?"

"I should go first. That's how Isaac and I trained. Plus, I've got better upper-body strength, so—"

"Do I need to remind you of all the times I've beat you?"

He arched an eyebrow, the sparkle of challenge in his eyes. "I've beaten you just as many. Besides, I'm taller. You might need my help reaching between the ledges."

Now I scowled, because he was right. Paul and I had practiced with him going first for this very reason. It was just that giving Cal any kind of power over me felt like swallowing acid.

"Fine, you go first."

He appeared pleased but knew me well enough not to gloat about it. Instead he replied, "Linda's right about the two of us being in sync though. I think it has to do with how well we fuck."

"Oh, Christ, can you shut up?" I did my best not to blush. Also, wasn't he aware that the cameras were rolling? Was he actively trying to get us fired?

He leaned close and lowered his voice to a whisper. "You know it's true."

I adjusted the microphone at my neck and endeavoured to ignore him. Cal turned to the camera and explained the stunt we were about to do, while I took several deep breaths in and out to centre myself. Michaela appeared with a bottle of water, and I thanked her before taking a long gulp.

"Good luck out there," she said.

I shot her a grin. "If I need luck, I'm in the wrong business."

She chuckled as I got ready to climb out onto the window ledge.

"We'll be pairing up to climb full circle around the building," Cal said. "No safety equipment, just our feet, hands, and pure determination."

Out of all of us, Cal and Trev were the showmen. They knew how to work a camera, how to mould our stunts into a narrative that was enjoyable for viewers to watch. However, where Trev came across funny and amiable, Cal sometimes seemed cocky and overconfident.

I knew it was a front, that deep down he had a heart. He did care a lot for his mum, after all. When we were together, I got to experience his caring side firsthand. It was a side not many people witnessed. Cal would do little favours for me, like bringing me food after a workout or giving me lifts home after a long day of filming. It didn't sound like much, but sometimes it was the little things that counted.

It was too bad we were both so argumentative and stubborn or we might've actually been perfect for each other.

Okay, that thought could get out of my head right now.

I forced myself back to the present.

Jimbo, one of the film crew, followed Cal and me as we climbed through the window and out onto the ledge. Cal went first, then held out his hand to help me through. I ignored it and climbed out by myself. James and Trev were on the floor below us, and Isaac and Paul on the floor below them. The loud, obnoxious buzz of the drone cam filled my ears as it hovered nearby, capturing us from an angle the camera crew couldn't reach.

"Whatever you do, don't look down," Cal said.

His warning only made my self-destructive side want to do it more. I glanced down quickly, felt a wobble of trepidation at the dramatic drop, then closed my eyes and centred myself again. I pressed my hand against the concrete and took several calming breaths.

"You okay?" Cal asked, his voice gentler now.

"Y-yes."

"I told you not to look down."

"You know whatever you say I'm going to do the opposite." And weirdly, I enjoyed the fear. I liked the idea that my skill was the only thing that could get me through this.

Cal's voice held a hint of amusement. "How could I forget. You ready for this?"

I opened my eyes and found his green ones peering down at me. For some reason, they gave me courage. "Ready as I'll ever be."

Barry counted us down from three, and we started climbing. I couldn't help admiring Cal's athleticism as he pulled himself across to the next ledge. Again, he reached a hand out to help me and I ignored it, demonstrating that I could climb from ledge to ledge perfectly well all on my own. I had to stretch my body to the max to bridge the gap, and it was hell on my arms and legs, but I managed it all the same.

I'd always been a climber. Even when I was little, I'd scaled trees and high walls, giving my parents heart attacks every time. Mum used to call me a "danger baby" because I was forever pulling stunts.

Cal and I managed the next ten or so ledges with little trouble. I started to get tired, but I knew my second wind would come. It always did. When I saw the finish line, something inside me kicked into gear.

"I love it when you get that look in your eye." Cal paused to catch his breath.

I glanced at him. "What look?"

"You know the one. When you're determined to win. We're already three ledges ahead of everyone else."

"Let's keep going then." I drew in a deep inhale as I readied myself.

"Wait," Cal said, and I paused as he reached out to touch my wrist strap. Some of the Velcro had come loose. His fingers slid against mine, and the feel of his skin, however small, made my heart race for a reason completely unrelated to the climb. His look was tender, and something about it caught me off guard.

"Thanks," I said, feeling a momentary rush of solidarity. Right now we were just two people working as a team not to fall to our deaths.

All the rivalry and arguments fell by the wayside, our bet was nothing but a far-off, abstract concept as we worked to make it to the finish line. Onlookers below cheered their encouragement. Inside the apartments, people smiled and waved from the windows as we went past. Above us, other people with their windows open, stared down in awe.

I knew what they were thinking, *Who are these crazy Brits, and why are they trying to kill themselves?* If any one of us fell right now, we'd be done for. It was a good thing we trained every day of our lives for stunts just like this one.

When we reached the final ledge, Cal stopped and gestured for me to go ahead. "Go on. Be first to the finish. You know you want to."

"No thanks. I only enjoy victories that I've won fair and square."

Cal's eyes crinkled at the edges in a smile. "Still stubborn as ever."

He pulled himself to the last ledge, and I followed. We were incredibly high up, but this time instead of looking down, I looked up at the sky and breathed deeply, unable to help the grin on my face.

"We did it," Cal exclaimed, surprising me when he pulled me into a hug. He held me tight to the side of his body, and for a second, I let myself enjoy his warmth.

"Get off," I complained, hating how he could tell I liked his closeness. I was so transparent sometimes. A few moments passed between us as we watched the others finish their climb.

"I bet the stars look incredible here at night," I blurted.

Cal's face went sultry. "Maybe we should come back later. Just the two of us."

Great. He was back to trying to win the bet. I wished he'd let it go, just for a couple of hours at least, so I could enjoy what we'd just achieved.

"Nice try," I said and climbed back through the window. Michaela was there to meet us, alongside several members of the film crew. She handed us bottles of energy drinks and congratulated us on our win.

Cal nudged me with his shoulder. "We should team up more often."

"I think once a season is enough for me," I shot back and headed downstairs to see Paul.

Yes, I was being cold, but it was necessary. There was a lot at stake here and I couldn't afford to let my defences down for a second.

Back at the house, a dinner of stew and freshly baked bread waited for us in the dining room. A bunch of the film crew had decided to eat out, so it was mostly the cast who gathered at the long table. I took a seat next to Michaela. James and Neil sat on the other side of me, while Trev, Paul, Isaac, and Cal sat on the opposite side of the table. Cal was directly across from me, which made it very near impossible not to look at him.

"You need to quit opening the window in our bedroom at night," James complained to Cal. "I was covered in mosquito bites this morning."

"Is that where they came from? A bunch of them flew into our room too," Trev said.

"I was hot, and the air conditioning took forever to kick in," Cal replied defensively. "I couldn't sleep with the heat."

"That's a terribly selfish approach," Paul said. "We'll all be covered in bites just so you can sleep better."

"I wasn't trying to be selfish. I forgot about the mosquitoes," Cal admitted.

"You're a wheat eater. It's not your fault," Paul said.

Cal shot him an amused look. "Is that some sort of obscure put-down?"

Paul shook his head. "There's a theory about the cultural differences between the East and the West. It's based on their main sources of carbohydrates. But I won't bore you with the details."

"No, go ahead, enlighten us," Cal encouraged. He rested his elbows on the table and steepled his fingers.

I could see Paul's complaint bothered him more then he wanted to admit. Selfish was something he got labelled with a lot in the group, so this was a sore spot for him. Cal was the only one of us who'd been raised an only child, and he displayed certain behaviours that showed it, i.e. not wanting to share things, complaining about not having his own bedroom when we travelled, etc. It was clear he was trying to do better, which even I could admit was kind of admirable.

"Well," Paul said, "there are distinct differences in how we cultivate rice as compared to wheat. Rice requires a complex irrigation system, and one farmer's use of water can affect the next. It's a group effort. Rice growers have to consider the whole community of farms, not just their own. Growing wheat, on the other hand, is a lot easier. You just need rainfall. You don't need to rely on the people who own the next farm over."

"I didn't know you were so into farming," James commented.

"I'm not," Paul replied. "I just find this particular theory interesting. Some people believe the growing techniques led to cultural differences. In Eastern countries where they eat more rice, like China, collectivism is much more prevalent. Whereas in the West where we eat a lot of wheat, we're very individualistic. We put ourselves first and everyone else comes second." He paused then addressed Cal. "This, essentially, is what I meant when I called you a wheat eater. You can't help being selfish. It's ingrained in the culture you were raised in."

"Oh, and where were you raised? Timbuktu?" Cal retorted.

"No, obviously not," Paul replied evenly. "But I read a lot of Chinese and Eastern philosophies."

"Sometimes I think if you'd been around in the seventies, you would've been one of those hippies who travelled from town to town, teaching people about peace and love, and eventually starting your own cult," I teased.

Paul slurped up some broth before pointing his spoon at me. "The only difference between a cult and a religion is time and money. Cults aren't my thing, but I think it'd be cool to have my own religion," he mused.

"Well, apparently gingers are dying out," James said. "Maybe one day people will start worshipping redheads because they're so rare."

Paul grinned. "Okay, it's been decided. I now declare myself your redheaded God. Feel free to worship at the altar of my ginger-ness."

I laughed then reached across the table, grabbed one of the open bottles of wine and poured a large glass. The wine here was amazing, and I'd been drinking quite a bit of it tonight. When I put the bottle back down, I noticed Cal watching me and remembered that idiotic diary cam I'd recorded. Probably best to make this glass my last one.

Cal fingered the pendant around his neck, the one I bought for him.

"Why do you still wear that?" I asked, my voice deceptively casual. "It really doesn't suit you at all. I don't know why I ever bought it."

He arched an eyebrow, a curious tilt to his mouth. "What do you care if I wear it? It's just a piece of jewellery."

"You should give it back," I went on, unable to hide my annoyance. Yes, I sounded immature, but Cal used that pendant as a way of getting to me. He used it to show he hadn't let go of what we used to have.

"It was a gift. You don't return gifts," Cal said, lifting his glass to take a leisurely sip.

I lowered my voice and eyed him keenly. "We both know you only wear it to taunt me."

Cal sat back, his posture relaxed. "You're wrong. I wear it because I'm fond of it, and I'm not giving it back."

"I guess I'll just have to wait until you take it off at night, then I'll sneak into your room and steal it."

"I don't take it off at night, so good luck with that. But feel free to sneak into my room any time." Infuriatingly, he winked.

I made a disgruntled noise in the back of my throat and endeavoured to finish my meal as quickly as possible. Cal didn't stop watching me, and I grew self-conscious under his quiet observation. He surprised me when he leaned forward, his hand resting on the table just a few inches from mine. His eyes started at my chest then rose slowly up to my mouth. On instinct, I wet my lips.

Cal spoke low, so only I could hear. "You want the truth?"

I put my glass down and tried not to let the wine in my system and the way he looked at me sway my judgement. "What truth?"

"About the pendant," he clarified. "I wear it because it reminds me of a time when I was happiest."

My pulse thrummed as his words sank in. All of a sudden I felt way too hot, and there was an itch under my skin that wouldn't quit. When I finally looked at him again, he stared me down, almost challenging me to respond.

Oh, to hell with not drinking. If I had to endure this level of frustration, then I deserved a drink. Or several. I snatched the wine bottle, stood from the table and marched upstairs to my room.

Once there, I refilled my glass, grabbed the video camera and hit the 'on' button. Barry instructed us to make a short diary entry at the end of each day, going over what we did, how we were feeling, etc. Well, it turned out I had some *feelings* to get off my chest.

I got comfy on the bed then held the camera up in front of me, selfie style. *"Hey, so today we ran at Ponte City. It's one of the tallest buildings we've ever filmed in, and I definitely had a touch of vertigo once or twice. Guess I should've taken Cal's advice when he told me not to look down. Speaking of which, he's been driving me absolutely crazy these last few days. I don't think I've ever met a more conceited, full of himself, cocky..."*

I trailed off, my irritation wavering. Cal might've been cocky, but I was a bitch to him tonight. I couldn't deny it. If he'd given me a gift during our relationship then asked for it back, I'd be more than a little pissed off. Yet he'd been calm, measured even. Also, his words from back in the dining room just wouldn't get out of my head.

I wear it because it reminds me of a time when I was happiest.

Just like that, I was plunged into the past, and no amount of wine could dull the memories.

Six
Callum
Three and a half years ago
Reykjavik, Iceland

"I bet I can beat you to the roof of this building," Leanne challenged, facing me as she walked backward down the street.

I advanced like a man possessed, while her cute, pixie-like face grinned with mischief. I wanted to grab her and kiss her. Too bad the cameras were rolling. I ran my gaze over her short black hair, a style I'd once considered boyish but now found sexy as fuck. I especially liked how it showcased her smooth neck. It just made me want to, I don't know, bite her or something.

"Not if I catch you first," I countered, and just like that the bet was on.

Leanne turned around and pulled herself up onto a wall at the back of a coffeehouse. In the blink of an eye, she was scaling the building, leaving me standing there with my dick in my hand.

Metaphorically speaking.

I hopped the wall and climbed to the next level.

The cameras could only film us from a distance now, but we both still wore our first-person cameras. We were in Iceland filming a Christmas special that would air later in the year. Leanne and I decided to wander off for a little bit, but unfortunately, two of the crew had come along with us, which meant I couldn't kiss or touch her like I wanted to.

I caught up to Leanne, but not in time to beat her to the roof. I made use of the divots in the corrugated steel, wedging each foot in between them for grip.

"I win." Leanne smiled wide.

I bowed to her, conceding defeat.

"I'd love to live here," she went on. "The air is so fresh and crisp."

"You say that now. In the winter it snows constantly and there are only a few hours of daylight."

"Well, when you put it like that, maybe not. I think I'd go mad cooped up indoors all the time."

I stared at her, again feeling that intense need to kiss her. The past few months we'd been sleeping together in secret. Since filming for the show had been practically constant, all we had were stolen, rushed moments and horny looks.

Her cheeks were flushed now. Not breaking eye contact, I reached up to turn off my first-person camera and switched off my microphone. I did the same with Leanne's, then ran a hand down her soft, warm cheek. I liked the way she trembled at my touch, those bright blue eyes staring up at me, infinitely fascinated with all the ways I turned her on. I liked how she made me feel powerful and in control, but also chaotic and out of control at the same time.

"What are you doing?" she whispered, as though the film crew below could hear us.

Only Jimbo and Celine could climb as well as we could. Luckily those two were off following the others right now.

"Kissing you like I've wanted to do all bloody day." I lowered my mouth to hers.

She gasped into the kiss, and I wrapped my arms around her. For some reason, it felt like I could never hold her tight enough. I slid my tongue along hers, coaxing her to open up to me. I was wild for her, and it wasn't just physical. I craved her smiles and her smart mouth, her snappy comebacks, and musical laughter. Most days we were surrounded by people, and all I wanted to do was take her back to my place so we could hang out, just be ourselves in a setting where we weren't always being observed.

I constantly longed to be alone with her, which was impossible when you had cameras following your every move.

"Hey! What's going on up there?" Noel the cameraman yelled.

See what I mean?

We broke apart, both of us breathless. I leaned close to whisper, "Come to my room tonight, after everyone goes to sleep."

Leanne didn't reply, only bit her lip and moved past me to climb back down. She flicked the switch to turn the camera around her neck back on. We walked back to the main street, and I followed her inside a shop selling tourist crap— keyrings and mugs and shit. I only had eyes for her. I was addicted to being with her, to the way she looked at me when we ran together.

She stopped at a jewellery display and picked up a necklace, fingering the pendant. "Oh! This is made from volcanic rock. How cool." She glanced at me and held up the chain. "I think this would really suit you."

I shook my head. "I'm not really a jewellery bloke."

Leanne rolled her eyes. "Don't be such a douche."

"I'm not. I just don't like it. It itches."

She chewed her lip, considering me. "I think I'll buy it for you anyway. That way you'll have a little keepsake of our time here."

Man, why did that make me feel all emotional and shit? It was actually true that I didn't wear jewellery, but if Leanne bought me something I'd wear it every single fucking day. Yeah, my feelings for her were intense. It was disconcerting considering I hadn't wanted her to join the cast at first. Now she felt as vital to me as breathing, and in the grand scheme of things, we'd only known each other a short while.

Before I could object, she sauntered over to the counter and paid for the chain. When she returned, she pulled off the wrapping and unhooked the clasp.

"Come here," she said, gesturing me to her.

She had to go up on her tiptoes to drape it around my neck, and when I felt the small lump of black rock fall against my chest, I was pretty sure I'd never take it off. I stared down at her, her thick lashes framing her feline eyes, her pink mouth begging to be kissed again.

"There you go. A little piece of Iceland to bring home with you," she whispered.

"I bet it was made in China," I teased.

Giggling, she slapped me on the chest. "Don't ruin this."

"Well, now I need to buy you something."

She scrunched up her nose. "No, you don't."

I moved behind her and whispered seductively in her ear, "Maybe I'll give you something that doesn't need to be bought, then."

Her throat moved as she swallowed. She removed her phone from her pocket and quickly typed out a message, then handed it to me: *The microphones can still hear us when you whisper.*

I typed a single word response and handed her back the phone: *So?*

She frowned and typed another message: *I don't want this show to be about us. I want it to be about parkour.*

Something about that response bothered me. I mean, the show was always going to be about parkour. A part of me wondered if she was ashamed to be with me, if that was why she was so keen to keep what was between us a secret. I knew what people thought when they looked at me. They thought I was some kind of tattooed scumbag, not a clean cut, respectable member of society. Was that why she wanted to keep us a secret?

A brick in my gut, I typed back another single word reply: *Okay.*

Later that night, there was a knock on my door. We were staying in a hotel, so each of us had our own room. I walked over and looked through the spy hole, grinning when I saw Leanne standing there in her oversized black hoodie and pyjama pants. Her room was just down the hall, but after our weird moment in the shop earlier today, I hadn't been sure if she'd come.

In the mood to torture her a little, I opened the door a smidge. "Sorry, I didn't order any room service." I closed the door again without even looking at her.

She gave a low swear and knocked quietly on the door, whisper hissing, "Let me in now or I'll never come to your room again, Cal."

The threat wiped the grin off my face. I opened the door quickly.

"You're a dick." She burst into the room, pushing me hard in the chest.

"What?" I chuckled. "I thought you were a porter who'd come to the wrong room."

She flopped down on the bed and folded her arms. "Sure, you did."

"It's an easy mistake to make. I didn't think you were the sort of girl who snuck into a boy's hotel room," I teased. She deserved a little torture since she was so keen not to have anyone find out about us. I'd be her dirty little secret, but I wasn't going to roll over and play dead.

"You know what?" She stood, her expression fierce as she headed back toward the door. "I thought I was, but now I'm revaluating my decision."

Wait? What? No. My teasing had officially backfired.

I stepped in front of her and gently clasped her shoulders, my voice a soft cajole. "Don't go. You're right. I'm a dick. Let me make it up to you."

If all she wanted from me was sex, then I was prepared to give it to her. I was prepared to do pretty much anything if it meant I got to be around her, feel the sun on my face when she smiled at me, the sharp yet pleasurable tightening in my chest when she gave me her full attention. I couldn't believe how emotionally needy I was for her, but I never felt more content than the times when we were alone together. She wanted my body, but I wanted more.

I wanted her heart.

I pressed my palm to the base of her spine and her breathing grew choppy.

She looked up at me from beneath her lashes. "Make it up to me how?"

I bent to suck her earlobe into my mouth, whispering, "Just watch."

And then I lowered myself to my knees.

Seven
Leanne
Present

"You look like crap," Paul said as he came up behind me.

I pressed my lips together. "Jeez, thanks a bunch."

"No, seriously, are you okay?" he went on, his face concerned.

I exhaled heavily. "I'm fine. Just didn't sleep very well last night." *Thanks to all the memories I let in.*

"Yeah," Paul agreed. "It always takes a while to get used to not sleeping in your own bed."

Today's schedule involved a freestyle run. Paul hopped aboard the minivan taking us into the city and went to sit next to Trev. Michaela and Neil sat at the front discussing work, while James and Isaac both listened to music on their headphones. The only available spot was next to Cal and I eyed it, torn.

"Leanne, do you want to sit back here?" Trev offered, obviously seeing my predicament. I frowned, not liking the idea of relying on the guys to keep me away from Cal all the time. I was a grown woman and I didn't need babysitting.

I shook my head. "I'm fine."

Trev narrowed his eyes a little but he didn't argue with me. Cal grinned wide as he pulled his rucksack onto his lap and patted the seat. I slumped down beside him and folded my arms.

"Hey, sexy," he purred, then chuckled when I scowled. "Fuck, I love it when you hate me."

"I'm tired. Can we please just sit in quiet?"

He leaned closer, nudging me with his shoulder. "Why are you tired? Not sleeping?"

"Something like that."

The glint in his eyes returned. "You always slept well with me."

"Can you not? One day, just give me one day when you don't try to push my buttons."

Cal didn't reply but continued to study me closely.

I turned my head to look out the window and watched the scenery go by. We were going to try to gain access to some rooftops in the city and see how far we could get. These types of runs were my favourite because they reminded me of the old days. Sure, I loved the challenge of competition, but sometimes I missed my anonymity. Now that we were on TV, everybody knew who we were. A lot of the time when I tried going for a run on my own, I'd end up having a bunch of people filming me on their smartphones.

Speaking of which, I pulled my phone out to check my messages. I had one from my mum asking how everything was going, and another from my sister, Lorna, with updates about my one-year-old nephew, Sam. He was the most adorable thing in my life. She'd even attached a picture of him with spaghetti sauce all over his hands and face.

My heart clenched, a sadness creeping in. Lorna didn't know how lucky she had it. Her husband, Jared, was one of the nicest guys I'd ever met, and they had the most perfect toddler. I couldn't imagine ever having anything like that.

I exhaled sadly and only realised Cal was still watching me when he said, "How's your mum and dad?"

I slipped my phone back in my pocket. "They're good."

"And your sister?"

"She's good too." I glanced at him and cleared my throat. "How's your mum been?"

A small smile tugged at Cal's lips. "Good. She just got herself a Pomeranian. Little fluff ball is nuts."

"Oh yeah? I bet it's cute though."

"Yeah, pretty cute. He follows Mum around everywhere she goes. She gets a real kick out of that." A pause. "She misses you, you know. Asks about you all the time."

I tensed. Cal's mum and I had always gotten along really well. "I miss her too," I admitted.

Cal shifted in place, his shoulder brushing mine. "You should come over and visit sometime. She'd love to see you."

I shifted uncomfortably. "I think it'd be a little weird to stay friends with my ex's mother."

"I don't care if you two are friends. Visit her whenever you like."

I swallowed, my eyes searching his. "You know it's not as simple as that."

His gaze didn't waver. "It can be if you let it."

I looked down, and the tiny tattoo on his inner wrist snagged my attention. Both his arms had full sleeves, so it wasn't very noticeable, but my eyes always seemed to wander to it.

After the first time we'd slept together, Cal brought me to a parlour to get my very first tattoo, a drawing of the solar system on the inside of my arm. It was still the only tattoo I had, and despite the other complications in our relationship, I still loved it.

Anyway, once the artist had finished with me, Cal had gotten his own ink, a tiny crown on the inside of his wrist with a swirly "L" inside. I'd gone a little crazy at him for getting my initial tattooed on him, but all he'd said was, *"Today was important. I wanted a reminder."*

Yeah, he could be kind of romantic when the mood took him—romantic and unpredictable.

Cal bent close to whisper, "What are you looking at, little one?"

I blinked out of my trance and sat back, wiping my expression clean of any emotion. "You should get that covered up."

Cal studied the small tattoo. "Why would I? It's one of my favourites."

I rolled my eyes. "Sure."

Without warning, he lifted my arm, then ran his fingers along the tattoo on my inner forearm. "I love this one too," he murmured. "Ever think of getting another?"

I jerked my arm away and rolled my sleeve down. Didn't need Cal seeing the goose bumps his touch solicited and getting ideas. "I think one tattoo is enough for me."

His mouth quirked. "Maybe you need me to inspire you again."

***

When we arrived in the city, Trev found an entrance at the back of an apartment building, and the six of us quickly managed to climb to the roof. It was almost midday and the sun was beating down on us. I pulled off my hoodie and tied it around my waist, noticing Cal's attention on my white vest top underneath. I arched an eyebrow at him.

"What?"

He scratched his neck. "Uh, nothing. You look good."

I hid my embarrassment at his compliment and turned around to jump several feet to the next rooftop. Had his comment been genuine, or merely an attempt to soften me up?

The neighbourhood was a concrete jungle. Across the way, there was a red brick building with a giant graffiti painting of Nelson Mandela shadowboxing.

"How awesome is that." Paul came to stand next to me, resting his elbow on my shoulder.

"I can't believe we're here. This city has such an intense vibe."

"Well, it's survived a lot. I guess all that creates an interesting atmosphere. I think all cities have their own soul."

"Hmm, I like that idea."

Paul always thought about things in unusual ways. It was a trait I loved because he gave me new perspectives I hadn't considered before.

I smiled up at him. "Has anyone ever told you you're pretty special?"

Paul flashed a grin. "Yes, but I never get tired of hearing it, so go ahead. Tell me more."

I giggled then noticed someone standing nearby. Cal's focus went from me to Paul, his mouth flattening into a thin line. Several months after our second break-up, Cal finally accepted that Paul and I were just friends. But even now, he was jealous of anyone who got to touch me, even if it was a purely platonic touch. The fact that we hadn't been together in almost a year just went to show how possessive he could be.

I ran ahead, needing to put some distance between us.

For the next half hour, we lost ourselves in the run. As the crew filmed us, we worked like a well-oiled machine, always in sequence. When one of us landed, the other one jumped.

I adored when all six of us got into the zone like this. It was common knowledge that humans released endorphins when they did something in sync with a group, and I definitely felt that way with parkour. With the exception of my troubled relationship with Cal, these boys were my brothers. I loved them like I loved my own family.

And okay, a part of me would always feel something for Cal too. I just, well, my feelings for him were too tangled up in pain. It was hard not to feel conflicted whenever I was around him.

We reached the end of a building, and I eyed the big drop to the next rooftop. Maybe ten or twelve feet. Trev suggested we each do a backflip down to the next level. He jumped first, followed by James, then Isaac. When Cal flipped, he landed a little awkwardly and his grimace of pain told me he'd hurt himself. Without thinking, I leapt down and was by his side in an instant.

He sat on the roof, swearing under his breath as I knelt before him. Trev, James, Isaac, and Paul gathered around, alongside Jimbo and Celine who were filming.

"Are you okay?" I asked, breathless.

Cal held his ankle. "Yeah, just twisted it."

"Aw, want me to kiss it better?" Trev asked, though I could tell he was just as relieved as the rest of us that Cal was okay. Injuries were a pain in the arse.

Everyone dispersed, but I stayed with Cal, suspicious he might be playing things down for the cameras. "Let me see your ankle," I insisted, reaching for the hem of his jeans.

He mustered a smirk, but underneath it, his face was notched in pain. "Gee, Leanne, I didn't know you cared."

"Course I care. Let me see."

He resisted but then finally gave in. When I pulled up his jeans, I saw he'd not only twisted his ankle, he scraped the crap out of it too. "You need to get a bandage on that."

His voice was husky. "Want to do it for me?"

I pulled his jeans back down. "I think I'll pass."

"You know what I miss?" he went on, voice low.

Against my will, his seductive tone drew me in. "What do you miss?"

"I miss those days when we used to just lie in bed, heavy petting and making out for hours."

Instantly, I flushed. In the beginning, I'd resisted letting Cal come to my place, but when I finally did, being alone together, away from the cameras and film crew, became addictive. We could get lost in each other for hours, sometimes days. I remembered the periods between filming when he'd come over to my place. We'd have Netflix marathons and fool around in bed all day. I straightened, not allowing myself to get swept away in the memories, which was clearly Cal's intent. I wasn't falling for it.

"Your ankle should heal up in a couple of days. Just go easy on it," I said flatly and walked away.

After we wrapped up filming, we went to eat at a nearby deli. It was big, with lots of locals about. I was sitting at a table with Paul, Cal, and Trev when a high-pitched squeal pierced the air.

What the hell was that?

I twisted in my seat, instantly recognising the group of women who'd just entered. They were some of our super dedicated fans from the UK who travelled to come see us when we filmed abroad. Since we'd gone so far afield this time, I hadn't expected them.

They were all in their early to mid-twenties, and I actually really liked most of them. There was just one girl who was obsessed with Cal to a level that was one step away from a stalker. Let's just say, she could be a little intense. Sometimes I felt like taking her aside and saying, *He's just a normal human like you and me. He's not perfect. In fact, I'm pretty sure he takes a dump every day too.*

That probably wouldn't go over so well. But this girl, she looked at Cal with stars in her eyes, and well, I refused to delve too much into why it bothered me. It just did. Besides, she didn't know him, not the real him.

I stood up and went over to say hello, even though I knew I wasn't the one they wanted to talk to. Actually, that was mostly the reason why I did it. It gave me a perverse sort of amusement to occupy their time when I knew they were looking over my shoulder, hoping to chat with the guys. It was a bitchy move, but you know what, I was a bitch sometimes, so there.

"Hey everyone! It's so great to see you. I can't believe you came all this way."

We exchanged the usual pleasantries, then Trev, Isaac, and James came over to say hello. The ladies beamed under their attention. I went back to finish my lunch, but when I reached the table, Cal grabbed my hand and pulled me onto his lap.

"What are you doing?" I hissed under my breath. "Let go of me."

"Please, just until they go. Olive is giving me her serial-killer stare."

"She's not a serial killer. She's just a fan."

"The same way Randall Evans is just a fan?" he countered.

Okay, so he had me there. Randall Evans was this really posh bloke from back home who came to a lot of our public appearances. He was in his thirties and was weirdly intense with me, similar to how Olive was with Cal. The vast majority of people who watched the show were perfectly normal and lovely, but when you had a large viewership, there were always going to be one or two oddballs.

Anyway, Randall was the sort of bloke who I suspected liked to be tied up and spanked by the women he slept with. I could come across pretty tough and no-nonsense on the show, which was probably why he was so interested in me.

I remembered all the times Cal had saved me from awkward encounters with Randall and decided to return the favour.

"Fine, I'll sit here, but only because you got Randall off my back last time."

"Thank you." Cal exhaled. He sounded genuinely grateful as he avoided eye contact with Olive.

And believe me, she was giving him some serious stare action from the other side of the deli. It appeared creepiness was not something confined to any one gender.

Paul sat on the other side of the table, on the phone with someone. He arched a questioning eyebrow when he saw where I was sitting. I mouthed the name "Olive" at him and he nodded, understanding.

Cal's hand rested on my upper thigh. His thumb brushed back and forth, but since it was under the table, no one could see. I stiffened.

"Can you quit that?"

He tilted his head to me. "Quit what?"

My voice was strained. "Quit touching me or I'll get up right now and leave you at the mercy of Olive."

Just like that, his hand dropped away. I tried to ignore how sitting on his lap like this gave me tingles and endeavoured to finish my sandwich. Nothing tasted better than carbs after a run, but all I could concentrate on was

Cal's smell, his clean, musky sweat. My brain made the connection that this was what he smelled like after sex and I let out a weird, unintentional noise that I'd literally never made before in my life.

"You okay?" Cal asked.

"Just got a piece of bread stuck in my throat," I lied, embarrassed.

I felt his breath on my neck when he responded quietly, "You know I'd do anything for you, right?"

My chest fluttered at his softly spoken words. There was some deeper meaning, but I refused to pick it apart. He was talking about sex, nothing more. "I don't need anything from you."

"Yes, you do. You just won't let yourself admit it."

"*Callum*," I said firmly, using his full name as a warning. I was doing him a favour here and he was pushing his luck.

Thankfully, or maybe not so thankfully, Olive interrupted us. She'd finally built up the courage to sidle her way over, taking the seat I'd previously occupied. "Hi, Callum," she breathed dreamily before turning to Paul. "Hi, Paul." He nodded at her, finishing up his phone call.

It amused me when her attention finally came to me, her distaste clear in her unhappy expression. "Leanne."

"Olive," I replied sweetly.

"So, Callum, how have you been liking Joburg?" she asked.

"I like it a lot. We've been having a good time here," he answered evenly.

I reached down to pinch his thigh. He was being way too stiff, and even if Olive was weird, he still needed to be nice to her. People watching our show was the only reason we had jobs. I would never be rude to a fan, not even Randall.

He pinched me back, and I choked down a yelp.

Olive's gaze wandered to his neck. She completely ignored the fact I was sitting on his lap. "Is that a new tattoo?" She gestured to the intricate blue and black design beneath his jawline.

She knew very well it wasn't new. I was pretty sure she'd catalogued each and every bit of ink on his body. The only ones left out, being those only the women he'd slept with had seen.

Cal's hand went to his neck. "No, I've had this one a while."

"Well, it's very sexy," Olive said.

My eyes nearly bugged out of their sockets. I felt Cal stiffen while Paul eyed me in amusement.

"It is very sexy," I agreed, deciding to torture him a little. "Though you should see the one on his left arse cheek. Now that, my friend, is a sight to behold."

If the way he gripped my thigh was anything to go by, Cal wanted to murder me right then, but he held his tongue. I thought Olive might get embarrassed, but no, she eyed Cal flirtatiously. "Well, maybe I will get to see it someday."

Seriously? I was sitting right on his lap, a very obvious display of "togetherness" and she was still flirting with him. Maybe Olive had a sixth sense and knew it was all pretend. Paul almost spat out the juice he just drank, and I swallowed tightly, trying not to laugh. I needed to stop looking at Paul. We had a shorthand of facial expressions and looking at him only made me want to laugh even more.

Cal coughed loudly, and then the most awkward string of words came out of his mouth. "Eh…uh…that's…okay."

"Olive," one of the other girls called. "Come on. We have to get to the hotel to check in."

She didn't look very happy about being interrupted but stood from the table all the same. "Maybe we could all get a drink together sometime this week," she suggested.

"Yeah, maybe," Cal replied and then she left, looking pleased with herself.

"You do realise she didn't hear maybe, she heard definitely," Paul said.

"Christ," Cal groaned as I slid off his lap and back into my own chair. He glanced at me somewhat mournfully, like he'd enjoyed having me there a little too much.

"You'll just have to do your best to avoid her," Paul went on.

"That's kind of hard when she has a knack for showing up out of the blue. Also, how did she not see you sitting right on my lap?" he asked me.

I shrugged. "Seems Olive fears no obstacles in her quest to get inside your tattooed pants."

He narrowed his gaze. "By the way, I don't have any tats on my arse."

I grinned. "I know. Just thought it was a nice touch."

On the drive back to the house, I made sure to grab a seat next to Paul, as far away from Cal as I could get. Sitting on his lap got me all hot and bothered, and I needed some space to get my head back on straight.

You can't sleep with him. If you do, you'll lose the bet. More importantly, you'll lose your job.

I reminded myself of these important facts as I settled into my seat. Paul put his earphones on, and I scrolled through the Instagram feed on my phone.

Neil and Michaela managed the *Running on Air* social media accounts, posting daily pictures and videos of us. I also had my own personal Facebook and Instagram pages, which I had a bit of a love/hate relationship with. I liked keeping in touch with fans and posting pictures but being well-known meant you inevitably attracted trolls. I tried my best to ignore the negative comments, but in spite of this, they often wormed their way into my head.

I plastered a smile on my face and snapped a selfie with Paul. When he saw I was taking a picture, he grinned.

"Ugh, you're so photogenic it makes me sick," I said.

"What?" he asked loudly over his music.

"Nothing. Never mind." I posted the selfie with a caption: *On our way home. Can you see how exhausted we are?*

A bunch of likes immediately rolled in. I had over half a million followers on Instagram, though Cal and Trev had more than a million each, mainly because they were favourites with our female fans. James, Isaac, and Paul had fewer, but they tended to post less. Hell, that's probably because they weren't lonely like I was. They didn't need daily affirmation to dull the void inside.

***

When we got back, I went straight to my room for a shower and change of clothes. An hour later, Michaela knocked on my door with some food so that I could eat alone. I could've hugged her.

When I finished eating, I checked my phone and saw there were a bunch of comments under the selfie I'd posted earlier. There were lots of nice ones from fans of the show, but one stood out. It was from Cal.

You're beautiful. x

My breath caught, and for a second my heart shimmered with warmth. But then I thought of the bet, and I knew the comment was designed to get under my skin. I couldn't believe that it almost worked. I looked underneath and laughed out loud when I saw Paul had replied with, *Thanks hon. You always know how to make a boy feel special.*

My humour was short-lived because someone else had left a comment: *Ur a slut.*

I would've ignored it like I usually did, but then I saw Cal had replied: *Fuck you. Leave another comment and see what happens.*

The troll responded immediately: *Fuck u 2 manwhore.*

What was Cal thinking, engaging with trolls? I knew exactly what. He had a hot temper. His natural instinct was to act now and think later. Just like at the TV Choice Awards, he went in all guns blazing. Still, I wasn't mad at him like I was then, because he was trying to defend me. His heart was in the right place. Or was he defending me so that I'd thank him, be grateful, let my guard down?

Ugh! I wished I'd never agreed to this bet. Even winning wouldn't make up for the amount of time I'd wasted internally agonising.

I put my phone away, deciding I was definitely done with social media for the night. I snuggled into my pillow and almost drifted off when there was a gentle knock on my door.

Must be Michaela.

I called, "Come in," then shot up in bed when Cal stepped inside. "What do you want?"

Cal closed the door behind him. "I came to check on you. You weren't at dinner."

"That doesn't mean there's anything wrong with me," I replied. "And by the way, what the hell did you think you were doing replying to that comment?"

He at least had the grace to look chagrined as he ran a hand over his stubble. "Eh, that was a moment of weakness. It won't happen again."

"See that it doesn't. In fact, quit commenting on my posts altogether."

Cal scowled and I saw a chord in him snap. "Maybe if you'd quit posting pictures with Paul all the time, I could actually think straight."

I blinked at him. "Are you seriously bringing this up again? Paul's my best friend. I thought you'd finally accepted that."

"He's still a bloke."

"That means absolutely nothing, Cal."

His eyes blazed. "I'm your friend. You don't post pictures with me."

"You're not my friend. You're my co-star."

"Fuck you. I'm your friend."

I got out of bed and stood toe-to-toe with him. "No, fuck *you,* and get out of my bedroom."

He glared at me, and I glared right back. We were locked in a stand-off for several moments before his face fell. He turned away, hands on his hips as he exhaled. "I'm sorry," he said, and turned back to me, his eyes soft now. "I didn't come in here to fight with you."

I huffed out a frustrated breath, while on the inside my heart raced. The old Cal rarely backed down during arguments, but more and more he seemed to be actively curtailing his temper. "What *did* you come in here for?"

His gaze went from me to the bed.

I laughed. "Think again because that's not happening."

"Are you a mind reader now? I was actually going to say I'd like to talk. I miss talking to you."

Despite my best effort, his gentle tone made me relent. I caught a glimpse of that dark, haunted look in his eyes and knew he needed not to be alone right now. I knew because I often went through the same thing, though I normally had a bottle of wine for company.

"Fine, but stay off my bed. You can sit on the armchair." I got back into bed and pulled the covers over me while Cal sat where instructed. The chair was narrow and didn't look very comfortable, but it was the most I was willing to offer. No way was he sitting in bed with me. That would definitely be asking for trouble.

A few moments of quiet elapsed. Then Cal gestured to his ankle. "Michaela bandaged me up, in case you were wondering."

"I wasn't, actually."

He gave a rumbly, affectionate laugh. "Are you jealous you didn't get to do it?"

"Not in the slightest. And besides, Michaela has zero interest in you."

"How do you know that?" He looked puzzled.

"We're girls. We talk." I was lying. Michaela and I had never discussed Cal, but I wanted him to think there was at least one female out there who was immune to his charms.

He eyed me, a sly grin emerging. "That means there's someone she *does* like. Who is it?"

I knew that look. I arched a brow. "As if I'd tell you."

Cal tapped a finger to his mouth. "Is it Paul?"

"I told you, my lips are sealed."

He started to list names. "Trev? Neil? James? Fuck! It's James, isn't it?"

I schooled my expression. "What makes you think that?"

"You have a tell. You do this little blink. It's cute."

"I don't have a tell."

"Yes, you do. You just did it again. So, Michaela has a crush on James, eh? Diana would lose her shit if she found out." Cal's eyes glinted with mischief.

I sighed and levelled him with a warning look. "Michaela didn't actually say anything to me. It's just something I noticed. It's obviously an innocent crush. She'll get over it." I pointed my finger at him. "So, don't you dare say anything to James. She'll be mortified if he finds out."

"Who said I was going to tell him?"

"I know you. You're as bad as Trev with gossiping."

"How about we make a little exchange, then? I'll give you my word I won't tell James if you do something for me."

I eyed him sceptically. "Something as in..."

"Come for a swim with me in the pool."

Ha! Did he think I was stupid? I played along just to torture him a little. "You know what? A swim sounds great, but I'll do you one better. We should skinny-dip."

Cal blinked, his mouth opening for a second. "You want to...uh..."

I barked a laugh. "Oh my God, you actually think I'm serious? I'm not going for a swim with you, Cal."

His face showed a hint of embarrassment, but he quickly recovered. "Then I'm afraid these gossiping lips will just have to go blabbing to all and sundry."

The seriousness in his eyes made me worry because I liked Michaela. I also felt somewhat protective of her since she was a few years younger than me. I narrowed my gaze at Cal. "Not a swim. Choose something else." I remembered our first morning here, and the frustration of sharing the pool with him, how distracting his body could be.

I saw the cogs in his head turning. "You know what? I'm drawing a blank."

"You're a sadist."

"Oh, come on. One little swim in the pool. What harm can it do?"

My temper flared. I was about to go off at him, but I reined it in. I thought of Michaela and how good a friend she'd become. I didn't want her to go through the embarrassment and awkwardness of having to work for James with him knowing about her crush. She didn't deserve that.

My attention returned to Cal and steel formed in my belly. You know what? Screw him, I could do this. My body might've reacted to his, but my brain knew what was at stake. Besides, it was late. No one would even know I swam with him because they were all in bed by now.

Resolved, I stared Cal dead in the eye. "Fine. One swim. You say absolutely nothing to James. You don't even fucking hint at it, you got me?"

"Yeah, Leanne, I've got you." His voice was seductively possessive.

I could do this. It was just another challenge, and I loved challenges. Besides, it was a swim in the pool. All I needed to do was swim far away from him.

Eight
Leanne

I followed Cal out to the swimming pool, relieved most of the lights were off in the house. A large Jacaranda tree obscured the view of the pool, so even if someone did happen to look out a window, they probably wouldn't be able to see much.

Not that there would be anything to see. It was just that, well, when you lived in a house with a small group of people, they gossiped, speculated, drew incorrect conclusions.

Cal turned around when he reached the pool and pulled off his T-shirt. "You seem nervous."

My look was steely. "Nope."

"Not even a little bit?" His eyes danced in the moonlight, his expression playful.

"Not even a little bit," I lied. On the inside I was bricking it, but I couldn't afford to show any weakness. If Cal caught so much as a flush or anxious wobble of my lip, he'd swoop in like a shark circling its prey.

He held my gaze while he reached for the fly of his jeans. He bit his lip, and just like that, butterflies filled my stomach. He shoved his jeans to the ground. There was a beat, and I could practically hear his calculation when he turned around and dropped his boxers too.

His confident posture said it all: *Game, set, match.*

I immediately regretted teasing him about skinny-dipping.

Cal stood naked in the dim light, and I squeezed my eyes shut. There he went again with his sly tactics. I was strong, but fuck, the sight of him standing in all his naked, tattooed, sculpted perfection was enough to break the world's strongest woman. I caught a glimpse of tenderness in his eyes, and it brought back memories of how he used to look at me when we were together. Like I was a goddess. Like I was the only woman in the world he could ever want, body, mind, and spirit.

Was that look real or fake? I couldn't tell. Maybe that was the core of my problem with him, I never knew how long his affection would last. One minute we were laughing and loving, the next we were fighting and hating.

I heard a splash and opened my eyes.

He hovered in the water, grinning up at me with a coaxing look. "Your turn."

Well, eff him if he thought he was winning this. I lifted my chin, stared him dead in the eye and started to undress. I wore a plain black sports bra and boy shorts under my pj's. I'd already decided they'd be better than my bikini, since they actually covered more skin.

Cal watched, his attention rapt, as I pulled off my top then my bottoms. When I stood in just my underwear, a warmth spread through me, a flicker of weakness, but I soldiered on. A low expletive left Cal's lips as I ran to the other end of the pool. When I was as far away from him as I could get, I dove in. As soon as I was submerged, I swam as fast as I could.

I knew he was coming for me, but if I kept moving, there was less chance of him catching up.

What the hell was I doing?

I thought I'd gotten off the roller coaster a year ago, but I suddenly realised I was still very much on the ride. This push and pull we shared had become a messed up yet integral part of my life, and our addiction to playing games would likely ruin us both.

I pumped my arms and legs towards the end of the pool and then back again, swimming laps. I heard Cal's deep, masculine chuckle, and my stomach fluttered. He knew exactly what I was doing. I stopped swimming but he wasn't chasing me anymore. He rested his arms across the edge of the pool, watching me.

"I wonder how many laps you can swim before you burn out."

"Didn't take you for a rope-a-dope fighter," I shot back.

"Oh, I'll be all too happy to grapple with you, babe." His eyes flashed with challenge.

I held his gaze. "Then why are you waiting for me to run out of energy?"

He didn't reply to that, instead swimming across the pool toward me. Instinctively, I backed up to the other side. My back hit the tiles as Cal hovered in the water before me. He reached out, but I held still, resisting any reaction when he touched my forehead.

He pushed the wet strands of my hair away from my face, then caressed my cheek. "I meant it when I said you're beautiful," he murmured.

"I thought you were talking about Paul," I said, scoffing weakly.

He gave a gravelly chuckle. "Oh, Paul's pretty, but you…" His words trailed off as his eyes wandered to my mouth. "You are something else entirely."

A moment passed. We both refused to be the one to look away first. I could practically feel his warmth through the water. Only five inches, maybe four separated us. He was so close I could smell him, so close my fingers itched to reach out and touch him, the traitors.

A dark cloud came over Cal, his expression intensifying. Oh no, I knew that look. *Don't do it. Don't say it.*

"Do you ever think about her?" he whispered.

A lump formed in my throat. There was no way I could answer with anything but honesty. "Every day." The words were more air than sound.

His gaze grew infinitely sad. "Me too."

My breath left me, and in that moment my body moved before my mind could intervene. I pulled him to me, wrapped my arms around his shoulders and hugged him tight. In less than a second, he melted into me, all his bad-boy bravado evaporating, replaced with a man in pain. His arms came around my waist to hug me back, his touch a salve to my loneliness.

I knew it couldn't last, but for a brief moment, I let myself have this comfort, this feeling of connection. No matter what happened between us, we'd always have this shared history. I acknowledged his pain with a hug, and he acknowledged mine by hugging me back.

And then, I remembered he was naked. His cock brushed my thigh, and I moved like I'd just been burned, sliding out of his embrace.

"You…um, you're not wearing any swim shorts."

A faint cheekiness lit up his eyes, humour washing away the moment of connection we had just shared. "That's correct."

"Well, it's…it's unhygienic."

One eyebrow lifted as his mouth formed a smirk. "Is it?"

"Yes."

"Duly noted."

I folded my arms across my chest, but it felt awkward in the water, so I quickly unfolded them again. I cleared my throat. "Well, have I fulfilled my promise? Are you going to keep Michaela's secret?"

His eyes were pure heat. "Yes, you have. And yes, I will."

I nodded soberly. "Good."

When I turned to climb out of the pool, Cal said, "You're going to kiss me by the end of this trip, Leanne. And you're going to do it because you want to."

I pulled myself out of the water and stood by the pool's edge, staring down at him. There was that intensity again, that hidden agenda. "If you think I'd risk my job for a kiss, you don't know me at all."

His confidence didn't waver. In fact, I'd never seen him look so sure. "I know you better than anyone."

I frowned in agitation. He'd gotten me to swim with him, wasn't that enough? Deciding not to engage him further, I grabbed my things and headed inside. What infuriated me most was he was right. He did know me better than anyone.

And that was why this bet was going to ruin me, because he knew exactly how to toy with me, and though I considered myself a better player, Cal had all the best tricks up his sleeve.

Nine
Leanne

I slept terribly.

After giving in to Cal last night and joining him in the pool, I tossed and turned, berating myself for going along with it. Honestly though, my heart had been in the right place, because now James wouldn't find out about Michaela's crush. Or at least if he did, it wouldn't be from Cal or me.

I'd let Cal think he had me right where he wanted me, because when it boiled down to it, midnight swims weren't sex. He could flirt with me, push my buttons, and yeah, I might even flirt back from time to time, but I wouldn't violate my contract, and that was all that really mattered.

After I dressed and ate a quick breakfast, I joined the others in the minivan. Today we were taking a little break to visit an amusement park. As usual, our filming schedule involved a few days of parkour followed by a day of frivolous fun to fill in the episodes. This was mostly because it was good to have some recovery time. But also, the viewers enjoyed seeing us hanging out and being normal twenty-something-year-olds just as much as they enjoyed seeing our stunts.

It was nice to leave the directors and producers and all the crew behind for a few hours. Sure, we were still being filmed, but only Jimbo and Celine were coming along to capture footage. It wasn't as intense or demanding to have two people follow us around as it was when we had ten.

I sat next to Michaela, who'd volunteered to come with us so Neil could have a day off. I'd told her she should take the day off too and we'd fend for ourselves, but she'd insisted. In front of us, James drove while Cal sat next to him. They were discussing James' and Diana's plan to spend their honeymoon in Miami. Michaela was replying to emails on her tablet, but I suspected she was listening too.

"We're going to have one of those Evian baths," James said.

"What the hell is that?" Cal questioned, his tone curious.

"It's exactly what it sounds like," James explained. "They fill a big fancy tub up with Evian water, light a few candles, and throw in some flower petals."

"How much does that cost?" I asked, joining the conversation.

James focused on driving as he mumbled his response. "$5,000."

"What?!" Cal practically yelled. "Even I think that's ridiculous and I once spent a grand on a bottle of champagne that I didn't drink."

"Diana's got her heart set on it. Apparently, Serena Williams swears by them."

"Serena Williams is a multi-millionaire," Cal said. "She can afford to take fancy Evian baths. You might be on TV, but I'm not sure $5,000 for a bath is going to be worth it. Unless Diana gives you the best blow job of your life afterward."

"Cal!" I exclaimed, seeing James' embarrassment as he ducked his head.

Cal flicked his gaze to mine in the overhead mirror. "You know I'm right."

"You only get to go on a honeymoon once," James said in an effort to justify the expense.

"I'm sure it'll be worth the money," I said, hoping to make him feel better. "Like, when you eat at a Michelin star restaurant, it's all about the experience. You're not just eating food, you're making a memory."

"Lots of people do those fancy treatments," Michaela added, lifting her head from her tablet. "My aunt once went to a spa where they treated her hair with Caviar conditioner. She said it never looked shinier afterward."

James shot us both a smile through his overhead mirror then focused back on driving.

Isaac, who was seated directly behind me, stuck his head through the seats. "I just texted my sister to tell her we're spending the day at Gold Reef," he said, full of excitement. "She's so jealous. We used to beg our mum to take us here every year, but she always said no. Leanne, are you going to come on the Anaconda? I heard it's a rush."

I turned to glance at him dubiously. "What's the Anaconda?"

"It's the scariest roller coaster in the park. My friend Junior peed his pants the first time he rode it, but he was only eleven at the time, so it's probably not *that* scary."

I chuckled. "You're really very excited for this."

His smile was wide, not a hint of embarrassment when he said, "Yes, yes I am."

I sometimes forgot that he was still only twenty.

When we arrived at the park, it was a riot of Saturday activity, with long queues of people waiting to get in. Admittedly, I felt a little excited myself. I'd never been to a theme park, and like all of us, I was a big fan of adrenaline rushes.

Trev held his selfie stick in front of him, taking a video for his million-plus Instagram followers. I considered taking a picture, but then remembered yesterday's selfie debacle and decided against it.

"Hey, come on! Everyone get in the shot," Trev called.

We all huddled together for a group selfie. Cal somehow managed to find his way next to me, his shoulder brushing mine. I thought about our late-night swim and remembered how tightly he'd held me. In spite of everything, it was the most peaceful I'd felt in a while. Well, until I'd remembered he was naked and trying to win a bet.

The first ride was a circular dingy where we all sailed down a man-made river together. I didn't mind getting splashed, though Michaela made a loud gasp of shock when the water hit her. James, who was sitting next to her, chuckled loudly, and she swiped him on the shoulder.

After a couple of rides, we grabbed burgers for lunch then headed to the roller coaster Isaac was most excited about, the Anaconda. Michaela didn't want to ride, so I offered to sit it out too.

On the way there, Cal jumped atop a bar partition and balanced himself, walking on the narrow strip and backflipping to the ground. Next, he did a spinning vault, followed by a palm spin flare and then a rail roll. His gaze flicked to me for a second, making sure I was watching. Was he trying to impress me or something? Nah, he just wanted attention. A bunch of people had stopped to film him on their camera phones.

Cal jumped and landed right in front of me, his breathing laboured. "Impressed?"

I feigned nonchalance. "You can't go a day without showing off."

He grinned playfully, then waved to the people who'd been filming him. "But they love me, they really love me."

"They love what you *do*. They don't love you."

"Ouch. Someone's got a mean streak in them today. Or are you jealous?"

"I'm not jealous. I could easily do what you just did. I simply don't feel the need to show off all the time."

Cal cocked his head, then frowned as his attention went to something behind me. "What's that?"

I turned to look, but there was nothing. Before I could react, he picked me up, threw me over his shoulder and ran towards the ride. I pummelled his back. "What are you doing! Let me down!"

"I'm showing you how to have some fun and stop being such a misery guts."

"Cal, I'm warning you, put me down right now." I gritted my teeth, wriggling in his tight hold, but I couldn't break free.

Michaela had arranged special passes, which meant no line. Cal carried me past the waiting crowds and plopped me down onto a seat.

"I told Michaela I'd stay with her," I protested.

"Michaela will be fine. You've been in a pissy mood with me all day. Maybe a little fear will snap you out of it."

"I jump off buildings for a living, Cal. I'm not afraid of a roller coaster."

"Oh yeah? When's the last time you were on one?"

My cheeks heated. "I've never been on one."

His eyes twinkled with mischief at this news. "Well, let's see what a bad bitch you are then."

Cal hopped into the seat next to me, and an attendant came to strap us in. I schooled my expression, not letting him see my trepidation as the ride slowly jolted forward.

Cal reached out to give my thigh a quick squeeze, his eyes alight with anticipation. "Here we go."

My heart was in my throat as the ride gained speed. I didn't think I was the sort of person to be freaked out by a roller coaster, but here I was, bricking it.

Sure, I could jump off a roof, but in that scenario, *I* was in control. I was the vehicle to get me from one point to another, and I knew and trusted my own body intrinsically. In this case, the roller coaster was in control, and the idea of being at the mercy of a mechanical device as it catapulted me through the air at top speed made me queasy. For a second, it reminded me of the feeling I got when I was with Cal, how I gave up all my control and got swept away in his wildness.

Cal was the roller coaster I'd been spending this entire trip trying to avoid riding.

I squeezed my eyes shut, praying for it all to be over. The seats were the kind where your legs dangled in the air, with your upper half strapped in. A million thoughts went through my head, as I wondered if anyone had ever died on this thing. I wouldn't be surprised if they had.

"This is amazing!" Cal yelled, though I could barely hear him over the noise of the ride.

The screams of the people behind us filled my ears and my anxiety ratcheted up a notch. Maybe if we weren't at the very front, it wouldn't be so terrifying. Or maybe I was just a wuss.

When the ride finally started to slow down, I opened my eyes and saw we were nearly back to the start again. Relief coursed through me. As soon we came to a stop, I released my safety belt and dove from my seat like a bat out of hell.

"Hey, Leanne!" Cal called, coming after me.

I didn't stop to wait for him, but he managed to catch up, his hand on my shoulder. "What's wrong?" he asked gently.

"You shouldn't have made me do that," I said, trying my best to keep the emotion out of my voice.

"I was just trying to help you have some fun."

I huffed a breath. "Well, that wasn't fun for me."

He dug his hands into his pockets, his voice quiet now. "It was just a roller coaster."

I finally turned to face him, unable to hide how upset I was. "Not everyone finds roller coasters fun, Cal. I don't like being thrown through the air at however many miles an hour. I don't need ups and downs or cheap thrills. I just need…"

Oh man, was I seriously having a breakdown over a stupid theme park ride?

Cal moved closer, his hand trailing down my arm. His palm was warm and his touch calmed me a little. "What do you need?" he asked very, very softly.

I blinked, my throat heavy as I stared up into his unfathomable green eyes. "I need control."

He studied me, brow furrowed, though I wasn't sure he understood precisely what I was talking about. "Okay."

I shook my head. "Just…just forget I said anything. I'm going to take a walk. I'll meet you all back at the minivan."

I went and, thankfully, Cal didn't try to follow me. I walked around the park for a while and tried to forget my humiliation that I'd emotionally come apart over a stupid ride. It was ridiculous how much I hated appearing weak in front of Cal. After all, I was human, and all humans had weaknesses. Why did having him see my vulnerabilities feel so scary?

Was there something wrong with me?

Was I incapable of opening myself up to someone and showing them my fears?

Was that why things never worked out with Cal and me in the first place?

I started to wonder if maybe the problem wasn't his unpredictability and temper, but rather my own issues with being seen as weak, and more importantly with suffering another loss. After we lost the baby, I told myself I'd never let something like that happen again. I'd never allow myself to be so powerless, to have the world rip something so vital away from me, leaving a gaping wound in its place.

My phone buzzed with a message from Paul, and it was a welcome reprieve from my agonised thoughts. The others were getting ready to leave, so I made my way back to the minivan. Once there, I picked a seat, put my earphones on and pulled up a movie-scene playlist on my phone, ignoring everyone.

1.) *The Last of the Mohicans*: Daniel Day-Lewis telling Cora he will find her.

2.) *Jane Eyre*: The final scene with Rochester.

Yeah, I was in a particular sort of mood. Cal sat two seats behind me, and I could practically feel his eyes scoring a hole in the back of my head, but he didn't try to talk to me. Maybe he knew I needed space and for once decided to give it.

Back at the house, I went straight to my room, which was becoming a habit. A little while later Michaela ducked her head in to say I had some press interviews over the phone. Inwardly, I groaned. Talking to journalists was the last thing I wanted to do right then, but I knew I had to.

The first couple of interviews went fine, mostly fluff pieces asking me my favourite brand of shampoo, or my go-to drink when training. Then, the final interviewer called. It was for a newspaper back home, and straight off the bat, I knew it was going to be a difficult conversation.

"So, the incident at the TV Choice Awards between Callum Davidson and Ben Young, did that have anything to do with you?" the interviewer asked.

He had one of those haughty public-school accents, which immediately got my back up.

"Not to my knowledge." I didn't feel any guilt about lying since he was obviously looking for a scandal.

"Several sources say you and Mr. Young looked very cosy during the event. There's even footage of you both sharing several drinks together. Given your past relationship with Callum, do you think this caused him to be jealous?"

"I have no idea what goes on inside Cal's head. You'd have to ask him that."

"Well, what about the out-of-court settlement that was made between Callum and Mr. Young, can you tell me anything about that?" There was an edge to his voice, probably because he wasn't getting anywhere with me.

"Like I said, you'd have to ask them."

The journalist cleared his throat. "Are you and Callum back together?"

"No. I'm not sure what would give you that idea." I instantly regretted my words because he was all too happy to explain exactly where he got the idea.

"Well, you might be aware that a lot of your followers on social media have been speculating up a storm about your current relationship status since just yesterday Callum commented on one of your selfies to say he thought you looked beautiful."

Well, crap. I hadn't even thought of the repercussions of that comment. Obviously, people were going to see it and talk. "Just because he gave me a compliment doesn't mean we're together."

"You can understand why it would make people believe you are though, can't you?"

"There are a lot of things I can understand," I said, avoiding an answer.

"Leanne, I'm just trying to get to the bottom of your relationship with Callum. Are you or aren't you together?"

I gritted my teeth. "We are not."

"Very well then. Thank you for your time."

"No, thank you," I clipped and hung up, then threw the phone across my bed. I couldn't afford for anyone to be printing interviews about Cal and me getting back together. If the network caught wind of rumours like those, I didn't know what might happen, especially since we were still in our one-year probationary period. If they wanted, they could get rid of us next season, cast some new faces. There were plenty of talented freerunners in London for them to choose from.

Okay, I was officially in a bad mood. And I needed a drink.

I headed to the kitchen and pulled open the fridge in search of alcohol, but there was nothing. In fact, I searched the entire house, and there wasn't a drop to be found. Irritated, I pulled up the number for a taxi service on my phone and booked a car to take me into the city. I knew this wasn't the best city to be wandering around alone at night, but I only planned to take a taxi straight to a bar, then straight back to the house.

When the car arrived, I managed to sneak out undetected. I told the driver to take me to the best bar he knew, though I probably should've been a little more specific because he stopped in a neighbourhood that didn't look too safe. Still, there were lots of people about, so it couldn't be that bad. In my experience, it was the abandoned places you had to be careful of.

Inside, the place was jam-packed with a Saturday-night crowd. The music was good, and the vibe seemed chill. Maybe the taxi driver had made a good choice after all.

I went to the bar and ordered a gin and tonic. Yes, tonight was a gin sort of night. I let the swell of music and chatter fill my ears, blocking out my thoughts while I soldiered my way through drink after drink. Nobody tried to talk to me, maybe because I had the look of a woman who wasn't there for conversation. I had one mission and that was blissful inebriation. I wanted to forget about that silly interview, about the emotions the roller coaster ride summoned in me, about how conflicted I was over Cal.

Something had changed in him, and it felt deliberate, like he was actively trying to be a better person. Why couldn't he just stay the same hot-tempered, argumentative, infuriatingly frustrating man I knew? That way it would be a whole lot easier to stick to our contract.

My phone buzzed in my pocket and I pulled it out. Michaela was calling, but I sent her to voice mail. Whatever she wanted, it could wait until morning. Right now I just needed to be alone with my thoughts and my gin.

I knocked back my drink then ordered another. I sat there until closing time and everyone was starting to leave. I decided I should probably make a move too. A little wobbly on my feet, I got up and headed outside.

When I'd arrived, there'd been lots of taxis on the road, but now there were none. I pulled out my phone.

"*Sawubona. Unjani?*"

I blinked drunkenly and looked up. A young guy about my age was smiling at me. I had no idea what he just said.

He looked friendly, but there was something off about his smile. Then I saw two other guys hovering behind him.

Crap. The guy who'd spoken looked at my phone, and I realised his intent. He was going to mug me.

It was 3 a.m. in Johannesburg, and I was drunk in a strange part of the city. I didn't even know the name of the street I was on. My first instinct was to tell them to fuck off and leave me alone, but then I'd reveal my accent. They'd know instantly I wasn't from here.

Not that I didn't look like an easy mark already.

I quickly glanced around. There was an alley behind the bar. Without hesitation, I shoved my phone back in my pocket and ran. I heard the three guys chasing me as I leapt atop a large dumpster, then climbed the back wall at the end of the alley. One of them tried to climb up too, but he didn't have much luck. Another one said something I didn't understand, but it sounded like a swear.

I saluted them with a wave, then climbed up onto the roof of the bar and ran to the next building. I jumped the six-foot gap easily, though my landing was sloppy, thanks to the gin. Adrenaline rushed through me, and I kept running, leaping from building to building, until I'd put a safe distance between the muggers and me. I sat down on a wall at the edge of an apartment block to catch my breath, the lights of the city twinkling before me.

I'd been so stupid to come out here on my own, not even figuring out the neighbourhood I was in before I'd decided to drink myself into oblivion. Now that the danger had been averted, a wooziness hit me. I barely managed not to puke.

I needed to figure out how to get back to the house, so I pulled out my phone. I had a tonne of missed calls from Michaela and Cal, not to mention a number of texts.

Cal: Where the hell are you?
Michaela: Answer your phone. Cal's been going crazy looking for you.

I was still scrolling through my messages when the phone started ringing in my hand. It was Cal. He was the last person I wanted to ask for help, but I kind of needed rescuing and I didn't want to wake up Paul.

"Hello?"

"Leanne, where are you?" Cal's voice was gritty, angry, worried.

Weirdly, hearing him was a relief.

I scratched the back of my head, looking around for a landmark. "Hey, so, um, I might've done something stupid." If I didn't have so much gin in my system, I never would've admitted that to Cal, but alcohol was like my truth serum.

"I'm coming to get you. Tell me where you are."

I pulled up my GPS coordinates and Cal said he'd be there as quick as he could. When I hung up, I lay down for a minute, just until the world stopped spinning. The fact I even made it up here in the state I was in was a miracle.

I looked up at the sky that was slowly starting to brighten, welcoming in a new day, and wished for stars. Stars reassured me. They made me feel like I wasn't the only tragic thing in the world. They showed me that you could still shine bright even after you'd died inside. That all wasn't lost just because you'd lost something.

I didn't know how much time had passed when I heard footsteps approach.

"What in the actual fuck happened to you?" Cal swore and kneeled before me.

He checked me over as I sat up. At least time had helped me sober up a little. Or maybe that was Cal being there.

"Eh, there was nothing to drink at the house, so I decided to go out and find a bar. Everything was fine, but I left it a bit late to go home and these three blokes tried to rob me. I managed to jump onto the roof and get away, but then I had no idea where I ended up, which is well, here. But obviously, you found me. So, it's all good."

Cal stared at me, pissed. "You little fucking idiot."

"Hey! I already admitted it was stupid. You don't need to rub my face in it."

He exhaled heavily. "Thank Christ nothing happened to you."

"No, thank Christ I know parkour."

His green eyes narrowed to slits. "What if they caught you? They might not have just wanted to rob you, Leanne." He looked furious, like he wanted to punch a wall or something. "If anything happened to you, I'd lose it. We all would."

Guilt ate at me. Cal was right, everybody would be devastated if I was hurt. I stared down at the street where there was a glowing sign on top of a closed supermarket. The minivan Cal drove here was parked outside it.

"Saw you taking a little nap up here on the edge of the roof. Also dumb, since you're clearly shit-faced and could roll right off if you weren't careful. Just out of curiosity, why are you going out of your way to get yourself killed?"

Our eyes met, and he seemed to realise the answer to that question was a lot more complicated than we had time for. I didn't respond, looking away. I felt way too exposed right then.

"You've been drinking an awful lot," Cal said, deciding to throw fuel on the fire.

I brought my gaze back to him. "And?"

"Why?" His stare was unrelenting.

I felt my eyes grow watery. "Because it helps."

Cal studied me so hard that lines formed between his eyebrows. A part of me wanted to jump off this roof and run away, but another part wanted to stay and savour his care and attention. This moment of truth had my heart pounding. Cal reached out and stroked my cheek. I blinked away a tear and it rolled down my face.

He wiped it away as he whispered, "How does it help?"

Honesty spewed right out of me. "It makes me forget."

His answering expression was something I couldn't put into words. It was pure emotional turmoil, like he wanted to take my pain away no matter the cost. But no, that wasn't right. Cal didn't do selfless things. Not for me.

He lifted my hand and brought it to his chest. "I'm sorry for making you ride that roller coaster today."

"I don't care about that anymore," I said, full of bluster.

"You were upset. I didn't like it."

I scoffed. "Course you didn't."

"For fuck's sake. I came all the way out here to rescue you. Can you just be real with me for one minute?"

I bit my lip, my throat growing heavy. "I don't need to be rescued," I whispered.

Cal swore under his breath. "That's not what I meant. You know it isn't. I just want you to acknowledge that there's a part of you, no matter how small, that actually gives a shit about me."

I met his gaze. "Why?"

"Because, with everything I'm made of, I give a shit about you."

The quiet rang in my ears before I finally spoke, "I...do care about you but..."

"But what?"

I bit my lip, held back the tears that wanted to fall. "When I'm with you, I don't feel in control of myself, and every time I've opened up to you, it's ended in pain. I can't go through that again."

Cal stood, his features hardening. It was clear he wasn't happy. "Come on, we better get back to the house."

I nodded sombrely and followed as he climbed the fire escape back down to the street. When we reached the minivan he paused, holding the keys in his hand.

"You seem to keep forgetting something, Leanne," he said and I held my breath, waiting for the rest. His eyes met mine, so green and heavy with emotion. "You're not the only one who suffered."

Without giving me a chance to respond, he pressed the button to open the car doors then slid into the driver's seat. I stood still for a second, the full realisation of my own selfishness dawning on me. He was right, he had suffered too. Each of our breakups had hurt him just as much as they hurt me.

I opened the door on my side and got in. I wanted to tell him I was sorry, but I couldn't. Maybe it was the lump in my throat.

Or maybe I was just a giant coward.

Ten
Callum
Three and a half years ago

My attention locked on her the moment she walked into the party.

Leanne wore a tight black top, dark jeans, and heeled boots. Her dark eye makeup brought out the aquamarine of her eyes, her short hair tousled. I couldn't look away. She was so sexy it physically hurt. This girl who I didn't even know a couple of months ago now took over ninety percent of my waking thoughts and a good portion of my sleeping ones.

This year Trev had decided last minute to throw a party at his place for New Year's Eve. There were drunk people everywhere, beautiful women, more than one of whom had given me the eye, but I wasn't interested. All I wanted was my scrappy little tomboy who gave me shit, then kissed me when no one else was watching.

We'd been seeing each other in secret for months, though I suspected Leanne might've confessed to Paul what was going on. Not that I cared. As far as I was concerned, we could shout that we were together from the rooftops. Unfortunately, Leanne was concerned it might mess with the dynamic of the show, and she was right. We had a good thing going and we didn't want to screw with it.

Now I finally had enough money to move Mum out of the shitbox we'd both been living in. I rented her a cosy two-bedroom house in the suburbs, and she was even able to quit her job. Since she'd worked in crappy jobs all her life just to feed and clothe me, it was about time she enjoyed a bit of leisure. That had always been the plan.

And since Mum was settled, I had all the time in the world to obsess over Leanne.

She moved through the room, stopping to talk with James. She hadn't seen me yet since I was skulking in the corner like an infatuated teenager. Unable to wait any longer, I made my way over, not so discreetly running my hand across her lower back.

"Hey," I murmured in her ear.

James gave me a funny look, but I didn't care. To be honest, I was pretty sure both he and Trev knew something was going on between Leanne and me, they just hadn't said anything. I was so gone for her I couldn't even censor myself anymore. People must've noticed how I looked at her.

Leanne cleared her throat, seeming uncomfortable with how forward I was being. I'd had a few beers, so it was kind of hard to hold back. All I wanted to do was touch her.

"I'm going to get a drink." She stepped away from us and headed toward the kitchen.

I glanced at James, who gave me a look that managed to be both stoic and admonishing at the same time.

I lifted an eyebrow. "What?"

"Close your mouth, Cal. You're drooling."

"Piss off."

"I'm not sure Leanne appreciates you feeling her up like that," he went on.

I gave him a cocky smile. "For your information, Leanne appreciates the fuck out of me."

He exhaled a heavy breath and shook his head. "Please don't tell me you're sleeping with her."

I lifted my chin. "What if I am?"

"You'll hurt her."

"How do you know she won't hurt me?"

Now James just looked cynical. "Have you ever had your heart broken?"

"There's a first time for everything."

"Leanne's not one of your playthings, Cal. She's our friend. You need to treat her with respect."

"I don't need to listen to this." I moved to walk away.

James caught me by the arm. His expression pled with me not to be a dick. "Just be careful with her, okay? Leanne's a good person. She doesn't deserve to be screwed around with."

All I did was nod in response. I found Leanne in the kitchen sipping a glass of wine and looking out the window. There was a bunch of other people there too, but I didn't recognise any of them. Trev had a knack for announcing a party at the very last minute and having dozens of random people show up.

"You hiding?" I asked as I approached.

"Just checking out Trev's view. This is a great spot."

"Mine's better. You should come over sometime."

In spite of our secret shagging, Leanne had never been to my place and I'd not yet been to hers. Not for my want of trying. She was keen to keep things as impersonal as possible, which okay, frustrated the shit out of me.

She shot me a grin. "Nice try."

"Would it really be so terrible if you stayed over at my place some night?"

"No, but that's not what this is about."

My jaw tightened because I got her insinuation. This was about sex and nothing else. At first, I'd been fine with that, but now I wanted more.

I gave a harsh laugh. "Do you know James just warned me not to screw you over?" *Ironic that it will probably be the opposite.*

Her eyes widened as she whisper-hissed, "How does James know about us?"

"Don't get your knickers in a twist. I didn't tell him. He's a perceptive bloke. He put two and two together."

"Shit," Leanne swore quietly and knocked back a gulp of wine.

"What's the big deal? Will the world stop turning if people find out about us?"

Her cheeks heated, which made me wonder if she was shy, if that was why she didn't want people knowing.

I leaned close and spoke quietly. "Are you embarrassed, or just shy to have everyone know you're fucking me?"

She wouldn't meet my gaze. "Shut up."

I grinned wide. "You are shy. That's adorable." I whispered my lips over her ear and she trembled. I reached down and took her hand. "Come with me."

"Where?"

I didn't reply, only led her out of the kitchen and toward Trev's spare bedroom. Pushing the door open, I made sure no one else was in there before I pulled Leanne inside. I turned over the lock, then wrapped my arms around her waist, pulling her arse flush with my crotch. I kissed her neck, and she let out a small, desperate moan and arched her hips. I was rock hard and desperate for her too.

I slipped my hand inside her top to massage her breast. When I pinched her nipple, she sighed and twisted in my arms, kissing me hungrily.

I smiled into the kiss. "Maybe you do like me after all."

She whimpered and slid her hand under my shirt. Her soft fingers trailed up my stomach, and I groaned. I loved it when she touched me back. I stepped forward, backing her up until she fell onto the bed and I climbed between her thighs. We continued to kiss, tongues clashing, breaths heaving.

Kissing her was my favourite thing. Yes, I adored fucking her, but foreplay with Leanne was addictive. She slowly opened up to me, becoming more and more aroused until eventually, much later, she came apart in my arms.

She tugged at my clothes, but I broke the kiss and drew away. I was sick of giving her everything and getting nothing in return. I gave her all of me, the good and the bad, but she held everything back. I wanted to break down that sky-high wall she'd built.

"Cal," she sighed, grabbing for the fly of my jeans. "Please."

"Tell me you like me."

She frowned, chest rising and falling with her breathing. "What?"

"Tell me you like me," I repeated.

Her frown deepened. "Why?"

"Because I like you. I like you a lot, and sometimes it feels like I'm just a body that gets you off. Like I could be anyone."

Leanne stared at me for a long time. "That's not true."

"Say it then."

"Fine. I like you."

"Not like that. Say it like you mean it."

Her eyelids fluttered, her attention on my collarbone when she whispered, "I like you."

I tipped her chin up. "Eyes up here, babe."

Finally, her gaze lifted. And then, for a second, the wall was gone, and her vulnerability shone through. "I like you, Callum. I like you so much it scares me."

A shimmering heat spread through my chest, while the fear in her voice made my throat ache. Did her feelings frighten her? Hearing the truth in her words was deeply satisfying. This wasn't a one-sided thing.

I caught her cheek in my hand and brought her mouth to mine. "Now, that wasn't so hard, was it?"

She moaned when I slid my tongue in slow, then ran my hand along her inner thigh. I pressed kisses to the tops of her breasts and undid her jeans. She pulled the buttons free on my shirt and tugged it off. She kissed my chest while I shoved down her underwear. I pulled my cock free and pushed inside her.

She gasped.

I pressed one hand to her throat and used the other to hold myself up while I fucked her. We were both still half dressed, impatient for each other. I had to have her. She sucked my earlobe into her mouth, then gave a bite. I growled at the spike of pain, thrusting faster. Her gentle breaths and sighs filled my ears, driving me to distraction. When I came, I kissed her again, my lips crushing hers harshly. She gripped my shoulders, her fingertips digging desperately into my skin, marking me.

"I really need to start using condoms with you," I said as I fell on top of her then rolled us on our sides. The first time we slept together, we'd been so eager we hadn't used protection, which had become a habit. I knew she was on the pill and we were both clean, but there was still a small chance she could get pregnant.

"I told you, I'm already on the pill," she said, echoing my own thoughts.

"But what if it doesn't work for some reason?"

She twisted in my arms, turning around to face me. "It's ninety-nine percent effective, Cal, I'm pretty sure we'll be okay."

"Ninety-nine percent? Really?"

She nodded, smiling like she found me adorable. Then, her face turned shy.

"Why are you looking at me like that?"

She shook her head, "It's nothing. I just…"

I admired the red flush that had risen to the surface of her skin. I traced it with my finger when I asked, "You just what?"

Her voice was small when she replied shyly, "I think I…I think I trust you."

Just like that, I was on top of the world. Leanne liked me, she trusted me. I couldn't help probing further. It was rare that she spoke openly about her feelings and I needed to know more.

"Why do you trust me?" I stroked her stomach, my hand wandering down to finger her clit.

She moved and shifted against me, her voice breathy. "Yes, keep doing that."

I kissed her neck, then brushed my lips across her ear, circling her clit with my thumb torturously slow. "Why do you trust me, Leanne?"

She let out the sexiest frustrated little growl. "I…I trust you because I never see you look at other women. And I trust you because you're always honest, even if it hurts my feelings."

Now I circled faster. It was deeply fulfilling to know she appreciated these things in me. I hadn't realised it, but she was right about me not looking at other girls. I didn't feel the need. She was the only one I wanted to look at.

And if she valued honesty, then I'd give it to her, always, no matter what, so long as she promised to stay mine.

I knew she was going to come when she got quiet. Leanne always grew quiet when she was close. She trembled when she orgasmed on my hand, and I kissed her neck as the waves petered out.

We lay in bed, and I held her tight.

A little while later, she pressed a kiss to the underside of my jaw. "It's almost midnight. We should go back out."

I glanced at the clock. It was two minutes to midnight. I had absolutely no desire to go back out to the party. I'd much rather stay right here where I was. Her lips continued their journey from my jaw to my neck, and I resisted the urge to climb on top of her and push deep inside. Instead, I pulled her mouth to mine and kissed her.

I put all I had into the kiss, all the feelings and emotions we hadn't yet spoken about. She had to feel what was between us, the tugging, drugging, falling sensation. It couldn't just be me.

Boisterous sounds came from outside as the clock struck twelve.

I broke our kiss to look down at her. "Happy New Year," I whispered, thumb trailing her bottom lip.

"Happy New Year, Cal," she replied.

I brought my mouth back to hers, trying to communicate all the things she wasn't ready to hear. She didn't even know it yet but I was going to make her mine. I was going to tear down all the barriers between us. Tonight I might've knocked down a few bricks, but soon I'd demolish the entire wall.

Eleven
Leanne
Present

The days blended into a predictable pattern: wake up, film, come home, eat, go to sleep alone. Things had been unresolved between Cal and me since our conversation on the roof, and I couldn't stop replaying it over in my head.

"I just want you to acknowledge that there's a part of you, no matter how small, that actually gives a shit about me."

"Why?"

"Because with everything I'm made of I give a shit about you."

His words created a void inside me, an ache that wouldn't seem to quit. My heart wanted to believe them, but then my head intervened, reminding me that Cal was playing a game.

It was late evening and we'd had a long day of filming, but I wasn't tired enough to sleep. Instead I wandered around the house, aimless.

"It's sad really, because there's a village somewhere being deprived of an idiot." Paul grinned widely as he threw the insult at Trev.

"At least my parents weren't cousins," Trev shot back and Paul barked a laugh.

I'd just entered the lounge, wondering why they were sitting here insulting each other.

"Coming from a bloke who couldn't get a whistle from a kettle," Paul retorted.

"Do you know what, I'm jealous of all the people who *haven't* met you."

"Nah, you're just mad because I wouldn't take you for a ride if you had pedals."

"I have a girlfriend who takes me for a ride regularly, thank you very much," Trev clapped back.

"Okay," I interrupted on a laugh. "I have to ask, what's going on?"

"We're trying to see who can come up with the corniest put down," Trev replied.

"So far I'm winning," Paul added.

"No way," Trev disagreed. "I haven't even told you I'm not as stupid as you look yet."

Paul chuckled loudly. "Did you get that one off Google?"

"I honestly can't decide which of you is weirder," I said as I sat down next to Trev.

"Him," they both said in unison then cracked themselves up laughing.

"You two seem way too giddy, are you high?" I questioned suspiciously.

"We're high on life, sorry if you're not evolved enough to understand," Paul retorted.

I heard the front door open and it sounded like a whole bunch of people just entered the house. There was giggling and chatter, the sound of high heels clicking on tile.

I got up and went to peek around the doorway. Glancing down the hall, I saw Linda welcoming in our fans. They'd been attending all our shoots in the city, but were headed home in the morning. I guess Linda invited them over for one last hurrah.

There were also a few women and men I didn't recognise, all of them young and good looking. I inwardly groaned. Linda was obviously trying to do some matchmaking and I wasn't in the mood.

"What's going on out there?" Trev asked curiously.

"Linda's brought some of the fans over," I whispered. "And a few locals too, it looks like."

"Really?" Paul questioned. "Are any of them hot?"

"I'll let you decide that for yourself. I'm going to my room."

"Oh, no you're not," Paul stood and caught hold of my wrist. "You've been hiding out in there way too much. You need to socialise."

"Linda didn't bring all those women here for me, but you guys have fun."

Paul manoeuvred me to take a look down the hall. "There are some blokes there too. You're staying."

I pulled my wrist from his hold and turned around, walking right into someone's hard chest. *Cal.* He must've entered the room through the patio doors while I'd been peeking down the hallway. Bringing his hands to my shoulders to steady me, he smiled.

It had a heady effect on me, since I hadn't been on the receiving end of many smiles from him lately. "Hey, buy me a drink first," I said, trying to deflect from how my cheeks heated.

His smile deepened.

I tried side-stepping him, but he moved quickly, blocking my exit. "Get out of my way."

He tilted his head. "Why? You in a hurry?"

Did he realise how much he was flustering me? I huffed a breath. "Yes, now move."

He bent close to whisper in my ear. "If you trip, fall and land on my lips, does that mean I win the bet?"

So, after days of nothing we were back to the bet? Weirdly, I was relieved he'd decided to engage with me again. Being teased and toyed with by Cal felt better than going days with him barely sparing me a second glance. Yes, I had issues.

Our tumultuous relationship really was half my fault, wasn't it?

I eyed him steadily. "In your dreams."

His grin was wolfish. "It was worth a try."

I grew agitated. "Can you please just get out of my way? Linda's brought a bunch of people over for a party and I need to get to my room before I'm stuck here."

Understanding dawned right at the same moment our producer ushered her guests into the lounge. "There they are! I invited everyone over for some drinks," she said. "I think it's the least we can do since they came all this way."

Cal's posture stiffened when he saw Olive and I had a brief moment of triumph as I went up on my tiptoes to whisper in *his* ear. "If you'd gotten out of my way, I might've had time to warn you."

Cal's expression was one of capitulation. He knew there was no escaping now. Some of the guesthouse staff came in with drinks, and seriously, what was Linda thinking? Bringing a bunch of fans over for a party with lots of booze and cameras watching was not her finest idea.

I stepped away just as Olive cornered Cal. I would've felt bad if it weren't for the fact that he'd hampered my escape. Isaac and James came downstairs, followed by Michaela and Neil. I grabbed two beers then went to sit next to Michaela, handing her one.

"Better settle in to watch. Tonight is going to be interesting," I said, clinking my bottle with hers.

"Do you guys normally have parties during filming?" she asked.

"Not always, but sometimes, yeah. If this ends in drama, I'm steering clear."

"Did somebody mention drama?" James said, coming to sit on the other side of me. Michaela gave him a shy smile and I wondered how he hadn't noticed her crush yet. Or maybe he had and decided to ignore it.

"It's a party, there's always drama," I replied. "But for once I'm not getting involved."

James nodded to Cal, who was still stuck talking to Olive. "Poor guy. Aren't you going to take pity on him and cut in?"

"Cal's a big boy. He can take care of himself. Besides, how do you know he's not interested in her?"

James arched an eyebrow. "Maybe because he looks as stiff as someone who just shit their pants and is hoping nobody notices."

Michaela and I chuckled. "He does look a little awkward," I admitted.

"Do you think she has a shrine of him at home? Maybe a giant poster of his face pinned to her bedroom ceiling?" James went on.

"Hey, we're not all into putting stuff on our bedroom ceilings," I teased and if his complexion wasn't so tan, I'm sure he would've been blushing.

"Shut up, Leanne," he grunted.

I laughed. "Just saying."

Michaela's voice was curious as she eyed him. "What have you got on your ceiling?"

James' face was pure mortification. "Nothing. Never mind." A pause as he narrowed his gaze at me. "How do you even know about that?"

"Cal told me." I also saw the mirrors on his bedroom ceiling for myself a few years ago, but I wasn't going to admit I'd snooped.

James sighed. "Of course he did."

"Okay, I'm still completely in the dark here," Michaela said.

"And that's where you're going to stay," James replied pointedly.

I nudged her shoulder and whispered, "Don't worry. I'll tell you later."

"Don't you dare," James warned.

Before I could tease him further, Linda appeared holding a glass of white wine. She was accompanied by a tall, good looking guy with a nose piercing and a man bun. "Leanne, come meet Bash. He's a professional photographer."

Great, she was trying to set me up. I knew it was going to happen at some point in the evening. Setups were the worst because I was no good at small talk.

"I believe they call this instant karma," James murmured, pleased.

I shot him an irritated look out the corner of my eye and stood to say hello to Bash. Maybe Paul was right about me needing to socialise more. My natural instinct these days was to be an antisocial grump and where was that getting me? A one-way ticket to loners-ville. It had been at least a year since anyone touched me, like *really* touched me, and that person had been Cal.

Okay, brain, we're not going there.

"Hi, it's nice to meet you," I said and shook his hand. He had a pleasant smile, straight white teeth, and he smelled really good too. Linda shot me a grin and a thumbs up then sauntered off.

"Linda says you're filming a TV show," Bash said as he lifted his beer bottle to his lips. "What's it about?"

"It's called *Running on Air*. Think *The Real Housewives*, except none of us are married and instead of going to parties and bitching about each other, we spend our time doing parkour and urban exploration."

Bash chuckled. "So, nothing like *The Real Housewives*, then?"

"I think I need to come up with a better comparison," I laughed self-deprecatingly.

This was going...kind of all right, all things considered. Bash was attractive and he had one of those interestingly sexy Afrikaner accents. It was too bad I kept getting distracted by how Cal watched us while Olive chattered at him on the other side of the room. His eyebrows drew together, gaze narrowed.

"There's a really hot guy over there glaring at me," Bash commented, clearly noticing too.

I studied Bash with new eyes. Was he gay? Linda clearly hadn't done her research. Oh man, I could have some fun here, but I wouldn't, because that wouldn't be fair to Bash. Though the urge to tell him glaring was how Cal showed attraction was strong. The angel on my shoulder fought against the devil.

"Sorry about that. He's my ex. He seems to imagine he still has some kind of claim over me. He also probably thinks you're flirting with me."

Bash chuckled. "No offence, but I'm more interested in the sexy nerd over there by the window. Unfortunately, he hasn't taken his eyes off his phone."

"None taken," I said, and looked to see who he was talking about. Neil sat on an armchair, fingers moving rapidly over the screen of his phone. He could be a bit of a workaholic. Bash describing him as a sexy nerd was interesting. I'd never outright fancied Neil, but he was good looking, with his floppy brown hair and hazel eyes. He always wore shirts and ties with jeans and navy Converse, like he was auditioning for an emo band circa 2005.

"Is he gay?" Bash asked.

I shook my head. "I don't think so."

He seemed disappointed as he let out a sigh. "Another one bites the dust."

"Leanne," Cal quietly uttered my name as he joined us. "Can I get you another drink?"

I held up my three-quarters full bottle of beer. "No, thanks. I'm good."

He turned his attention to Bash, expression cold. "We haven't met yet. I'm Callum."

Bash smiled despite Cal's iciness, his tone flirtatious when he replied, "The pleasure is mine."

I saw it the moment Cal realised his error and felt a strong urge to say, *see what happens when you assume, you ass*. Cal scratched the back of his neck, a tell-tale sign he was taken off guard. "Do you live around here?" he asked, deciding to go for casual conversation now that he knew his initial presumption was incorrect. I savoured his moment of embarrassment.

"Yeah, I've lived in Joburg for a few years," Bash replied.

"Bash is a photographer," I added just as Olive cut in.

"Cal, you left me all by myself over there."

His lips tightened in annoyance, before he proceeded to introduce Olive to Bash. Cal's hand came to rest on my shoulder. "Leanne, I forgot we have that conference call with Tanya in a couple of minutes."

I glanced at him and he widened his eyes meaningfully, but for once his scheming worked to my benefit. I slapped my hand to my forehead. "Right. We better go." I looked to Bash and Olive. "We'll be back as soon as we can."

We approached the double sliding doors, but Paul intercepted us, his expression suspicious. "Where are you two off to?"

"We have a conference call with Tanya. It has to do with our contracts," Cal lied smoothly.

Paul looked to me, studying me a moment. "Is that true?"

I cleared my throat. "Yes, there were some last-minute details that we needed to go through." I felt bad lying to him, but I really wanted to escape this party. Besides, it wasn't like me and Cal were sneaking off for sex. Paul seemed to believe us as he stepped away and went back to the attractive blonde he'd been talking to.

We entered the garden, passing by the pool. "Want to go for another swim?" Cal asked huskily.

"I think I'll pass."

"Hey, I just helped you escape that party. You owe me one."

"No, I don't."

"Okay, well, you can at least let me hang out in your room for a while," he went on.

I arched an eyebrow. "Why?"

"Because no one will think to come looking for me there."

My expression said *pull the other one*. "Of course they will. My room is like, the second place they'll come looking for you."

He shoved his hands in his pockets and gave me a cheeky grin. "Busted."

I shook my head, trying hard not to be charmed by him, and turned in the direction of the back door that led to the kitchen and the staff quarters. If I could sneak through there, I might be able to make it to my room without actually bumping into anyone.

"Have I mentioned that you look really pretty today?" Cal said, heavy on my heels.

I tilted my head to him, recognising the devilish glint in his eye all too well. "Have *I* mentioned that I'm now immune to your charms? Better save your compliments for someone who doesn't know all your tactics already."

His face fell as he muttered, "It's not a tactic."

"Okay, sure."

Before I could react, Cal stepped in front of me, his expression intense "You're so fucking pretty it hurts to look at you. I'm not lying," he said vehemently and I blinked in surprise.

My pulse sped at the ferocity of his compliment. Had I hurt his feelings? I didn't know what to say. A second passed, then two.

"You always think the worst of me," he went on, voice glum.

I frowned. "I know. I'm sorry." Remorse niggled at me and I felt bad for being so dismissive. "I'm a bitch." Cal stared at me for a long, long moment. His eyes wandered over my head as I let out a flat laugh. "I see you aren't going to disagree with me."

He didn't respond, instead grabbing my arm and pulling me around a corner into a narrow window nook. My chest smashed into his as I blurted, "What the hell are you—"

His hand clasped over my mouth to quiet me. I glanced up at him and his eyes communicated with mine, *don't breathe a word*. I held still, our bodies flush in the small space. His scent and warmth surrounded me and for a second I forgot myself. My hand came to rest on the upper part of his chest. His eyes wandered to my fingers and I saw his breath catch. My attention went to his sculpted lips and I couldn't look away.

I was broken from the spell when heavy footsteps sounded. Two fans walked by arm in arm, determination in their gait. They were friends of Olive's.

"I think I saw him go this way," one of them said.

"Oh em gee, do you think we could sneak into his room?" another asked and my jaw tightened, but I kept quiet until they were gone.

"Those sneaky little bitches," I said angrily.

Cal sighed. "Guess I'm hiding on the roof until they leave."

In that moment, I felt sorry for him, which was probably why I said what I did next. "You can come to hang out in my room for a bit." He started to smile, so I held up a finger. "Only until they go. You're not staying the night."

He placed a hand to his chest. "As soon as they leave I'm gone. Scout's honour."

I scoffed as I turned and led the way to my room. "Like you were ever a boy scout."

When we reached my room, the space suddenly felt a lot smaller with Cal there. He sat down on the armchair and I turned the TV on as a distraction. Me and Cal sitting alone in a quiet room could lead to personal conversations, which in turn could lead to…well, us taking our clothes off. Our feelings for one another had always been very much tangled up in desire, but was that all it ever was? Just sexual attraction? For some reason, I found that thought depressing.

But no, it wasn't true. I definitely remembered coming close to falling for Cal, and it was entirely separate from how attracted I was to him physically.

I sat on the bed and pulled out my tablet to check my emails. Nothing exciting. Next, I checked my social media accounts, but there wasn't anything to keep my attention from the fact that Cal was just a few feet away. I chanced a peek and found him engrossed in his phone. He must've sensed my attention when his gaze flicked up. I looked away immediately and pretended to read an email.

"Can I get your opinion?" Cal asked and came to sit next to me on the bed. I was taken off guard by his closeness as he held his phone out to me. "What do you think of this?"

He'd pulled up a sketch of a skyscraper, depicted in an artistic style where each pane of glass seemed to shimmer with refracted light.

"That's amazing. Who drew this?"

"You remember Kev? The bloke who did your tattoo?"

My memory summoned up an image of a tall, scary looking man covered in ink and piercings. Cal's tattoo artist was an intimidating character, but he was a teddy bear underneath the tough exterior.

"Is this going to be your next one?" I asked, looking back to the drawing on the screen.

Cal nodded. "Don't you recognise the building?"

I studied the picture more closely before I realised it was One Canada Square. The second tallest building in London. Back while filming the first season, Cal, Trev and I had gone out one night and managed to sneak past security to get to the top of the 770-foot-tall skyscraper in the centre of London. It had been a complete rush and also something to tick off all our bucket lists. Thinking back on it, though, we were so lucky we hadn't gotten arrested.

"That was an amazing night," I breathed, still staring at the sketch. "Where are you getting this?"

Cal bent to lift his leg. He pulled up the hem of his jeans to reveal a blank section on his shin. "Right here."

I sucked in a breath. "That'll hurt."

He shrugged, eyes flashing briefly to mine. "I'm used to it."

Somehow, I felt like there was a double meaning to that statement. I sat back, putting some space between us. "Are you just going to keep getting tattoos until you have no room left?"

"Well, I draw the line at my face, but the rest of my body is fair game."

And what a body it was. A work of art, and not only because of the ink that graced his skin. "Do you enjoy the pain? Is it addictive?"

"Not the pain, no. It's like adding to a collection. All of them signify something of meaning in my life."

That's why he got the tattoo of a crown after you first slept together, my brain reminded me. I told it to shut up.

Cal's attention wandered over me, lingering on my mouth and I braced myself. He was sitting too close, being too real, and I needed some distance. Hell, I needed a freaking ocean between us for all the ways his proximity corrupted my thoughts, pulling up memories like files on a hard drive. If I really wanted to torture myself, I could click into them, pour over all the captivating details stored within.

I shifted back further on the bed and he seemed to get the message. His expression regretful, he returned to the armchair and I brought my attention back to my tablet screen.

We didn't talk after that, but I was aware of him the entire time he was in my room. Two hours later the music that had been playing downstairs turned off and I heard some cars pulling up to the house. I got up from the bed and went to the window, tugging the blinds open a tiny bit to peek out.

"Looks like everyone's leaving," I said.

When I turned around Cal was already standing. He tucked his phone in his jeans pocket. "Thanks for letting me hide out," he said, eyes searching mine, like he hoped I might invite him to stay longer.

I swallowed and nodded. "Sure, no worries."

He gave me one last longing glance before he turned and left the room, the door closing behind him with a quiet snick. I was surprised he hadn't tried to push things with me tonight. We'd been alone in my room for hours, but he hadn't made any effort to win the bet. Instead, he'd been on his best behaviour. I looked around the room, but I couldn't ignore a blatant fact.

Now that he was gone, the space felt very, very empty.

Twelve
Leanne

Regular as clockwork there was a knock on my door at 7 a.m. Michaela had called me to get up for filming, and I groaned into my pillow. My sleep pattern was all messed up, my ability to switch off my thoughts practically non-existent at this point. Most nights I'd only been getting a couple of hours of broken sleep.

Before heading downstairs for breakfast, I popped on my sunglasses—that way the cameras wouldn't pick up on how shitty I looked.

"Hey, where's the other Blues Brother?" Trev called cheekily when I entered the dining room. I was too tired to respond, but he kept going. "I'm taking about Callum, in case you were wondering. Are you copying him now? I thought he was the only one pretentious enough to wear sunglasses indoors."

"I got a shitty night's sleep, if you must know," I said, not liking the insinuation that Cal was rubbing off on me. He already occupied the majority of my thoughts. I grabbed a bowl of oatmeal and some fruit, then took a seat next to Paul just as Barry entered with a pretty, slightly overweight woman with long brown hair.

"Everyone, this is Autumn Hayes. She's a podcaster from New York who's come to shadow you for the day for an episode she's recording. As you know, the show has started running on Netflix in the US and you've garnered quite an audience over there."

Paul shot her a wide grin and tipped his invisible cap. "Hello, Miss Hayes."

Autumn, who I guessed to be around our age, gave a polite smile. "Hi. It's a pleasure to meet you all."

"The pleasure is ours," Paul said, laying it on thick.

"You're such a flirt," I said to him under my breath.

"Hey, I'm just glad to see a female. This house has far too much testosterone," he whispered back playfully. He wasn't wrong.

"You came all the way from New York just to follow us around?" Isaac questioned, eyebrows raised.

Autumn nodded sheepishly. "Yes, actually, I did."

He grinned in that amiable way of his. "Well then, we'd better show you a good time."

"The minivans leave in thirty minutes," Barry said abruptly, not one to waste time on pleasantries, then left the room. Autumn stood there, looking a little uncomfortable in his absence, so I took pity on her.

"Do you want some coffee?" I offered and patted the seat next to me.

A tiny flicker of relief passed over her features. She nodded gratefully and took a seat. "Coffee sounds fantastic. I didn't get a chance to grab any before I left my hotel."

"Well, go ahead," I replied, gesturing to the carafe. "I'm Leanne, by the way."

"Yes, I know who you are. I'm a big fan of the show."

"Oh yeah?" Isaac pulled up a chair at the table. "Be honest. I'm your favourite, right?"

She gave a quiet laugh. "I don't think I've chosen a favourite yet." A pause before she continued. "So, um, what's the plan for today?"

"We're filming at the Three Castles. It's an abandoned building in the city," Isaac replied. "But if you want to see the real Joburg, my cousin Thato is taking me spinning later tonight. You're welcome to come along."

"What's spinning?" Autumn asked. She sounded genuinely curious.

"It used to be illegal, but now it's considered a sport," Isaac explained. "Basically, it's when you spin a modified car around a track real fast."

"My brother Lee used to do that when we were kids," Trev said.

"Well, it's really popular in my township," Isaac went on. "Everybody's invited. Maybe some of the crew could come and film."

Cal entered the room just then and we made brief eye contact as he sat at the table and buttered himself a slice of toast. I thought of last night, the way he'd looked at my mouth like he wanted to devour me, and shivered. If he'd tried to kiss me, I wasn't sure I would've been able to resist, and that was the scary part. To be perfectly honest, I was impressed by the fact that he didn't try anything, since he wasn't exactly known for his restraint.

Cal glanced at Autumn curiously. "Who are you?"

Predictably, she flushed. Cal was the heartthrob of the show, and she'd mentioned she was a fan. Although, his greetings could do with some work. *Who are you?* wasn't the friendliest way to welcome someone.

Holding her hand out, she introduced herself. "I'm Autumn Hayes. I run the podcast, *Autumn Talks TV*. I'm here to shadow you all for an episode I'm making about your show."

Cal shook her hand. "Will you be recording us?"

Autumn nodded enthusiastically. "With your permission, yes, but just audio. I want to try and get to know you guys, how you all work together as a group. I've done a lot of research on your stats and you have a large following in the US already. And Leanne, your approval rating among gay men is off the charts."

I frowned at her quizzically and lowered my sunglasses. "Gay men?"

"Yes, they adore you. You're like their parkour Lady Gaga, or, I don't know, Barbara Streisand."

Well, that was kind of cool.

Paul chuckled. "From now on I'm calling you Babs."

I shot him a narrowed-eyed look. "Don't even think about it."

"The gay male audience are also big fans of you guys," Autumn went on. "But they have a particular soft spot for Leanne."

"Aw, Babs, isn't that sweet," Paul said playfully.

I punched him in the arm. "Call me that one more time. Go on. See what happens."

Paul made a show of zipping his lips and holding his arm, like I'd actually punched him hard. "Don't go all Joe Pesci in *Goodfellas* on me." He looked to Autumn. "It's true what they say about short people having hot tempers."

Cal gave a low chuckle and I shot him a sharp look. "What are you laughing at? If I'm Joe Pesci, then you're Naomi Campbell."

"Hey!" he protested. "I'll have you know I've never once tried to throw a phone at anyone's head."

I flattened my lips to keep from smiling and returned my attention to Autumn. "So, how many listeners do you have on your podcast?"

"I'm coming up on almost 250,000 regular listeners," she answered with a note of pride.

"Really? That's amazing."

She nodded. "I started the podcast a couple of years ago, basically just to talk about my favourite shows. Somehow it grew bigger than I ever expected. Now I get paid to watch TV and Netflix all day, then record myself talking about it."

"That's living the dream right there," Paul said, smiling at her. I think she got a little flustered because she lowered her gaze. A moment later she dug in her bag to pull out a handheld recorder and asked shyly, "Do you all mind if I start recording now?"

"No, go for it," Paul told her, still with that smile. Something about the way he looked at her made me think he thought she was cute. *Interesting.*

On the drive into the city, Autumn sat next to Isaac, and he was talking her ear off about the history of the city, pointing out buildings of interest as we passed by.

I clicked onto Instagram and scrolled through my likes and comments.

Paul bent close to speak quietly in my ear, "Celebrity is a mask that eats into the face."

I startled and gave him a disgruntled look. "Lovely imagery, you little weirdo."

"It's a quote from the writer John Updike," he explained. "Don't pay too much attention to all that," he gestured to my phone. "Before long the real world will be meaningless, and the only meaning you'll find will be in tiny little love hearts and complimentary comments from strangers. And then, when all that goes away, because everything goes away eventually, what will you have left?"

This was typical Paul speak. He often liked to pipe up with random philosophical ramblings. "You talk like I need this." I held up my phone. "It's just a distraction. I can give it up whenever I like."

Before I could react, he swiped the phone from my hand and shoved it in the pocket of his jeans. "Okay then, in that case, I'll keep this for the day."

I reached right into his pocket to take it back. "No, you won't."

Paul chuckled. "See what I mean? You're addicted."

"What do you think of Autumn?" I asked, deciding to change the subject.

Paul's attention went to where she sat a few rows in front of us. "She seems nice."

"Just nice?"

"Yes, what's wrong with nice?"

"So, you don't think she's pretty?"

"She's pretty. You're pretty too. Lots of people are pretty."

"You should ask her out," I suggested. "I bet she'd say yes."

"Maybe, but she flies home tomorrow. Plus, she lives in New York. Long distance isn't really my thing."

He did have a point there. "That's it. As soon as we get home, I'm setting you up with someone. You haven't had a proper girlfriend in ages."

"Well, I wouldn't say no to a date with your sister. Has she decided to ditch that fool she's married to yet?" Paul teased. He'd always thought Lorna was hot.

"Unfortunately for you, she's still happily married."

He sighed. "Just my luck."

When we arrived at our destination, my eyes were inexplicably drawn to Cal as he pulled off his hoodie and shoved it in his backpack. The short sleeves of his T-shirt showcased his tattooed, muscular arms. Somehow, even the black tracksuit pants he wore were sexy.

Okay, enough was enough. I was officially vowing to ignore my contradicting feelings and attraction for Cal for the day. I was going to get out of my head and just run. Today, I was going to have some fun for a change.

Catching up with Isaac, I said, "Hey, I'll come with you and your cousin tonight. I've always wanted to see someone spin a car."

"Yes! You're going to have the best time, I promise," he said with a grin.

I gave him a thumbs up and walked ahead. The Three Castles was an abandoned building from the late 1800s that used to be a cigarette factory. It didn't look like a factory though, it looked like, well, a castle. The lower level was full of graffiti and overgrowth, while the upper levels still looked like something out of a medieval play. It was completely unexpected and was going to look great on camera.

One of the advantages of being a part of this show was that the behind-the-scenes people usually got permission for us to film in locations that were closed off to the public. Sometimes they didn't have to, but when we were entering a place like this, it was typically required. Anyway, it meant we didn't need to worry about getting into trouble.

I took a look around and managed to climb through one of the windows that wasn't boarded up.

"Leanne, will you wait? We haven't set up properly for filming yet," Barry called.

I ignored him. I just needed to keep moving.

On the inside the place was a wreck, the brick crumbling away. The decay appealed to me, the knowledge that even though the building was in disrepair, it still survived. I climbed to the very top of the building and ran along the turreted roof. I jumped from the areas where the bricks jutted out, just like stepping stones.

Down below, the others still hung about outside. It felt nice to have a moment to myself. I sucked in a deep breath and looked up at the sky. Today it was clear blue, almost azure, a dot of white clouds here and there, as though drawn from an artist's palette.

"Hey, Leanne!" someone called. I glanced down and good Christ, Autumn was awkwardly trying to climb one of the lower walls. I jumped down to help her before she hurt herself.

"It's probably not a good idea for you to be up here. Our insurance is already through the roof, what with all the accidents me and the boys get ourselves into."

"I was just wondering if we could have a chat?"

"Sure, but you don't need to break your neck for it," I said and caught her right before she almost tripped over a loose plank of wood.

A whoosh of air escaped her. "Crap, thank you. I'm such a klutz."

"Come on, we can find a quiet spot over here." I led her to one of the boarded-up windows. "What did you want to talk about?"

Autumn pushed some of the loose strands that had fallen from her ponytail out of her face. "You're the only girl in the group. I thought that you might have some interesting perspectives."

"Such as?"

She gave a light chuckle. "Well, what's it like to share a space with five gorgeous guys?"

I gave her a cynical look. "It's an orgy a minute. Next question."

She flushed bright red, her expression apologetic. "Sorry, that was nosy, wasn't it?"

I waved her off, deciding to go easy on her. "Don't worry about it. A lot of people don't get that just because I spend all my time around five good-looking guys, it doesn't mean I want to shag them."

With the exception of Cal, I'd never had a single sexual thought about any of my co-stars. Sometimes it bothered me that that was all people ever wanted to know about. I looked back to Autumn.

"There's a lot more to me than simply being the lone female in this group. I'm a freerunner. I also love astronomy. I have a fondness for science fiction novels and a weird obsession with movie clips."

"Oh!" Autumn exclaimed. "What's your favourite movie clip?"

I grinned. "I can't answer that. There are too many."

"Well, personally, I can watch Mr. Darcy dive into that lake all day long."

"Right." I chuckled. "You can never go wrong with a bit of Colin Firth."

Autumn cleared her throat. "So, can you tell me a little bit about parkour? I love watching you guys, but I have to admit I don't know a whole bunch about the sport."

"Technically, it's more of a discipline than a sport. Parkour is all about getting from one point to another in the quickest, most efficient way possible. But with freerunning, there's a little more showing off, lots of backflips and fancy looking tricks. Then there's urban exploration, which is what we're doing right now. We pick abandoned, often forgotten about buildings, or spots where it's dangerous to go and explore them."

"Sounds like it takes a lot of courage."

"It does, but mostly it takes a certain type of person. All of us get off on a little risk."

"So, it's an adrenaline rush?"

"Definitely."

She nodded and looked away, adjusting something on her recorder before she continued, "Do you mind if we talk a little about Callum? It's totally fine if you don't want to."

I hesitated, then said, "What do you want to know? If you've watched the show, then I'm sure you know all about us."

"I guess I just don't get it."

I frowned. "What don't you get?"

Autumn shrugged. "Why you two hate each other so much."

I clammed up. "We don't hate each other."

Her eyes widened with interest. "Oh, well, it's just that, it can come across that way on screen sometimes."

She was right. A lot of our arguments had made it onto the show, mostly because when I got riled up about something I tended to forget there were cameras watching. Cal did too.

I gave her the simple explanation. "We're both very hot-headed. I guess that's why we never worked out in the end."

Autumn's face was empathetic. "If it's any consolation, I still have hope for you guys. I've literally only spent a few hours with you, but the way he looks at you is special. You don't see a lot of men looking at women the way Callum looks at you." She gave a self-deprecating laugh. "Or maybe I'm just a hopeless romantic."

"What way does he look at me?" I asked curiously, the question tumbling out before I could stop it. So much for spending the day not thinking about Cal.

She thought on it a second, her face turning wistful. "Like you're his everything."

My heart gave a hard, lung bashing thump. The past few weeks, Cal had been very forward with me, his attention often overwhelming. I mostly put it down to him trying to break me, win our bet, but what did it mean if Autumn observed him looking at me like that when I didn't know he was watching? More specifically, when *he* didn't know he was being watched?

I dragged myself from my thoughts, willing my heart to stop racing. "Is there anything else you'd like to talk about."

She gave an enthusiastic nod and we spoke about how I got into parkour from a young age. I saw some teenagers doing it in my local park and became spellbound. I told her how being able to do things with my body few others could held a strong appeal. I'd always craved independence, having moved out of my parent's house at eighteen. Parkour was another form of independence. It made your body strong, gave it escape routes few people had access to.

Somewhere along the way, I launched into what happened to me when I went to that bar. Autumn leaned forward, engrossed.

"I was leaving and three guys approached me. They wanted to steal my phone, probably my wallet too. If I didn't know parkour, I wouldn't have been able to get away from them. But I did, which meant I lost them easily."

"Wow, that's amazing. It's too bad they didn't get it all on camera. It would've made for an exciting action scene."

"I doubt anyone would try to rob me with a film crew following me around."

Autumn shook her head at herself. "Right. My bad. But seriously, more women should take up parkour. They always say that if you encounter a thief, your best bet is to drop your stuff and run."

"True, but parkour comes with risks. It's easy to injure yourself if you don't know what you're doing."

"Have you ever gotten injured?" Autumn questioned with interest.

I looked away, the lie solemn on my lips. "Small things, but nothing serious."

Over her shoulder, Cal and Paul appeared.

"There you two are. We thought we lost you," Paul said, while Cal eyed Autumn suspiciously, probably wondering what we'd been talking about. He shot me a questioning look and I reminded myself that today was a Callum Davidson free zone.

I moved by him and climbed to the top of the building again. Paul followed, then completed a backflip.

"Wow, that was incredible," Autumn exclaimed, clapping.

He shot her a wink. "Glad you're impressed."

I went to sit on the edge of the wall and realised belatedly that I was wearing my first-person camera. What I'd told Autumn about sneaking into the city alone to go to a bar that night was recorded, and I knew I was going to get a scolding from Barry over that one when he went through the footage.

"Hey, so, who's coming spinning?" Isaac asked once filming wrapped up for the day.

"Not me. I'm in the mood for a quiet night. I've got a book and a bubble bath with my name on it," Paul said. Out the corner of my eye, Autumn stood off to the side, looking a little disappointed.

I shook my head at him. "Okay, Grandad."

Isaac looked to me. "Leanne, you're coming, right?"

"Yep. Lead the way."

Unexpectedly, Cal added, "I'll come too. Sounds like it could be fun."

I knew he was only tagging along because I was, though considering what Autumn said to me during our chat, I wasn't feeling as hostile towards him as usual.

In fact, I wasn't feeling hostile at all.

Isaac rubbed his hands together and smiled wide. "Fantastic. Let's go."

Thirteen
Leanne

In the end, James, Michaela, Autumn, Isaac, Cal, and I all climbed into a minivan to drive to Soweto, the township where Isaac grew up. Jimbo came along to capture some footage since word got out to Barry and he thought it could make for some interesting TV.

Neil dropped us off a little ways into the township, and we decided to get taxis home later so he didn't have to drive back into the city to get us.

Isaac led us past row upon row of one-story houses. Some were more dilapidated than others, but most were surrounded by high walls at the front. At first the houses were mostly brick, but the further we got, I saw more that were made from corrugated steel or a hodgepodge of different materials.

I knew that townships were supposed to be some of the poorest neighbourhoods in South Africa, and this one, in particular, had over a million people living in it. Cal walked beside me, and I could see him taking it all in, the same as me.

I didn't know what I expected, but even though the area was poor, it didn't feel like the people were miserable. Lots of them were going about their business, chatting with their neighbours or hanging out with friends. When it came down to it, it didn't seem a whole lot dissimilar from any working-class neighbourhood back in London. The setting and culture were different, but the people were the same, just living their lives.

Paul always said that the problem with most people nowadays was that they tended to fixate on division and forget a simple fact. That in spite of cultural or racial differences, at our core, we were all human. And all any of us wanted was to be loved, to be safe, to have a roof over our heads.

I applied that theory to myself. I had a roof over my head, I was safe, my family loved me. Maybe I just needed to focus on that instead of agonising over Cal and pining for what was missing. The problem was, I tended to obsess over the bad instead of being thankful for the good.

We reached an open area where a large crowd had gathered. I heard a car engine revving in the distance. A guy who looked to be in his late twenties came running up to us.

He pulled Isaac into a big hug, smiling widely. "Look how much you've grown!" he exclaimed, and I guessed this was his cousin, Thato. Isaac introduced everyone, ending with Autumn. "She's a podcaster from New York who came to record an episode about us. Can you believe it?"

"Whuut? New York City?" Thato said playfully, teasing Isaac when he poked him in the side. "You've made it to the big time now, cousin."

"Shut up." Isaac pushed him off. "And this is Jimbo. He's going to film us tonight. I hope that's okay."

"Of course it's okay. Everyone is gonna be trying to get on camera. They'll love it."

We approached the gathered crowd, and a few people gave us curious glances, especially Jimbo with his camera. I went up on my tiptoes to see what was happening and saw a tall guy get into an old BMW. He slammed the door shut and revved the engine.

Cal came to stand next to me. "Want to get up on my shoulders? You'll be able to see better."

I cast him some side-eye. "I can see just fine from here."

"Your loss."

The guy in the car started driving, but instead of going in a straight line he spun the car around in a circle. People cheered him on, the wheels kicking up dust as the car spun faster and faster until steam started coming out of the engine.

"That doesn't look entirely safe," Michaela said.

"But it does look fun." James grinned at her.

"My friend is up next. If you want, I can ask if she'll let you two ride with her," Thato offered.

Michaela shook her head vehemently. "No, thank you."

"Oh, come on. Live a little," Thato encouraged.

James' grin widened. "Yeah, live a little."

She glanced up at him, nibbling her lip, hesitant. "I don't know."

"Nandi is the best. She's never had an accident," Thato reassured, while Michaela seemed to be having an inner struggle.

"You should do it," I said, hoping to bolster her confidence. "It'll be fun."

Michaela glanced at me, then steeled herself as she looked back to Thato and James. "Okay, I'm in."

A few minutes later, Thato's friend Nandi got into her car, while Thato sat in the front passenger seat beside her. James and Michaela climbed in the back. As soon as the car started spinning, Michaela grabbed hold of James' upper arm. I was pretty sure she kept her eyes closed the entire time, and it reminded me of when I'd ridden the roller coaster.

I glanced at Cal, remembering how sorry he'd been afterward. His entire focus was on the car as it spun, and I took a second to admire his profile. He really was stunning, especially in the low light. The sky darkened to nighttime, and it cast shadows on his face, highlighting his cheekbones and the strong line of his jaw.

"You're staring," Cal said and I startled then cleared my throat, feeling embarrassed to be caught.

"Right. Sorry."

He cast me a side glance. "You can look. I don't mind."

Conflicted, I returned my attention to the car. When it finally stopped spinning, James climbed out first, followed by Michaela, who stumbled a little on her feet. James caught her just in time.

"Thanks," she said as she steadied herself, her cheeks pink.

They smiled at each other, and there was something intimate about it. It felt like a bit of an intrusion to watch.

"I think Michaela might not be the only one with a crush," Cal said from next to me.

My eyes widened. "Don't say that. If it's true, it's a disaster waiting to happen."

He didn't have time to say more, because a second later a commotion broke out on the other side of the track. It came from nowhere. A bunch of people were yelling at each other, and a ball of panic coiled in my belly. What was going on?

One minute everything was normal and the next, chaos. A man threw a punch at another, and then the entire group started in on each other. Before I could react, Cal grabbed my hand and started dragging me away from the crowd.

Other people had the same idea, and we got caught up in a horde. I looked around for the others, but I couldn't see anyone. After a few minutes, the group dispersed in different directions, and Cal and I were alone.

I realised I was still holding his hand and let go immediately. "What the hell was that?" I asked, breathless.

"I have no idea. Looked like two blokes were fighting over a girl, and then a bunch of other people got involved."

"Fuck, it escalated quick. We need to find the others."

"I'll call James," Cal said, pulling out his phone.

We kept walking. This place was gigantic, and we were never going to find our way out on our own. I pulled my phone out to call for a taxi. It seemed like the best option. When I looked at my screen, I already had a text from Isaac.

Isaac: *Are you okay? I'm with Jimbo and Autumn. We're going to hang out at my uncle's house for a bit.*

Leanne: *I'm with Cal. We're okay. Gonna get a taxi back to the house.*

Isaac: *Good. I'm sorry about the fight. That doesn't usually happen. Have you heard from James or Michaela?*

Leanne: *No, Cal's calling James now. Will keep you updated. What happened back there?*

Isaac: *A girl cheated on her boyfriend, and the boyfriend confronted the guy she cheated with. Usual stupid drama. Text me as soon as you hear from the others.*

Leanne: *Will do.*

After ordering a taxi, I put my phone back in my pocket. Cal was still trying to get through to James with no success. I tried Michaela's phone but got no answer either.

"Hopefully they're together," I said, chewing worriedly on my lip.

"I'm sure they are," Cal reassured.

A minute later the taxi pulled up, and we climbed into the back. It was full dark out now, and other than the radio playing low, Cal and I were quiet on the drive. A thick atmosphere pervaded the space, just like it always did when we were alone. I really needed a drink. When I saw a bar up ahead, I leaned toward the driver.

"Could you stop here?" I asked.

"What are you doing?" Cal frowned.

"I'm getting out here for a little bit. You can head back to the house though."

He looked out the window and saw we'd stopped at a bar. "You think I'm letting you go in there alone? Do I need to remind you what happened the last time you went drinking in this city on your own?"

"I'll be fine." I climbed out of the taxi.

"I'm coming with you." Cal handed the driver some money. The guy looked a little disgruntled that we'd decided not to go all the way to the house, which would've been a much larger fare.

I ignored Cal as I went inside, headed straight to the bar and asked for a gin and tonic.

"Make that two," Cal said over my shoulder.

The bar wasn't too crowded, with just a few patrons sitting at tables or playing pool in the back. The woman behind the counter placed two gin and tonics in front of us. I pulled out my wallet to pay, but Cal was faster.

Fine. If he wanted to bother me with his presence, then the least he could do was buy my drink. I was distracted when my phone buzzed with a text from Michaela and I sighed in relief.

Michaela: *Hey! The signal on my phone is patchy out here. I'm with James. We're safe.*

I held the screen up for Cal to see and texted Isaac to let him know they were okay. Then I texted Michaela the name of the bar, inviting her and James to come join us, mainly because I could do with some buffers.

"My dad's been trying to get in touch," Cal confessed as I slid my phone back in my pocket. His expression showed a rare flash of vulnerability, which made me automatically lower my defences.

I knew a little about Cal's dad, how he left him and his mum to fend for themselves when he was barely two years old. Cal always swore he'd never turn out like him, so I guessed he wasn't someone he wanted in his life now that he was grown. It reminded me of something cruel I'd said to him a long time ago, and my stomach twisted.

"When's the last time you spoke to him?"

"Not for years. Ever since I've been on TV, he's tried calling at least once a year. A sniff of money in the air and all the rats come out of the woodwork."

"I'm sorry."

Cal lifted a shoulder and took a sip of his drink. "Don't be. It's not difficult to ignore a call. I just wish he'd get the message and fuck off."

I drew in a breath for courage. "No, I mean, I'm sorry for something I said to you once. About your dad. I don't think I ever apologised."

Cal's expression was questioning. My voice was tiny. "After the...the miscarriage, I told you you'd probably just end up like your dad and abandon us anyway."

The muscles in his face moved in a way that showed I'd touched a nerve. Man, I was an idiot for bringing this up. Old wounds should be left in the past where they belonged.

"I won't lie," Cal spoke finally. "It fucking hurt when you said that, but you were grieving."

"I was awful to you back then."

"Yeah well, I forgave you, didn't I?"

"Maybe you shouldn't have." I remembered how he'd visited me every day at the hospital, and when I was finally able to go home, I broke up with him. It was a callous, selfish thing to do, but I'd been in a very dark head space at the time.

Cal stared at his glass, then lifted his gaze to me, his expression troubled, "When it comes to you, Leanne, there's not much I wouldn't forgive."

Emotion caught in my throat. "That's seriously fucked up."

Cal didn't respond, just continued staring at me, his eyes beautiful and sad. I had to change the subject, otherwise, I was liable to drown in past regrets. "Are you sure you don't want to talk to your dad?"

Just like that, his features hardened and he sat up straighter. "Hundred percent. I made it this far without him. And I definitely don't need him now that my life's finally on the up-and-up."

I turned my attention to my drink, downing it in just a few gulps. I gestured to the bartender for another. It had been a long day and one of the main reasons I needed a drink was sitting right next to me.

We sat in silence for a while. Every time I ordered a drink, Cal did too. He was breaking his two-drink rule, but I didn't call him out on it. I had a feeling the last few weeks had been just as rough for him as they'd been for me.

"Can I ask you something?" Cal said, breaking the silence. His tone got my back up because I sensed whatever he wanted to ask would require more than a simple yes or no answer.

"Seems you have me cornered here, so go ahead," I replied.

"You're not cornered. You could sit here and not talk to me if you wanted."

"Just ask your question, Cal."

There was a beat of quiet and then, "When we were together the first time, why didn't you ever want anyone to know?"

I caught the eye of the woman behind the bar. "Can we have a round of shots? Tequila if you have it."

She nodded and went about lining up the glasses before pouring out the liquor.

"Leanne, what are you—"

I held up a finger, silencing Cal, and he watched as I knocked back both shots, his expression tense. "Okay," I began, exhaling heavily. "Now I'm tipsy enough to answer that question. So, let's cast our minds back a couple of years. I'm twenty-one, a nobody, and I get a part in a reality TV show that has the potential to change my life. *But* I'm silly enough to start sleeping with one of my co-stars before the show even goes to air. I'm the only girl in a cast and crew that's mostly men. If we were completely open about our relationship, what would people think?"

Cal opened his mouth, but I cut him off again. "I'll tell you what they'd think. They'd think I'd only gotten the job because I was sleeping with one of the guys."

"But us being together had nothing to do with you getting the part," Cal argued, his intense eyes searing me.

"That doesn't matter. It's what people think that matters, and people would think I'd slept my way in. I wanted to be judged based on my skill as a freerunner. I didn't want people gossiping about my sex life."

Ironically though, my effort to keep us secret had all been for nothing. We couldn't hide the truth from the cameras, and those pesky lenses picked up on what was between us right from the beginning. By the time we started filming Season 2, everyone knew about mine and Cal's personal relationship.

"You have no idea, have you?" he said, still looking at me way too closely.

I glanced at him. "No idea of what?"

"That when you're on-screen, nobody can doubt your talent. The reason you're on the show shines through, no matter what gossips want to think. When they watch you, it's undeniable. I knew it from the moment you auditioned for us."

This softer side to Cal, the one who was free and easy with his compliments, really was making it harder and harder to resist him. If Paul or Trev could see us now, sitting at a bar getting drunk and talking about our past, they'd probably smack us both across the face for being so stupid. Technically, we were risking our jobs every time we were alone together.

I schooled my expression and tried to kill the intimate vibes. "Stop trying to butter me up. It won't work."

"I'm just telling you the truth, Leanne."

There he went again with the longing gaze. *Resist, resist, resist!*

"Yeah well, you should just go back to toying with me. It's what I'm used to. This nice version of you is weird."

"I was never as bad as you like to imagine. I only acted the way I did because you kept pushing me away."

"That doesn't mean you weren't pretty fucking cruel sometimes," I countered.

"Okay, give me an example." He wasn't backing down. Good. Arguing would definitely kill any intimacy between us.

I twisted in my stool to face him. "All right then. How about that night, a few weeks after we…" my voice cracked for a second before I forced myself to continue, "…after we lost the baby. We had to attend the launch party for the show, and you kissed that girl. That was definitely cruel given the timing."

Cal dragged a hand through his hair. "The only reason I kissed her was because you'd been pushing me away for weeks. You hurt me, so I hurt you back. I never even slept with her. I was using her to get back at you."

My stomach clenched as I remembered just how much he'd hurt me, but he was right, I had pushed him away. "Isn't tit for tat a little immature?"

"Not as immature as ignoring a shared traumatic experience and pretending it never happened," Cal countered.

His bullet hit home and emotion clogged in my throat. Arguing with him had definitely backfired because now I was genuinely upset. He had no idea how depressed I was back then, how my guilt ate at me worse each day. It had taken months to feel even a tiny bit like myself again.

I stood from my stool, turned around to leave, took a few steps, changed my mind, then walked back. "I was dying inside and you know it." I hated how my voice held all my pain right there on the surface.

Cal reached out to grab my wrist, his touch gentle. "We both were."

I glared at him. "At least I didn't resort to using other guys to make you jealous."

"You do now."

I shook my head in disbelief. "You're deluded."

"So, the way you're nice to every bloke you meet and cold with me, that doesn't count?"

I gaped at him. "I'm sorry if I'm nice to people who are nice to me."

Cal eyed me pointedly. "It's not about you being nice to people who are nice to you. It's about you purposely being cold with me to keep me at a constant distance."

Refusing to continue this discussion any longer, I turned to the bar and ordered another shot of tequila.

"Gin and tequila? Are you trying to make yourself sick?" Cal grunted, his voice tight.

"What I'm doing is none of your business."

He swore under his breath and nodded to the bartender. "Double that order."

The bartender didn't argue, but she did eye us warily. I knew what she was thinking: *I hope these two nutjobs don't cause a scene.* Well, any more of a scene than what we were causing already.

Cal picked up a shot glass at the same time I did. I glared at him when I knocked it back. He returned my glare with one of his own. He really was going to drive me crazy tonight, taking everything I gave and giving it right back to me. There would always be a part of me that admired his stubbornness, no matter how much it irritated me because I was stubborn too.

In fact, I'm not sure there ever existed two more aggravating humans. Perhaps we deserved each other.

Cal polished off his shot then strode across the bar to the jukebox. It was a relief to have a moment alone. But then, when I heard "Can't Hold Us" by Macklemore come through the speakers, I knew he'd decided to play dirty. This was our song. It made me think of the short periods of time when we'd been happy. Well, the periods where I'd deluded myself into believing we were. Maybe I just didn't have that gene, the one that let you hold onto something good. Instead I was gifted with the gene for destruction.

Cal returned to his stool. I didn't comment on the song because I knew he wanted me to.

"So, if I'm such an awful person for you to be with, tell me what sort of man you're looking for?" he said.

I blinked at him. "Who said I'm looking?"

He arched an eyebrow. "We're all looking, even when we say we aren't."

I fingered the rim of my almost empty gin glass, feeling drunk enough to speak openly. "Just someone who's kind, and who takes my feelings into consideration. Someone who makes me laugh and supports me."

Cal nodded, eyes on the shelves of booze behind the bar. He didn't look at me and I couldn't help asking, "How about you?"

He glanced at me, shook his head and stared at the shelves again. "Nah, you don't want to know."

"Try me."

He swivelled on his stool to face me, piercing me with his stare. We were so close his thighs were on either side of mine, almost touching. "You."

I scoffed. "Okay."

"I'm not lying."

"I thought you liked tall, beautiful blondes who play tennis," I shot back cuttingly. I knew it was petty to bring up Mia Popov, but Cal was wearing me down and this was one of the last weapons left in my arsenal.

Cal's eyes narrowed. "Why do you still think I was with her? Didn't you hear the story about her claiming she had a one-night stand with a footballer? His wife almost divorced him until she found out he and Mia weren't even in the same country on the night it was supposed to have happened. The woman is a pathological liar."

I frowned, my chest deflating. "No, I never heard that." Cal had always been adamant there was nothing between him and Mia, but I'd jumped to conclusions, let my paranoia get the best of me. I'd believed rumours over what he claimed was the truth. What the hell was wrong with me?

"You can look up the story for yourself," he said gently. "It happened about a month ago."

My gaze flashed to his. "Why didn't you tell me?"

"You'd already hung, drawn, and quartered me, Leanne. What's the point in coming back to you almost a year later for a re-trial?"

I turned away, a million self-recriminations building up inside me. Was I actually the bad person in our relationship? I always thought we fell apart because Cal was so immature, preferring to fight than talk things through. But maybe he wasn't the problem at all.

Maybe it was me.

Cal's voice drew me from my thoughts. "Just to make things clear, my perfect woman is short, cranky, and sexy as fuck."

My pulse pounded, cheeks heating at the compliment and the gravelly way he spoke. My plan to argue with him had completely backfired. Cal was far too much of a worthy opponent.

"And where is your perfect man? Does he exist?" Cal went on, leaning in close. I got a whiff of his cologne, intoxicating as ever.

"I don't know yet." Try as I might, I couldn't look away. His eyes held mine captive.

Cal plucked an ice cube from his glass, lifted my arm and ran the ice from the inside of my wrist, all the way up to the crease of my elbow. I shivered and he spoke low, "You think you want some nice guy, but when it comes down to it, the man you want in the day isn't the same man you want at night. You can't have it both ways."

"Are you saying the man I want in the streets isn't the same man I want in the sheets?" I said, making a joke to lighten the mood.

Cal's lips twitched and I could tell he was trying not to smile. A second passed, our eyes still held, "You've never had better than me. Say it."

"In bed? Yes. When it comes to my mental health, that's a whole other story."

Immediately, he withdrew, and I suspected I'd pissed him off again. He ran a hand down his face as he let out a tired laugh. "You have no idea."

"No idea of what?"

His look was fiery intensity. "You have no idea that nobody's ever cared about you like I do."

My entire body stilled. Was it just me or had the bar gotten significantly hotter? "You're just saying that because you're trying to win our bet," I refuted.

"Is that what you think tonight has been about? Fuck the bet. I only came up with it in the first place because…" He stopped himself, like he hadn't meant to say that.

My chest thrummed. "You only came up with it because of what?"

"Never mind. You wouldn't believe me anyway."

"Try me."

Cal stared at me for so long, so many emotions flashing behind his eyes that I was afraid of what his answer might be. "We Don't Talk Anymore" by Charlie Puth came on and I wondered if he'd chosen this one specifically for the lyrics. Ironically, we'd done a whole lot of talking tonight.

"You've curated quite the playlist there," I said, changing the subject. Whatever he'd planned to tell me, I didn't know if I could handle hearing it right now.

"Just dance with me," he said, his voice a soft, quiet caress.

He'd been wearing me down all night, and that combined with the alcohol in my system propelled me to take his hand. He led me over to a completely empty dance floor and slid his arms around my waist, their warmth familiar. I knew every part of him, his scent, his body language, even his facial expressions. And tonight I'd learned a new one: longing mixed with pain. It had been there all along, I was just too blind to see it.

Everything we shared together was catalogued in my head, branded into my brain whether I liked it or not. When we'd first broken up, I couldn't watch any of the TV shows or movies we'd watched together, couldn't listen to the music or go to the pubs and restaurants that were our favourites. I had to give up so many good things because my broken heart had turned them all to poison.

I wondered if Cal had given them up too. I tried to convince myself he didn't hurt over our breakups like I did, but more and more I saw that wasn't true. An ache built in my chest as I wished the thought away.

His hands rested at the base of my spine. I stared at his collarbone, overwhelmed by his closeness and a feeling of futile hope. A hope that one day I wouldn't be so torn apart inside.

Lifting my gaze, I found him already looking at me. "Cal?"

His response was a rumble from deep in his throat. "Hmm?"

"Do you think I'm a bad person?"

He stared at me for so long I wasn't sure if he'd answer. "You're flawed. That doesn't make you bad."

I swallowed back the lump in my throat because I hadn't realised just how much I needed to hear that.

Cal studied me, perturbed. "Why would you think you're a bad person?"

All of a sudden, my words came pouring out. "Because I feel like everyone else has life figured out and I resent them for it. It's like they understand some secret formula that I never will," I trailed off, looking down, then forced myself to look back at him. "But mostly I think I'm a bad person because I pushed you away when you needed me most."

His expression changed, like he couldn't believe I'd actually just admitted that. Hell, I couldn't believe it myself.

"You needed me just as much as I needed you," Cal said, bringing his hand up to touch my cheek. "And nobody has life figured out. We're all just taking stabs in the dark, learning as we go along. I mean, just look at me. If there ever was a poster boy for fucking things up, I'm him."

Unbidden, a tear trickled down my cheek. "Why are you being so nice to me? I've been horrible to you all night."

"Because I told you, I care about you, Leanne. I care about you more than you know."

His words blazed a fire inside me. I couldn't stop staring at his mouth. It felt like I'd discovered so many new things about him tonight and I just...I just wanted to kiss him. He didn't deserve what I'd done to him in the past, but I didn't have the words to describe how sorry I was.

I hovered close and his eyes grew hooded when he saw my intent. Our breaths mingled, and then...

"There you are! It took us forever to find this place," Michaela announced and I immediately pulled away from Cal. She and James came toward us, suspicion written all over their faces. Both of them knew about our contract and it suddenly dawned on me how close we'd come to violating it.

Them turning up right now saved our bacon.

So why wasn't I relieved? My feelings for Cal and my guilt for pushing him away clouded over everything else. I hated what I'd done to him, now more than ever. There were so many things I wished I could go back and alter.

Unfortunately, no matter how painful, there was no changing the past.

Fourteen
Callum
Three years ago

I hadn't seen Leanne in almost a month. Not since she was released from the hospital, and not since she broke up with me at her parents' house. It was driving me crazy. I needed to talk to her, but all my calls and texts went unanswered. Paul said to give her space, that she needed to rest and come to terms with losing the baby.

She's not the only one who lost something, I wanted to yell. Like, was this shit not supposed to affect me too? Was I supposed to just lick my wounds and get over it? I wanted us to do this together, to share the pain and find a way to heal, but she'd completely iced me out.

We finished up the final week of filming and the show was going to air soon. Things were moving fast. Leanne had been on sick leave, but I heard she was coming back to join us for promos. We had weeks of interviews and appearances lined up and I was eager to see her.

Who was I fooling? Eager was too tame a word. I was on a knife's edge.

Our first press conference was today. Journalists from magazines and news outlets across the country would be there, but all I cared about was seeing Leanne, making sure she was okay. Holding her.

I showed up with Trev and James and we were led to a green room where a bunch of people involved in the show were waiting. Frantically, I scanned the space. Leanne sat on a couch next to Paul, the two of them deep in chat.

I resented how close they were, especially now.

She went to him for comfort when she should've been coming to me.

Well, that shit ended today.

"Leanne," I said, my voice strained.

She looked up, her expression flat. "Hi, Callum."

I scratched my jaw. "How have you been?"

Her gaze lowered. "I've been okay." I hated how she sounded, gone was her usual feistiness. Contrary to what she said, she didn't sound okay.

"Can we go somewhere after this? Grab lunch maybe?"

She hesitated to answer, and Paul jumped in, like he was her protector and I was the villain of the piece. Hell, maybe I was. It was my fault this happened to her. To *us*. But that didn't mean I was going to give up on what we had before it all went to shit.

"I'm taking Leanne home after the conference," Paul said.

I turned to him irritably. "Are you her bodyguard?"

He didn't back down. "I'm her friend."

Before I could respond, our press agent interrupted to say it was time for us to go out to the conference hall. We all shuffled out of the room and I met Leanne's gaze, but she quickly looked away. If she thought she could just avoid and ignore me and I'd give up, she had another thing coming.

Quickly zipping by Paul, I made sure to grab the seat next to hers at the long table. There were fifty to sixty journalists in the room, alongside a bunch of photographers up front snapping pictures. This was it, the fifteen minutes of fame I'd been working for. I needed to make as much money as I could before those minutes ran out, but all I could think about was the woman sitting beside me and where we stood.

"I miss you," I said quietly and her posture stiffened as she stared dead ahead. "Jesus, are you not even going to look at me now?"

She cast me a quick side glance. "Can you just stop? This is already hard enough, you don't need to make things worse."

"You've been ignoring me for weeks. Do you even give a shit what I've been going through?"

Now she turned to me, her eyes fierce. "What *you've* been going through?"

"Ladies and gentlemen, we're so pleased you could all join us today to meet the cast of Channel 4's up-and-coming reality show, *Running on Air*," our press agent began, introducing us one by one.

Trev answered most of the questions. This whole thing was his brainchild. I always knew I wanted to do something big with my life, better mine and Mum's situation. I just never knew what that was until I found parkour. Then I met Trev and he never shut up about his idea for a reality show. It captured my imagination and his dream became my dream. We spent years working towards this moment right here, but the precipice of success we were currently standing on didn't taste as sweet as I anticipated.

I'd give it all up in a heartbeat if Leanne would just give me the time of day.

"This sounds like a pretty risky concept. Were there any accidents on set?" a journalist asked and I swear every single one of us froze. Barry wanted to use the footage of that day on the docks to add drama to the show. We all said fuck that and threatened to stage a walkout. In the end, they relented and agreed to cut the entire day of filming from the final edit.

"We've been practicing for years," Trev replied. "Sure, there are accidents from time to time, but so far we've been lucky."

I shot him a grateful look and he gave a small nod. It was nice to know he had our backs. When I looked at Leanne, she seemed to have retreated in on herself. I reached out to squeeze her hand, but she pulled it from my grasp.

"Please don't touch me," she said, her voice quiet but firm, cutting me to the quick.

When the conference ended, Leanne stood immediately and hurried from the room. I ran after her and she was already at the end of the long corridor by the time I caught up.

"Leanne, wait. Can we please just talk for a minute?"

She stopped but didn't turn around to face me, her shoulders slumped. "I already told you I can't be with you anymore, Cal. Just accept it."

Oh, hell no.

I stepped in front of her, glaring down. "Running away is for cowards."

She exhaled tiredly, like she had the weight of the world on her shoulders. Didn't she realise that all I wanted was to relieve some of the load? When her blue eyes met mine, she looked infinitely sad, infinitely broken. I wanted to pull her into my arms and sweep her away from all the pain.

"Come here," I whispered, arms open.

For a second, I thought she would, but then her expression flattened. "I meant it when I said I can't be with you. I'm sorry."

With that, she turned and walked away. She might as well have had my heart right under her shoes.

For the next few weeks, every time I saw her, she gave me the silent treatment. It was maddening, but I accepted it. I respected that she needed space and kept my distance. I knew she only did it because she was hurting, but did hurting me back make her feel better somehow? I didn't get it. And I was a fireball of rage, just barely holding it together. Anytime anyone said something even remotely annoying I was biting their head off. I was irritable, snappish, and grouchy. All because Leanne was freezing me out.

Tonight was the launch party for the show and I honestly would rather be anywhere else. Normally, I loved parties, but if I had to see Leanne and pretend like we never happened, I was liable to finally lose my shit. For real this time.

The party was being held in a swanky venue in Soho and lots of important TV people were there. I wore a suit (at Mum's behest) and determined to be on my best behaviour. Only problem was, there was free flowing booze and I'd partaken in a little too much. When I spotted Leanne, Paul was by her side as per fucking usual. Seriously, if the bloke wasn't my friend, I'd have punched his lights out by now.

A tall brunette walked by, looking me up and down. I could tell she was interested, but my libido was flatlining these days. I was too depressed to get hard, and that was a serious travesty. Not to mention embarrassing.

Leanne wore a sleeveless, backless black top, exposing her smooth, flawless skin. Was she trying to torture me? She and Paul stood with our agent, Tanya, while I knocked back a shot of whiskey and summoned up the courage to approach them.

"Hey! You lot enjoying yourselves?" I said, my voice too loud, too boisterous.

"Hi, Callum," Tanya greeted. "We're having a good time. And you?"

From Leanne's expression, she knew I was already steaming drunk and well on my way to blackout levels. Her pink lips flattened to a thin line as she folded her arms and gave a faint shake of her head like I was some kind of scumbag.

That sent me over the edge and I couldn't contain the poison that spewed from my lips. "Try smiling, babe. You'll give yourself wrinkles if you keep scowling like that all the time."

"Cal, don't start," Paul interjected, and I turned to face him.

"Who asked you?"

Now Paul was giving me the scumbag headshake too. He draped his arm around Leanne's shoulders and led her away. "Oh, so you're both too good for me, huh? Whatever. Like I give a shit."

"Callum," Tanya spoke quietly. "Maybe you should go grab a glass of water. Try sobering up a little."

I scoffed, arched a derisive eyebrow and scanned the room for the brunette who'd given me a come-hither look. If Leanne didn't want me, then I'd show her that someone else did.

It didn't take too long to find her, and she was all too willing to keep me company. I threw my arm around her waist and we talked about some bullshit, how she'd love to go out sometime, etc, etc. When I spotted Leanne watching me, I didn't waste any time pulling the brunette in for a quick, sloppy kiss. I broke away only to see Leanne storming out of the party.

A sobering moment pimp slapped me right across the face. I'd really gone and screwed up now.

"Hey, come back," the brunette called, but I was already on the move, chasing after Leanne. I found her outside trying to flag down a taxi. It was a busy time of night, though, and nobody was stopping for her.

"I'm sorry," I said and her shoulders stiffened. Quick as a flash she turned around and came at me, pushing me in the chest.

"You're a dickhead."

I caught her wrists. Leanne was small, but she hit hard. "You've been freezing me out for weeks and it's driving me crazy."

Tears started to run down her cheeks and my chest deflated. "I'm here, don't cry." I tried pulling her into my arms, but she pushed me off.

"No! Don't you dare!"

Now I got angry. "You said we were over. So why do you care if I kiss someone else?"

"I don't care. Kiss whoever you want."

"You're a terrible liar."

"I'm not lying." Her face reddened, her features drawn in rage, and somehow I knew the next blow was going to hurt. "You know what, Cal? What happened is probably for the best. If we had a kid together, you'd just end up stepping out on it the same as your dad did."

The punch hit home. K-fucking-O. I swallowed down my fury like bile in my throat. "That was a low blow."

Instantly, she looked remorseful, but I wouldn't let her take back what she said. All I wanted was to comfort her, share our pain so that it wasn't such a heavy burden. But she just wanted to ignore it and pretend we never existed.

Now she reached out, her hand at my elbow. "Cal, I—"

This time I was the one to pull away. "Don't bother. Message received. You don't want me. You don't need to worry about me bothering you anymore. We can work together for the sake of the show, but that's it. I'm done trying."

I turned and walked back into the party, leaving Leanne standing alone on the busy city street. Inside I was met with Paul's disapproving frown.

"Whatever lecture you plan to give me, don't bother. You win. I'm done," I said, shoving past him.

He caught up to me and got in my face. "Why can't you just give her space? You're both hurting right now and you need to sort through what you're feeling. Leanne will find her way back to you eventually."

"Oh yeah, and how long's that going to take?"

"As long as she needs." A pause as he eyed me meaningfully. "As long as you *both* need." Well, he was wrong on that front. I didn't need any time without Leanne. The last few weeks had already been long enough, thank you very much.

Still, his pleading, sad eyes knocked my temper down a notch. I dragged a hand through my hair and swore loudly. "*Fuuuck!* I've screwed everything up."

There was a flicker of sympathy on his face. "No, you haven't. If you can just figure out a way to be the bigger person, she'll come back to you."

I stared at him, hopeless. "What if I can't do that? What if it isn't in me?"

Paul settled a hand on my shoulder. "He who has a why to live can bear almost any how."

I blew out a breath. That was some profound shit. "Where do you come up with this stuff?"

Paul gave a small smile. "Don't credit me. It's a Nietzsche quote. Sometimes life is rough, but if you keep your focus on the end goal, you'll make it through."

"So you're saying I need to wait things out?"

"Yes. Leanne has feelings, big feelings. I can tell. But she's grieving right now. She's not herself."

What he said made me feel a little less angry about her saying I'd end up the same as my old man. I was no delicate flower, but that comment *hurt*.

"Come on. Let's go back inside and do the rounds. Those bigwig TV people aren't going to flatter themselves."

I took one last look outside, but Leanne was gone. Following Paul inside, I determined to stay the course. Before all this happened, I'd been falling for her, and I suspected she'd been falling for me too.

Leanne had my heart and I wouldn't let her sabotage us. She could throw everything at me she had in her arsenal. I wasn't giving up on her.

I wasn't giving up on *us*.

Fifteen
Present
Leanne

I woke to a steady knock on my door. "Wakey, wakey, rise and shine," Neil called cheerfully.

I groaned and looked at the clock next to my bed. I'd officially gotten less than three hours sleep and every muscle in my body screamed. After we got back to the house last night, I'd tossed and turned, unable to nod off. My conversation with Cal had been too raw, my mind on alert, running through all the ways I wished we'd both kept our mouths shut.

Now I had all these thoughts swirling around in my head, about how Cal felt for me, how I felt for him, how it didn't matter anyway because we were contractually obliged not to be together.

I climbed out of bed, showered, threw on some jeans and a T-shirt, then went downstairs. I couldn't stomach breakfast just yet. Instead I drank several glasses of water, then poured myself some black coffee. Even after my caffeine fix, I still felt like death.

"You look like you could do with a two-week holiday on a beach in the Caribbean," Linda joked as she sidled up to me.

I gave her a wan smile. "Something like that."

Her expression turned to one of concern. "How are you feeling? Do you need anything?"

"I'll be fine. I just drank too much last night."

"A little hair of the dog will sort you right out," Linda suggested, but I shook my head.

"I don't think that's a good idea."

She waved me away. "Don't suffer unnecessarily. I'll have a few bottles sent to your room."

"No, seriously," I began, but she shushed me with a hand on my shoulder.

"It's already done."

When I returned to my room to grab my things before we headed out for the day, someone had set up a mini-fridge beside the dresser. I looked inside and it was fully stocked with booze. I was tempted to take Linda's advice but decided against it. Freerunning and alcohol were not a good mix.

On my way out of my room, I bumped into Michaela.

"Leanne, hey," she greeted, pulling her hair into a ponytail. She had tired circles under her eyes, and I wondered what happened when she and James were alone last night.

"So, I forgot to ask, but did you and James get lost yesterday? You were missing for a few hours."

"Oh," she said, hesitating. "Um, we didn't really go anywhere. We just spent most of our time trying to find you guys."

Somehow, I felt like she was omitting a few details, but I didn't probe. We stepped into the minivan and James was sitting in the front. I noticed he looked just as tired as Michaela. Something had definitely happened with them last night that she didn't want to tell me. I just had no idea what.

James gave her a warm smile, but she didn't sit next to him, instead sliding in beside me. Cal sat at the back next to Trev, sunglasses on, expression unreadable. After our conversation and almost kiss last night, I thought staying away from him today was a good idea. Smart.

The van dropped us off in a public park. There were lots of people out and about. My body was sore from my hangover, but I forced myself to perform. The cameras followed as I climbed to the top of a high concrete wall, then completed a backflip down to the ground. Trev, Paul, and James were goofing around on some outdoor exercise equipment, while Cal and Isaac were just behind me. I climbed the wall again, this time walking along the narrow edge. It led to a building that looked like a library. When I was as high as I could get, I jumped to a lower wall, but my step was off and I scraped my shin on the concrete. Swearing loudly, I bent down to check the damage.

"What happened?" Isaac called from a few feet away.

"I'm fine. It's just a scrape."

"Come down and let me have a look," Neil said.

Last year he'd taken a course in First Aid, since being our assistant usually meant tending to small wounds and mishaps. If we were filming a dangerous stunt, we had a medical team on standby. But not for more casual filming days like today.

I sat on the grass while Neil pulled out his First Aid kit. He took his time dressing my wound, and I winced when he pressed antiseptic to it.

"This is a little more than just a scrape," he chided.

"I'm tough. I can take it," I replied, sucking in a harsh breath.

"I think you have the highest pain threshold of the whole group. The last time Callum twisted his ankle I swear he almost cried like a baby."

I chuckled, and speaking of Cal, he hovered nearby, his eyes narrowed on Neil. Here we went again with his stupid suspicion that there was something between us.

"Don't look now, but Cal's staring at you like he wants to rip your head off."

"Oh, so it must be Monday," Neil joked, not letting hostility from Cal phase him. It basically came with the job at this point.

"I'm sorry he's such an arsehole to you all the time. It's mainly my fault. He thinks you fancy me. It's ridiculous."

Neil's hands stilled for a moment, and then he resumed his work. *Oh man, what was that pause about?*

"What if I do fancy you?" he said quietly.

I froze, my eyes widening.

Neil looked at me and shook his head in self-deprecation. "*Okay*, well, you look mortified. So pretend I never said anything."

"No," I rushed to reply. "I'm not mortified. I'm just… surprised. I didn't expect you to say that."

Neil sat back, looking away again. "I shouldn't have. I work for you. It's unprofessional and I completely understand if you want to fire me now. It's just that I've liked you for a long time, Leanne, and I'm sick of hiding it. I guess I just needed to put it out there and deal with the consequences."

I reached out and grabbed his hand. "No way would I ever fire you. You're an amazing assistant, but…"

"But you don't feel the same way. It's all right. I get it."

"Quit trying to read my mind. It's just that there's always been so much drama between Cal and me that I've never really had a chance to catch my breath."

Some of Neil's confidence returned. He really was handsome. Not the kind that was noticeable right away. It was something that shone through the more you got to know him. The way his eyes crinkled when he smiled, his self-depreciation and warm personality.

Crap, maybe I did like Neil. Last night I'd told Cal my perfect man was someone who was kind, who I could rely on and trust. Neil was all of those things and more.

"So…?" He hedged.

"Sorry. I'm just going through a weird period right now. Can we wait until we get back to London and talk then?"

In translation: I had unresolved feelings for my ex and we were in some kind of emotional limbo that I needed to figure out before I got involved with anyone else.

Relief flooded his features and he nodded, so reasonable. Was this what it would be like to be with someone who I didn't feel compelled to fight and argue with all the time? Could a relationship actually be easy with someone who wasn't Callum Davidson?

My stupid heart ached in protest at the very question. All it ever seemed to want was Cal, especially after the sweet things he said last night. Silly heart. I needed to retrain it somehow.

"Leanne, can we talk for a minute?" Cal asked, interrupting.

I glanced from him to Neil, who gently patted my shin. "You're good to go."

I shot him a grateful smile and stood to face Cal. "What do you want to talk about?"

"Not here," he said, grabbing my hand and leading me across the park behind the library building. Once we were out of sight, I stopped and folded my arms.

"You were holding Neil's hand," Cal said, his words laced with frustration.

I arched an eyebrow. "And?"

Cal gestured wildly. "And can we please stop playing this game? When you talk to him, it drives me crazy, especially when he looks at you all puppy-dog-eyed. I can't stand it, okay? So, you win. I thought after last night..." he raked a hand through his hair. "I thought we were past this."

"I wasn't playing any game," I said, speaking sincerely. I didn't like seeing him so stressed out. "Neil and I were having a private conversation, and you shouldn't have been watching us in the first place."

"Don't give me that. *Of course* I fucking watched you. I always watch you. There is literally no situation where I can make myself not watch you, Leanne."

I saw a flash of insanity in his eyes and knew it spelled trouble. Before I had the chance to slip away, Cal advanced on me. Lighting quick, he took my face in his hands. His eyes flitted back and forth between mine, searching, then dipped to my mouth. I thought he was going to kiss me, but then, abruptly he let go and moved away.

"I'm sorry. I shouldn't have grabbed you like that."

Right then, I saw that he was suffering, and I didn't have it in me to keep being cold. I stepped forward and gripped his forearm, my voice gentle. "You want to quit playing games? Okay, no more games. I promise. But that means the bet is off too. Anything we do around each other from now on will be free from manipulation. Do we have a deal?"

The sheer relief that flooded him made me wonder why he even made the bet with me in the first place.

Cal exhaled heavily, his eyes finding mine. "Yes, we have a deal."

Unable to resist, I pulled him into a hug, squeezing tight. The hug wasn't sexual; it represented a truce, a waving of the white flag. Besides, if I was going to consider starting something with Neil in the future, then I really needed to put my baggage with Cal to bed. No more bets, no more torturing one another.

We needed closure.

I stepped out of his arms and walked back toward the others. In my peripheral, I saw Celine standing over by a tree. She'd been filming us the whole time, and our microphones would've picked up the conversation. *Great.* This shit making it into the show was all I bloody needed. They were probably filming my conversation with Neil too, and I could just see how Barry would spin the storyline into some kind of love triangle.

I knew it was hard to believe, but when you were being filmed all day long it was easy to forget the cameras. They became part of the scenery and you found yourself speaking and doing things as openly as you would in private.

When we finally got home after a long day of filming, I'd never been more excited to fall into bed. Not only was I physically exhausted, but I was also emotionally stretched thin. It was days like these where I wished for a boyfriend, a real one, who could hug me, rub my feet, and run me a bubble bath. Sometimes being alone was bliss, but other times it just felt like there was this gaping chasm in my chest that yearned for physical comfort and intimacy.

So yeah, pretty miserable.

Since everyone had decided to go out for dinner, the house was quiet. Needing sleep, I'd declined to tag along. It had been a hot day and I was sweaty, so I took a quick shower then wrapped up in the thick white complementary bathrobe the guesthouse had provided. Hair still wet, I flopped onto the bed, but as soon as I closed my eyes, my stomach rumbled loudly. Aside from the small sandwich I'd had at lunch, I'd eaten nothing else all day.

Deciding sleep could wait another twenty minutes, I went down to the kitchen and found some leftovers in the fridge. I opened up a container of meat stew, dumped it in a bowl and popped it into the microwave. I buttered two thick slices of bread and dunked them in the stew, eating every scrap in record time.

"Leanne." Cal stood in the doorway.

My first instinct was to reply with something snarky, like, *Jeez, sneak up on me like a creepy silent ninja, why don't you.* But then I remembered our truce. We're weren't going to verbally spar anymore. We were simply going to talk like normal, mature adults.

"I thought you went out to dinner with the others," I said.

Cal shook his head. "Nah, didn't fancy it."

I nodded and rinsed my dishes in the sink, eager to return to my room. My gait was stiff, my movements slow, but I only had myself to blame. Cal had been right when he said mixing gin and tequila was a bad idea.

"Hold up," Cal said, eyes on my leg. "Are you sure you didn't do any real damage when you fell today?"

"I just need sleep. I didn't get much last night, so my muscles are stiff."

"You're walking like an eighty-year-old woman."

I ignored his comment and continued down the hall at a snail's pace. Much to my dismay, he followed. When I reached my room, I dropped onto the bed face first. The firm mattress felt like heaven, and I practically moaned as I snuggled into the pillow. I thought I heard Cal mutter a low swearword, but I couldn't be entirely sure since I was so exhausted.

"You should let me give you a massage," he said, which immediately woke me up.

Cal had given me massages many times in the past, and not just the sexy variety. In our line of work, they really did do wonders for recovery and Cal was excellent at giving them. Of course, that didn't mean I was letting him anywhere near me right now. I was quite literally naked under this bathrobe, and truce or no truce, letting him touch me was a bad idea.

"No, thank you," I said and closed my eyes, hoping he got the hint.

When I didn't hear him leave right away, I twisted my head to the side and saw him standing just inside the doorway.

"If you let me give you a massage, you're going to feel a million times better in the morning. If you don't, you'll probably just feel worse."

I knew he was right, but that didn't mean I was going to say yes. "I'm not risking the others coming back and catching you in my room. Now please, just go."

His deep exhale punctuated his frustration. "Let me do something nice for you for once."

I groaned into the pillow. Couldn't he just leave? No, he had to continue standing there, pestering me, tempting me with his deep voice and skilled hands.

"If I let you do this, will you promise to leave me alone after? I'm so tired if I weren't already lying down, I'd keel over."

Cal's eyes turned soft. For once I saw no calculation, no antagonism or hidden agenda, just him. He closed the door and went into the bathroom before emerging with my toiletries bag. He rifled through it without asking permission, and I let him because again, I was tired. He found a small bottle of lotion and uncapped the lid.

I closed my eyes, feeling like a dead weight was pulling me down. A moment later Cal pushed up the hem of my bathrobe until it rested at my upper thighs. Like a splash of cold water to the face, I immediately perked up. His fingertips brushed the skin at the back of my legs feather light and then I felt the cool sensation of lotion. He rubbed it in firmly, and though a moment ago I'd been on the cusp of falling asleep, I was now more awake than I'd ever been.

How could I not be with Cal's hands on me? His touch was clinical, all business. And yet it was a futile effort not to feel the electric buzz that seemed to fizzle out of him and into me. He started first at the base of my calf, kneading the muscles there and releasing all the aches and tension.

"How does that feel?" he asked.

In spite of his clinical touch, I knew instantly from the throaty quality of his voice that he was alert to the buzz between us just the same as I was. It would always be there, even if we'd been apart for decades. I don't know why either of us actually believed he could touch me like this and we wouldn't feel anything. The fact that it had been so long since we'd been together physically only made matters worse.

I squeezed my eyes shut, trying to enjoy the soothing strokes, the firm way he massaged me, but the itchy need to touch him back was overwhelming. This right here was pure torture, and I'd walked into it willingly.

Cal worked his way up my leg. When he reached my thigh muscles, a whoosh of breath escaped me. He dug into a particularly tight spot, relieving the ache, and it was wonderful.

"Jesus Christ, that feels amazing," I blurted into the pillow before I could censor myself.

Cal's low chuckle vibrated through me as he continued to work miracles with his hands. Butterflies invaded my stomach when his hand brushed under the hem of the bathrobe. It was the briefest, softest touch, there and gone, but it still burned through me, leaving my self-control in ashes.

Without a word Cal moved to the other leg, again starting at the calf. I exhaled a breath. With his hands lower, my tension should have eased, but having his hands so close to my private parts, even for a second, was extremely frustrating.

"You've got the softest skin," he murmured. He paused mid-stroke, and then he continued to massage me like he hadn't made the comment at all.

I was so wet, all because of his touch. I squeezed my thighs together and tried to ignore how arousing this was.

When he dug his fingers into my upper thigh, I had to bite my pillow because I wanted to moan so hard. It was impossible to stay quiet when something felt this good. Sharp arousal built in me. I would do anything to make his hand move higher.

I was certain I was delirious with exhaustion when I uttered a strangled. "Please."

"What do you need, Leanne?" Cal's low, silky voice caressed me.

"Shit," I swore when he found another tight knot and eased it out. "Nothing, nothing," I said, backtracking.

He was silent for a long while after that, and I was so glad that my face was smashed into the pillow because at least that way Cal couldn't see how red I was. A few minutes later he finished the massage and moved away from the bed, still quiet.

I could hear him just standing there, so I turned my head to look at him. "What's wrong?"

He gave a joyless laugh. "You want me to write you a list?"

I blew out a breath and my eyes moved lower, his erection plain as day. *Um, wow.* Arousal simmered through me, my body still buzzing with need.

I spoke before I even knew what I was saying. "Come here."

Cal's jaw twitched before he uttered a raspy, "No."

Few things had the ability to surprise me, but Cal's response just now knocked me for six. I stared at him, mouth hanging open. "No?"

He dropped his head, his eyes on the floor when he muttered gruffly. "Get some sleep, Leanne." With that he turned and left the room, closing the door with a soft snick. I threw my head back into the pillow, my heart racing.

Had that actually just happened?

I lay there, stunned. I'd more or less offered Cal sex on a platter, because when he touched me I *clearly* wasn't in my right mind. But he...he declined. He'd never denied me before and it was a sobering experience. I was finally getting a taste of my own medicine. Was that what he was trying to do, or did he have another goal that was less clear to me? One thing was for sure, he really wasn't playing anymore. He could've won an epic victory just now and he walked away from it. I swallowed tightly, my emotions on overdrive. An inconvenient, niggling question prodded at me, and it wouldn't let up.

By making the bet, had Cal's goal been to win, or had it been to lose?

Sixteen
Leanne

Two surprisingly uneventful days passed.

Cal and I didn't talk about what happened in my bedroom after the massage, and I was glad he didn't bring it up. A lot of embarrassment and confusion still lingered, but thankfully we were kept busy with work, so I didn't have too much time to fixate and obsess over his rejection.

On Thursday we were scheduled to visit a game reserve just a couple hours outside of the city. Paul was all hyped up to see the elephants, peppering me with facts along the journey.

"Did you know that elephants are the only mammals in the world that can't jump?"

"Well, I'm not surprised, have you seen the size of them?"

"They can run really fast though. They also greet each other by wrapping their trunks together."

"Uh huh," I said, half my attention on my phone. I was scrolling through my news feed when I saw Cal had posted an old picture of us. It was from the early days of filming the first season. We were at the gym, having just completed a workout when he'd snapped a selfie. I remembered it because he told me I looked beautiful right before he took it. I didn't know how to feel about him still keeping photos of us on his phone. It just felt…weird. Then again, maybe I was a hypocrite since I hadn't deleted my photos either.

"I think they're my spirit animal," Paul said, still talking about elephants. "There's just something so soulful about them. When they pass by a place where one of their loved ones died, they stop and observe a few minutes of silence. Such noble creatures."

"My spirit animal is a dolphin," Michaela said, turning around in her seat to face us. "If they sense a person is sad, they'll play with them to try and cheer them up. Like, I can't even with that."

Paul nodded. "Dolphins are considered to be the empaths of the animal kingdom."

"It's my dream to swim with them one day." Michaela glanced at me. "What's your spirit animal, Leanne?"

"I don't know. A honey badger?"

Paul chuckled. "Oh yeah, I can definitely see that."

"Hey, it's not just because they're violent psychopaths," I joked. "They're also notoriously inventive escape artists. I saw a video where these people were trying to keep a honey badger trapped in an enclosure, but he kept finding new ways to escape. They thought if they got him a girlfriend, he'd be happy to stay put and mate, but when they put a female in the two of them just teamed up together to escape."

Neil, who was sitting next to Michaela, laughed. "That's pretty badass, but I think you're more of an arctic fox."

I shot him a quizzical look. "Why's that?"

"They're survivors. They're also small and cute."

"Aww! Leanne, the cute little fox," Paul cooed and pinched my cheek. I swiped his hand away. Paul gave Neil a considering look. "You'd be a beaver since you're such a hard worker."

Neil shot him a lopsided smile. "I'll take that as a compliment…I think."

"They build dams. That's pretty admirable."

"They're still rodents," Neil said.

"What about you?" Paul called over to James, who was sitting across the aisle.

He pulled out his earbud. "What?"

"Your spirit animal. What would it be?"

James' face said, *you're interrupting my audiobook for this?* "I have no idea."

"He's definitely a lion," Michaela blurted. By the look on her face, she hadn't meant to say that out loud.

James' attention went to her, a hint of a smile shaping his lips while she looked anywhere but at him.

I decided to save her from further scrutiny, interjecting, "James is more of a grizzly bear."

"No way," Paul argued. "If anyone's a grizzly, it's Callum. They're all attack first, think later. You know, big hot-tempered bastards. Total Callum Davidson."

"Who's talking about me?" Cal shouted from the back of the minivan.

I wondered if grizzlies also had the uncanny ability to hear their name being said while wearing headphones.

"Your spirit animal is a grizzly bear. It's been decided," Paul replied.

"Fuck yeah, it is." Cal seemed pleased with this, unaware of the reason *why* Paul chose the animal to describe him. Personally, I saw him more like a black panther; beautiful, sleek, stealthy in their attack.

"What about me?" Trev asked, the conversation catching his interest too.

"You're a chimpanzee, definitely," James said.

Trev grinned. "I always considered myself a Jack Russell Terrier on account of my habit for humping people's legs."

"Please send Reya my condolences," Paul deadpanned.

"No need. She loves it," Trev replied cheekily.

It was late evening when we arrived at the game reserve, and one of those open-air buses was waiting for us.

A tour guide talked about how this was the fifth largest reserve in all of South Africa, and how we might spot some of the Big Five: lions, rhinos, buffalos, leopards, and elephants. Paul gave a little hoot at the mention of the latter, and I couldn't help smiling at his excitement. He was like a kid on Christmas morning when it came to elephants.

I took a seat in front of Cal and twisted around to eye him. "Why did you post that picture of us?"

He turned his attention from the scenery to me. "I like it."

"I look like a sweaty mess. Please take it down."

Of course, that wasn't the real reason. In fact, most of the time I could give a shit if I looked bad in pictures. I didn't owe it to anyone to be pretty. I just didn't want to think about all of Cal's million-plus followers scrutinizing his reasons for posting it, the same as they'd done when he commented on my selfie with Paul the other week. I also didn't want anyone at the network getting the wrong idea. Though ironically, I was the one they had to worry about, since Cal had proven he could say no when I offered him sex, even with a throbbing erection in his pants.

Okay, so maybe I was still a little sore about the rejection. "I thought we agreed not to play any more games."

"We did, but I'm not playing games. Like I said, I like the picture, so I posted it," he said evenly.

Feeling grumpy, I turned back around and refocused on the tour guide. A little while later we saw a giant herd of antelope running in the distance. They were fawn coloured, majestic looking creatures with large horns.

A warm hand squeezed my shoulder before Cal leaned in, his breath tickling my ear. "Look," he whispered and pointed to a spot in the distance. At first, I couldn't make it out, but then I saw something spotted and furry move along a fallen tree trunk. The leopard came into view and I caught my breath. This wasn't like when you saw exotic animals at the zoo, bored and depressed. This was a predator in its natural habitat, and I couldn't look away.

"Ladies and gentleman, if I could direct your attention to our left," the tour guide said excitedly, pointing out the leopard. "You're very lucky today. Leopards are endangered and not many of our visitors get to see them in the wild."

It didn't come very close to the bus, but for a second I could've sworn it looked right at me before it disappeared off behind the trees. Maybe I just wasn't around nature often enough, but something about its wildness completely enthralled me. I suddenly realised it was the same fascination I'd felt for Cal in the beginning. He was an untamed, wild, unpredictable thing that I willingly let devour me, body and soul. Not only that, I *wanted* to be devoured.

It dawned on me that my addiction to risk wasn't just about challenging myself physically. I was also addicted to emotional risk, and that was why Cal and I had so many ups and downs. A deeply-seated, unconscious part of me craved the thrill and excitement of breaking up and getting back together. That's why I offered him sex the other night. My risk-seeking emotions were ready to repeat the cycle.

I was the problem.

And I needed to break the cycle.

The tour was almost over when we saw a herd of elephants far in the distance. The sun was setting, casting a low golden light over the enormous creatures. Paul almost lost his shit, snapping pictures and commenting on how beautiful they were. He was too adorable sometimes.

At the end of the tour, I was a little disappointed that we didn't get to see a lion, but I still couldn't get the leopard out of my head, nor the personal revelations it brought on.

It was easy to point out flaws in others, but less so when they were your own.

I tried to quit agonising and focus on the fact that we were spending the night at a five-star luxury lodge. The building looked to be built from stone with a thatched roof, the front all lit up with torches. Two women dressed in hotel uniforms stood by the front door to welcome us.

They gave us the guided tour, and I had to admit the place was impressive. There was a porch that wrapped around the entire building, and each bedroom opened up onto a view of the reserve beyond. There were even private outdoor showers and baths.

"You might catch a glimpse of the giraffes if you wake up early enough in the morning," one of the women said. "They often pass by this way."

"Uh, I have a question," Trev said. "Why haven't we been staying here the entire time?"

"Because today was a treat. Tomorrow it's back to the grind," Barry was all too happy to inform him.

Michaela and I were sharing a room, and I couldn't wait until morning so that I could see the view in all its glory. We took turns showering before heading out onto the porch where dinner was being served. I felt like I was in some romance movie from the eighties starring Kathleen Turner. Well, minus the romance.

Everyone was seated by the time we arrived, and the food was just about to be served. Cal sat directly across from me again, and I noticed he'd showered too, his hair still damp. He'd changed into a white shirt that emphasised the colour in the tattoos on his neck. He caught me staring, and I looked away. Heat claimed my cheeks, so I concentrated on the server who held up a bottle of wine.

"Would you like to taste the wine, sir?" he asked Cal, who nodded and took a sip, then announced, "Yep, it's a red."

I bit back a laugh as the server frowned then went ahead and filled everyone's glasses.

We were served a soup starter and the main was a curry dish called Bobotie that reminded me a little of a spicy Moussaka.

"Well, I don't know about you lot, but I for one can't wait to shower bare arse nekkid outdoors tomorrow morning," Trev announced.

"No better way to greet the day," Paul chuckled.

"Ugh, you've just put me right off my food," Cal added with a laugh.

"Just make sure none of the other guests have a view of you," Barry warned from the far end of the table where he, Linda, and Ken were discussing plans for the next day of filming. "I don't want a public indecency suit on my hands."

"If anyone cops a look at my fun and frolics, it's their own fault for spying in the first place," Trev replied.

It took me a second to translate his cockney slang. Then I grimaced. "Nice visual."

Trev shot me an offended look. "Well, quit visualising, you dirty bird."

I shook my head, half tempted to flick some of my Bobotie at him. When the main course was finished, dessert was brought out, a type of sponge pudding with cream sauce. Just like everything else, it was delicious.

There was a clink of cutlery on glass before Trev stood to address the table, "Well, since I have you all here, there's actually something I've wanted to share. I was going to wait until we were home, but now seems like as good a time as any."

"If you say you're quitting the show, I'll lose my shit right here right now," Paul teased.

"I'm not quitting the show," Trev said. A big grin slowly spread across his face. "It's about Reya and me. We're going to have a baby."

"What? You're serious?" Paul said with a wide smile

"That's great news!" James stood to go and pull Trev into a hug. "I'm made up for you."

Slowly, everyone stood to congratulate Trev. I thought I was the only one still sitting, but then I noticed Cal sat deathly still across from me. Our eyes met, and in them I saw my own pain reflected back. A thousand words were exchanged in that one look.

Cal's throat moved as he swallowed. He seemed to steel himself, then finally pushed up from his seat to go and tell Trev congratulations. I didn't have his strength, and although I really was happy for Trev and Reya, I just didn't have it in me to go to him. Instead I slunk away from the table like a ghost.

All things considered, I'd been having an okay day, but those few words from Trev plunged me right back into the abyss. My stomach twisted. I felt ill, feelings and memories I normally did so well to repress rising to the surface.

Stumbling through the lodge, I found the bar where a number of guests were having drinks. I scanned the liquor options as a barman appeared to take my order. "Would it be possible to have a bottle of tequila and some glasses sent to my room?"

I just wanted to be alone. I didn't want to sit at a bar while the staff watched in disapproval as I drank myself into a stupor.

"Yes, of course. If you could just provide your room number, I'll take care of that right away."

I mustered a smile I didn't feel. "Perfect. Thanks."

Back in my room, it only took a few minutes for my bottle to arrive. A youngish guy in a polo shirt handed me a tray and I tipped him handsomely. Sitting on the edge of the bed, I didn't even bother with the glasses and instead drank right from the bottle. I heard some shuffling at the door and remembered Michaela and I were sharing.

I made a dash for the door that led outside and closed it behind me, then walked out to the edge of the patio and sat down. The quiet darkness that surrounded me soothed my deafening thoughts. I took a long gulp and it burned my oesophagus all the way down. I kept going, drinking to kill the memories.

I looked up at the sky. There was even less light pollution out here than at the house back in Johannesburg. I could see so many stars, sparkling like jewels in the dark. Andromeda was the clearest I'd ever seen it. In a place like this, there was no need for telescopes.

In mythology, Andromeda was the daughter of Cassiopeia and Cepheus, the king and queen of Aethopia. In her vanity, Cassiopeia declared herself more beautiful than the daughters of the sea god, Nereus. To punish her for this, Poseidon chained Andromeda to a rock on the coast so that she could be eaten by a sea monster. But then she was rescued by Perseus, slayer of monsters. They got married and lived happily ever after. When Andromeda died, Athena placed her in the sky where she would be immortalised in the stars…

Now, why couldn't I be rescued by some noble warrior hero? Instead I was being slowly eaten alive by the sea monster of my own devising.

"Leanne," a voice called.

I stood up and turned around, the tequila sloshing around in the bottle. "I spoke too soon! Here comes Perseus now to save me."

Cal appeared out of the darkness, his expression stern. "What on earth are you talking about?"

"Nothing. Leave me alone." I slumped back down onto the patio.

Cal lowered himself to sit beside me. "I searched the entire lodge for you."

"Oh."

"Why did you leave? Trev's worried he upset you."

"It's not his fault. He can't help if I'm a mess."

Wordlessly, Cal wrapped his arm around me, and I welcomed the comfort, even if I knew I shouldn't. He pulled me close and I rested my head on his shoulder. He took the bottle and swallowed a long gulp. The sounds of the South African night echoed around us, punctuating our own silence.

I broke it when I asked, "Do you think this ever gets any easier?"

Cal took a moment to answer. When he did, his voice was raw in a way I'd only heard a few times. "I honestly don't think so. People say grief evolves and changes, but I'm still waiting for that to happen. So far, it's never been anything but a gut punch."

He'd literally just articulated everything I felt in words I'd never been able to find for myself.

"Maybe everyone's just lying," I said, my voice flat.

I was a different person since we lost the baby, we both were, and I wondered if we'd been more careful, if I hadn't gotten pregnant, would Cal and I still be together now? Would I have pushed him away like I did, or would we have had some version of a happily ever after?

We were quiet again, sitting there, Cal with his arm around me. I guess it was true that misery loved company because mine seemed to revel in the fact that there was someone here to share it. It stretched out its tendrils and latched on. I gazed out at the reserve, the darkness was so vast it was eerie. I tried to see all the things that I knew were lurking nearby.

A jolt hit me when I saw a flicker of something, like the reflective lens of a cat's eye glimmering in the dark. But these eyes were too big to belong to your average house cat.

Okay, the tequila was officially playing tricks on me.

"Did you see that?" I asked, a tremor in my voice.

"What?" Cal asked low.

I frowned, peering out, forcing my eyes to see. "I think there's something out there."

"We're in the middle of an African plain. There are a lot of things out there, Leanne."

"M-maybe we should go inside," I said, wobbling as I tried to stand.

Cal stood and grabbed my elbows to steady me, his eyes holding mine. They were green, so beautifully vibrant, and all I saw in them was care and concern.

I didn't deserve it. No matter how difficult he could be, I was the one who'd brought this pain on us. I was the one who'd been careless, who hadn't paid enough attention to my own body to know something was different, who'd taken a risk. And afterward, when Cal needed emotional support just as much as I did, I'd been the one who pushed him away.

Seventeen
Leanne

The need to vomit woke me up.

Michaela was sleeping soundly next to me in the giant bed. Careful not to wake her, I pushed the covers off and ran across the suite before locking myself in the bathroom. My knees hit the cold tiled floor milliseconds before I emptied my guts right into the toilet bowl.

Ugh.

This is what happens when you drink an entire bottle of Tequila, you stupid little fucker.

I mentally berated myself while my body did its best to purge everything inside.

I kept thinking this had to be the last heave, but my body kept going, like it knew what I'd put in there was poison and it wanted everything *out*. Tears streamed down my face as I shivered, waves of nausea rippling through me. There had never been a more pathetic sight than me slumped on the bathroom floor of a five-star lodge praying to whatever all-seeing being was up there to make this stop.

Maybe the moon was God and the stars its angels, my still drunk brain mused before my body heaved again. I was sick of doing this to myself, sick of wallowing in self-hatred and regret. It needed to stop and I needed to quit using alcohol as a crutch. The same thing happened when my sister Lorna announced she was having my nephew. I'd spiralled then too. Was I going to break down every time someone close to me got pregnant?

I couldn't live like that.

I needed to accept my mistakes, forgive myself, and move on.

I flushed the toilet then opened the window, cleaned myself up and brushed my teeth. When I went back out into the bedroom, Michaela was still sleeping. I grabbed my phone, pushed open the patio door and stepped outside. It was almost six o'clock, the early morning sun and soft breeze gentle on my nauseated skin. I knew it was way too early to call home, but I needed to hear my mum's voice.

Yes, I'd always been independent, but sometimes I just needed my mum. She was a kind, gentle woman. My sister, Lorna, had taken after her, whereas I was much more like my dad; wary, suspicious, disagreeable. When it came to my parents, opposites had definitely attracted. They were fire and water.

Cal and I were fire and fire. We burned bright but were doomed to self-destruct. There was never any water to stem the flames.

Mum answered after several rings, her voice tired. "Leanne? Have you any idea what time it is?"

It wasn't even five o'clock in the morning in London and I felt guilty for waking her, but I needed this.

"I'm sorry, Mum," I said, and just like that I started crying. "I just needed to hear your voice. I miss you."

"Oh, honey," she said, hearing my distress. "What's the matter?"

And just like a dam breaking, I told her everything. Mum was the sort of person you could tell anything and know you wouldn't be judged for it. I told her what had been going on with Cal, the things I'd realised about myself, how I didn't think I ever really got over the miscarriage.

"Leanne," Mum said softly. "Why don't you come home now? I'm sure if you explain everything to Barry, he'll understand. You're not in the right state of mind to keep working."

"No, we're almost done filming. I just need to finish up the season and then I can focus on fixing myself," I said, determined.

"You're not broken, darling. You've just never allowed yourself to heal." Her words were a soothing balm to my distress. My parents and sister had spent the last three years trying to convince me to slow down, talk to a therapist, sort my head out, but I always fought against it. I thought if I kept moving forward then what happened in the past couldn't drag me down. But it *was* dragging on me, slowly, insidiously, a small bit every day.

I stared out at the view, endless miles of South African plain. The morning light took away all the mystery shrouded darkness of the night before. It was beautiful, and I was so lucky just to be here, in such a magnificent place. I was lucky to have my dream job and to work with a bunch of guys who were family to me. And yes, that included Cal. No matter what, we'd always share a connection. We couldn't erase the chain of loss that linked us.

And though we both blamed ourselves for what happened, none of it was anyone's fault. Learning how to accept that truth was the challenge that lay ahead of me.

I hung up the phone with Mum, promising to check in with her tomorrow. Then I sat in the quiet. Last night out here had felt eerie, dangerous even. But now the sun had risen, and it was only peaceful. I needed to figure out how to let my own sun rise, to finally find some peace.

In the distance, I spotted a lone giraffe. With its long, elegant neck, it walked slow, as though taking in the scenery. It was too far away to get a decent picture, so I just sat there and watched, tried to exist in the moment and not think about the hurdles to come.

A cold, clammy sweat covered my skin and even the idea of drinking a glass of water made me feel ill, never mind eating anything. I knew I was in no state to film today and would need to go to Barry and ask for the day off.

Fun!

Back in the room, I put on some clothes and went in search of our director, who thankfully was already awake. I lied and told him I had "lady issues", so I'd stay here at the lodge an extra few hours and take a bus back to the city tonight. I think he agreed merely to escape me going into more detail about what exactly "lady issues" entailed. When I returned to my room, Michaela was by the mirror, clipping a necklace around her neck.

"Hey, um, can you do me a favour and go down to reception? I need you to book me a late checkout."

"Sure, but…you don't look too hot, Leanne. Is everything okay?"

I shook my head. "I drank too much last night, but don't tell Barry. He's given me the day off. He thinks it's period cramps."

Her soft, kind eyes dipped down as she came and rubbed my shoulder. "It will probably be good for you to have some time to yourself anyway. Get into bed and relax. I'll book the late checkout and order up some breakfast."

"Thank you," I exhaled. "You're the best."

She went, and I shoved off my jeans before climbing into bed. A little while later there was a knock on the door. Too sick to get up and answer it, I called for whoever it was to come in. The same guy who'd delivered the tequila last night carried a breakfast tray into the room. When he left, I decided I was still too nauseous to eat, so I rolled over and drifted, not quite asleep, not quite awake.

I didn't know how much time passed when I was disturbed by another knock. Thinking it was Michaela giving me a moment to make myself decent, I simply called for her to come in. She didn't. The knocking continued, so I groaned and climbed out of bed. Opening the door a few inches, I found Cal standing there. He wore jeans and a T-shirt, sunglasses in place.

"What do you want?"

"Barry said you're sick."

"Yes, but I'll be fine. It's just the tequila flu."

His lips twitched in amusement before his expression turned serious. In my current state, I'd almost forgotten he'd sat with me outside last night, drunk as a skunk and bemoaning my pathetic existence. I couldn't remember leaving him, or how I'd gotten back to my room, but the look on his face told me I'd said or done something I'd be embarrassed about if I could actually remember it.

I winced. "What did I do?"

Cal's mouth formed a concerned frown as he slid his sunglasses up his head. "You, uh…" A pause as he scratched the back of his neck. "You didn't *do* anything."

"Then what did I say?"

"You were drunk."

"Cal, just tell me."

He glanced down at the floor then back to me. His eyes wandered to my bare legs before rising to my face. "You asked me to hold you while you slept."

Oh, God. I groaned and turned around, leaving the door open while I went to grab a glass of water from the table. My breakfast tray still sat there, untouched. I downed the glass in two gulps then poured another, suddenly thirstier than I'd ever been. Since he hadn't shared my bed, he clearly said no. This season had completely unravelled me. I started it determined to stay as far away from Cal as possible. Now it seemed we'd switched roles.

"You were sharing with Michaela anyway, so—"

I slammed the empty glass down on the table, already embarrassed enough without having to listen to his explanation. "I'm staying here an extra few hours. You should go. I'm sure everyone's downstairs getting ready to leave."

"They are, but I think I'll stay here too. Take care of you," he said, voice soft. I couldn't handle him talking to me like that right now, because my willpower was as weak as my stomach. The idea of Cal staying here with me, making me feel cared for was tempting, but I couldn't do it. Besides, I didn't deserve his comfort. I'd done this to myself.

"You don't need to stay. A few hours rest and I'll be right as rain."

He studied me a long moment, then finally said, "Okay, but if you need anything, call me."

I nodded weakly and he turned to leave. I don't know why, but when he reached the door, I blurted, "I'm going to see a therapist when we get home."

Cal's expression morphed into a mixture of concern and relief. "Good, that's..." he paused to clear his throat, "good."

"I think it's about time I finally addressed my issues."

He held my gaze, not breathing a word. Then, in a flash, he strode back to me. Silently, he took my face in his hands and pressed a chaste kiss to my forehead. He exhaled, dropped his hands and walked back to the door. Not facing me, he repeated, "I'm just a call away."

"I know," I breathed and then he was gone.

I managed to push down a slice of dry toast and a cup of tea. When I got back into bed, it was hard to fall asleep because I just kept thinking of Cal. For the first time, I wondered if I actually deserved him. Given all the crap I'd put him through these last few years, probably not. Sure, he hadn't been the easiest person to be with either, what with his jealous behaviour and short temper, but in spite of this, he'd always been open and willing to try and make things work.

I was the stubborn one who said no, too frightened of being hurt again.

To distract myself, I pulled up a movie scene playlist on my phone and watched Jennifer Hudson sing about betrayal in *Dream Girls*. I watched Drew Barrymore's evil stepmother rip her wings in *Ever After*. I watched the little old man's wife die at the start of *Up*. They were all scenes that made me cry. It felt cathartic to feel someone else's pain, even if they were all fictional.

Finally, I drifted off for a few hours and woke up feeling a little better. I took a bath, then later I sat outside and watched a herd of antelope in the distance. Maybe they were the same ones from yesterday. I realised I rarely did this anymore. I didn't often have days where I stopped and just took a moment to breathe.

I rode a bus full of tourists back to the city that evening and it was late when I arrived at the house. I climbed from my taxi and hitched my backpack over my shoulder when something caught my eye. Someone was sitting up on the roof.

Cal.

I dropped my bag on the porch and climbed the wall at the side of the house before hopping over onto the roof.

I thought I was being stealthy and ninja-like, but without even turning to look at me Cal spoke, "What are you doing up here, Leanne?"

"I could ask you the same question."

"You're not the only one who needs alone time."

I swallowed. "Do you want me to leave?"

Finally, he looked at me, his eyes travelling up my body. He shook his head then turned his attention to the sky. I sat down next to him, resting my arms on my knees.

"I'm trying to pick out constellations," he said after a few moments of quiet.

He was? It still made my chest flutter to think he'd taken an interest in astronomy because of me. The idea of Cal sitting down and taking the time to read a book really got my libido fired up. There was just something sexy about a man who read.

"Can you see Aquila?" I asked. "It's one of my favourites."

Cal's shoulder nudged mine. "Show me."

There was an intensity in his voice that made me shiver. I pointed up at the sky, mapping out the pattern for him. "It's the shape of an eagle," I said.

"I see it," he replied quietly, pausing before he continued, "Why are you so fascinated by stars?"

I smiled wistfully. "I think the question should really be, why aren't more people fascinated by them? Every night we can see these miraculous balls of gas that are literally billions of years old right above our heads and nobody takes a minute to stop and realise how incredible that is. How small we are in comparison. Our entire lives are only a fraction of a fraction of a second in the life of a star, maybe even a fraction of a fraction of a fraction of a second. When I think about that, at least for a small moment, all my silly, petty little worries seem so pointless. If I could just figure out a way to extend the moment..."

His face was tender. "We all worry, Leanne. It's part of being human."

I shook my head. A few years ago, I never would've expected Cal to speak like this. He'd matured in a way that made me feel inadequate by comparison. "When did you get to be so wise?"

He didn't answer, and instead reached out, touching his fingers to the spot beneath my eye. When he withdrew, he held a fallen eyelash on the tip of his finger. "Make a wish."

I closed my eyes. I didn't even need to think about it. I knew what I wanted.

I wish for Callum Davidson to find happiness. Because after everything we've been through, he deserves it.

I blew on the eyelash.

He studied me. "Not going to tell me what you wished for?"

"Everybody knows wishes need to be kept secret, otherwise they don't come true."

Cal chuckled softly. "That's right. My bad."

I looked away. Down below the pool was empty and all lit up, the reflection of the water glimmering against the lights.

"How are you feeling?" Cal asked.

"Better than this morning. I just, well, I'm looking forward to wrapping up this season so I can get home and work on some stuff. It's been a long time coming."

I felt him studying my profile and tried to ignore how his assessment made me feel so laid bare. It always did. "You said something else last night," he murmured.

I stiffened, unable to meet his gaze. "What did I say?"

It took him a moment to answer, like he struggled to form the right words. In the end, it became apparent that there weren't any. "You said you blame yourself for losing our baby."

Just like that, tears formed and I sniffled. "Yeah, well, that's one of the things I need to work on."

Cal's voice was scratchy. "The, uh, the day it happened, I spoke to your sister."

I glanced at him. "I didn't know that."

"She told me that what happened wasn't anybody's fault. It took me a long time to accept that. I'm still not sure I have fully."

Now I looked at him. "Why? You weren't the one who jumped that day."

"Yes, but if it weren't for me, all you would've suffered was a few broken ribs. I should've taken better care with you."

I shook my head. "That's ridiculous."

"Is it as ridiculous as you blaming yourself for jumping when you had absolutely no idea you were pregnant?" he countered fiercely. I had no response. Cal's expression softened as he swore and pulled me to him. "Come here."

He wrapped his arm around me while I rested my head on his shoulder. His warmth was a comfort I badly needed. I felt him press a kiss to my temple and suppressed a shiver.

"I guess we both need to learn to forgive ourselves," I said in the quietest voice.

"Yeah," Cal breathed, staring out into the distance. "I guess we do."

Eighteen
Leanne

"So, if our planet is within the observable universe, and the multiverse is outside of our universe, then what's outside of the multiverse?" Paul asked.

"Well," I replied. "That's the whole point of the multiverse theory. It describes everything that exists, even the stuff we haven't discovered yet." If I was honest, it made me infinitely sad to know those discoveries wouldn't happen until long after I was dead and gone, if they ever did at all.

"But no matter how big it is, there *has* to be something outside of it, right? There's always something outside of something else," Paul argued.

"What weed have you been smoking?" James asked with a chuckle.

"I'm trying to explain astronomy to him," I said. "But he keeps bamboozling me with questions."

Currently, we were outside the FNB Stadium close to Soweto. Our challenge was to find a way of climbing to the roof. It was night and we all wore dark clothes. Even though the filming was legit, I still felt a little like an intruder, like we were up to no good. It gave me that excited thrill in my stomach.

The giant stadium stood empty, thousands upon thousands of vacant seats going up. We walked down the centre of the pitch, while Isaac ran ahead and did three perfect backflips. Cal walked close by. After our heart-to-heart last night, things had been pretty good between us, friendly even.

All of a sudden, Trev ran by us shouting, "Last one to the top has to pay for dinner."

That got us all moving. I started to run, then yelped when someone scooped me up and threw me over their shoulder. "Cal! Let me down!"

"Hold tight. I see a shortcut."

Instead of protesting, I wrapped my arms around his neck and let him carry me. He held my legs and sped forward, jumping on board a lift and hitting the button for the top floor.

"I'm pretty sure this is cheating," I said as I slid down his back.

Cal winked. "There's no such thing as cheating when you haven't set any rules."

"I bow down to you, master," I chuckled. Cal smirked and I suddenly realised how that sounded. "Uh, I mean...."

He batted his eyelashes. "Yes?"

I pushed him lightly on the shoulder. "You know. Shut up."

The door pinged open and we stepped out, reaching the top tier of the seating area before everyone else. Trev arrived a few seconds later, breathless. "I should've known you'd cheat."

"Still won, didn't I?" Cal replied cockily.

"Cheaters don't win," Trev griped and went to check out the wall behind the last row of seats. There were bars running across the ceiling. Trev jumped to try to grab hold of one but missed by less than an inch.

James, Isaac, and Paul joined us, in that order, which meant Paul had to buy dinner.

"If I'm paying, we're eating at McDonald's," he announced then narrowed his gaze at Cal and me. "Technically you two should pay for cheating."

"You call it cheating. I call it thinking outside the box," Cal said and grinned. We made brief eye contact before I quickly looked away. Something had definitely shifted between us. I felt light, like a mental weight had been lifted.

Trev jumped again, this time managing to grab hold of the bar. He swung his body up then climbed over to the skylight windows.

"Gonna see if I can get one of these open," he said.

In the end, he used one of his old tricks to pry a window open, since he used to steal cars when he was a teenager. Opening locked car doors, opening locked windows, it's all the same, right? Let's just say, Trev was the only one of us who'd taken up parkour because it was useful when running away from the law.

Cal climbed up after him, reaching down to give me a hand. I put my hand in his and let him pull me up. We climbed through the window and then, just like that we were on the roof of a gigantic football stadium.

"Is it just me, or does the air feel a little thinner up here?" Paul asked.

"It's called altitude," Isaac said, emerging through the window.

I looked out at the twinkling city lights, breathless. Cal came and rested his elbow on my shoulder, quietly looking out too. I felt his heat, his closeness.

"That's it. We're doing Wembley Stadium when we get home," James announced. "I can't believe we never thought of it before."

Trev lifted the first-person camera around his neck and turned in a circle to capture the full three-sixty view. It was too risky for the crew to follow us up here, so we had to rely on our own cameras to capture the footage. There was also a drone that Jimbo operated to capture us from above.

I shivered, having forgotten to wear a jacket. It was so warm during the day that I never seemed to anticipate the coldness at night.

"Are you cold?" Cal asked, noticing me shiver.

"I'll be fine," I said, but he was already taking off his hoodie and tugging it over my head. It was way too big, the fabric swimming on me, but I had to admit it did keep the chill out. Plus, it smelled like Cal, which was a whole other level of comfort mixed with awkward.

Paul noticed, his gaze narrowing in suspicion as he pulled me aside. "What's going on with you two?"

I shrugged casually. "Nothing." *Everything.*

Paul didn't look like he believed me, and rightly so. "I'm not going to tell you how to live your life, but just think about what you're doing, okay?" His caring blue eyes were etched in concern and I swallowed down a lump of guilt. Paul's words were a reminder that no matter how I might feel for Cal, I had a job to protect. There were bigger factors at play, factors that could result in a loss of livelihood.

I nodded, the thought sobering. "Okay."

"I just want what's best for you," Paul said, squeezing my shoulder before going to join Trev and James.

I followed and we ran a lap around the circumference of the roof, goofing about and taking turns to film each other. Then we sat down for a while to get some good shots of the view.

It was a thrill to be so high up.

When we finally climbed back down, Barry congratulated us on a great shoot. Neil eyed me, his eyebrows drawn together as he noticed what I was wearing. I remonstrated myself, wishing I'd never accepted Cal's offer in the first place. That familiar guilt pinched at me again, because I'd made Neil a promise that we'd talk about possibly dating when we got home and now here I was wearing my ex's hoodie.

I was officially a horrible person.

I considered going to him and explaining that I'd simply gotten cold up on the roof and that's why I was wearing it, but that would just make things more awkward. Besides, deep down I knew it wasn't simply a friendly gesture. I'd seen how Cal's eyes shone with possession when I put it on, and I did it anyway. I could've taken it off when Paul warned me to be careful, but I didn't want to, and that was the part that worried me most.

Was I falling back into old habits? Somehow, it didn't feel like it. Whatever was going on with us, it felt different. Somehow, we'd evolved. I just didn't know where that evolution would lead.

We stopped at a burger bar to get takeout, then back at the house we all sat in the dining room to eat. It was nice to hang out together, but I still felt shitty about the whole Neil situation. A part of me just wanted to tell him I was an awful human and that he was better off not putting his eggs in my dysfunctional basket.

When Trev went to the kitchen to grab some drinks, I followed and pulled him aside.

"Hey, um, I'm sorry for being a bitch yesterday and not congratulating you on the baby news. It was a dick move."

Trev shook his head. "Nah, I was the dick. I didn't even think that my news might upset you."

I gave a soft smile. "I really am happy for you and Reya. You'll make great parents."

He waggled his brow. "Now we just need to organise that shotgun wedding."

I laughed and headed to my room to check my phone. I'd forgotten to take it out with me tonight, so I probably had a whole bunch of messages and notifications. On my way there, I noticed Cal's bedroom door was open, and on his bed sat his diary cam. I wondered if he'd been recording entries like the rest of us, and my curiosity got the best of me.

Stepping into the room, I closed the door and picked up the camera. I definitely shouldn't be doing this, but technically, whatever he'd recorded was going to end up on the show, so I'd see it eventually anyway. Right?

Right.

Turning the camera on, I navigated to the videos. There were several of him sitting on his bed, grudgingly talking to the camera. Thinking it would be funny to see him force himself to do something he considered a waste of time, I hit play on the most recent entry. The date and time stamp showed it had been recorded two nights ago, while we'd been visiting the game reserve.

Downstairs everyone was finishing up with dinner, so I had to be quick. My conscience niggled at me, telling me this was wrong. Then again, I was fairly sure if Cal saw my camera laying around, he wouldn't hesitate for a second to look at it too.

The recording began with Cal placing the camera on the bed facing upward, so it caught him from a low angle. He blew out a breath, ran a hand over his face then stared into the lens. I couldn't help noticing how sexy the direct eye contact was, like he was looking right at me. No wonder girls who watched the show like Olive became obsessed.

"I won't lie, today has been rough." He paused, glanced away then back. "I wasn't going to talk about Leanne on here, but fuck it, I have to talk to someone."

My pulse pounded at the mention of my name. My conscience butted in again, urging me to stop the video, but my curiosity won out.

"Things have been tense between us this whole trip, which is probably my fault. I thought if I could figure out a way to prove I'd changed, that I wanted more from her than just sex, she'd see I was worth giving one last chance. I even came up with this ridiculous scheme to show her I was willing to give up everything just for her. We have this thing where we make bets, try to beat each other. I thought that if I made a bet with her and let her win, she'd see that I don't care about beating her anymore. I thought that I could make her see I'd give up every victory just to have her finally be mine again."

My mind raced. He'd made the bet with the specific intention of losing? I'll admit the thought had occurred to me but it hadn't made sense at the time. Now it did. He planned to lose to prove he'd changed. His voice brought my attention back to the video.

"It was a stupid idea anyway," he said, blowing out a breath. "You can't trick people into seeing you've changed. I know that now. I just..." his eyes burned with longing "I've been in love with her for such a long time, but I feel like if I tell her, she'll refuse to believe it. She'll come up with some reason to prove I'm lying."

Time stood still as his words echoed around my skull. *He loved me?* Emotion sat heavy in my throat.

"She...I guess deep down she doesn't want to get hurt again, so she comes up with ways and excuses not to give us a chance." He laughed sadly. "When I'm around her I *just want to be close to her, touch her, anything. She thinks she has to be tough with me, keep up a wall, like I could ever hurt her. She doesn't realise that since we met, I haven't even slept with anyone else. Not a single person. I mean, what's the point when she's constantly in my head and my heart?"*

Cal went quiet, then swore under his breath and picked up the camera.

"Christ, what am I doing? How do you delete this shit?"

He seemed to be fiddling around with it for a minute before the screen went blank. Clearly, he thought he'd deleted the video but hadn't.

My entire body buzzed.

Cal had never told me he loved me before. Not in so many words. It was something he'd always held back, and now I knew why. He thought I wouldn't want to hear it. Tears welled in my eyes. He'd put himself through emotional torture the last few weeks just to prove himself to me, and in return, I'd given him a hard time. He...he *loved* me. I'd heard the genuine honesty in his voice, goose bumps still lingered on my skin just hearing him say those words.

Also, he hadn't slept with anyone but me in the past three years? A brick sank in my gut as I remembered how brutally we'd fought when I accused him of sleeping with Mia Popov. He'd been telling the truth all along...

Sniffling and wiping the tears from my eyes, I turned the camera off, put it back where I found it and snuck out of the room.

A swarm of bees took flight in my chest. I tried to bat them away, but they persisted, stinging at me, pushing home a truth I couldn't ignore.

We weren't supposed to be together, could lose our jobs if we were, but I couldn't live a lie anymore. Screw the consequences. Callum Davidson was in love with me, and I'd done nothing but make him suffer. He'd spent the last few weeks trying to prove he was worthy.

Well, now it was my turn to prove myself worthy of him.

Nineteen
Leanne

It was our final full day of filming. Last night's escapades on the roof of the football stadium would make up the grand finale of the season. So today was casual, capturing extra footage to fill the episodes we'd already recorded.

While I got dressed, I was completely wrapped up in thoughts of Cal. Watching that video last night had really done a number on me. I was full of fluttery, excited, swoony feelings. Every time I thought of him, I smiled. Like, what the hell? I didn't smile when I thought of Cal. I scowled. Fretted. Struggled to prepare an arsenal of snappy comebacks, but now...

Now I knew he fucking *loved* me.

I mean, anyone would be in a tizzy to know they were secretly loved.

It was a new and addictive feeling. I always thought Cal lusted and obsessed over me. That it was a challenge to peel away my layers one by one. That he took a perverse pleasure in fighting and fucking. But that wasn't true, at least, not entirely. I'd been wilfully blind, too stubborn to see the truth.

Now I had to go out there, look him in the eye and know what he felt for me. The knowledge changed so many of the principles and rules I'd mentally set for myself. Luckily, I'd decided to set some new ones.

Cal wanted a chance with me, that's what the whole bet had been about. Well, he was going to finally get one.

I still had his hoodie from last night, and I knew I should return it, but I didn't want to, not yet. Hastily, I pulled it on over my vest top then headed downstairs where the minivans were waiting to take us into the city.

I was last to climb aboard. Cal sat in the third row and I took the empty seat next to him. His eyes landed on me, making a slow ascent up my body when he saw I was still wearing his hoodie. "Morning."

"Morning," I replied with a wide smile, belly fluttering at the way he perused me.

He studied me a beat longer than normal, probably wondering why I was being so chipper and not snapping at him to keep his eyes up top.

At the back of my mind, I was worried he'd be mad at me for watching the video without his permission. But right now I wanted to focus on figuring out a way to get him to admit how he felt. I just didn't know how to go about it. I could hardly just come out and say, *So, you're in love with me, eh?*

It was a little strange that we'd never spoken of love. At the height of our relationship, we'd been obsessively infatuated, but we'd always been so busy screwing, fighting, or making up to have those serious conversations.

And then, well, I'd had the miscarriage and a dark cloud hung over all our interactions.

"You're staring," Cal said, glancing up at me from the screen of his phone.

I cleared my throat, embarrassed to be caught smiling at him like a loon. "Sorry, it's just…uh, your hair is a mess."

He cocked an eyebrow. "My hair?"

"Yes, your hair. Come here, I'll fix it for you." I shifted closer on the seat, our thighs brushing as I reached up and ran my hands through the floppy, silky strands. Cal kept his hair buzzed short at the back and sides and long on top.

"Have you ever noticed that we have almost the exact same haircut?" I said in amusement. He tilted his head to give me better access, eyeing me with a lazy, sexy gaze. I got the sense he enjoyed me fondling his hair just as much as I enjoyed touching it.

His lips twitched. "Maybe we go to the same barber."

I chuckled softly, running my fingers through the strands one last time before announcing. "There. Much better."

Cal's attention went to my hoodie again. Well, *his* hoodie. "You're still wearing it."

I gave a cheeky grin. "Yeah. I like it. I think I'll keep it."

He smirked. "Don't I get a say?"

I shook my head. "Nope."

His eyes gleamed in challenge. "Maybe I want it back."

"No, you don't," I replied, flirtatious. I needed to stop, but all I could think about was how sexy he looked right now, how much I wanted to kiss him, run my hands over the tattoos inked on his neck, feel the corded muscles beneath.

Something shifted in the air between us and a quiet moment elapsed. Neither one of us dropped our gaze.

"Well," I said. "Can I keep it?"

Cal's eyes wandered from my collarbone to my chin. "That depends," he murmured huskily.

"On?"

His eyes flicked up. "How much do you like it?"

"I *really* like it."

His voice dipped lower. "Does it feel good?"

My thighs clenched as I whispered, "Yes."

He leaned forward, his mouth a hair's breadth away from mine. "How good does it feel?"

Our breaths mingled, and I could smell the minty waft of his toothpaste. A sigh escaped me. Seriously, I was on the verge of moaning and we were literally only talking. "Really fucking good."

Cal swallowed, a flicker of uncertainty in his eyes before the sexy glint returned. He reached out and tugged at the edge of the hood around my neck. His knuckles brushed my skin and I almost trembled. I wanted him to touch me so badly. Cal brought his lips to my ear and whispered, "I guess I'll just have to give it to you then."

Jesus. It was a good thing I was already sitting down because the gravelly quality in his voice made my knees weak. I finally dragged my eyes away from his, looking anywhere but at him. A flush broke out on my skin when I felt him watching me. I could tell he was wondering what had brought on this sudden flirtatiousness.

When we arrived in the city, Trev was determined to get to the roof of one particular building, but Barry said no, we didn't have a permit. The Carlton hotel had been empty and abandoned for years. I kind of wished we could explore it too, but you didn't go against Barry's orders.

Instead, we shot on the roofs of several apartment buildings. We were down on the street taking a break when I spotted Neil and Cal talking and my stomach flipped. I wasn't close enough to hear, but Cal's jaw was set tight and Neil's expression was serious.

What were they saying?

I waited until Neil left before sidling over to Cal and noisily clearing my throat. He bent to fix his laces, a smile in his voice when he asked, "Something bothering you, Leanne?"

My cheeks heated. "Just wondering what you and Neil were talking about."

Cal glanced at me, amusement playing on his lips, but he didn't respond.

"Seemed like it was serious," I hedged.

"It was."

"And?"

"And what Neil and I discuss is our business."

I groaned. "Fine, keep your secrets." I grabbed hold of a bar that stuck horizontally out of a signpost and swung my body up. I hung out of it like a petulant monkey while Cal sighed and came to stand in front of me.

"You're a moody little thing," he murmured.

I swung back and forth, pretending not to hear him. "Can you move? I'm trying to test my upper body strength."

Instead of moving out of the way, Cal came to stand directly in front of me. "You want to play? Let's play."

I squealed in surprise when he grabbed me by the hips, stopping me mid-swing. His arms came around my waist where the hoodie had ridden up and the shock of his roughened skin sent a spark of awareness through me. Cal made a gruff sound in the back of his throat and our eyes locked. His thumb lightly grazed my hip and I tightened my grip on the bar. If I let myself drop even a centimetre, my crotch would be flush with his.

"Neil asked me if there's still something between us," he revealed.

My heart pounded loudly in my ears, both from the topic and how Cal was holding me. "What did you say?"

"I told him that was up to you." His voice was soft, his eyes questioning, and I suddenly felt like I couldn't breathe.

"Oh." A pause as I gathered my thoughts. "I guess—"

"Callum! Leanne! We need you over here," Barry shouted, interrupting the moment.

Cal let go of me and I instantly missed the heat of him. I dropped to the ground and followed him over to join the others.

Barry was about to call action when I stepped close to Cal. Put it down to how warm and fuzzy I was feeling for him, but I had the sudden urge to pay him a compliment. "You look hot today."

He blinked, glancing at me in surprise, and then the cameras were rolling. Cal studied me like he wondered what I was up to. "Not that I'm complaining, but what's gotten into you?"

I gave an elusive smile, like I knew a secret, which I did. "I don't know, you tell me."

Then I turned and ran. The adrenaline rush pulsed in my veins as I made it to the roof of one building then leapt through the air and landed on the next. I barely even felt the impact of my landing because I was riding a wave. Cal chased me, and the thrill of his pursuit made every nerve ending in my body tingle in anticipation.

Unlike when I'd run from him in the past, this time I wanted to be caught.

When I reached the edge of the building, I paused to catch my breath, and just like that he was on me, his voice in my ear, "Don't toy with me, Leanne. Not unless you want to get fucked."

A shiver tickled at the back of my neck. I turned so that my mouth was close to his. "If you remember, I already offered you that and you said no."

Evidently, he didn't have a response. I grinned and ran away. He chased. He always did.

It was a few hours before we got back to the house. I sat next to Cal at the dining table for dinner. The caterers had set out some freshly baked bread. It was so delicious it practically melted in my mouth. Sensing Cal's attention, I tore off another piece and held it out to him.

"You need to taste this. It's amazing."

His curious expression told me he still hadn't got used to my sudden flirtatiousness. Then, his gaze heated as he lowered his mouth and bit the bread right out of my hand. My breath caught when his lower lip brushed my finger and I forgot all the other people sitting at the table. I was entranced by Cal. Then I felt eyes on me. Neil watched us uncomfortably from across the table. A lump formed in my throat and guilt ate at me. I needed to talk to him because stringing him along like this was wrong.

Shifting away from Cal, I pulled my phone from my pocket to send Neil a text.

Leanne: Can we talk?

I watched him take out his phone to read the message and then his eyes met mine. He nodded and stood from the table. I stood too and followed him outside. The noise of crickets and insects filled my ears when I approached Neil. He stood by the pool, eyes on the water.

"I'm sorry," I said, remorseful. "I've been a bitch."

Neil gave me a look that said he agreed, but he was too nice to ever say it aloud. Instead, he shoved his hands in his pockets and asked, "What did you want to talk about?"

My stomach twisted. "I shouldn't have led you on."

Neil frowned. "You didn't."

"Yes, I did. I told you we'd talk when we got back to London, but obviously I'm still wrapped up in Cal and—"

"It's not your fault if you love someone, Leanne," Neil said sadly, and the starkness of his statement shocked me out of whatever I'd been about to say next.

"I...I don't," I protested weakly, but deep down I knew it was a lie. Loving Cal was such a scary prospect that I had a hard time accepting it was true, even if it was as clear as the stars shining above our heads.

Neil gave a joyless laugh. "Do you honestly believe that?"

My entire body slumped. I sat down on a sun lounger and let out a tired sigh. Neil filled the space next to me, his voice solid, reassuring. "It's okay to love him, you know. I feel like you try to ignore it. Hell, *I* try to ignore it because I like you so much, but I'm starting to realise that nobody's ever going to come close to how you feel about him."

"But we've always been such a disaster."

"You forget I've known you both from the beginning. You were young and figuring out your relationship. One minute you were two normal people and the next you were famous. Then the worst thing happened and whatever might've been, well…" Neil trailed off.

"It was lost," I finished for him.

"Yeah," Neil agreed. He sounded tired.

"I've always thought of Cal and me as toxic," I said. "We fight so much."

"You fight because your feelings are strong. People who are indifferent don't fight."

"That's not true. Lots of people who love each other don't fight. We fight because we don't know how else to be. We fight because we're a pair of stubborn pricks who don't know how to compromise or back down."

"Then maybe you need to learn," Neil suggested.

I couldn't believe how selfless he was being, sitting here giving me advice when all I'd given him was false hope. Maybe it was just a selfish instinct to alleviate my guilt, but I really wanted him to be happy, to find someone. If anyone deserved happiness, it was Neil. He was one of the kindest, hardest-working, most selfless people I knew.

And he was right about Cal and me. We had passion figured out, but harmony was something we never really had a chance to work on.

I was broken from my train of thought when Neil stood. "You have a lot to think about. I'll leave you."

I glanced up at him. "Are we still friends?"

His smile was soft as he reached out to briefly squeeze my shoulder. "Always."

I watched him walk back to the house.

It's not your fault if you love someone, Leanne.

Neil's statement was stuck in my head. It seemed so obvious. I thought about Cal all the time, I was trying to be a better person, someone he deserved.

Of course you love him. There's never been anyone else but him.

I sat there for a long time, so long most of the lights in the house gradually went off. We flew home to London in the morning, and the idea of not seeing Cal every day gave me a pang in my chest.

I was going to miss him. We lived in the same city, sure, but it wasn't the same as living in each other's pockets. It was ironic that I'd started this trip counting down the days until it was over. Now I didn't want to go home.

My phone buzzed with a message from Trev. It appeared to be a group text.

Trev: Meet me in the dining room. Wear dark clothes.

Well, that didn't sound ominous at all. Wondering what all the cloak and dagger was about, I made my way inside. I already wore dark pants and Cal's hoodie, so I didn't need to get changed. When I entered the dining room, Trev, Cal, Paul, James, and Isaac were waiting.

I glanced between the five of them. "What's going on?"

Trev grinned impishly. "We're breaking into the Carlton."

"The abandoned hotel?" I questioned. "But Barry said we couldn't get a permit."

"Fuck Barry and his permits. We need something exciting to finish off this season."

I chewed my lip, considering it. If we got caught, we'd be in so much trouble. But if we managed to get in and out undetected, it could make for an amazing episode. I looked to Cal for guidance and he seemed to be thinking the same thing. My decision made, I turned back to Trev. "Okay, I'm in. Let's do this."

"Hell yeah," he exclaimed, high-fiving me.

James grabbed the keys to one of the minivans and we snuck out of the house without alerting any suspicions. Most of the crew were asleep in their rooms, so the place was quiet.

We drove into the city and the dark, fifty-floor hotel loomed forebodingly above us as we parked across the street. I spotted two security guards sitting outside and my chest deflated.

"How are we going to get past them?"

"Easy," Trev replied and pulled an envelope filled with cash from his pocket. Paul filmed us as we headed across the street as a group. Isaac spoke to the security guards and there was a short back and forth before some joke was exchanged and then they took the bribe. They let us by and just like that, we were in.

"What did you say to them?" I asked and Isaac looked a little sheepish, a grin tugging at his lips.

"I might've insinuated you were dumb European tourists looking for a thrill."

I laughed and slapped him on the shoulder. "You did not!"

He lifted his hands. "Hey, I got us in, didn't I?"

I looked around while James held up a flashlight, illuminating the crumbling, dated interior, and a spooky chill trickled down my spine. This building was a place trapped in time, and there was something incredibly eerie about it. The reception area was like something from a seventies horror flick; someone checks in unaware that they're the only guest and all the workers are ghosts.

I also tried not to think of the creepy crawlies that were probably scurrying by our feet in the dark. The air was stale, an unpleasant mixture of mould, damp, and stagnant dust.

"Did you know there was a murder here once?" Isaac said, and I shivered, glancing at him.

"Really?"

He nodded. "Yes, in the late nineties. The rumour goes that two workers were caught drinking on duty by their manager, so they killed him."

My eyes widened. "That's extreme."

"This city has always been an extreme place," Isaac said solemnly. "Guess that's why my mum left."

"And your dad, where is he?" I asked. Isaac never really spoke about him.

"He died when me and my sisters were young," he replied, but I didn't probe further. I got the sense it wasn't something he wanted to discuss.

"This place is definitely haunted," Paul said.

James turned to him. "Don't tell me you believe in ghosts."

"It's one of many theories," Paul answered. "Some of us go to heaven, some of us go to hell, but some of us are unlucky enough to get stuck in limbo, and that's where ghosts come in."

"I thought you believed in reincarnation," I said.

"Reincarnation is my *preferred* philosophy, but there's always a chance I'm wrong."

"It kind of goes without saying we'll see a ghost tonight. I mean, look at this place," Trev interjected, appearing in front of us as he held his phone under his chin, torchlight on, illuminating himself in a spectre-like fashion.

I swiped at him. "Quit that."

He chuckled and moved out of the way.

"Don't worry," Cal murmured, suddenly beside me. His hand came to rest at the base of my spine. "I'll keep you safe from ghosts."

His warmth trickled into me, and strangely, his promise did make me feel safer. I flushed and noticed Paul had the camera trained on us. It was on night mode, so I knew he could see where Cal's hand rested. Just like last night when Cal gave me his hoodie, he looked concerned. Paul was my best friend and I knew he was only worried for me, but I couldn't deny my heart any longer. I loved Cal, and I wasn't going to let some TV executives dictate our relationship. If they wanted us off the show, then I'd just have to accept it.

I was still only twenty-five. Definitely young enough to start over in my career if it came to that. A part in a reality TV show wasn't worth giving up the love of my life for.

The thought was shocking, but I couldn't deny it was the truth.

With a new and heightened awareness of the man beside me, I walked up a creaky staircase covered in dirty, dusty carpet. On instinct, I slid my fingers through Cal's to hold his hand. He paused and I could barely make him out, but I sensed his surprise.

"Is this okay?" I whispered.

"Yeah, it's okay," he answered, voice gruff. Little electric shocks went through me at the feel of his rough palm on mine. No one could see us in the dark and it gave me a thrill.

Hand in hand, we continued our exploration. I honestly didn't expect this place to have such an unnerving vibe. It felt both creepy and mysterious. Lots of good and bad people had come and gone through the hotel's doors, all with their own lives and stories to tell. I imagined the building rising and falling many times before eventually dwelling in its current abandoned state.

Cal must've noticed me shiver when he asked, "You okay?"

"This place has bad juju. I can feel it."

"Maybe we should've come in the day time," James said.

"It's definitely a lot creepier at night," Paul agreed.

"We'll be fine," Trev reassured. "We just need to figure out a way to the roof."

We explored a little then discovered a large ballroom. There was a weird scratching sound and I held tighter onto Cal's hand, goose bumps rising on my skin.

"What the hell is that?" James whispered.

"It's probably just an animal. A fox or something," Trev said.

"Let's get out of here. I don't want to find out," Isaac replied.

We left the ballroom and started the climb to the top. We were all in excellent shape but climbing fifty floors was no joke. Paul filmed the entire time, counting each floor for the audience and narrating what we saw. We were only a couple of floors from the top when I had to stop to take a break. I needed to sit down, but I was afraid if I sat on the floor there might be cockroaches, or worse, rats.

Why the hell had I agreed to this idea again?

Oh, right. For the show. Had to keep our audience entertained.

I knew Barry would be pissed when he found out, but if the footage was good, he'd forgive us. Eventually.

"C'mere," Cal said as he lowered his shoulder. "I'll carry you the rest of the way."

I shook my head. "You're tired too. It's fine. I can handle it."

"It's just a few floors, Leanne. Come on," he said and pulled me onto his back. I was reluctant at first, but when I draped my arms around his neck and he took my weight, it was a relief. I inhaled deeply, loving his smell, the warmth of his skin, his strong arms as they held me.

"Hold on," he said and then we were on the move again.

Feeling safe in the dark, I nuzzled his neck, soliciting a sharp inhale. His hand flexed at the back of my knee. He let me down when we made it to the roof and James put his torch on the ground, facing up to illuminate the space. On the opposite end of the roof, we discovered what used to be a swimming pool and lounge area. It was down a level, sort of sunken, and surrounded by high walls.

"I bet you'd get one hell of a suntan up here," Trev said, looking around.

"This must've been for the VIPs," Paul added. "I wonder if any famous people ever sunbathed up here."

"Mick Jagger visited once. Oh, and Margaret Thatcher," Isaac said.

"Okay, now I'm imagining Thatcher in a bikini. Thanks for that," James chuckled.

"I thought you loved those strict, authoritarian types," Trev teased. "You should thank him for the masturbation material."

"Nah, James has a secret liking for the shy ones," Cal countered and I elbowed him in the stomach. He was referring to Michaela, clearly, but I'd already warned him not to say anything.

Paul looked puzzled. "Eh, Diana is anything but shy."

"Can we all quit discussing my private life?" James asked, casting Cal an irritable glance.

"I just want to know if you're jerking it as much as I am," Trev replied, his grin relentless.

I scrunched up my face. "Ugh, please."

"What? It's completely natural," he went on. "I've been going at it hell for leather over here, twice if not three times a day."

"Hey! We share a bedroom," Paul complained.

"Don't worry," Trev winked. "I always wait until you're sound asleep."

Paul put his hand to his chest, feigning outrage. "I feel defiled."

Cal gave a low chuckle. "Okay, I think we need to get this show on the road." He moved by me and precision jumped at least twelve feet down to the swimming pool level. Trev, James, and Isaac followed, and I stood next to Paul while he filmed.

We were quiet a moment, watching the others take turns running and jumping back up the surrounding walls.

"So, you and Cal?" Paul said, casting me a curious glance.

I shifted from foot to foot, antsy. "What?"

"Don't play dumb. I saw you two holding hands."

So much for no one being able to see us in the dark. I sucked in a deep breath for courage. "Don't faint or anything, but...I think I'm in love with him."

"Wow, she finally admits it," he said, not at all surprised. *What the hell?* It was disconcerting to think both Paul *and* Neil could see I loved Cal when I didn't even know it myself. "Have you told him yet?"

I shook my head and chewed my lip. "Not yet."

Paul turned to me, his expression serious now. "Well, whatever you do, be careful, and try to make sure nobody else finds out. Not until you can figure something out about those contracts you both signed."

"What is there to figure out? I can't wait a whole year to be with him."

Paul squeezed my hand. "Then I guess you're going to have to make a tough decision. Just remember I'm here for you, whatever you need."

"Hey! Get over here you two!" Trev shouted, interrupting our talk. He stood at the far side of the roof, on the very edge of the outer wall.

"Guess we should go do our jobs," I said, nudging Paul then launched myself diagonally through the air before landing on the wall. I looked out then down. Heights didn't typically faze me, but I still got a faint wobble in my belly thinking how high up we were. It wasn't unpleasant, in fact, it was part of the thrill, the danger.

Paul captured us as we ran, jumping from one wall to the next. The view up here was panoramic, the city lights twinkling below. When it was time to leave we'd almost made it back to the ground floor when I saw a flash of light. Someone shouted in heavily accented English, "Who's there?" and my stomach dropped.

"Fuck," Cal swore, his arm going protectively around my waist.

"Looks like those security guards sold us out to the coppers," Trev said.

"Everyone turn off your flashlights," James whispered.

Footsteps sounded as we turned in the opposite direction to find another way out. My heart pounded, palms sweaty. We were breaking the law by being here and I did not want to get arrested in a foreign country.

Without any lights to find our way, the place was a dark maze. I stayed close to Cal, James on the other side of me, while Trev, Isaac, and Paul were ahead of us. The shouting and flashlights behind us drew closer. We entered what appeared to be a storage closet. There was only one small window close to the ceiling. Trev reached up and miraculously, it opened. He gestured for Isaac to climb through, followed by Paul, then James. By the sound of how close our pursuers were, there wasn't going to be enough time for everyone to get out.

My heart pounded as I made a rash decision.

"I'm too short to reach the window. You go first then pull me up," I said, pushing Cal forward. I didn't give him a chance to argue, and just as he climbed through the window, the room was illuminated in cold, white light.

I slammed the window shut and turned over the lock.

"Leanne! What are you doing?!" Cal yelled and banged on the glass at the same time a policeman ordered, "Stop right there."

I met Cal's furious gaze. "Go and get help!"

He looked like he wanted to strangle me, but I'd locked the window and I wasn't going to let him back in. If this was what I had to do to prevent Cal from being arrested, then so be it. This was my chance to prove that I deserved him. I'd take the fall so he didn't have to.

"Well, fuck," Trev swore.

It was just me and him left and the two policemen had their guns trained on us. Icy cold fear seized my veins. I hadn't actually seen a gun before in real life. Most police back home didn't carry them, so it was shocking to have one aimed right at me. There was something about staring down the barrel that sent a horrifying tremble through my entire body. My life didn't exactly flash before my eyes, but I definitely had a thought like, *this could be it for me.*

"Put your hands in the air," one of them shouted, still aiming at us while the other one came and handcuffed Trev first, then me. Trev wasn't half as freaked out as I was, but then again, he'd had many brushes with the law in his previous life as a car thief.

It gave me a small measure of relief that the others managed to get away. At least they could go get help. And Cal, well, I was sure he'd thank me when I finally explained my reasoning for saving him.

Trev and I were escorted out of the building and loaded into a police van to be brought to the station. I saw someone charging towards us just as we pulled away. It was Cal. He'd made a mad dash from the back of the building, but he wasn't fast enough.

"Why did you do it?" Trev questioned, eyeing me curiously. I knew what he was asking. He wanted to know why I'd made Cal go first.

I exhaled tiredly. "I've treated him really badly this last year when he didn't do anything to deserve it. Taking the fall tonight is part of my penance."

"I'm not sure he'll see it that way," Trev said and my stomach twisted. Had I just made an epic mistake?

A few minutes went by before I asked, "What's going to happen to us?" I was nervous now, the full weight of my actions suddenly dawning on me.

Trev scratched his jaw. "Not sure how things operate over here, but we should play it cool. I'm hoping the police are corrupt enough that Barry will be able to pay them to let us off."

I gave a flat laugh. "Do you know him at all? Barry will probably leave us in jail to stew for a few days just to teach us a lesson."

"Yeah, I wouldn't put it past him."

A short while later, the van came to a halt. I listened as someone climbed out then the back door slid open abruptly.

"Hey, thanks for the ride," Trev said jovially. "We can make our own way home from here."

The policeman stared at him, unamused, as he hustled us out of the van.

"Well, that went over like a lead balloon," Trev bent to whisper to me as we walked into the station, still in cuffs. "You can tell the seriousness of the situation by how much banter a cop will indulge in. This guy didn't even crack a smile."

"So, you're saying we're screwed?"

"Let's just see how this plays out first before we start to panic."

Inside, the station was big and there seemed to be a lot of people waiting to be processed. After they booked us, taking away our phones and personal belongings, I was separated from Trev to be put into the women's section.

"Just keep it together," he said in a reassuring voice. "We'll be out of here in no time."

I wasn't so sure about that.

I was put in a large cell with a bunch of other women. It was crowded, hot, and humid. Some women were visibly distressed while others didn't seem too bothered. I found a free spot on the floor and sat down, holding my knees to my chest and trying not to make eye contact with anyone.

I was all for new experiences, but this was definitely past my comfort level.

Swallowing hard, I took a deep breath in and out and hoped I got out of here soon.

Twenty
Leanne

It was almost morning. There was still no sign of anybody coming to get me and panic truly began to set in. Was Trev still being held or had he been released? The stress of not knowing was killing me.

The walls had definitely started to close in a little and a wave of nausea hit me.

Every time I tried talking to the police officers on duty, they wouldn't answer my questions. I also wasn't given an opportunity to make a phone call.

On the plus side, it wasn't like in the movies, where you were stuck in a cell with some psychopath who'd killed people and decided you were next. We were just a bunch of women who'd ended up here by doing something bad or dumb, possibly both.

Anyway, I kept my mouth shut and stayed to myself until I came up with a way to get out of here.

My thoughts meandered to paranoid, fearful places, as I concocted hellish scenarios in my head. What if everyone had gone home and decided to just leave me here?

Leanne's a resourceful girl. She'll figure something out, they'd say as they hopped into cabs to the airport.

Traitorous bastards.

Okay, I was officially losing it.

I smelled terrible and probably looked even worse. I held my head in my hands, feeling sorry for myself. Stupid Trev and his risky ideas. Sometimes it didn't always pay off to take chances.

I was deep in a pit of self-pity when I heard someone shout, "Where is she? I need to see her!"

Callum.

Just like that, my spirits lifted. They hadn't forgotten about me. I jumped to my feet and ran to the bars, going up on my tiptoes to try and see what was happening. A second later a policewoman appeared in front of me and unlocked the cell.

"You're free to go," she said before letting me out and escorting me down the corridor. My legs and butt ached from sitting on the hard floor for hours and I felt sweaty and gross, but the sheer relief of knowing I was getting out of here rushed through my veins. We reached the lobby area and Cal came barrelling toward me. He knocked the wind out of me when he pulled me into his arms, lifted me up and held on tight.

"If you ever do something like this again, I'll kill you myself," he growled, lips pressing into my hair. The comfort of being in his arms flooded me, and tears leaked down my face. "I thought you left me."

Cal swore and took my face in his hands, his expression fierce yet tender. "I'd never leave you. Not ever."

I swallowed and he wiped a tear from my cheek. "Oh, Leanne, come here," he murmured and pulled me to him again. I breathed him in, savoured the feel of him, his reassuring warmth. When I looked over his shoulder, I saw the others. Trev, Paul, James, and Isaac gathered round, Neil and Michaela too, all of them looking relieved to see me. Jimbo stood nearby, filming our reunion. Barry was nowhere to be seen. I imagined he was already on his first-class flight back to London, stewing over what we'd done.

"Hey, you're not the only one who needs to hug her," Paul complained, and Cal grudgingly released me from his hold. I hugged my friend and he gave me a firm squeeze. "We've all been scared half to death. The police who arrested you caught wind that you and Trev were on TV back in the UK and said they'd let you go if we paid them twenty grand," Paul rambled. "Can you believe that crap? And after we already paid off those security guards, too. They're obviously running some kind of scam."

My eyes widened. "What the hell?"

"Yeah, we didn't know how we were going to pull the money together on the quick—"

I held a hand up, cutting him off. "Hold on a second, you paid twenty grand to get Trev and me out of here?"

"Well, technically, Cal paid it. He had the money wired directly from his account."

I turned to gape at him. "You did what?"

He put his hands on my hips, pulling me back into him as he shot Paul an annoyed glare. Clearly, he hadn't planned on telling me about the money. "Don't worry about it. We got you out, that's all that matters." His voice lowered to an almost threatening whisper. "Although you better believe we're going to talk about you locking that window."

I ignored his threat, instead arguing, "It's too much. I'm paying you back."

"Like fuck you are."

I swiped him on the chest. "Cal, I'm paying it."

His eyes gleamed in challenge. "You can try."

I looked around at my friends, feeling misty-eyed again. "Did you all miss your flights home to be here?"

"We were hardly going to leave when you were still in jail," James said.

"We're family," Paul added, coming to give my hair a ruffle. "Besides, I don't think any of us wanted to share a flight home with Barry. I swear he almost popped a blood vessel when he heard what happened."

I chuckled, a feeling of love and affection for all of them swelling in my chest. I was having a serious *Finding Nemo* reunion scene moment. "I love you guys, do you know that?"

"Well, we are pretty amazing," Isaac said with a grin.

Okay, now I was crying again.

"Come on," Cal said, his arm firmly around my waist. "Let's go get something to eat. You must be starving."

I smiled up at him. "I could eat a horse."

His face was full of tenderness. "That's my girl."

Back at the house, I took a shower and changed into some leggings and a loose T-shirt. I was too wired to sleep, so I went out to sit by the pool, the sun warm on my skin.

Michaela and Neil were booking new flights home for everyone tomorrow, so at least I could take the day to rest and forget about the stress of spending a night in jail. It was almost ten o'clock, but after being awake all night, everyone had gone to bed.

"There you are," Cal said. "I've been searching all over the house for you. Aren't you exhausted?"

My chest tightened at the sight of him. I traced his features; masculine lips, strong jaw, a deep scar over his left eyebrow that he got from a bike accident as a kid. I longed to press my lips to it, taste his skin on my tongue.

"I'm too wired to sleep," I replied and he came to sit next to me.

His hand caressed my cheek and I looked up, recognisable heat in his eyes.

"This is probably going to get me into a world of trouble, but fuck it, after last night I can't stay away from you anymore."

He pulled my face to his and kissed me. His mouth was hungry, his tongue melding with mine. I was frozen, shocked by the taste of him after all this time. It felt like it had been both seconds and an eternity since we last kissed and the weight of how much I'd missed him fell on top of me at once.

I love you.

The thought came unbidden. I needed to tell him. I just had to find the right moment.

My hands fisted in his T-shirt. I gasped when Cal picked me up and instinctively, I wrapped my legs around his waist. He groaned when I ran my hand up the back of his neck, scratching my nails into the base of his skull. Fire burned between us and I almost lost myself when my brain won the battle over my heart. Breaking the kiss, I drew away from him. I had a confession to make.

"I watched the video," I revealed then covered my mouth with my hands.

Cal's expression was questioning, his voice breathless from our kiss, "What video?"

"The one on your diary cam. The one where you said you love me."

Twenty-One
Leanne

Cal frowned and scratched his neck in confusion. "But...I deleted that."

"You didn't. I watched it. I'm sorry."

I saw his face run the gamut of emotions as it dawned on him that he really hadn't deleted the video. A video where he'd revealed his true intentions with our bet, where he'd poured his heart out thinking no one else would ever see it. When he didn't say anything, I worried I'd messed up royally.

"Are you mad?" I chewed my lip, nervous.

A frown caused a line to deepen between his eyebrows. When he finally looked at me, his eyes were wild. "Fuck yeah, I'm mad that you watched it, Leanne. I'm also mad that you made me climb out that window last night so that you'd get arrested instead of me."

"But don't you get it? I did that because of what you said in the video," I explained, my voice desperate. Cal's frown intensified. My nerves caused me to ramble. "You said you made the bet with me because you planned to lose. You wanted to show me you'd give up any victory to prove that I was more important."

"You *are* more important." Cal's voice was gruff.

I stared at the ground, shame eating at me. "I've pushed you away for an entire year for something you didn't even do. Hell, I pushed you away the first time, and all you'd wanted was to help me through what happened. I'm a horrible, mistrustful, selfish person but you still went out of your way to fight for me, for us. So I took the fall for you last night as a way of saying sorry. I did it to prove that I can be selfless too." I paused as I swallowed down the lump in my throat. "I still have a long way to go, but I did it to prove that I deserve you."

Cal shook his head. He was pacing now, shoulders tense. "You don't need to prove anything. Yes, you pushed me away, but I've hardly been perfect. I've been jealous and possessive. Christ, Leanne, I accused you of sleeping with Paul. *Paul!* Even now I know there's nothing between you, but I still feel crazy when you two are close."

I rose and took a step towards him, reaching out to touch his hand. "But you've spent the last few weeks actively trying to be better. I see that now."

He gave a faint shake of his head. "Honestly, half the time I can't even tell if I'm succeeding or failing."

"You're succeeding."

His breath left him all at once, his expression tortured, eyes penetrating. "I've missed you."

The simple sentiment hit me like a sledgehammer, my heart going a mile a minute. "I've missed you too. And I'm sorry. For pushing you away. For watching the video. For everything I've ever done to hurt you, I'm truly sorry."

His fingers linked with mine, his tone self-deprecating. "Like I wouldn't have watched your diary cam given half the chance."

Our eyes locked and we stood in silence before I whispered, "Is it true what you said?"

His eyes turned fierce. "Of course it's fucking true."

My heart caught in my throat, my voice tiny. "I need to hear you say it."

Cal moved closer, his voice a dark caress. "Leanne, I think I've loved you since the day we met. You challenged me to outshine you and stole my goddamn heart right there."

I blinked and a tear fell down my cheek. Cal reached up to wipe it away, his voice scratchy, emotion lacing every word. "We've always been so busy loading our bullets we never realised we were already covered in battle scars." His hand moved down over my shoulder to my neck, his fingertips brushing my collarbone. "But I always took every bullet you wanted to shoot at me, because being hated by you felt better than being loved by anyone else."

"I don't hate you," I breathed. "I never have. The truth is I..." my voice broke and another tear fell. My throat was clogged, but I finally managed to push the words out. "The truth is I love you too."

Cal stole the air from my lungs when he grabbed my face and crushed his lips to mine in a fierce, heart-stopping kiss. He broke away to push me down onto a sun lounger then knelt before me, eyes bright with passion.

I stared at him, chest heaving, my attention rapt. He pushed up the hem of my T-shirt, his fingers tracing the scar on my hip. "I remember when you got this. It was summer and you fell on a piece of broken glass during a stunt," he murmured reverently. Next, his hand clasped my ankle. "And when you broke your ankle in Manchester that time I swear I went crazy with worry." His hand travelled back up my body, dipping under my T-shirt to stroke my stomach. He didn't need to say what injury he was thinking of now. Three years ago I broke my ribs, and when the doctor told me I'd been pregnant, that my baby was lost, my heart broke too.

So had Cal's.

He knew all my scars, inside and out, and I knew all of his. Pain was a part of our history, but we wouldn't let it ruin us. Not anymore.

In a flurry of need, we tore at each other's clothes, not even caring that we were out in the open, the only privacy between us and the house a giant jacaranda tree, its purple blooms vibrant under the morning sun. Cal kissed his way up my inner thigh, his voice a hungry rasp, *"Finally."*

I gasped when his lips met my sex. No preamble. Cal's tongue laved at me and I gripped the armrests, head thrown back, pleasure rippling through me. He splayed his fingers out over my stomach.

"Please," I begged. I wanted him to touch me everywhere. My nipples beaded, begging for attention.

Cool air wafted over my bare skin, tickling at my nerve endings. Cal devoured me with a look before his mouth went back between my legs. He held my gaze and circled my clit with his tongue. Reaching up, he caressed my breast then pinched my nipple. I arched my spine. This felt so good. I was going to come so soon, *too soon.*

I didn't want this to end quickly, but I couldn't hold back.

I came with a sharp, keening cry and Cal continued to tongue me, slower now, softer, exquisitely drawing out each wave.

His mouth curved into a satisfied smile as his hands gripped my hips possessively. "That was fast."

My cheeks heated. "It's been a while."

"I've missed your taste," he purred, planting kisses on my inner thigh.

"Come here," I said, needy.

I ran my hand down his stomach, marvelling at his tattoos. Trailing my fingers along the pattern on his neck, I pressed a kiss to the underside of his jaw and he trembled, swearing under his breath.

"You might not be the only who comes fast," he said as I nuzzled his cheek and he groaned. "You have no idea how much I've missed you."

"Yeah?" I said, meeting his gaze as I reached down to palm his cock. He was rock hard.

He buried his face in my neck, his gravelly voice vibrating through me. "Fuck, keep touching me."

I positioned him at my entrance. He pushed in the tiniest bit and I moaned at the stretch. It really had been too long. No wonder Cal made me come so quickly. My body had been completely neglected.

"Wait, wait, we need a condom," Cal grunted.

"I'm on the pill," I countered and his expression darkened. "Seriously," I went on, breathless, needing him, "I never miss a pill, not anymore, not after…"

My words trailed off when he brought his lips to mine and kissed me slowly, gently. Breaking away for a second, he whispered, "Are you sure?"

Biting my lip, I nodded. Cal exhaled, like he was mentally berating himself, but then he moulded his lips to mine again and pushed fully inside. I moaned in pleasure as he started to fuck me slow. I exhaled harshly and begged him for more, harder, faster, but he kept up his slow, even tempo, like he was savouring every second. I got lost in his eyes and then found his rhythm. Every time he exhaled, I inhaled, every time he inhaled, I exhaled. We were in sync. I felt connected to him on a cosmic level.

Cal wasn't fucking me. He was making love to me, and emotion swelled in my chest. It was torturous but perfect. Every part of me was primed for release. He literally only needed to touch my clit and I'd go off like a trigger.

Cal held himself up, eyes on mine. "I forgot how well we fit."

"You feel so good," I moaned, biting my lip.

His expression was strained and I knew he was close. He kissed me again, hips still moving slow, when I felt his wet heat fill me. He caught the lip I'd just bitten in his and groaned, his gorgeous weight bearing down on me. I loved being surrounded by him like this. Cal was larger than life, and sex only amplified that quality.

I happily drowned in him, his scent, his strength, how alive he was.

Wrapping my arms around his shoulders, I cradled him to my chest and listened to his breathing. Cal took my hand and pressed my fingers to the left side of his chest.

"You feel that? My heart beats like crazy for you," he said, voice raspy.

I focused on the rhythm of his pulse, and a feeling of peace swept over me as I drifted off to sleep.

I woke up a little while later. Cal still slept, his big body spooning mine. The realisation that we were completely naked in broad daylight hit me. I panicked and sat upright, wondering if anybody was awake to see us. Fumbling for my clothes, I found my phone in my pocket and checked the time. It was almost midday. We'd been out here for nearly two hours. I pulled on my top then tried to wake up Cal. Nudging his shoulder, he stirred then blinked.

When he saw me, he grinned sexily and pulled me to him for a kiss. I melted under his attentive lips but quickly broke away. His eyes were molten lava and I was in danger of getting lost in their depths.

I cleared my throat. "Um, you should probably put some clothes on."

He dragged his hand through his hair, his eyes dancing in amusement as he gave a low chuckle. "Yeah, I probably should." He grabbed his jeans, then his T-shirt, his voice gravelly when he said, "This morning was incredible."

I flushed and looked away, spotting Linda coming out of the house. "Crap, there's Linda. Okay, I'm going to my room to take a shower." I'd just had one a few hours ago, but I smelled like sex. Cal's scent and sweat were all over me.

I made to leave, but he caught my wrist, gaze searing me as he bent to steal one last kiss. "Love you," he purred and my heart did a somersault.

"Love you too," I replied quietly and he smiled gloriously.

"I'll never get tired of hearing you say that."

I couldn't help smiling back, chest full of butterflies as I hurried over to the house. I felt so different, light, like I was walking on air.

"Hi, Linda," I said. "Why didn't you fly home this morning with the others?"

Her face showed concern. "I heard about what happened to you and Trevor, so I stayed to make sure everything was okay. How are you feeling?"

"I'm good. It was a rough night, but we survived."

She came at me, surprising me with a hug. "I'm so glad you're safe." I was taken aback by how much she cared.

"Thanks. I'm sorry you missed your flight."

"Think nothing of it."

We parted and I headed to my room, undressing and turning on the shower. I stepped under the spray and sighed when the hot water hit me. This morning I'd used muscles that hadn't seen action in a while, and my body ached. I saw a shadow and knew it was Cal.

"Pulling a Norman Bates. Classy," I teased. His deep laughter simmered through my bones. Without warning, he pulled open the shower door and stepped inside, fully dressed. The spray soaked his clothes instantly.

"What are you doing! Get out!" I said in a fit of giggles.

His mouth curved in a delicious smile. "Nah, I think I'll stay."

His eyes trailed down my naked, wet body and lust marked his features. I swallowed and tried to ignore how big he was, how his presence filled the tiny space, how surrounded and turned on I felt. Instantly, my nipples beaded. Cal noticed.

"What do you want?" I asked, my voice thick with arousal as water trickled down my face. Cal groaned, his hand coming up to trace my lips. My mouth fell open and I moaned when he slipped a finger inside. My head fell back against the tiles and Cal's eyelids lowered, sex in his gaze.

I wanted him again.

I swirled my tongue around his finger and he pressed his body to mine. "You like that?" he asked, gravelly.

"Mmmm," I moaned. My nipples brushed the rough, soaked fabric that clung to his chest and it was torture. I needed his touch *everywhere*.

He added another finger, slowly feeding them in and out as he lowered his mouth to my aching nipple and sucked. I held his head there, needing *something, everything, more*. Cal growled as he dragged his lips across my breast.

"You want something else in that hot little mouth?" he asked and my sex clenched. I nodded and the dark look that came over him almost did me in. His fingers left my mouth, replaced with his lips. He kissed me roughly, thoroughly. Instinctively, I broke away and lowered to my knees. A string of expletives erupted from him as I shoved his wet jeans down his thighs to free his cock. He hadn't bothered putting on boxers in his rush to get dressed out by the pool.

His erection throbbed as I softly pressed my lips to his shaft. Then, torturously slow, I sucked his head into my mouth and took as much of him as I could without gagging. I soaked in his reactions. One of my favourite things about giving Cal blow jobs was how reactive he was, how vocal. He told me how incredible I looked, how beautiful my mouth felt, all the while his expression was tight with exquisite male tension and arousal.

I loved how I could do this to him.

Swirling my tongue around the head of his cock repeatedly, I gripped his firm backside and took him in deep. He made a sound of pure masculine pleasure as I bobbed my head up and down. I kept sucking him, working him up to a crescendo until his cum filled my mouth. I swallowed. He picked me up and kissed me in a way that made my bones melt.

He broke away, breathless. "Thank you. That was fucking perfect."

I started to pull off the rest of his clothes.

"Don't worry. You'll have lots of chances to repay me," I said with a playful smile.

He smiled back, and this time he was the one who got down on his knees.

***

Much, much later, I woke up in my bed and Cal was spooning me. I snuggled closer and savoured his warm, comforting skin.

"It feels so good to be able to hold you," he whispered, lips brushing my ear, causing pinpricks of pleasure to skitter down my spine.

"I still can't believe you spent twenty grand to get me and Trev out of jail." Yes, I wasn't letting that drop.

"You're going to have to start believing it, because you're not paying me back."

I smiled. "You underestimate my sneakiness. I'll figure out a way."

Cal pressed his lips to the back of my neck. "Good luck with that."

All of a sudden, I was no longer sleepy. I arched my spine, pressing my backside into Cal and felt his erection stir. He swore under his breath.

"Go back to sleep, Leanne."

I twisted around to meet his hooded gaze. "Make love to me again."

His expression was torn and I frowned. "What's wrong?"

Cal's eyes went to my mouth regretfully. "I have a proposition."

My eyebrows lifted. "Oh?"

"I want us to date."

"*Okay...*"

"I mean properly," he was quick to elaborate. "I want us to start over. We never got a chance to do things normally. We were sleeping together before I ever took you out for a meal. We did everything the wrong way around."

I studied him, curious. "So what you're saying is, you want a do-over?" I asked, slightly disbelieving. This was a weird conversation to be having since we were both completely naked under the covers.

Then, as the full meaning of what he was saying sank in, my heart shimmered with gold. My impatient, brooding, and argumentative man had come up with an idea to take things slow. I was suddenly overcome with how much of a gentleman he was being.

"Does that mean no sex?" I asked, trailing a finger from his neck to his collarbone.

Cal caught my chin and brought my gaze to his. "As much as it pains me to say it, yes, it means no sex until the time is right."

My lips tilted in the tiniest grin, moving my thigh against his. He groaned in frustration. "When do classy ladies usually put out these days? The third date or the fourth?"

Cal's thumb brushed back and forth over my chin, his voice husky. "Oh, I'd say they wait until at least date five or six."

"That's a lot of dates."

He made a humming noise in the back of his throat, his eyelids lowered and I got a little lost. I swear I couldn't be more turned on. "It is, but I'm trying to teach myself delayed gratification," he said finally.

"Well then," I breathed with a sexy lilt, bringing my lips so close to his our breaths mingled. "You'd better get the hell out of my bed."

Cal never looked so tortured. It took a long moment, but he finally climbed off the bed. He pulled on his clothes, which were still damp from the shower, his expression pained.

"This could either be the best or the worst decision I've ever made," he said, leaning down to press a chaste kiss to my forehead. He looked regretful as he backed away towards the door. "See you in the morning, Leanne."

"See you in the morning, Callum."

***

Michaela woke me the next day for our flight. I'd slept like the dead, in spite of the bed feeling decidedly empty after Cal left. I was all sorts of giddy and excited about the idea of him taking me out for dates. Where would we go? I'd never really gone on a proper date before. When I was a teenager, the most romantic thing a boy could do was buy me a Coke and take me behind some bushes for sloppy kisses.

My longest relationship was with a bloke named Ricky, who would mostly just pull up to my house in his Ford Fiesta, drive me somewhere secluded, then shag me in the back seat. All I remember him talking about was alloy wheels and Formula One racing. Needless to say, I had a lasting and strong aversion to car sex.

But the idea of being taken out by Cal, of being romanced by him, had my stomach all aflutter.

We were in a rush to get to the airport and I only felt like I had time to exhale when I was seated on the plane. Just like on the way over, my seat was across from Cal's, but this time I didn't mind having him close. The fact that we were taking things slow, rewinding the clock, gave me a heightened awareness of him, even more so than usual.

Like, when he rested his head back and closed his eyes, I couldn't resist staring at his handsome profile. Or when he rolled his shirt sleeves up to his elbows, I couldn't stop staring at his tattoos, especially the one with my initial. Perhaps for the first time, it didn't make me feel weird. In fact, I liked having a permanent mark on him.

By the time we landed, I was so ready to get home to my flat. I was excited to sleep in my own bed, work out at our gym, just basically get back into a regular routine.

We'd collected our bags from the luggage carousel and were just about to exit through the arrivals gate when I heard a commotion. The sliding doors opened and flashing lights almost blinded me.

"They must have caught wind of yours and Trev's arrest," Cal said, his voice terse. He stood next to me, his hand coming to rest on my lower back and I inwardly groaned. This was all we needed, a bunch of paparazzi looking for some juicy story about why two of the stars of *Running on Air* were held in a South African jail cell overnight.

"Callum! Leanne! Callum!" they shouted and I momentarily wondered why none of them were calling Trev's name.

"Leanne, do you have anything to say about the photos?" one of the paparazzi asked, snagging my attention. He was one of our regulars, a medium height, dark-haired guy named Bill who was actually pretty cool all things considered. He was definitely one of the politer ones.

"Can you please back up?" Michaela requested, standing in front of us. "Callum and Leanne have just gotten off an eleven-hour flight and they're exhausted, so you can understand why they aren't answering questions right now."

I pushed by her, a cold tremor running down my spine. Something about this felt off. "What photos?" I asked and Bill stared at me like, *shit, she doesn't know*. I felt Cal's hostility aimed at the people surrounding us while he stood at my back and Bill pulled out his phone. The whole time to our left and right, we were being filmed and snapped.

"These pictures leaked a couple of hours ago," Bill said and I snatched the phone from his hand.

Immediately, my stomach dropped, a wave of nausea washing over me as I flicked through picture after picture of Cal and me. They'd been taken from a distance, but there was no mistaking our nakedness, nor what we were doing.

Someone had taken pictures of us having sex by the pool at the guesthouse. Shame and panic threatened to overwhelm me. Cal pulled the phone from my hand, a string of swearwords leaving his mouth in a trail of fury. He shoved the phone back into Bill's hand and swept me away from the paps.

Before I knew it, we were in a taxi heading into the city. "I think I'm going to puke," I muttered and the driver shot me a dirty look through his overhead mirror.

"You get sick in my taxi and you'll be paying for the cleanup."

Cal's arm came around my shoulders as he scowled at the cabbie and pulled me to him. "Whoever took those pictures is going to fucking regret it," he grunted.

"Cal, our *parents* are going to see them," I whispered, feeling both embarrassed and ashamed.

He caught my chin, a warning in his eyes. "Don't you dare. There's no shame in what we were doing. It's the person who took the pictures who should be ashamed. No one else."

His arms tightened around me and my mind raced. Then, a horrifying realisation struck me as I turned to him. "Oh my God, what about the contracts? We're going to be fired."

Cal stared at me, the colour draining from his face as the fact sunk in.

We were so bloody screwed.

Twenty-Two
Leanne

I'd just gotten home from a long and exhausting meeting with a boardroom full of lawyers and television executives when my phone rang with yet another call from my mum.

I'd spent over an hour talking with her, my dad, and my sister last night, explaining to them about the pictures. They were more concerned for me than for their own embarrassment, not caring what family and neighbours might think. It only reinforced to me how amazing they were.

I was incredibly lucky to have such a great and supportive family. But still, the fact that pictures of me having sex were circulating on the internet killed me a little inside. I felt violated, laid bare. Outrage and embarrassment mingled inside me, a toxic mix.

Unsurprisingly, the last twenty-four hours had been manic. Several times I found my fingers itching to pick up a drink, drown my sorrows in liquor, but I resisted. I was in the middle of a media shitstorm and I needed to keep a clear head.

"Hi, Mum," I said, bringing the phone to my ear as I dropped my wallet and keys on the kitchen counter.

"Hello honey, how did the meeting go? I've been worried sick."

I let out a long, beleaguered sigh. "Well, the good news is they didn't fire us."

"Oh, thank goodness."

"The bad news is they're docking our fee by twenty-five percent because we violated our contracts. Plus, we're going to be on yearly contracts indefinitely instead of three years like the rest of the cast. Tanya tried her best to fight our corner, but there wasn't a whole lot she could do given the circumstances."

She made a huffing noise of irritation. "I wished you'd discussed it with myself and your father before you signed that thing. It was incredibly unethical for them to have you agree to something like that in the first place."

"Yeah well, I can't take it back now. To be honest, I think they're secretly glad all this happened. The story is everywhere, which means embarrassment and shame for Cal and me, but big publicity for the show."

"It's bloody disgusting," Mum said, furious. "I hope they're going to find out who did this. It's a blatant invasion of privacy, not to mention breaking the law."

I sighed, running a hand down my face. "You have no idea what people will do for a viral story these days."

"Vultures, the lot of them," Mum griped. "I hope you've turned off all those social media accounts of yours. It's not healthy for you to be looking at them right now, honey."

"Uh, yeah," I lied, scratching my head. I wished I had the strength not to look online, but my curiosity got the better of me. Now I had all these awful comments swirling around in my head.

She's way too ugly for Callum. What does he see in her?

Where's the sex tape? I wanna see that whore cum.

She looks like a terrible lay.

"It's for the best," Mum said, interrupting my thoughts. "No good can come of reading comments online. How is Callum holding up, and his poor mother?"

"He's angry, which is understandable. He's with his mum now. I think she's pretty upset about the whole thing.

They only have each other since his dad's not in the picture, so it's tough."

"Well, send her my love. Oh, before I forget, your dad and I would like it if you came to stay with us, just for a few days until this blows over."

It was going to take more than a few days for this to blow over, but I decided not to burst her bubble. Besides, spending some time at my parents' house actually sounded pretty good.

"Yeah, okay. I'll come tomorrow."

We hung up and I went into my living room to flop down on the couch. When I arrived at my apartment building, there'd been a number of reporters outside, but I ignored them and told the doorman to not, under any circumstances let anyone up to my apartment. That was probably why I got a frustrated text from Paul saying how he couldn't get in. I completely forgot he was coming over.

I called down to the front desk and they quickly let him in. I opened my door just as he stepped off the lift. He opened his arms and pulled me into a hug. "How've you been?"

"Shitty, but better now that you're here."

He lifted a brown paper bag. "I brought noodles."

"You're a godsend. Come on, I'll plate them up."

Paul and I sat at my table and ate while discussing all the drama of the leaked pictures.

"They'll be talking about something else in no time, just you wait and see," he reassured.

All through our conversation, my phone wouldn't quit buzzing with notifications, but I refused to look. When Paul went to use the bathroom, I couldn't resist taking a peek. There were a million tags and comments clogging up my timeline. The comments were the worst.

If I were her, I'd kill myself.

That one really hit home and like the flick of a switch, I started to cry. Since the airport I'd held in all my feelings, trying to stay strong. I couldn't believe it was one comment from some careless, faceless person that broke me.

"Oh, Leanne," Paul said sadly when he emerged from the bathroom. He pulled my phone from my hand, looked at the screen and cursed.

"Fucking sociopaths."

"How can people be so cruel? Don't they realise I'm a person too?" I said with a sob.

Paul took my hands in his, his eyes steady and full of care. "It's called deindividualization. When people are in a crowd, or anonymous on the internet, they don't feel culpable for their actions, so they'll do or say things they might not if they were speaking to you one-on-one. People can say the cruellest things on the internet and there are no consequences. It's the epidemic of our generation."

"But why would they even want to?" I sniffled. "I would never feel the need to go online and put someone down like that."

"It's not that they go online with that exact intention. But when they find themselves in a position to comment, the devil on their shoulder pushes them to say something nasty. There's a certain relief in spreading misery when a part of you feels miserable about something in your own life. And we all feel something's missing, no matter how good we have it."

"Not you though. You're one of the happiest people I know."

For a second, there was a flicker behind his eyes, but it was gone in an instant. "Like I said, we all have something we're dealing with. We just keep it on the inside. This whole internet shaming thing replaces the catharsis we used to get from watching executions. There's a Latin phrase that translates to "bread and circuses". In Roman times, a law was passed to provide grain to the poorest citizens, and they were provided entertainment in the form of gladiatorial games. So, the larger population was well fed and distracted, happy for people to fight to the death because it was fun and safe to watch from afar."

"So what you're saying we is, in over two thousand years the format has changed, but we haven't?"

Paul shrugged. "Pretty much."

I gave a small smile. When he explained things so intellectually, it broke me away from my feelings, helped me to look at things from a more logical, level-headed perspective. "How'd you get to be so smart?"

He grinned. "Simple. I read books."

I thought about all the people who were writing vile things about Cal and me. I thought about their lives and how they might be unhappy. Somehow, it made my own suffering feel less. They didn't know me, not the real me. They didn't know what I'd been through. They might as well have been talking about a blank page, just something to channel all their worst thoughts onto, to distract themselves.

Bread and circuses.

My phone started ringing and as soon as I saw Cal's name on the screen, I picked up.

"Hey." *Why did I sound so breathy?*

"It's good to hear your voice," he replied, sounding as exhausted as I felt.

A smile tugged at my lips. It seemed ironic that Cal was the one thing in my life right now that made me feel peaceful, when for so long it had been the opposite. "You saw me at the meeting a couple of hours ago."

"It's not the same," he replied, and it sounded like he closed a door before his voice lowered. "I just want to be alone with you, be inside you."

My chest tingled and sharp arousal built between my legs, all from the sexy quality of his voice. Those pictures leaking might've thrown a spanner in the works of our everyday lives, but they did nothing to quell our feelings for one another. I glanced at Paul and he waggled his brows, blatantly earwigging, so I stood and went into my bedroom, closing the door. "I thought we were taking things slow."

"We are," he said, then sighed. "It's just been insanity since we landed. I need something to take the edge off. Guess I'll just have to use my hand."

"Coming isn't the only way to take the edge off," I whispered.

Cal laughed deeply. "Oh? What other options are there?"

"A workout always helps."

He gave a low chuckle. "Maybe I'll try that."

I cleared my throat and asked, "So, um, how have you been? Are you okay?" I wasn't the only who'd had their privacy violated. I just hoped Cal hadn't been letting all the online comments get to him like I had.

I heard him exhale heavily. "I'm tired, but I'll survive. I'll be better once we can finally spend some time together. Are you free tomorrow night?"

"Why?" I asked with a hint of flirtation. "Do you want to take me out?"

"I want to do a lot more than that, but for now, yes, I'd like to take you out."

I flushed, smiling widely, but then I remembered I promised I'd visit Mum and Dad. "I can't," I said, regretful. "I'm going to stay at my parents' place for a few days. The press has been outside my apartment day and night. I need to get away."

"Yeah, they've been outside mine too. Some of them have even been at Mum's house, hassling her."

"That's horrible."

"You're lucky your parents live outside of London."

I hesitated, then offered. "Why don't you come with me?"

He sounded surprised. "To your parents' house?"

"Yes, you could sleep on the couch..."

He gave a low chuckle. "As tempting as that sounds, I don't want to leave Mum alone right now."

"How is she?"

He sighed gently. "She's holding up. But I can't leave her at the mercy of all those reporters. I'm staying with her until this all dies down."

"Please tell her I'm thinking of her."

"I will. You should come to visit when you're back. She wants to see you."

"Okay. I will."

A moment of silence fell before Cal said, "So I guess our date's on the back burner for a little bit?"

"Yes," I replied, relieved he wasn't annoyed about putting things off.

"I miss you already," he breathed, low and husky.

"I miss you too," I replied.

"I'll see you when you get back. And Leanne?"

"Yes?"

"Dream of me."

I hung up, butterflies invading my insides. He was being so sweet and patient, and seeing this new side to him had me feeling all sorts of loved up. Spending a few days without him was going to be tough, but I needed to spend time with my family. Recalibrate and armour myself against the fact that my privacy had been breached in a way that couldn't ever be taken back.

I couldn't stop fixating on who took those pictures. It just didn't make sense. The only person who came close to being a suspect was Autumn Hayes, the podcaster who'd spent the day with us, but she'd gone back to New York long before the pictures were taken. Plus, even if she had been there, I just didn't get that vibe from her.

That left only one other possibility and the very idea made my stomach twist.

This had been an inside job.

Twenty-Three
Leanne

"Hey! Don't do that!" I said, giggling while my nephew pulled at my ear. I sat on my parents' living room floor, my chubby one-year-old nephew in my lap. His big blue eyes were a balm for the soul. My parents babysat Sam most weekdays while my sister, Lorna and her husband worked, but this week I'd taken him captive. He was the cutest, cuddliest little boy in the world. Caring for him erased my anxiety, put all my worries into perspective.

"Whoosh!" I said, lifting him into the air before lowering him back down. His baby giggle healed my heart. I gave him a couple more whooshes and belly kisses before Mum came into the room.

"You'll make him dizzy if you keep doing that," she warned.

"But it makes him laugh. I love hearing his laugh," I said.

Mum sat down on the sofa, watching us. I wondered if she was thinking the same thing I was. That if life had taken a different turn, I could've had a toddler of my own right now. Would I have been a good mother? Would Cal have been a good dad? Sure, we were young, but neither of us ever shied away from a challenge. I was pretty sure we would've given our all to parenting. The thought made me sad, but hopeful.

Maybe one day...

I couldn't believe I was even thinking about it, but being home with my family helped me put things into perspective. Being around people who loved me made me realise that I didn't always have to focus on what I'd lost, but instead on all the amazing things I had.

In the city, I hadn't noticed how much I was drowning, unable to resist checking my phone to see what awful new things people were saying about Cal and me. As soon as I stepped in the door to my parents' house, my dad confiscated my phone, deleted every last one of my social media apps then handed it back to me.

At first, I'd been outraged and the first day was rough, but now I existed in blissful unawareness. The only thing I used my phone for was chatting with Cal, and we'd been texting up a storm. Everything felt new and fresh, in spite of all the ugliness that was out there in the media. I think the shock and fear of being arrested back in Johannesburg, combined with the horror of the leaked pictures made us truly realise what we meant to each other. That all the petty fights and rivalries were pointless in the face of true adversity.

Speaking of, my phone buzzed with a text and I handed Sam over to Mum. Every time Cal texted me, I got an excited flutter in my belly. His messages felt like little gifts throughout the day.

Callum: Just finished five gruelling hours of narration. My brain has given up hope.

I chuckled. When we finished filming on location, we had to complete hours of in-studio narration. This meant sitting in a chair and describing things from weeks ago like they were happening in real time. It took some getting used to, and like Cal said, your brain felt like mush afterward.

Leanne: Don't remind me. I have to go in next week to do mine.

Callum: RIP Leanne's brain.

Callum: Btw, I hired a private investigator to find out who took the pictures.

My heart froze as I read his text.

Leanne: Really? Do you think they'll be able to find who did it?

The last couple of days I'd sort of made my peace with everything. Finding the person who took those pictures couldn't change what happened. Besides, we'd hired a company that specialised in erasing things from the internet, videos, pictures, social media posts, and such. Up until a week ago, I had no clue these sorts of companies existed. Now I knew you could pay someone to clean up your misguided online past. In mine and Cal's case, we just wanted the photos gone. Since it was still a hot topic, people reposted them each time they were deleted, but after a couple of months they'd get bored and quit.

I hoped.

Callum: Most likely scenario is that they work for the show. How else could they have gotten onto the grounds of the house to take pictures? Whoever it was needs to be fired.

His text echoed my own suspicions. The guesthouse had been surrounded by walls and the security cameras hadn't shown anyone breaking in or out. Was there some unhappy, disgruntled member of the film crew who'd decided to cash in? It really upset me to think someone we worked with could do this.

The next morning, I regretfully said goodbye to my family and headed home. As nice as it was to spend time with them, I needed to work and get back to regular life. Mum had helped me find a therapist in the city, who I planned to see a few times a month. Not only did I still need to sort through old personal issues, but I was also keen to unwrap all the feelings I'd been having since the photos leaked. My past experience taught me that keeping things bottled up never led anywhere good.

I was at the studio, having just finished my first narration session, when I spotted Cal coming down the corridor. His face lit up when he saw me and I couldn't help smiling too.

"Fancy meeting you here," I greeted.

"Is it creepy that I had Michaela check your schedule?" he asked and made a funny face.

I laughed. "A little." I couldn't drag my eyes away from his.

Cal took a step closer, taking my hand and running his thumb along the inside of my wrist. "I was wondering if you wanted to grab lunch?"

I suppressed a shudder and tried to keep my voice steady. "Does this count as a date?"

His lips twitched. "If you'd like."

"Well, okay then."

He kept hold of my hand as he led me outside to where he'd parked his Ducati. Cal slid his helmet on before removing something from his rucksack. "I got this for you," he said, producing a small black helmet. Open-mouthed, I took it and saw the little crown with a swirly L inside, the same as his tattoo.

"Did you get this custom made?"

He nodded, smiling fondly. "Do you like it?"

"I love it," I breathed, attempting and failing to get it on.

"Here, let me," Cal murmured, coming and taking the helmet. He settled it properly on my head then clipped it around my chin. His fingers grazed me and I trembled.

"There, perfect," he whispered before turning to climb on the bike.

I got on behind him and wrapped my arms around his waist. The air rushed past my ears as Cal overtook several cars and then we were zooming along the Thames. He chose a small, mostly empty café for lunch. A woman working behind the counter did a double take when she saw us, looking a little starstruck. Cal leaned an elbow on the counter and flashed her his most charming, underwear eviscerating smile.

"Hey, what's your name, babe?"

She blinked then cleared her throat. "Amy."

Cal leaned closer and for once I watched him work his charm on someone else. "Well, Amy, I'd be forever in your debt if you could wait until after we're gone to post about this online. In fact, I'll even take a selfie with you after we finish eating, but you gotta wait until we leave."

"Uh, yeah, sure," she breathed.

Cal winked. "I knew you'd be cool."

Huh. I wished I could use the same tactic when I didn't want people posting online that they'd spotted me out and about, but I didn't have Cal's magic charm. In fact, charm was something that was completely absent from my DNA. I remembered something Cal said to me back in Johannesburg and grinned.

My perfect woman is short, cranky, and sexy as fuck.

With every year that passed, I was learning to accept myself for who I was. I wouldn't fight against my instincts anymore, because that had only ever made me miserable. I thought staying away from Cal would help me avoid pain, but ironically, in doing so, I'd suffered worse.

We sat in a private nook at the back of the cafe. Cal ordered a pastrami on rye and I ordered the basil tortellini. A minute or two of companionable silence went by before Cal's attention wandered from my top all the way up to my face. "You look pretty today."

I cocked an eyebrow. "Are you charming me like you just charmed the waitress?"

He flashed a playful grin. "You think I'm lying?"

I looked down at the ripped jeans and plaid shirt I wore. "My outfit doesn't exactly scream 'pretty,'" I said. *Okay, maybe I was fishing for a compliment. Just a little.*

"The outfit doesn't matter. You look pretty no matter what you wear." He paused, a certain gleam in his eye. "Though now that you mention it. I do have this fantasy about you in a skirt."

My eyes widened. "Oh?"

Cal shook his head, teasing. "Nah, never mind."

I swallowed, heart hammering at the idea of him fantasising about me. "Tell me."

He looked back, his lips shaping into a sexy smirk. "I had a dream about us once." He waggled his eyebrows and my pulse raced. "You were wearing a skirt and came to sit on my lap. I ran my hand up your thigh and—"

"Okay, I get it. No need to elaborate further," I flushed.

His deep chuckle set my arousal on a low simmer while Amy arrived with our food. "Enjoy," she said as she glanced at Cal, then at me. I plastered on a bland expression, and she hovered awkwardly before finally leaving us.

"Looks like you made a new fan. Better be careful or we might have another Olive on our hands."

He scoffed. "I already have at least fifteen Olives. They send messages daily."

I lifted an eyebrow. "Really? What do they say?"

Cal shook his head. "You don't want to know. Mostly I have Neil reply."

"You have Neil reply?" I asked, incredulous. "What does *he* say to them?"

"Just polite stuff. If they get too flirty, he steers the conversation to more neutral ground."

"Do you read the conversations?"

"Not all of them."

"Seems like you're putting a lot of trust in a guy you don't have the best relationship with. He could be writing them all kinds of messages and you wouldn't even know."

"Neil values his job too much to do something like that. Speaking of, I haven't seen him giving you puppy-dog eyes lately."

I sat up straight, not liking being reminded of how I treated Neil. "Yeah, we talked. He knows nothing can happen between us."

Cal eyed me a long moment, his expression serious. "Good. It's about time he found out who you belong to."

I reached out to swipe him on the arm, all the while heat travelled from my chest all the way up my neck. "Hey! I don't 'belong' to anyone. This isn't the Victorian era."

Cal's only response was a cocky, possessive smirk and I rolled my eyes. He might've learned to control his temper, to stop and think before resorting to a fight, but I liked that there was still a hint of the old him, the confident, tattooed, wild boy I'd first fallen for.

He'd always be there under the surface, but now he'd matured. Gone was the boy, replaced with a man I knew I couldn't live without.

When we finished eating, he gave me a ride back to my building. I was a little disappointed when he didn't even try to kiss me, but I reminded myself that technically this was only our first date. People didn't kiss until the second or third date, right?

Man, these rules were confusing.

Twenty-Four
Leanne

The following morning, I was surprised when I got a call from Cal's mum inviting me over for tea. Judy and I had always gotten along really well. So much so that it made me sad when Cal and I stopped seeing each other because it meant I had to stop seeing her too.

I told her I'd be over in an hour or so, then I donned sunglasses and a hoodie before heading out. Instead of leaving through the front door, I took the stairs up to the roof, jumped to the next building, then climbed down the fire escape. This had been my go-to way of leaving my apartment ever since I got back since there was still a bunch of reporters holding a vigil outside my place.

Too bad for them that I knew parkour and was an excellent escape artist.

Cal's mum lived in a small two-bedroom period house just outside the city. His ambition had always been to make enough money to give her a good life and he'd definitely succeeded.

I knocked on the door and she threw it open, arms outstretched. "Leanne, come here and give me a hug. It's so good to see you."

"It's good to see you too," I said, stepping into her hug.

Judy was a warm, friendly woman, very non-judgemental and very easy to talk to. She'd had a rough go of it in life being a single mum and I got the sense she channelled all her love into Cal. She treated him like her little prince growing up and this was probably where some of his cockiness came from. On the positive side, it's also where he got his loyalty and his ability to love so completely it could feel overwhelming.

When we first started sleeping together, Cal's appetite for sex and his need to be around me all the time felt like an obsession. Now I understood him better and knew that was how he showed he cared.

Callum Davidson was definitely an all-or-nothing sort of bloke.

"How are you holding up?" Judy asked as we sat down at her kitchen table and she poured us some tea. She'd also set out a plate of biscuits. I picked one up and dunked it in my tea.

"I'm doing good, all things considered. Been having a bit of a social media detox until people find something new to talk about."

"I wish my son could take a leaf out of your book. He's been driving himself mad trying to figure out who took those pictures. Even hired a private investigator."

I grew a touch uncomfortable at her mentioning the pictures. My parents and sister had refused to look at them, but I wondered if Judy had seen. The idea of her seeing Cal and I like that made me cringe to the very core of my being. She must've noticed my discomfort because she reached out to pat my hand.

"Don't worry, pet. It's nothing I haven't seen before. Though it's not exactly something a mother expects when she opens her morning paper."

Oh my God. She *had* seen them, or well, whatever censored version was printed in the paper. At least she hadn't gone out of her way to look them up. That definitely would've been weird.

"I'm still getting used to the idea of people seeing us like that. It's not a nice feeling," I said quietly.

"You shouldn't have to get used to it. It infuriates me."

I blew out a breath. "Yeah, it's hard to imagine that someone would invade our privacy like that."

A moment of quiet passed. I sipped some tea and felt Judy studying me. When I looked at her, her expression was serious. "My son loves you, you know."

I almost choked on my sip of tea. It wasn't that I didn't already know Cal loved me, it just felt strange to hear someone else say it. But in a good way. Warmth spread through me, my cheeks colouring as I stared at my teacup and spoke quietly, "I love him too."

Judy's gaze sharpened now, a warning in her voice. "I know you do, and don't take this the wrong way, but I just have to say it. If you ever break his heart again, you'll have me to deal with."

I blinked in surprise. Who knew Judy had a tough centre underneath that kind, unassuming exterior? So this was why she'd invited me over for tea. It was a ballsy move and I was kind of impressed.

"I'd rather cut off my own hand than hurt him again," I said and she nodded. It appeared that was the right answer.

A second later, the front door opened, Cal calling out, "Mum, we're back. Fluffy took three shits on his walk today. Three! How can one tiny dog hold so much…"

His words died when he entered the kitchen and saw me sitting there. Cal had his mum's Pomeranian on a leash, and he looked, well, oddly sexy. It was cute that he walked his mum's dog for her. Cal met my gaze then cleared his throat, bending down to let Fluffy off his leash. The dog went bounding up to Judy and hopped on her lap to lick her face.

"I need to give him his monthly bath," Judy said, lifting the dog as she stood, "but you two sit and catch up. I'm sure you have a lot to talk about."

She left the room and amusement played on Cal's lips. "Seems Mum's decided to do some meddling."

"Actually," I said. "I think she invited me over to tell me I'll be facing her wrath if I ever hurt you again."

Cal's eyed widened. "She did *what*?"

I laughed. "Don't worry about it. If I were in her position, I'd do exactly the same thing."

Cal shook his head, running a hand down his face. "She's nuts."

"She just loves you."

He stared out the window a moment before tilting his head to me. "So assuming my mum's craziness hasn't put you off, are you up for going out tomorrow night?"

A smile tugged at my lips. "Sure, I'd love to."

My answer appeared to please him, his eyes heating. "Good. I'll pick you up at six."

On my way home, I took a walk, in a mood to wander. I stopped at the window of a women's boutique and saw an amazing black dress. It came to just above the knee, but what really made it risqué was the see-through black panel that dipped low at the neck. I'd never been one for dresses, but I couldn't stop thinking about that dream Cal had. Every time it popped into my head, I grew flushed, and well, turned on.

On a whim, I went inside and tried it on. Then, I bought it. What? It wasn't like I planned on wearing it for our date. But maybe someday I *would* wear it. On Cal's birthday. As a treat.

The following night, Cal took me to the Sky Garden restaurant. The food was incredible and I couldn't believe how perfectly the date went. Cal was a gentleman and we didn't have a single argument. Actually, a part of me was disappointed in the 'gentleman' bit, but I went along with it. It was hard getting used to him actively trying to *not* have sex with me.

A week later he took me to a fancy cinema near Notting Hill to see the latest superhero movie. I rested my head on his shoulder and he draped his arm around me. You could cut the sexual tension with a knife, but he didn't so much as try to kiss my cheek.

I might've been getting a little paranoid.

Which brought us to now, our fourth date. I stood in front of the mirror wearing *the dress*. I knew it was a sly move, but I was feeling a little neglected. I missed his touch, his lips.

I tousled my hair with some product, put on some foundation and eye makeup and stared at my reflection. I looked hot. Maybe a little too hot. I wasn't sure what Cal was going to do with all this hotness, but we'd soon find out.

When Cal texted that he was outside I buzzed him up, palms sweaty, pulse pounding. I was excited to see him. Or more accurately, I was excited for him to see me. He'd never seen me so dressed up before.

There was a knock on the door and I hurried to open it. When I did, I felt a tad embarrassed because Cal was dressed casually in jeans, a T-shirt, and a navy jacket. On our last two dates, he'd worn shirts and trousers that I suspected were tailor-made, which left me feeling underdressed. Now I had the opposite problem.

He gave me a slow perusal from head to toe, heat simmering behind his eyes, and I knew the dress had worked. Cal's expression darkened, and I wondered if maybe I'd bitten off more than I could chew.

"That looks new," he said, pulling his lower lip between his teeth, still standing in my doorway.

I swallowed thickly. "It is."

Cal tilted his head, like a wild animal gauging its prey. He took one step inside my apartment, then two. Gazing down at me, he murmured, "Are you trying to tempt me, Leanne?"

Summoning my courage, I stared at the floor then glanced up at him from beneath my lashes, my voice sultry. "I wouldn't dream of it, *Callum*."

He smiled, showing teeth. Somehow, that felt like a threat. Shivers trickled down my spine, every part of me aware of him.

"We better get going," he said and held out his hand. I grabbed my jacket then laced my fingers with his. As soon as our palms met electric shocks travelled up my arm. A few photographers were still hanging around outside. They leapt into action when they spotted us, snapping pictures and calling out questions.

"Where are you off to, Callum?"

"Leanne, you look amazing. Give us a smile for the camera."

"Are you two back together then?"

We ignored them and I realised my error when we arrived at Cal's Ducati. Riding on the back of a motorbike in a dress this short was asking for trouble.

"What's wrong?" Cal said, holding out my helmet. It still warmed my heart that he'd had it custom made for me.

I bit my lip, gesturing to my skirt and then to the bike. His eyebrows jumped and he rubbed his jaw when realisation sank in. He pulled me closer to whisper in my ear, "Don't worry. I won't let you flash anyone."

"That's easy for you to say."

His deep chuckle vibrated through my chest. "Come on. You'll be fine."

I reluctantly climbed aboard, my bare thighs pressing flush to his jeans. His hand came down, clasping my thigh. His thumb brushed lightly over my knee before it returned to the handlebar. I hoped he didn't notice how his touch made me tremble. The skirt of my dress hitched up, just barely covering my underwear. I futilely prayed the paps didn't get any pictures. Then again, it wasn't like the entire country hadn't already seen a whole lot more.

Being exposed like that left scars on the inside, but those scars were slowly healing, leaving behind tougher skin. I was stronger now. And if people thought they could break me with a few embarrassing photographs they had another thing coming.

I would never be that fragile again. Life had toughened me, and I was glad for all the rough seas. Now my skin was Kevlar and no cruel online comments, leaked photos, or unflattering articles could breach it.

The photographers tried to follow us in their cars, but Cal did some fancy manoeuvring on his bike and we managed to lose them. He pulled into Regent's Park and we walked to a spot on Primrose Hill that had great views over the city. My chest thrummed when I saw he'd made us a picnic. He laid a blanket out on the grass.

"Makes sense that the one time I wear a dress our date is outdoors."

He shot me a hot look. "You'll just have to keep close to me for warmth."

I shook my head, a smile pulling at my lips and watched as he set out the food. The view up here really was beautiful. The sky was starting to darken, and you could see the city skyline all lit up in the distance. Cal had gone out of his way to pick a romantic spot and my heart didn't know what to do with itself.

We ate sandwiches and sipped on wine, talking about this and that. Toward the end of the date, Cal levelled me with a serious look.

"So there's something important I need to do, and I wanted you to be here to witness it."

"Okay," I said, my curiosity piqued as he pulled out his phone to make a call. He put it on loudspeaker and it started to ring.

"Who are you calling?" I questioned, brow furrowed.

He reached out to place a hand on my knee, his face stern. "Just listen."

What was going on? A voice answered "Callum?" and it took me a second to realise it was our producer, Linda.

"Hi, Linda. I was just calling to discuss possible locations for the next season."

"Oh," she replied, her tone relaxing. "Right, well, we've been considering Hong Kong, though New York is an option too."

"Hong Kong would be amazing," Cal replied. "Have you ever been?"

"No, actually," she gushed. "I've been pushing for it hard. I think the visuals there will be incredible."

"Well," Cal responded casually. "It's too bad you won't get to go."

There was a pause on the other end, then, "What do you mean?"

Cal lifted the phone closer to his mouth, seeming to take great pleasure when he said, "What I'm talking about is you're fucking fired."

"Excuse me?" she questioned, voice rising.

I stared at Cal, wide-eyed, still no clue what was going on and why he thought he could fire Linda. The only people we really had authority to fire was our assistants.

"I said you're fired. I know it was you who took those photos," he said and deathly silence came from the other end of the line. My mouth fell open. Linda had been behind the pictures? What the hell?

Linda cleared her throat, obviously trying to keep her voice neutral. "Listen, Callum, I'm not sure what you think you know, but you're mistaken."

"I have a copy of the cheque you received from the website you sold the pictures to," Cal said, sounding bored. "So don't bother trying to deny it. And don't bother going above my head either. I've already gotten permission to be the one to fire you, so you better go clear out your desk. Also, a little piece of advice, you should probably lawyer up, because I'll be hitting you with a lawsuit very fucking soon."

With that, he hung up. Our eyes met, and I had a million questions.

"How did you—"

"Remember that private investigator I hired?" I nodded. "Well, he did some digging and found out the pictures came from Linda's personal computer and that she got a hundred grand for selling them."

My head swam. "But…why would she do that?"

Cal's eyes turned to slits. "It seems she thought the scandal would bring in more viewers. The money was just a bonus."

My memory worked overtime as I rifled through all my interactions with her. Linda always seemed so nice, eager to help with whatever I needed. But now looking back on it, I saw it from a very different angle. Over the years, she always encouraged me to confront Cal when I was mad at him. She pushed for us to have scenes together when she knew our contracts forbade us from having a relationship.

She even stocked a mini-fridge full of alcohol in my bedroom, because if I were getting drunk behind the scenes, it would lead to on-camera drama.

I remembered her leaving the house on the morning the pictures were taken, how she'd hugged me and expressed her concern, all the while she was scheming behind our backs.

"That bitch," I hissed, suddenly furious. "I can't believe I didn't see through her."

Cal's arm came to rest around my shoulders as he pulled me to him. "Don't blame yourself. None of us could've predicted she'd sink so low."

"But it's not like the show isn't killing it in the ratings."

Cal sighed, his hand rubbing up and down my arm. "In her mind, it's her job to make sure we keep killing it, even if it means throwing the stars of her own show under the bus."

I huffed. "It's like we can't even trust anyone anymore."

"We can trust each other," Cal said and I glanced up at him. In spite of all our differences, it was true that he was one of the most loyal people I'd ever known. Every time I gave him shit, he stood by and took it. Well, actually, he gave me shit right back, but maybe that's what I needed. Someone who would fight me when I was being a bitch instead of lying and pretending everything was hunky dory.

I got a little lost in his eyes and didn't even realise how close our mouths were. His breath washed over my skin and instinctively, I kissed him. A slight tremor went through Cal's body as he held completely still. My lips coaxed his to respond, but he didn't react for a long moment. Then, finally, he emitted the loudest, most masculine groan as he captured my face in his hands and pulled me in for a spine-tingling, toe-curling kiss.

I drowned in that kiss, was drugged by it.

Cal's warm hand travelled up my leg; he ran his fingers along the inside of my thigh, brushing the edge of my underwear and I swear I almost came.

"You'll be the death of me," Cal breathed, reluctantly drawing away. He ran a hand through his hair and stared broodingly out at the view.

"Sorry, I forgot you'd converted to Puritanism," I teased in an effort to lighten the mood and nudged his shoulder with mine.

The edge of his mouth lifted in a smirk and he pulled me back into him, pressing his lips to the top of my head. "Quit trying to corrupt me. It won't work." A pause as his thumb brushed my hip. "Even if you are wearing the sexiest fucking dress I've ever seen."

"That was mean of me," I admitted.

We sat close, Cal's arm around me, and the quietness of the park trickled over my senses. Cal must've noticed my skin prickle because he pulled another blanket from his bag and draped it around us both. I rested my head on his shoulder and exhaled, feeling truly peaceful for the first time in a while.

The following morning, I went to the gym and Cal was already there with Trev and Paul. The three of them were over on the bars, working on their upper bodies. I started some cardio on the treadmill, my attention wandering to Cal every once in a while. One time I looked over and he caught me. I flushed and looked away.

For the rest of my workout, I was determined not to get distracted by him, and I did well until I was leaving the shower room and he filled the doorway.

"Hey."

"Hey," I said. "Good workout?"

He nodded, chest rising and falling from whatever laborious exercise he'd just completed. "Yeah, you?"

"It was good. Uh," I paused, feeling self-conscious. "Do you want to come over to my place tonight to watch a movie?"

He moved closer, his hand coming up to brush a wet strand of hair back from my face. "You mean Netflix and chill?"

"Well, the 'chill' is optional," I said with a hint of flirtation.

He made a humming noise in the back of his throat. "Hmm, that depends."

"On?"

"What movie will we be watching?"

"I haven't decided yet."

"A woman of mystery."

"Something like that."

Cal bent and pressed a kiss to my cheek. "I'll be over around seven. And I'll bring food."

I exhaled. "Okay, great, see you at seven."

Cal moved by me to use the showers and I stood still. For some reason, my feet wouldn't move. That probably had a lot to do with the fact that he'd just pulled off his T-shirt. I watched as his hand went to his pants, then paused. He obviously sensed my presence when he spoke, his back to me.

"What does a bloke have to do to get a little privacy around here?"

I made a dramatic sigh. "You're no fun." When I left, his laughter followed.

I was a ball of nervous energy as I went around my flat, tidying up and trying to set the scene before Cal arrived. Technically, this was our fifth date. I was still trying to figure out whether or not to light candles when there was a knock on my door. I hurried to open it and there he stood. There weren't words to describe how handsome he looked.

I wore leggings and an oversized jumper. After last night, I didn't want to dress up and make him think I was trying to tempt him again. Now I was going for the casual *I couldn't care less if you find me sexy* approach. A little bit of reverse psychology never hurt anyone.

"Whatever you brought smells amazing," I said as he followed me to the kitchen.

"It's Mexican enchiladas. I got them from this great new restaurant. You're going to love them."

I helped him unpack the food and then we sat down on my sofa, scrolling through Netflix to find something to watch. In the end, we settled on *Deadpool*, since neither of us had seen it yet. We ate and laughed our way through the movie.

"Oh my God, I'm definitely adding this scene to my "so wrong it's funny" playlist," I said, chuckling as we watched Deadpool grow a tiny hand after he lost his old one. Cal smiled at me.

"I forgot about your playlists. What else is on that one?"

"Hmm, there's the record throwing scene from *Shaun of the Dead*."

Cal nodded. "Hilarious."

"Also, the hotel role-play scene from *The Office*."

Cal almost spat out the mouthful of water he just drank. "I forgot about that one!"

We were distracted from the movie for a while, getting lost in our conversation so much we had to rewind it back.

When we were done eating, I snuggled into Cal and his arm came around me. I savoured his smell; his cologne was woodsy with a hint of amber. Whenever I got a whiff of it, my mind automatically went to sexy places.

I took his hand and traced the lines of his tattoos with my fingertips. On this wrist, there was a blank space next to the tiny crown. I traced the L on the inside.

"I couldn't believe it when you got this," I whispered, then glanced up at him, our faces close.

His fingers touched mine, then led them over to the blank spot. "I've actually been thinking of getting another one here," he replied softly.

I sucked in some air. "Oh?"

His eyes were gentle. "I think we should both get the same thing." Using my finger, he drew a small heart, then he drew another small heart inside that one, and an even smaller one inside the second. He moved my finger to the edge. "Here it'll say, *always in our hearts.*"

My breath left me as emotion caught in my throat. He was talking about our baby. A tear trickled down my face as I continued to stare up at him. He wiped it away and I swear I couldn't love him more than I did in that moment.

"Keep looking at me like that and I'll get down on one knee," he murmured and my eyes widened. The idea of Cal proposing set my heart racing. Now he chuckled low. "No need to look so terrified. It'd be foolish of me to ask you to marry me."

My face fell. "It would?"

"Well," he said, leaning close. "We're only on our fifth date."

I laughed, and he caught my chin, silencing me with a kiss. I moaned when his tongue met mine and I melted into him. He leaned over me, pushing me back onto the couch and settling his hips between my thighs. His stiff length pressed into me and I ached to have him closer. We kissed for what felt like ages, Cal's hips moving against me in a tantalising rhythm. I needed him to touch me, put an end to the torture.

Breaking away, Cal dropped his face to the crook of my neck. I stroked his hair away from his face and he tilted his head a little to look up at me, eyes calculating.

Finally, he breathed, "Fuck it, I'm not a saint."

Before I could react, he lifted me off the couch, carried me into my bedroom and laid me down on the bed. Bracing himself over me, he brought his lips to mine and we kissed again, long and slow. His hands trailed up my body, lifting my top so my abdomen was exposed. He lowered himself and pressed kisses to my bare stomach.

I whimpered when he pressed his face between my legs, his breath hot against the fabric of my leggings. His sexy eyes met mine before he nuzzled me and I let out a gasp, my clit aching for more.

"Cal, please," I breathed out and he chuckled huskily.

Pulling down the hem of my leggings, he kissed my hip bone, teasing, his touches light as feathers. Every nerve ending in my body was primed. Cal pushed himself up again and gave me those sultry bedroom eyes before his hand dipped inside my pants. I gasped. He fingered my clit slowly, carefully, like he was taking his time. His fingers sped up, bringing me to the cusp of orgasm, but then slowed back down. He knew my body so well, knew all my tells, that he could predict when I was about to come. I both loved and hated how he teased me.

I moaned in frustration, which seemed to bring him great pleasure.

"Kiss me," I urged and he obliged. I fumbled with the fly of his jeans and he groaned when I slid my hand in to palm his cock.

"Christ," he said, breathing laboured.

"I need you."

Something about my plea set him off and he tore at my clothes. Within seconds we were both naked. Cal's eyes traced my body, worshipful. He held himself above me, took my mouth in another kiss, then pushed inside. He filled me perfectly. All the places that had been aching for him rejoiced. His hand came up to grip my neck and my nipples beaded at the possessive gesture. His hips moved in and out as he made love to me with wild abandon. It felt like his lips, teeth, tongue, and hands were everywhere at once.

He consumed me.

I stared at the ink on his skin as his muscles strained and pumped. His tattoos moved like paintings coming to life. My fingers gripped his upper arm then moved down. Next, I touched his chin, his jaw, then his collarbone and shoulder.

"You're beautiful," I said, gasping when he fucked me harder.

His expression was intense, his mouth suddenly at my ear. "What about on the inside?" he asked, a raw vulnerability in his voice. Emotion caught in my throat.

"You're beautiful on the inside too."

He kissed me then, long and deep, like he was thankful to me for finally, truly seeing him. I moaned into the kiss and Cal thrust faster. His movements stilled when he came, never breaking our kiss. I ran my hands up and down his muscular back, expecting him to fall away. Instead, he reached between our bodies, his fingers circling my clit. I dug my nails into his skin as he spread his cum over my folds, his finger dipping inside me a moment before returning to my clit.

"Come for me, Leanne," he ground out.

"I'm almost there," I cried, feet digging into the bed, spine arched. Cal devoured me with his eyes and I came with a loud moan. He made a satisfied noise. "Good girl. Now come here."

Cal cradled me in his arms. I sat between his legs, my back resting against his front. He toyed with my nipples and I stretched out like a lazy cat. He sucked my earlobe into his mouth then murmured huskily, "Was that as good for you as it was for me?"

I decided to play with him. "Eh, it was okay." He pinched my nipple and I squealed past a giggle. "Hey!"

His voice was a low, masculine threat. "Keep lying to yourself. I should be your lawyer I'm so good at getting you off."

I barked a laugh, twisting to face him. "Oh my God, how long were holding onto that one?"

His lips twitched. "A while."

I smiled wide then leaned up to press a light kiss to his mouth. "I don't think I could love you more."

He squeezed my hips, his voice a sexy challenge. "Why don't you show me?"

***

I woke early the next morning with Cal stretched out in my bed. I was going to have to invest in a bigger one because there definitely wasn't enough space for both of us. Soft light streamed through the curtains and I admired how his lashes cast shadows on his face. His straight nose, strong jaw, sculpted lips, and high cheekbones were a work of light and dark.

He looked so peaceful lying there, his head on my pillow. After last night, everything smelled like him, like *us*, and my skin prickled with awareness. I lay watching him for a while, running my fingertips in circles across his chest until he finally opened his eyes. They were bright, startling green, something that always had a potent effect on me.

"Morning," I whispered.

He smiled a breathtakingly gorgeous smile. "Were you watching me sleep?"

I smirked. "Maybe."

"Little pervert." He pulled me to him when my phone buzzed with a text. Still in his arms, I reached over to check who it was from.

Paul: Autumn Hayes' podcast just went live. You should give it a listen.

There was a link, so I clicked on it, and the intro music for the podcast started to play.

"What's that?" Cal asked, his mouth on my neck.

"Remember Autumn? Her podcast episode about us just went out."

Cal and I were quiet as we listened. Unlike in person, where she was a little awkward, Autumn was all confidence in the recording.

"Hello, and welcome to episode 256 of Autumn Talks TV. I'm Autumn Hayes and today we're going to discuss all things Running on Air. *Yes, that's right, the latest reality TV import from Britain that has us all completely obsessed! I was lucky enough to get to travel to Johannesburg to meet the cast, where filming for the fourth season of the show was underway...*

Cal and I spent the next hour listening to Autumn talk about her love for the show, interlacing some recordings of chats she'd had with each of us. I noticed that she hadn't included the part where we'd discussed my relationship with Cal. She also didn't talk about our leaked photos, only bringing them up briefly to say she thought it was unfair to invade our privacy before swiftly moving on. I thought that was pretty cool of her.

Then I remembered how I'd wanted to set her up with Paul. Hmmm...she lived in New York and that was one of the top location choices for our next season. Maybe...

I was distracted from my plotting when Cal switched off the podcast and gently bit my shoulder, his hand wandering down my body. I sighed, wanting nothing more than to spend the entire day in bed with him, but there was something else more important we needed to do.

I grabbed his hand, pausing its descent.

"Wait," I said, already breathing heavily.

"What is it, beautiful?" he purred.

I met his gaze, my voice heavy with emotion. "We should go get those tattoos."

He climbed on top of me now, hands caressing my cheeks as his eyes wandered back and forth between mine. I saw just how much my statement touched him, his eyes soft with tenderness. "Okay, then," Cal breathed. "Let's go."

Epilogue
Leanne
Several months later

I stared down at the small tattoo on my wrist and smiled. Cal had the exact same one in the exact same spot. Three hearts, four words.

Always in our hearts.

It had been a couple of months since we got them, but it felt like a part of me now, like it had always been there. And it reassured me. I'd never forget what we lost, but I wouldn't let it drown me anymore either.

It was a cold night, but the heavy black clothing I wore staved off the chill. We were filming a Christmas special for the show and the icy wind bit at my ears. I stood atop a building in the heart of London's financial district. Neil was in front of me, attaching my mic and first-person camera. In spite of him promising he was still my friend, things had been distant between us. I wished I could figure out a way to fix things, but I was with Cal now, and having a friendship with a guy who used to crush on me was uncomfortable territory.

There was also the fact that he worked for me, which made things extra awkward. Still, I wanted to at least be amicable.

"Hey," I said, drawing his attention away from the mic he was fixing. "Cal mentioned something about having you reply to his fan mail."

Neil blinked, seeming to stiffen as he looked away. "Uh, yeah."

"That can't be too much fun."

"It's fine."

"I can tell him to get someone else to do it," I said, hoping the favour might put me in his good graces.

"*No*," Neil blurted, then seemed to catch himself. He shifted uncomfortably on his feet. "I mean, I don't mind doing it."

"Oh," I said, surprised by how vehement he sounded. "Well, if you ever feel like you have too much on your plate, just let me know and I'll assign some of your duties to Michaela."

"I can manage what's on my plate just fine, Leanne," he said, giving the mic and camera one last check before stepping away. "There. You're all set."

I frowned at his retreating figure. It sounded like…well, it sounded like he actually *wanted* to reply to Cal's fan mail. Weird. Before I had more time to ponder the thought, Paul appeared in front of me, a big excited smile on his face.

"Tonight is going to be amazing. I think this is actually one of the best concepts we've ever had," he said and I smiled back at him, happy for the compliment. The concept for this special had actually been mine, and I was nervous for it all to turn out how I envisioned in my head. It was the middle of the night and we wore black bodysuits with lights that glowed in the dark when you turned them on. The cameras would catch only the glowing lights, our running bodies invisible to the naked eye.

"Anybody know why Neil's in such a bad mood?" Michaela asked as she approached. "I asked him what time it was, and he told me he wasn't my personal timekeeper."

"Oh, harsh," Paul chuckled.

"That actually might be my fault. I think I pissed him off," I said.

Michaela appeared curious. "What did you say to him?"

I frowned. "It's complicated."

"Is everybody ready?" James asked, joining us. He'd been on the other side of the roof with Barry, who had just barely forgiven us for what happened in Joburg. The man could hold a serious grudge. He started coming around when I came to him with my idea for the special though. Not to toot my own horn, but it was a pretty great concept.

"Almost," I replied.

"Wait, your handgrip is loose," Michaela said, stepping close to James to fix the Velcro that hung open.

He looked down at her, a fond expression on his face. "Thanks."

She appeared to swallow, her voice tiny. "No problem."

Across the way, Diana eyed them, her features drawn tight. Since we were shooting in London, she'd come down to watch. Right now, she wore a long burgundy winter coat and a hat with fur trim. I couldn't tell whether her expression was frosty because of the cold or because of how James looked at Michaela. Whatever the reason, I was determined to stay out of it. The wedding was in a few short weeks, so yeah, I just hoped Michaela and James had gotten whatever was between them under control by then.

Trev, Isaac, and Cal approached, and my boyfriend pulled me into his arms. We were both in a really good place right now and I was excited to see what the future held. Cal's hand ran lightly across my shoulder blades and down my back to rest at the base of my spine. My stomach fluttered, and I wondered if there would ever be a time when I didn't feel this way when he touched me. I didn't think so.

"Places everybody," Barry called and Cal bent down to press a kiss on my lips.

"Love you," he whispered, eyes shining in the dark.

"Love you too," I whispered back and then it was time to take our places.

Barry shouted, "Action!" and off we went.

Ahead of me, Isaac shot through the air. The first time I met him, we clicked instantly. His passion and ambition to be a professional freerunner won me over. And his family's story was inspiring. His mother left South Africa with no money and three small children in search of a better life. She had no idea that a few short years later her son would make a big start on realising those dreams.

I chuckled when Trev passed me by, making a funny face. He was the undisputed leader of our group. Years before any of us ever thought we'd be on TV, Trev was an orphan in a family of four brothers living in an impoverished, crime-ridden part of London. His elder brother, Lee, decided to get the family out of that world and Trev began to work on his idea for a reality TV show. If it weren't for him, none of us would even be here right now.

Then there was James, our rock, the most measured and reliable member of our little group. Quite like Isaac's mum, his grandparents left Trinidad in the early 1960s to emigrate to London and start new lives. Two generations later James was born. In school, he was naturally athletic and took to running track. Then he discovered parkour and the rest was history.

Paul came up behind me, briefly squeezing my hand. He was my best friend, my manic pixie dream boy, the one who could make me smile even when I was at my lowest. Paul was a ray of sunshine; quirky, philosophical, and always able to show you a new way of looking at things. I wanted more than anything for him to find someone to love him like he deserved to be loved.

Lastly, Cal came and ran alongside me. He was my partner, my soul mate, my everything. Even before I properly knew him, he'd entranced me. Then we met, and my world was turned upside down. Our relationship both off the air and on had always been a tumultuous one, but I felt like we'd finally found a happy balance. It was still scary because he had my whole heart in the palm of his hand, but all I could do was hope he'd be careful with it.

Above our heads, three drones captured us from several angles. I ran ahead of Cal and he took up the rear. I'd painstakingly mapped out our run, choosing this spot because it had the perfect combination of buildings, allowing us to run in a very particular pattern.

At first glance, the viewers might not see it, as we ran in seemingly random directions, but as the cameras switched to the overhead view, it would become clear. Our glowing suits were painting a picture below that could only truly be appreciated from above.

We left a sparkling flare at each point in the run, depicting all the stars in Andromeda, one of the first constellations I ever managed to find on my telescope.

With a thrill I lit the final flare, signifying the brightest star, Alpha Andromedae, also known as Sirrah. It was ninety-seven light years away with a luminosity two-hundred times brighter than the sun.

In my mind, if something that magnificent could exist, then I was pretty lucky to be alive to witness it.

I placed the final flare on the ground and glanced again at my tattoo, three little hearts inked into my skin, and whispered into the darkness, "If you had been born, I would've named you Sirrah, a star that's brighter than the sun."

I went and joined the others, holding Cal's hand and taking a moment to enjoy the little piece of art we'd created. It filled my heart with joy that it had all gone exactly how I envisioned. Then I looked up into the eyes of the man who'd stuck by me through thick and thin, never giving up on the idea of us even when I pushed him away over and over again.

Tonight, we ran on air.

And tomorrow, we'd do it again.

The location might change, but one thing would stay the same.

I'd never stop holding his hand.

END.

Running on Air is a spin-off series featuring characters first seen in the final book in the Hearts Series, *Hearts on Air*. This book is about Trev and Reya, who you met in *Off the Air*. If you are intrigued to know their full story, read on for a sneak peek...

I was busking on the street, singing an "ironic" cover of *Wrecking Ball* when I opened my eyes and saw him.

Trevor Cross, one of my best friends/bane of my existence sat with his legs dangling off the edge of a shop rooftop. He was my best friend because he was one of the most hilarious and fun people to be around. And he was the bane of my existence because he was a hyper-active livewire who, for some reason, enjoyed being in my company. Dealing with him sometimes felt like trying to circumnavigate a mine field. I changed the lyrics as I sang and wondered if he'd notice.

You came in like a wrecking ball.

That was Trev down to a T. *Destructive. Addictive. Fascinating. Frustrating.* Too full of energy to ever pin down. At times he wrecked me. Other times he built me up. Our relationship was...complicated. And yet, we'd never even kissed.

He often liked to turn up unannounced like this. He knew my routine off by heart, so if he wanted to he could always find me. I busked every afternoon, Tuesday to Saturday, and in the evenings I gave private piano lessons. I usually played a club gig on Saturday nights, then had Sunday and Monday off. I tended to make a pretty steady income week on week.

Trevor watched me with a serious look on his face, his head tilted to one side as though in contemplation. He'd heard me sing countless times before, so I didn't really get what was different today.

Most of the time, I got one of two Trevors. The flamboyant, loud-mouthed, piss-taking one normally came out when we were around other people, while the more serious, introspective, thoughtful one made an appearance when it was just the two of us. If I wasn't acquainted with his more low-key side, then we probably wouldn't have stayed friends this long. There was only so much hyperactivity a person could handle.

We met almost two and a half years ago through my girlfriend, Karla, who at the time was having a clandestine relationship with Trevor's brother, Lee. Trev latched onto me from the very first night we met, charming me, making me laugh, making me feel like the most important and interesting person in the world. I'd come to learn that's what he did. His liveliness made you feel like a better version of yourself, someone far more exciting than who you really were.

When I finished the song Trev effortlessly jumped down from his spot on the roof, a skill honed through his years of dedication to parkour. As he crossed the street he pulled a lollipop from his pocket, ripped off the packaging and stuck it in his mouth.

"To what do I owe this pleasure?" I asked once he reached me.

His mischievous blue eyes caught the light in a way that almost made them appear otherworldly. He took his time sucking on the lolly, then pulled it out with a loud popping sound.

"Just came to check up on my favourite girl. I haven't heard you sing that one before. Never took you for a Miley fan," he grinned, goading me.

"Course I am. She's got more grit than Taylor," I answered, smiling as I moved to pack up my keyboard. Trev came forward and pushed my hands away when I went to fold up the stand.

"I've got it. You go grab your cash before someone tries to steal it."

"Okay, um, thanks," I said and went to pick up the hat I left out for passers-by to throw money in. Once everything was packed, Trev lifted my keyboard case and gestured for me to lead the way.

"Come on, I'll walk you home."

"Somebody's feeling very helpful today. What are you after?" I asked, suspicious.

He put his hand to his heart as though offended. "Can't a fella help out his best friend simply because he feels like it?"

"Yes, a fella can. You, on the other hand, always seem to have something up your sleeve."

He let out a slow breath, his gaze moving lazily over my features, down to my chest and then back up again. I was used to him looking at my boobs. It was par for the course with him. And since I'd been born with an ample pair, it seemed like a losing battle to get someone like Trev not to ogle them. I ran my hands down my long burgundy dress, feeling self-conscious. He wasn't ogling me light-heartedly like he normally did. Today there was more heat behind it, and it put me on edge.

So, here's a confession. When I first met Trev I was hopelessly infatuated with him. I mean, show me a twenty-two-year-old girl who wouldn't be. Trev was tall, dark haired, light eyed, athletically muscular and had a great sense of humour. Plus, he was never short on charm or compliments. All this meant I developed a gigantic crush. Little did I know, all he was after was friendship.

It should've been more obvious to me, but at the time I had my head in the clouds. Trev didn't go for women who looked like me. He liked them petite and blonde, while I was anything but. Anyway, it took me a few months to come to the heart-breaking realisation that he wasn't interested in me romantically. After that, I made my peace with the situation and moved on. Now I was a twenty-four-year-old woman who knew better than to put her eggs in the Trevor Cross basket.

But today…today he was looking at me in a way he never had before and it was making me feel strange. Too hot, and itchy – real itchy.

He was uncharacteristically silent as he went back to sucking on his lolly.

I eyed him. "What's up with you?"

"Nothing."

"Come on. You're being weird. Well, weirder than usual."

He shoved one hand in his jeans pocket. "I guess I'm just a little bit restless. I feel like doing something crazy, something exciting. It's Friday and I don't have a shift at Lee's until the day after tomorrow. How about we go out and have some fun? Throw caution to the wind."

I smiled fondly at his enthusiastic hand gesture. "Like how?"

"Like…" he paused, pondering it a moment before he continued, "Okay, how about this. We both make a pact to stay out for the entire night, and we can't go home until we've done at least three things we've never done before."

I gave him a suspicious look. "I don't know. I think your idea of exciting is a lot more extreme than mine."

He came around to stand in front of me and I stopped in place. "What if I promise not to make you do anything you don't want to? Come on, Reyrey, have an adventure with me. You know you won't regret it."

I wasn't too sure about that. Still, after only a few moments of hesitation I gave in, unable to resist that boyish grin of his, especially when he called me Reyrey. I hated it, but also secretly kind of loved it. "Fine. I'll do it."

"Yes! Okay, now all you have to do is suck on the lollipop to make it official," he held it out to me in challenge, then winked. "It's strawberry. Your favourite."

I knew he thought I wouldn't do it, which kind of made me want to prove him wrong. Instead of pushing the proffered lolly out of the way, I plucked it from his fingers, stuck it in my mouth and took a long suck.

When I popped it from my lips I shot him a cheeky grin. "Mmm, delicious."

Trev's mouth fell open and I delighted in the fact that I'd surprised him. I arched a brow in challenge, waiting for him to comment, but all he did was stare at my mouth like he never noticed how fascinating it was before. Shivers ran up my arms and I started to regret my gutsy move.

He took a step closer, his eyelids hooded, and asked quietly, "I know I'm probably gonna get a slap for this, but would you consider sucking my cock like you just sucked that lolly as one of the things you've never done before?"

Now it was my turn to be surprised. And turn bright red. And get goosebumps over every inch of my body. I mean, he'd said stuff like this to me in the past, but it had always been in jest. Today I wasn't so sure. It felt like if I said yes, he'd actually go ahead with it. And it was difficult to breathe normally when the image of giving my best friend a blowjob was etched in my mind. Swallowing hard,

I shook my head and plastered on a breezy expression, "Nice try, but I think I'll pass."

Trev threw his arm around my shoulders then bent to whisper in my ear, "Spoilsport."

I tried to ignore how his breath hit my skin, and how his voice gave me tingles.

When we arrived at my building, I stepped ahead of him to swipe my fob over the door entry system. Living in a three-hundred square foot studio apartment could be stifling and demoralising at times, but it was the only thing that was within my budget. When I was in college I lived in a house share, and believe it or not, this was actually a step up.

I wanted to sing for a living, and I knew I'd be miserable doing anything else, so for that reason I had to make sacrifices.

At first I'd been too embarrassed to bring Trev here, because the building was old and a little musty, and when you lived in such a small place all of your possessions were sort of on show. It was like bringing people right inside your bedroom. Awkward. Too close.

Keeping Trev away was a losing battle though, and eventually he wore me down. He actually liked the place, thought it was cosy. But that was probably because he'd grown up in a tiny council house with his three brothers all sleeping in one room. Hell, he probably considered my place spacious in comparison.

Anyway, I tried to keep the place nice and take pride in it, even though it wasn't much. At least I could hold my head high and be proud of my little home.

As soon as we got in Trev flopped down onto my bed. He pulled his phone from his pocket, probably to check Facebook or something, while I went to put my things away and freshen up in the bathroom. When I returned he was still on his phone. I took a moment to soak him in, because the visual of him lying so casually on my bed was always...interesting.

Sure, I'd made my peace with the fact that he didn't fancy me, but I couldn't help finding him attractive. He just was. He was pretty, too, for a bloke. His lips were full and red, his lashes long and dark, and his skin pale and flawless. Being of Spanish descent, I was his opposite: dark eyed and tan. Perhaps that was why I'd always been so taken with his looks.

I dropped down beside him and asked, "What are you looking at?"

He turned the screen so I could see and I scrunched up my face. "An underground rave? Not sure that's my thing."

"But it's held in an old abandoned tube station. Neither one of us has been to a rave in a tube station before. We should do it."

I shrugged and gave it some thought. I wasn't a big fan of rave music, but I did like to dance. Perhaps it wouldn't be so bad. "Okay, then. We'll go, but you have to stick with me. I hate being left alone at those things."

Trev shot me a serious look. "Of course I'll stick with you. I wouldn't leave you on your own. It's not safe."

His sincerity made me feel a little less wary and I gave him a grateful smile. This close I could smell him, and involuntarily I leaned in to sniff his neck.

"Did you just smell me?" he asked with amusement.

I blinked, realising how odd that was. "Um, yeah, sorry. Is that new cologne?"

"Acqua di Gio. You like it?"

"I really do."

He grinned. "Good." Leaning in, he brought his nose to my neck and inhaled deeply. The action caused my stomach to clench and my chest to flutter. I thought I even felt his lips touch my skin for a second.

"You don't smell so bad yourself."

"Thanks."

He winked. "I'm all about returning the favour. Do you need to do anything else before we leave?"

I shook my head and he pulled me up from the bed. Before I knew it we were on the tube, heading for destinations unknown.

"It's too early for the rave, so I thought we'd go get something to eat first."

"Good idea. I'm starving."

Trev grinned devilishly and I knew it meant all was not as it seemed, but I decided not to question him. For some reason I felt like truly embracing his idea of throwing caution to the wind. I did need material for some new songs, after all. Maybe this night of new experiences would be the perfect inspiration.

Yes, God help me, for the next couple of hours I was going to let Trevor Cross be my guide.

Continue the story in Hearts on Air (Hearts Book #6).

About the Author

L.H. Cosway lives in Dublin, Ireland. Her inspiration to write comes from music. Her favourite things in life include writing stories, vintage clothing, dark cabaret music, food, musical comedy, and of course, books. She thinks that imperfect people are the most interesting kind. They tell the best stories.

Find L.H. Cosway online!

www.lhcoswayauthor.com
www.facebook.com/LHCosway
www.twitter.com/LHCosway
www.instagram.com/l.h.cosway

Books by L.H. Cosway

Contemporary Romance
Painted Faces
Killer Queen
The Nature of Cruelty
Still Life with Strings
Showmance
Fauxmance

The Cracks Duet
A Crack in Everything (#1)
How the Light Gets In (#2)

The Hearts Series
Six of Hearts (#1)
Hearts of Fire (#2)
King of Hearts (#3)
Hearts of Blue (#4)
Thief of Hearts (#5)
Cross My Heart (5.75)
Hearts on Air (#6)

The Rugby Series with Penny Reid
The Hooker & the Hermit (#1)
The Player & the Pixie (#2)
The Cad & the Co-ed (#3)
The Varlet & the Voyeur (#4)

Urban Fantasy
Tegan's Blood (The Ultimate Power Series #1)
Tegan's Return (The Ultimate Power Series #2)
Tegan's Magic (The Ultimate Power Series #3)

Tegan's Power (The Ultimate Power Series #4)

Made in the USA
Lexington, KY
13 March 2019